RAVES FOR BILLIE LETTS AND
THE HONK AND HOLLER OPENING SOON

"SERVES UP LAUGHS AND TEARS WHILE REMINDING THE READER THAT IT IS NEVER TOO LATE TO FIND WHAT YOU ALWAYS WANTED."
—*San Antonio Express News*

"A TOUCHING STORY of people who discover the true meaning of home in the most unlikely of places."
—*Good Housekeeping*

"LETTS'S CHARACTERS ARE ENDEARING."
—*Los Angeles Times*

"BILLIE LETTS HAS A FRESH AND ENGAGING VOICE."
—Anne Rivers Siddons

"A SWEET AND COMIC NOVEL . . . IT POSITIVELY CHARMS. . . . 'Honk' if you love romance."
—*Sunday New York Post*

"A WARM, SENTIMENTAL TALE, ABUNDANT WITH QUIRKY DETAIL AND HOMESPUN WISDOM, which emphasizes not only the power of romantic love but the healing powers of community as well."
—*Publishers Weekly*

more . . .

Also by Billie Letts

Where the Heart Is

Billie Letts

THE HONK AND HOLLER OPENING SOON

WARNER BOOKS

A Time Warner Company

Grateful acknowledgments are given to the following:

B.R. Flories estate for portions of lyrics from "Stop the Presses," music and lyrics by Shawn Letts. Copyright © 1986. All rights reserved. Used by permission of Bret McCormick.

Shawn Letts for portions of lyrics from "I Knew I Could Count on You," music and lyrics by Shawn Letts. Copyright © 1992. All rights reserved. Used by permission.

Shawn Letts for portions of lyrics from "Lost Love and Heartbreak," music and lyrics by Shawn Letts. Copyright © 1992. All rights reserved. Used by permission.

Brentwood—Benson Music Publishing, Inc. for portions of lyrics from "Farther Along," by J. R. Baxter, Jr., and W. B. Stevens. Copyright © 1937 Stamps Baxter Music/BMI. All rights reserved. Used by permission of Brentwood—Benson Music Publishing Inc.

Peermusic/Red River Songs, Inc., for portions of lyrics from "Take Me Back to Tulsa," by Bob Willis and Tommy Duncan. Copyright © 1941 by Peer International Corporation, Inc./Red River Songs, Inc. Copyright renewed 1968. International copyright secured. Used by permission.

Thompson and Thompson for permission to reprint an excerpt from "Heritage," by Countee Cullen, published in *Color.* Copyright © 1925 by Harper & Bros. Copyright renewed 1952 by Ida M. Culllen. Used by permission.

Warner Books, Inc., 1271 Avenue of the Americas, New York, NY 10020
Visit our Web site at www.warnerbooks.com

 A Time Warner Company

Printed in the United States of America
First Trade Printing: May 1999

3 4 5 6 7 8 9 10

The Library of Congress has cataloged the hardcover edition as follows:

Library of Congress Cataloging-in-Publication Data

Letts Billie.
    The Honk and Holler opening soon / Billie Letts.
        p. cm.
    ISBN 0-446-52158-2
    I. Title.
    PS3562.E856H66   1998
813' .54—dc21   97-51230
                                                          CIP

ISBN: 0-446-67505-9 (pbk.)

Cover design and illustration by Wendell Minor

For Holly Wantuch

who soared beyond our reach . . .
but left us grounded in her light and joy

Acknowledgments

My appreciation to Kevin Dancer who shared with me some special moments of the nineteen years he's spent in a wheelchair; Doan Hoang and Nien Thi Truong for leading me through their language; Dr. Friede Wells and Dr. Phyllis Engles who kept me straight on wounds to dogs, horses and humans; Kenneth "Butch" Rose, Major SF, Ret., who served thirty-one months in Vietnam and worked to protect me from my own ignorance; Howard Starks, my reader, my friend; and Vicky Ellis who performs magic with a computer; my sons for believing in me; and Dennis, my cherished critic.

Also, special thanks to Barbara Santee, Jeff Kyle, David Knight, Rhonda and Jimmy Grider, Wes Dunson, Betty Gayle Cooper, Narrie Harris, Molly Griffis, Kim Doner, Ray Don Letts, Brad Cushman, Georgeann Vineyard, Peggy Fielding and John Aherne.

And finally, my gratitude to my agent, Elaine Markson, and my editor, Jamie Raab—exceptional women with great courage, extraordinary talent and marvelous humor.

THE HONK
AND **HOLLER**
OPENING
SOON

December 1985

CANEY SWITCHED on the light over his bed and reached for the last of last night's coffee . . . one cold oily swallow at the bottom of a chipped stoneware mug.

He'd been trying to convince himself he was still asleep ever since he'd heard the rattle of trash cans behind the cafe sometime around three. At least he supposed it was three. Molly O had unplugged the clock on his dresser so she could plug in two sets of lights she'd strung around a scrawny Christmas tree standing in the corner.

Caney had told her he didn't want a tree in his room. He said the one she put up out front beside the jukebox was one too many, but telling Molly O not to do something was like telling a four-year-old not to stick a bean up her nose. So when she started dragging in sacks of pinecones and tangled strands of red tinsel, Caney kept his mouth shut and stayed out of her way. He'd lost enough battles to know when to give up.

Encouraged by his silence, Molly O had thrown herself into a decorating frenzy. After she finished with the trees, she hung aluminum stars from the ceiling fan, but they got tangled around the blades, causing the motor to short out.

She draped silver icicles over a length of clothesline stretched across the center of the room, but every time the door opened, ici-

cles slipped off the line and drifted down onto plates of spaghetti
or bowls of vegetable stew.

She brought in a box of old frizzy-haired Barbies that had belonged to her daughter, adorned each one with mistletoe and
perched them on top of all the napkin holders. She had to position
them straddle legged, as if they were doing splits, the only way she
could manage to tape them down, but the ungainly pose brought
lewd comments from a drilling crew that came in for breakfast
each morning.

Undaunted by minor flaws and small minds, Molly O pressed
on. She carted in candy canes, holiday plants and plastic elves. She
hung wreaths, strung popcorn and tacked up cardboard bells.

Finally, she made a trip to Wal-Mart where she found a nativity
scene made in Taiwan. She arranged it in the center of the lunch
counter and placed the tiny baby Jesus, who looked oddly Orien-
tal, into the bamboo manger.

Finished, Molly O surveyed the Honk and said it looked like a
Christmas wonderland. Caney said it looked like a Chinese carnival.

But Christmas was not on his mind as he squirmed, then threw
back the covers, sending a paperback sailing off the bed. After a
mumbled apology to Louis L'Amour, Caney rubbed at his temples
where a headache was just beginning to build.

He thought once again about sleep, but figured it was useless.
He knew if he turned off the light and sank back into his pillow,
the same old pictures would play in his head, reruns in which he
was the only performer . . . a one-man show.

Three hundred miles away, at a rest stop near Kansas City, Vena
Takes Horse cracked the window of the passenger door, lit a Winston and blew the smoke into the cold predawn air. The driver of
the eighteen-wheeler, a shriveled little man who called himself
Cobweb, was asleep in the bed behind the seat. He had tried to get
Vena to crawl into the back with him, but when she told him to
go to hell, he hadn't insisted. He said he reckoned sleep would do
him more good than sex, then left her sitting alone up in the front.

He'd picked her up on Interstate 59 just south of Sioux Falls, but they hadn't said much to each other. Cobweb spent most of his talk on his CB, which was fine with Vena. She didn't care much for conversation anyway.

She tossed the last of her cigarette out the window, then put her head back and closed her eyes. She hadn't slept since South Dakota and hoped, now, that sleep would take her, but each time a truck rolled by on the highway, something tightened in her chest that caused her heart to quicken. She wasn't good at staying still.

She thought of trying to get another lift, but a hard rain had begun to fall just before they stopped and she had seen specks of ice in the drops that smacked against the windshield. The cold didn't bother her much, but she didn't like the rain. She didn't like the rain at all.

When she finally decided to give up on sleep, she lifted her duffel bag onto the seat beside her and fished out a half-eaten Hershey, but before she could peel back the wrapper, she heard a noise, a strange sound she couldn't identify.

At first she thought it might have come from Cobweb, a whimpering sound men sometimes make when they dream, when they're not afraid to be afraid. But when she heard it again, she knew it came from outside, from somewhere in the dark.

If she could have convinced herself that what she heard was the whine of tires hugging the wet road or the ping of ice pellets ricocheting off the truck . . . if she could have made herself believe that, then she wouldn't have crawled out of the cab and climbed to the ground, wouldn't have felt the sting of rain and sleet pelting her face, plastering her hair to her head.

She started toward the light poles ringing the rest stop, but when she heard the sound again, certain it came from the highway, she turned and headed in that direction.

She could hear it more clearly now, a high-pitched mournful wail. As she crossed the grassy strip separating the rest stop from the interstate, a car rounded a curve, headlights sweeping across the darkness as it veered suddenly toward the median, and in a brief slice of light, a moment before the car's passing, she saw something lying on the highway.

She started to run then, but when she reached the shoulder of the road, when she saw what was out there, she slowed, the way people do when dread needs an extra breath.

In the middle of the far lane was a small black dog, one leg ripped off at the bend of a knee where a tendril of slick gray vein protruded, leaking blood onto the wet pavement. The dog, flattened on its side, was trying to lick life into five lifeless pups, vapors of steam rising from their still-warm bodies . . . and as Vena started across the road, the dog looked up, found her face with its eyes and managed one weak wag of its limp black tail.

Just down the road from Caney's place, in the Cozy Oaks Trailer Park, Molly O peered out the window of her fifty-foot Skyline, giving some serious thought to sneaking next door and ripping down the wind chimes that were about to drive her nuts. She might have done it, too, but she was afraid the silence would wake up the whole neighborhood.

She had been up since three and had known from the first that the day was going to be a disaster. And she was right.

She'd started out by grabbing a tube of Ben-Gay instead of toothpaste, cracking her hip against a dresser drawer and losing one of her new fake nails down the drain. But that was just the beginning.

She found mouse droppings on the kitchen cabinet, a quart of soured milk in the fridge, exactly four squares of toilet tissue left on the roll and a crimson rash running up her neck.

What she didn't find was the mate to her one fuzzy house shoe, enough water pressure to wash the taste of Ben-Gay from her mouth or an extra roll of toilet paper.

She could have blamed her troubles on insomnia—three hours of half sleep and distressing dreams she couldn't shake until she got up and looked through Brenda's old scrapbook. But a bad night was nothing new for Molly O. She'd been living with insomnia for so long that it was as familiar as her cowlick, as comfortable as her faded chenille robe.

No, her problem was worse than a restless night, more serious than a rash. Her problem was Christmas. Christmas without

Brenda. And while the photographs she had looked at earlier had soothed the sting of bad dreams, the images of Brenda would be with her for the rest of the day.

> *Brenda, hair the color of quince, face set in defiant scowl, posted under a Christmas tree . . . a three-year-old sentry waiting up for Sandra Claus*

At first, Molly O had tried to turn Christmas off. Just think of December as another gray month, the last thirty-one days of the year, four long weeks in which her propane bill would double. But she couldn't avoid the Christmas parade down Main Street, couldn't ignore the plywood reindeer on the lawn at City Hall, couldn't shut out the sounds of the Methodist carolers singing "Joy to the World."

> *Brenda at ten, straw-thin legs crossed in a movie star pose, ankle-strap shoes too adult for her feet, head haloed in copper curls, mouth painted sunburst coral with a tube of forbidden lipstick*

But like a spoiled child demanding attention, Christmas insisted on having its own way. *Christmas was coming*—with its scent of pine needles and jingle of bells—and there was nothing Molly O could do to stop it. She couldn't hide from it or get around it, but she had to find a way to get through it, so she devised another plan.

She would perform her own Christmas miracle to renew a joyless heart.

> *Brenda at thirteen, hair by Clairol—raven black, eyelids shadowed midnight blue, short leather skirt hugging her thighs as she climbs into a pickup, flashing a woman's smile at the grinning boy behind the wheel*

With renewed spirit and firm resolve, Molly O started her new campaign by dropping five dollars in the Salvation Army bucket, then taking a racing car set and two Dr. Seuss books to the firehouse for the Toys for Tots collection. She bought two trees from the Kiwanis lot, then pulled out cardboard boxes full of lights and ornaments.

She watched *Miracle on 34th Street,* addressed Christmas cards and made a pan of fudge. Then she sat down and cried.

> *Brenda at fifteen, cowboy booted, western suited, hair bleached, teased and pomped, bottle of Coors in one hand, guitar in the other, wedged between two slim-hipped musicians, standing beside a beat-up VW van with* BRENDA B AND THE BAD AXE BOYS *painted on the side*

Depressed by the sight of so much Christmas, Molly O loaded up everything and took it to the Honk where she spent three days decorating for Caney. She had pretended to enjoy it and forced herself to smile. But it didn't work. The spirit she faked was left at the cafe like an apron she could slip in and out of. Here in her own trailer, there was nothing to suggest that Christmas was just days away. Nothing at all.

> *Brenda, hair the color of quince*
> *a three-year-old sentry*
> *waiting up for Sandra Claus*
>   *   *   *

Bui Khanh emptied the closet quickly, but he had little to take—a windbreaker, three pairs of pants, a half dozen wrinkled shirts . . . ill-fitting castoffs from the Goodwill where he shopped. He tossed everything into a paper sack, then scooped out the contents of a dresser drawer.

He had just stepped into the kitchen when he heard a car roll to a stop in the alley behind his apartment. He switched off the light, then slipped to the window.

He knew the police would come, but had hoped it would not be so soon, hoped he would already be gone.

He had seen the Houston police many times in the neighborhoods of Little Saigon. Big men with hard voices and hard eyes.

Once he had seen two of them with their guns drawn, yelling words he couldn't understand at a Thai boy in front of the U Minh Import Shop.

Bui held his breath as he inched aside a stiff window shade.

The sight of a man standing ten feet away caused his knees to buckle. But when his eyes adjusted to the darkness of the alley, he recognized the familiarity of another Vietnamese face as the man staggered against the car, fumbled open his fly and relieved himself.

Bui backed away from the window and waited for his breathing to slow. He wanted to sit down and close his eyes, but he knew if he did, he would see again the woman with yellow hair.

He could not remember her car pulling out of the darkness and into the path of his own, did not remember the jolt of the wheel in his hand or the tearing of metal as the cars came to rest at the side of the road. But he would never forget the face of the woman with yellow hair as she stumbled from her car and started to shout.

Bui told her he would take her to a doctor and promised to pay the bill, but when he tried to wipe the blood from her hair, she grabbed his arm and screamed words he had never heard.

He tried to explain, told her he had no license and no insurance for the car. Then he gave her all the money in his pocket, but she kept shouting and pointing to her car.

Bui tried again to tell her, to make her understand, but he didn't have enough American words. And when he heard the sound of distant sirens, the Vietnamese words came too fast and too loud. When he reached for her arm and begged her to listen, she scratched at his face and tore the collar of his shirt.

He wished he could have helped her, could have found the right words, but the woman was still shouting when he ran away. And now, standing in the empty kitchen, he knew wishing was too late.

The car in the alley was gone when he peeked through the window again, but he left the room in darkness as he felt his way to a corner cabinet, empty except for a heavy bag of rice. Working quickly, he untied the bag, then ran his hand deep inside and pulled out a thick leather pouch. He didn't take time to open it. He could tell from the heft of it that the money was still inside.

The kitchen held nothing else of value—no microwave or toaster, not even a coffeepot. Bui had made do with one blackened saucepan, three plastic glasses and a stack of plastic containers from the Cafe Lotus where he worked.

He had planned to buy nice dishes later, when Nguyet came— white china bowls and teacups edged in gold. He would buy beautiful chopsticks made of ivory and a tray painted with red flowers, and Nguyet would prepare *rau cải xaō* and *cóm chiên vói sauciss,* not the canned fish and frozen pizzas he sometimes ate.

Nguyet wouldn't like American food, not at first, but Bui would teach her the taste of fried chicken and baked apples. He would show her how Americans ate eggs with forks and explain why they wanted their tea with ice. She wouldn't understand, not in the beginning, but he would help her and she would be all right. When she was with him again, everything would be all right.

The living room was even darker than the kitchen, but Bui didn't need light to see where he was going. He had been there many times in the dark. And now, before he left, he would go there once more.

The shrine, on a rickety wooden table in a corner of the room, was small and plain. But when he lit the candle, the stone Buddha cast a giant shadow against the wall. Bui lit three sticks of incense over the candle flame, then stepped back and knelt on the floor.

He bowed his head and waved the incense three times toward the altar, then, with his hands pressed against his forehead, he prayed. He prayed for his ancestors, he prayed for Nguyet and he prayed for the woman with yellow hair.

Chapter Two

CANEY LOWERED HIMSELF into the nearly full tub, eased into the steaming water little by little, letting the warmth spread over his belly, then up his chest, around his back, as he slipped down and down until he was submerged up to his chin. He leaned his head back against the cold enamel, closed his eyes and saw himself floating in a clear stream, carried along by the current, the sun on his face . . . his body light, drifting, free.

He liked being there, in that stream. Thought of how fine it would be to stay all day . . . forever. Because when he was there, he didn't have to worry about the fry cook showing up or the ice maker shutting down, didn't have to think about the roof that had been leaking for six months or the meat bill that was ninety days past due.

But Caney knew he didn't have a chance, not a chance in hell. If he stayed in that stream, just drifted along, some disaster would spoil it, something would end it all.

He'd drift into a nest of snakes or get sucked down a hole or crash into a jagged boulder. He didn't know how or why, but he knew it would all turn bad because that's the way dreams worked.

He scooted himself up in the tub, reached to a shelf above his head and grabbed for his cigarettes. He was expecting to find a half pack of Camels; instead, he discovered a prickly pear cactus Molly O had adorned with sprigs of holly and sprinkled with plastic snow.

The thorn that pierced the pad of his thumb was just a little shorter than the one that ran under his fingernail, the one that caused him to yell.

When he jerked his hand down, he ripped the shelf loose and everything on it slid off and tumbled into the tub with him. A bottle of Prell, two rolls of Charmin and a half pack of Camels floated around him like bathtub toys.

"Jesus Christ," he said as he surveyed the mess he was sitting in. Plastic snowflakes and holly drifted across his belly, the Charmin settled to the bottom of the tub and dirt from the cactus pot turned the bathwater brown.

"Jesus Christ," he repeated, then shook his head in disgust.

He couldn't decide whether to drain the tub and start all over or just skip the whole thing. But he knew for certain that with or without a bath, he needed a smoke and it wouldn't come from the soggy package floating between his ankles.

He wrapped his hands around the rubber grips on the sides of the tub, took a ragged breath and began to lift himself out of the water.

Great knots of muscle hardened like gristle as he started to rise. Veins swelled into dark ridges, and thick ropes of tendons corded and bulged as he raised pound after pound of resisting bone, flesh, body.

Beads of sweat popped into rivulets that streamed in his eyes, and his skin purpled as the veins in his neck gorged to bursting. And with his jaw clamped and lips stretched into a grimace, he made some sound of pain deep in his throat.

He quivered as he reached the last of it, as he strained to gain the final few inches. Then it was over.

With his arms fully extended, his weight in perfect balance, he hung in midair . . . back straight, head up, muscles rigid. And for a moment, for just one sweet moment, he was one of Louis L'Amour's cowboys, gloved hands gripping the rails of a loading chute as he settled himself onto the back of a lean stallion. Flawless . . . except for his legs hanging heavy and still beneath him.

Then, with a practiced twist, Caney shifted his weight, slid his hips onto the side of the tub and reached for his wheelchair.

Chapter Three

THE ONLY LIGHT in the cafe came from a neon beer sign in the front window. But Caney liked the faint red glow that veiled the stains on the ceiling and smoothed the cracks in the linoleum.

He rolled to a stop behind the counter and slid a pack of Camels out of the cigarette rack. With a book of matches he found in the windowsill, he lit his first smoke of the day as he watched the sky beginning to lighten in the east.

The wind was picking up, sudden gusts sailing paper cups and beer cans across the parking lot, lashing at the branches of a pine tree that towered over the cafe. When something heavy banged against the roof, Caney ducked his head, waiting for the sky to fall.

But it was the sound of the wind that got to him, the sound that raised goosebumps up the back of his neck.

When he was little, the sound of a howling wind would shake him from sleep and send him racing to the bed of his ancient great-aunt who believed nothing good came of bad weather.

"Night creatures ride on the wind, boy," she would whisper as she settled him against her brittle hip and covered him with quilts that smelled of lavender talc.

But all that had changed. And so had Caney Paxton. He could no longer recall the scent of lavender . . . his legs had forgotten the magic of running . . . and he hadn't been welcomed into a woman's bed for a very long time.

When the wind started to whine around the door and through the heating vents, Caney decided to crank up the jukebox. If anyone could outwhine an Oklahoma windstorm, it was Merle Haggard singing about low-down women and low-life men.

Caney popped open the cash register and dug out a handful of quarters, then wheeled from behind the counter, heading for the jukebox, when the front door flew open.

A blast of wind howled as it swooped and swirled into the Honk, giving new life to the dark fears of Caney's childhood, new voice to an aunt long dead . . . a voice that whispered against the rushing air.

Night creatures ride on the wind, boy.

Dizzy with dread, Caney whirled, his pulse pounding in his ears, his voice stunned to silence by the banshee that loomed in the doorway, her long dark cloak billowing around her. With her hair whipping at her face, her lips stretched into a B-movie grimace, the shrillness of her scream echoed inside the dim light of the Honk.

"Molly O, what the hell are you yelling about?"

"Caney Paxton!" Molly O clutched at her heart while she worked to regain her breath. "I think you've gave me a thrombosis."

"Well, if your heart stops before you close that door, then I'm pretty sure my pecker's gonna freeze off."

"Oh," she said, noticing for the first time that Caney was naked. "Honey, you ought to have something on your feet."

"My feet? It's not my feet I'm worried about."

"What in the world are you doing out here without any clothes on? You know what time it is?"

"No, but if you'll shut that door . . ."

"Caney, are you okay?" she asked, her voice registering concern. "That kidney infection's come back, hasn't it? I knew I should've refilled your prescription soon as—"

"My kidneys are fine! My feet are fine!" Then Caney glanced down at his lap. "But this little baby here is about to ice over."

"Well, I don't wonder. It's freezing in here." Molly O slammed the door, snapped on the lights, then fiddled with the thermostat until the heater kicked on.

"You started coffee yet?" she asked as she peeled off her coat.

"Nope."

"Good." She hung her coat on a rack in the corner, then bent to a cracked mirror propped on a low, narrow shelf. "I can't abide a naked man in the kitchen." She smoothed her hair, then wiped at a smudge of rouge on one cheek. "Dewey O'Keefe, God rest his soul, thought he couldn't cook a lick unless he was naked." Molly O ran her tongue over her teeth once, checking for lipstick.

"By the way," Caney said, "what are you doing here so early?"

"Couldn't sleep."

"Those dreams again?"

"No. Everything's fine." Molly O shot him her top-of-the-morning smile, but not even Merle Norman could help her pull it off. Lips shiny with Wild Poppy, cheeks flushed with Woodland Rose, skin dusted with Perfectly Porcelain . . . none of it could hide the lines that webbed her brow or the dark half-moons beneath her eyes or the tightness that pulled at her mouth.

"Feeling all right?"

"Great," she said as she slipped into her cheerful Christmas apron, the skirt too tight across her hips, the bodice too narrow to cover her Maidenform double D's. But this morning, the apron fit her better than the Christmas cheer.

"Insomnia?" The question Caney intended sounded more like an accusation.

"Too excited about Christmas, I guess." She tried to put some sparkle into it. "Still got so much to do."

"Well, I hope to God you're all finished decorating."

"Yeah, at least I'm done with that. But I haven't wrapped not one gift and I've still got to—"

"Look, you want to take the day off, that's fine with me. I mean, it's not like we're overrun with business here. Nothing I can't handle."

"Oh no!" she said too fast. "I'll get it all done. Always do. Matter of fact, I been thinking about helping you out this weekend. No sense in having Wanda Sue come in."

"This weekend? Christmas?"

"Well, yeah. But you know what you can expect from Wanda Sue. Sitting on her butt, drinking coffee. And you know for sure Henry Brister's gonna show up for Christmas dinner. Can't get a fork of mashed potatoes in his mouth, let alone the rest of it. You think Wanda Sue's gonna cut up Henry's turkey? You think she's gonna do that?"

"What about Brenda? Thought you were going to Nashville. Thought you two were going to spend Christmas together."

"That's not going to work out the way we planned."

"You mean—"

"See, Brenda's got some auditions coming up. . . ."

"On Christmas?"

"And she's having new head shots made. Same photographer who shoots Tanya Tucker's pictures."

"But why can't you go on to Nashville? I can't figure out why you—"

"You don't know nothing about show business, Caney. Nothing at all."

Caney knew Molly O wasn't telling him the whole story, not by a long shot. But when she stepped behind the counter and began to spoon coffee into a filter, he knew the conversation had come to a close.

"Now," Molly O said, "we gonna get this place opened up or what?"

Chapter Four

MOLLY O HAD long ago given up trying to help Caney get dressed each morning, so she stood by and watched as he rocked back on the bed, then wrestled his way into a pair of Wranglers by rolling first onto one hip and then the other.

About the most she could do was make sure he had matched socks, clean jeans and a fresh denim shirt every morning. If she didn't, he'd simply slide into whatever he'd worn the day before and the one before that. Clothes held no more interest for Caney than food or the weather or the time of day.

When someone began to bang on the front door of the Honk, Caney shook his head in disgust.

"Why the hell can't he wait till we're open?"

"Guess he's hungry," Molly O said as she peeled plastic off a shirt just back from the cleaners. "Life don't like to wait long for his breakfast."

Life Halstead, the most regular of the regulars, was always the first customer of the day and nearly always the last.

"He's hungry, all right," Caney said. "But it's not food he's after."

"Then why does he show up here for breakfast, dinner and supper, seven days a week?"

"No mystery there." Caney popped his head through the neck of an undershirt, then worked his arms into the sleeves which strained against his biceps. "You know he comes to see you."

Molly O took a few seconds to consider Caney's remark, then she pitched his shirt at him. "You ought to be ashamed of yourself, Caney. Why, Reba's not been in the ground more'n six months."

"Well, I doubt Life's spending much time checking the calendar."

"He's just lonesome, that's all. Sold off most of his land and some of his cattle, so he doesn't have much to keep him busy. That's why he comes here . . . to eat, have a little company, read the morning paper."

"Life doesn't read the paper. He just props it in front of him so you won't know he's watching you."

"You're beginning to sound like Wanda Sue. Biggest gossip in town."

"Not gossip. Fact."

"Caney, you know how old Life is?"

"What's that got to do with it?"

Molly O stepped closer to the bed and lowered her voice, though there was little danger Life could hear her above the racket he was making out front.

"The man is old enough to die," she said.

"Hell, we're all old enough to die."

"Yeah, but some's older than others."

"Looks to me like Life's still got some kick left in him."

"I doubt it. He's had two heart attacks. Gallbladder's gone bad. And he's about half-deaf."

"Too many damaged parts, huh?" Caney hauled one leg onto the bed, then stuffed his lifeless foot into a stretched gray sock. "Well, that'll damned sure take a man out of the game, won't it?"

The question hung between them long enough to fill the room with silence. Even the banging out front had stopped.

"Honey, I—"

"You'd better go open the door or we're gonna lose our first customer of the day," Caney said as he reached for his other sock. "And we can't afford to let Life get away from us, can we?"

By the time Caney had finished dressing and rolled into the cafe, Life Halstead was hunkered over his second cup of coffee and a greasy plate streaked with cold egg yolk. Though his face was half-hidden behind the morning paper, his eyes were firmly fixed on Molly O's bottom as she bent to swipe at crumbs on a tabletop.

"Morning, Life," Caney said.

"Yes, it is." Life cut his eyes back to the paper, but he was clearly not as engrossed by the print as he was by the way Molly O's skirt stretched across her hips. "A fine morning."

But Caney could see little evidence of a fine morning. A steady rain had started to fall, and the wind, straight out of the north, scattered scraps of yesterday's garbage across the parking lot.

"Raccoons got into the trash again last night," Caney said. "We got crap blowing from here to Texas."

"I wouldn't worry about it," Life said. "A little more crap in Texas ain't gonna make much difference." Obviously pleased with this contribution of humor, Life smiled.

When Caney heard the old Plymouth pull up and park, he didn't even have to turn to know who was coming in.

Soldier Starr and Quinton Roach were always the first of the coffee drinkers to arrive, settling in at their regular table just before seven, the same table they had occupied every morning since the day the Honk opened. The third member of their group, Hooks Red Eagle, usually showed up at seven-thirty, the galvanized tub in the bed of his pickup teeming with catfish. Hooks, always on the lake before dawn to run his trotline, sold fish to Caney from time to time and gave the rest to his neighbors, having no taste for fish himself.

All three men were Cherokees, all in their late sixties . . . friends from boyhood, and all veterans of World War II, the one subject they never discussed, their conversations centering instead on tribal politics, weather and women. Though they had long suspected the three topics were connected in some mysterious way, they had yet to discover it.

"Hey, Caney," Soldier said, "I figured we were going to have to go down to the Dairy Queen to find a cup of coffee this morning."

Caney looked puzzled. "Dairy Queen's not open yet."

"Looks like you're not either."

"What?"

"You forgot to turn on the sign."

"Oh." Caney stirred a spoon of sugar into his coffee, then reached over the cash register and flipped a switch on the wall.

The sign out front, once the biggest and brightest in the county, tilted and trembled against the wind. Pelted by too many BBs and battered by too many storms, it attracted no more attention now than a dozen others along this stretch of highway. Now, even the brilliance of the neon had faded.

But twelve years earlier—when the awnings were bright, when the stainless-steel kitchen gleamed, when the countertop and tile glistened—Caney hadn't had to be reminded about the sign. Then, when even "Opening Soon" had been a fresh joke, Caney's fingers would tingle with excitement as he reached for the switch that would turn it on. And when the first bright neon blazed in the morning sky, he would stare wide-eyed with the wonder of a boy watching his first Roman candle explode in the air.

The day the sign had been delivered and installed, Caney turned twenty, still young enough to laugh about mistakes. But after eighteen months in a VA hospital, he was not as familiar with laughter as he had once been.

Caney had designed the building with the help of Wink Webster, an amputee in the ward who had done some drafting in high school. And from the day the foundation was poured, Molly O made sure they got to "watch" the building going up by sending them snapshots she took of the construction site each week.

Then, the morning before Caney's discharge, he called Leon's Neon in Tulsa where he had the sign made. He told Leon exactly what he wanted: THE HONK AND HOLLER in ten-inch letters, red neon against a white background. After all the details were settled, Caney wrote a check for the deposit and put it in the mail.

That might have been the end of it if the guys in the ward hadn't smuggled in some beer and bourbon that afternoon to give Caney a "getting-the-hell-out-of-here" party. And the sign might have been perfect if Caney hadn't drunk half a case of Coors and if he hadn't listened to Wink, who drank the other half.

"Hell, Caney," Wink said, "if you're going to put that sign up now, you ought to add 'Opening Soon' to it. Then everyone who drives by will know something big is going to happen."

"You think so?"

"Sure. They'll figure there's going to be some kind of grand opening. Prizes, free food. That sort of thing."

"That's not a bad idea."

"Maybe a band. Have a dance out there on the parking lot."

"Yeah. I like that," Caney said, his entrepreneurial spirit fueled by a dozen cans of beer.

"You'll draw a big crowd, too, if you'll tell those carhops you hire to wear short skirts."

"Real short!"

"And halter tops."

"Those stretchy kind."

"Go call that guy. . . ."

"Leon?"

"Yeah. Call him before it's too late."

"Well . . ."

"Look. Just tell him you've decided on a little change in design. Tell him you want to add 'Opening Soon.' Now how he does it is up to him, of course, but if it was me, I'd hand-letter a sign to hook on the bottom of the neon. Then, once you're open, just unhook it, toss it in the trash and you're in business."

"Okay! Soon's I finish this beer, I'm gonna call Leon."

Three weeks later, Leon delivered and installed the sign. THE HONK AND HOLLER OPENING SOON. Mounted on steel, anchored in concrete. Six hundred dollars of red neon. Nonrefundable.

At first, living with the sign was easy. While Caney was doing the hiring, ordering stock, having menus printed, "Opening Soon" made sense. And the grand opening *was* grand—free hotdogs, a rock band and carhops in halter tops.

But as soon as the hoopla ended and the Honk and Holler was in business, "Opening Soon" gave the locals something to laugh about.

Caney didn't mind, though, not in the beginning. Not when old pickups and new Firebirds and jacked-up Camaros circled the lot, waiting for a parking spot. Not when knots of teens in tight jeans fed handfuls of quarters into the jukebox. Not when long-legged carhops juggled trays of chili cheeseburgers and frosted mugs of cherry-pickle-lemon-lime-orange until two o'clock every morning.

But all that had changed.

And now THE HONK AND HOLLER OPENING SOON was just another tired old joke.

Chapter Five

THE LUNCH CROWD at the Honk wouldn't have filled a Volkswagen van. Two checkers from the Piggly Wiggly; a telephone repairman out of Muskogee; Cash Garnette, who auctioned livestock at the sale barn; a kid cutting classes at the high school; Wilma Driver, who sold real estate for Century 21; and, of course, Life Halstead.

They'd all cleared out except for Wilma who was waiting on a steak sandwich to take home to her ailing husband, Rex.

"He was up all night," Wilma said. "Why, I didn't get any sleep at all. And I had a house to show Big Fib Fry at nine this morning. Going way below appraisal, too."

"How's he feeling now?" Molly O asked.

"Big Fib?"

"No, Rex."

"Oh, still complaining. Says his . . . thing is swollen. Made me touch it to see if it had fever in it."

Molly O shook her head, a gesture of sympathy either for Rex and his fevered penis or for Wilma, who had been made to touch it.

"He runs to the bathroom every five minutes. And would you

believe he pees through my tea strainer?" Wilma's mouth puckered with distaste.

"Took my second husband three weeks to pass his," Molly O said.

"Three weeks?" Wilma's voice was filled with outrage.

"Wasn't bigger'n a plantar's wart. 'Bout as ugly, too. But you'd of thought he had a diamond. Kept it in a little drawstring pouch, showed it to everyone in town."

"Well, I haven't got three weeks to spare. Rex is just going to have to understand that I've got a career, kidney stone or not. And as far as him showing it off like some Cracker Jack prize? That would not look good for me or Century 21. Would not look good at all."

"Oh, oh," Molly O said. "Duncan's loose again."

Wilma reached for the phone. "I'll call Ellen so she won't worry."

"Afternoon, Duncan," Molly O said as a gaunt old man shuffled inside, but he offered no response, and, of course, she expected none.

She knew what he was there for, knew he would begin moving silently around the dining room and kitchen, measuring counter-tops, shelving, cabinets, windows, doors.

Duncan Renfro, a carpenter for over fifty years, had helped build the Honk, as well as many of the houses and businesses around town. But now, robbed of memory by Alzheimer's, unable to recall the familiarity of faces and neighborhoods he had known for a life-time, powerless to voice even his own name, he was aware of only one thing—the importance of accurate dimensions.

So from time to time, whenever he was able to slip away from the confines of home, he drifted into the Honk, fumbled in his pocket for one of the half dozen tape measures he carried and set to work doing the one job he could still remember.

Then, retrieved like a lost pet, he was led home by his wife, Ellen, a wife he no longer recognized and a home he was connected to only by inches.

When Caney came out of the kitchen, he said, "Hey, Duncan.

How's it going?" but the old man, busy measuring the pass-through, never looked up.

"Did you call Ellen?" Caney asked Molly O.

"I did," Wilma answered. "She's on her way."

Caney handed Wilma her sandwich in a paper bag. "Guess you wanted mustard on this. Didn't think to ask."

"Caney, why are you doing the cooking again?" Wilma asked. "Thought you hired a new cook."

"I did. He showed up just long enough to draw twenty dollars against his pay and make off with ten pounds of round steak and a gallon of chili peppers."

"Now what do you suppose he's going to do with a gallon of—"

Wilma's question was cut short by the sound of air brakes as an eighteen-wheeler bounced off the highway and pulled onto the edge of the parking lot. Before the rig had even stopped rolling, the passenger door of the cab opened and a woman in a short yellow dress, a faded jean jacket and red cowboy boots climbed out.

"Now there's a fashion statement," Wilma said.

The red boots had barely touched ground before the truck began to move.

"He's in a hell of a hurry to get back on the road."

"Maybe he's just in a hurry to get shed of her," Molly O said.

The woman dropped a limp duffel bag at her feet, then readjusted a bundle in her arms, tucking corners of a stained blanket around whatever she was carrying.

"What's that she's got wrapped up?" Wilma asked. "Is that a baby?"

"Look's like it's dead," Molly O whispered.

Wilma screeched, "She's carrying a dead baby?"

"No," Molly O said with little certainty. "I think it's a cat."

"Now why in the hell would she be carrying around a dead cat?" Caney asked.

"We don't know if it's dead," Molly O said in a voice that appealed for reason. "It might just be asleep."

The woman picked up the duffel bag and started toward the cafe.

"Well, whatever it is, we're fixing to find out."

The woman looked like she had nowhere to go, but she moved like she was in a hurry to get there. She reminded Caney of a coyote. Fast. Wary. And tough.

Just as she neared the front door, she stopped and peered into the window.

"She sees us watching her." Molly O grabbed a rag and began to polish the dials of the coffeemaker. "Look busy!"

Wilma, in a frantic attempt to busy herself, plunked her butt onto a stool at the counter, yanked her husband's steak sandwich out of the bag and snapped off a mouthful with the exaggerated gestures of a silent film star. But Caney, quiet and unmoving, stared back at the woman through the window.

Her face seemed to be all hard edges and sharp angles—an unyielding jaw, defiant chin, the tight, straight line of uncurled lips.

Caney had known her kind before, could tell what she had been . . . the girl in third grade who went without eating rather than line up for free lunches, the one who stood alone in the corner of the playground, staring down an alley at something the others could never see . . . the girl at fourteen who smoked in the bathroom and inked H-A-T-E into the back of her hand . . . the girl in high school who drifted away long before senior pictures ever made it into the yearbook.

She was trouble, Caney had no doubt about that. But she was something else, too . . . something Caney couldn't put a name to.

Without glancing up, Molly O asked, "What's she doing out there?"

"Reading," Caney said.

The front window of the Honk was plastered with signs—notices of garage sales and pancake suppers, lost dogs and free kittens, ads for houses to rent, guitar lessons, mobile homes for sale, fliers announcing talent contests, county fairs and cattle auctions, posters for the United Way and Mary Kay.

Most had been taped to the glass so long that the paper had

curled and yellowed with age. But the woman outside didn't move until she had studied each one.

By the time she stepped inside, the coffeemaker sparkled and all that remained of Rex's steak sandwich was the mustard in the corner of Wilma's mouth.

The woman stood in the doorway for a long time, taking it all in until she had to move aside for an old man measuring the door frame.

"Can I help you?" Molly O asked.

"I'm here about the job," she said.

"What job?"

"Carhop."

"Oh, we don't use them anymore. What made you think we needed a carhop?"

The woman went to the window and peeled a small rippled sign off the glass. CARHOP WANTED. The lettering, once bold and black, had faded to gray.

"Well, that's been there for ages," Molly O said. "Eight or nine years, I guess."

Then Wilma asked, "What have you got in the blanket?" Her tone sounded a bit accusatory, but if this stranger was transporting a dead baby, Wilma believed she had a right to know.

"A dog."

"Is it sick?"

"She lost a leg."

"Oh, poor little thing." Wilma knew that sympathy would reflect well on her and Century 21. And she had long ago learned that appearances could be deceiving, especially in the real estate business. She would never forget the man dressed like a rag picker who had pulled fifty thousand dollars out of a paper sack to pay cash for a brick duplex with bad plumbing.

"Let me hold her for you," Wilma said, her voice dripping with solicitude.

After a few hesitant moments, the woman gingerly eased the small bundle of dog and blanket into Wilma's arms.

"Look," the woman said to Molly O, "I really need a job."

"Well, like I told you—"

"I'm looking for some steady help in the kitchen," Caney said.

Molly O sent a spoon clattering to the floor and shot Caney a slit-eyed stare of caution.

"Can you cook?" Caney asked.

"Nothing you'd want to eat."

Molly O winked at Wilma, clearly encouraged by the woman's confession.

"But I'm good at the curb. I can make you money out there."

"Wish I could help you out," Caney said, "but I'm only looking to hire a cook. Someone permanent."

"I'll work for tips."

"You wouldn't make anything," Molly O warned.

"I'm sorry, lady, but—"

"Vena. Vena Takes Horse."

"Takes Horse." Wilma looked puzzled. "Is that Cherokee or Choctaw?"

"Crow."

"Well, truth is, Vena," Caney said, testing the name, "we don't have enough business in here to turn a profit most months. But out there . . ." He inclined his head toward the parking lot, a man pointing out the wasteland.

"I'll take my chances."

Molly O shook her head. "Why, you wouldn't snag a customer a week."

"You don't have anything to lose, then, do you? I mean, if I'm just working for tips, then it won't cost you a dime, will it?"

"Besides, Sunday is Christmas!" Molly O's voice was edged with desperation now. "You can't expect to do any business out there on Christmas weekend."

Just then a banged-up red Mustang with a twelve-point buck strapped across the hood pulled in and made a wide half-circle around the parking lot, slowing as it headed back toward the highway.

"Glad they're not staying," Molly O said. "A deer with a bullet in its head and a little blood smeared across its face would not enhance our dining atmosphere."

But when the car idled to a stop, Vena shot out the door and headed across the parking lot. The driver, a heavyset man in an orange hunting vest, had already opened his door and planted one foot on the ground before Vena reached him and talked him back into the car.

"I'll bet you a doughnut he stopped to ask directions," Molly O said.

The man slammed the door, then rolled down the window. His passengers, a woman and little girl in the front and a man and two teenage boys in the back, listened as Vena leaned in the window and spoke.

"I thought deer season was over," Wilma said.

"Not for bow hunters," Caney told her.

As soon as Vena turned away and started back to the cafe, the man rolled up his window and restarted the engine.

Molly O mocked a laugh and said, "Well, so much for curb service."

But then, instead of leaving, the driver maneuvered the Mustang into a tight turn and pulled into one of the parking spots right in front of the Honk.

"Eight hamburgers, hold the onions on two," Vena yelled as she came through the door. "Two chili dogs, five orders of fries, three Cokes and two coffees."

Caney spun his chair and wheeled toward the kitchen.

"Oh, yeah," Vena said, "you got any doughnuts?"

"Nope," Caney said. "Molly O just bought the last one."

Chapter Six

$\mathcal{B}$Y FOUR-THIRTY, Vena had snagged three cars, two pickups and a van filled with a covey of Blue Birds—a dozen little girls whose discovery of a "real" carhop was just too "cool." The driver, a stern-looking Bird Leader, tried her best to convince the brood that eating inside her brand-new Dodge Caravan would not be nearly as "cool" as going inside, but they had seen too many reruns of *American Graffiti*. She didn't have a prayer.

Just before sunset Caney ran out of hamburger buns when a gang of 4-H boys jammed into the cab of an old GMC reordered three times. The boys stuffed themselves with burgers less for the pleasure of eating than for the excitement of watching Vena cross the lot, the wind pasting her thin yellow dress against her crotch.

But she couldn't catch everyone who pulled in. The regulars went on inside where they eyed Vena curiously as she prepared trays and picked up her orders. Each time she went out the door, though, they fired questions at Caney and Molly O about the sudden appearance of the new carhop. Most stayed longer than usual, lingering over Thursday's special of liver and onions, their conversations enlivened by the dramatic turn of events at the Honk.

Sam Kellam, not quite as regular as the regulars, was out of his truck and halfway to the door when Vena passed him with a tray of foot-longs and fries. He paused and watched her stride across the lot before he went inside.

Sam had just turned forty, but lean and handsome, he made forty look good. Some said he had the hard, mean eyes of his daddy. But they didn't say it when Sam was around.

An Old Testament fanatic, Kyle Kellam had kept his boys in line with fear of retribution, though they feared God's punishment far less than they feared their daddy's. But on the night of Sam's sixteenth birthday, he made the mistake of diluting his fear with bourbon, and when he staggered home at two in the morning, he found his father waiting for him in the yard.

Kyle, in a brutal rage, stripped Sam, beat him with a cattle prod, then hauled him to town and chained him, naked and bleeding, to the door of Christ Temple where he was discovered the next morning as the congregation arrived for church.

Sam left town that same day and stayed gone for eight years. No one knew where he was or how he found out his daddy had died, but on the day of the funeral, Sam showed up, walked straight to the coffin and spit on Kyle Kellam's face.

Whatever meanness was born in that boy chained to the door of a church at sixteen had taken root like a spiny cactus that had flourished on nothing more than heat for the past twenty-four years.

As he slid onto a stool near the door, he tossed two dollars on the counter, but kept his eyes on Vena while she hooked the tray into the window of a gray Cutlass.

"You looking for a beer, Sam?"

"If they're still putting alcohol in it, I am."

As Caney popped the top from a bottle of Budweiser, Sam watched Vena make change for the teenage driver of the Olds, a boy who looked too young to drive.

After Sam took a long pull at the bottle, he lit a cigarette, then went at the beer again before he glanced back outside at Vena.

"Where'd you find the squaw, Caney?"

"What?" Caney said, momentarily distracted by a popping noise coming from the ice machine.

Sam tilted the nearly empty bottle and used it to point toward Vena. "Nice ass," he said, then downed the last of the beer and wiped his mouth with the back of his hand. "Real nice-looking piece of ass."

Caney was surprised to feel his jaw tighten with anger. He shifted forward in his chair, his face just inches away from Sam's.

"You figure that's any of your business, Sam? Seems to me—"

"Caney!" Molly O yelled.

Caney pivoted to see Molly O standing in a puddle of water running from beneath the ice maker.

"Look at this mess," she said.

But Caney was, at the moment, little concerned with busted tubing spouting water onto the floor.

When he turned back to the counter, Sam was already out the door. Through the front window, Caney saw him brush against Vena as he walked to his truck.

A minute later, when Vena came back inside, Caney found he still had Sam's two dollars wadded tightly in his fist.

At seven-thirty Vena picked up her last customers of the night, a couple in their sixties drinking whiskey from paper cups. They had intended a quick stop to use the john, but when they encountered Vena at the curb, they decided to stay. After their business inside the Honk was finished, they returned to their car where they ordered steak finger baskets, glasses of ice and Coke.

Though the food was largely ignored, they reordered fresh setups twice and stayed until closing time.

When Caney turned off the sign at nine, the pockets of Vena's jacket jangled with change, tips which totaled eleven dollars and eighty-three cents.

"You want to buy some of this silver?" Vena asked Caney as she dropped two handfuls of change onto the counter.

"Sure. I'll take whatever you got."

"Well, you didn't exactly make your fortune, did you?" Molly O said, barely able to keep the I-told-you-so tone out of her voice.

"No," Vena answered as she stacked quarters four high, "but it's better than nothing."

Molly O, who usually left around seven, the tail end of the supper run, had spent the past two hours finding work that demanded her attention. She had emptied all the salt and pepper shakers, then washed and dried each one before she refilled them. As soon as Life Halstead had cleared out, she wiped down all the stools at the counter with Pine Sol. She reorganized everything in the freezer, then changed the shelf paper in a cabinet where they kept clean cups and saucers.

Caney had asked her a couple of times why she was staying so late, but rather than admit her determination to outlast Vena, she had pointed out work long overdue, work she couldn't put off any longer.

Now, with Vena about to make an exit, Molly O got busy cleaning the plastic menu covers stacked on the counter, a job that would keep her as near Caney as possible.

"Here's ten dollars," Vena said, shoving stacks of silver across the counter.

Caney opened the cash register. "Look," he said as he handed her two fives, "I don't feel right not paying you a salary, but—"

"I told you I'd work for tips."

"Well, at least let me feed you. I can sure as hell afford to do that."

"I've already cleaned the grill," Molly O said.

"That's okay. I'm not hungry."

Caney said, "You haven't had a bite since you got here." Then he pushed a package wrapped in foil across the counter to Vena. "I fixed you a couple of ham-and-cheese sandwiches."

"Thanks."

"How about a cup of coffee?" Caney offered.

"Just emptied the pot," Molly O said.

"I've got to go, anyway."

"You want a Coke?" Caney asked. "A bottle of beer?"

Vena shook her head. "I'll just go get the dog," she said as she turned and walked away.

Earlier in the day, right after her first customers left, Vena had settled the dog in a small utility room next to the kitchen. Each time she'd checked, the dog was asleep. But she'd had to wake it twice—once for the medicine and again when she replaced the soiled pad inside the blanket.

Now, though, the dog was awake, and as Vena eased it into a cardboard box she'd found behind the cafe, it began to whimper.

"It's okay," she said as she shouldered her duffel bag and cradled the box beneath her arm. "Don't be scared."

"How's she doing?" Caney asked when Vena came from the back.

"Not so good."

"You think she'd eat some ground beef?"

"No. She couldn't handle that right now."

"How about—"

"I've got something for her."

Vena stuffed the sandwiches inside her bag while she headed for the door.

"Why don't you let Molly O give you a ride?" Caney said. Then, to Molly O, "You're about ready to leave, aren't you?"

"Not yet. I've still got a few more things to do."

"I'll walk." Vena said. "It's not that far."

"Okay." Caney shrugged. "I guess we'll see you tomorrow."

"Sure." Then, as she was closing the door, Vena said good-bye.

Caney, rolling his chair to the window, watched her as she crossed the parking lot. She moved quickly, away from the light, like an animal sensing safety in the cover of darkness.

Molly O finally broke the silence when she picked up the menus and tapped them against the counter until they fell evenly, between her fingers, into a neat stack. But Caney, undistracted, continued to stare out the window even after Vena had disappeared into the night.

"Well," Molly O said, her voice tinged with relief, "we've seen the last of that one."

"You don't think she'll be back?" Caney asked, still peering into the shadows edging the road.

"Not if we're lucky."

Caney turned then, studying Molly O's face. "What's going on with you, huh?"

"With me?"

"Yeah. You've been pissed since she walked in. I don't get it."

"No." Molly O slapped the menus onto the counter, sending most of them flying to the floor. "Apparently you don't."

"Then why don't you tell me."

"She's trouble, Caney. Real trouble."

"She didn't cause me any trouble, but she's damned sure got you riled up. What I don't know is why."

"Why?" Molly O pulled off her apron, jerking at ties and clawing at straps like a woman coming out of a straitjacket. "Because she's a liar and a thief."

"What are you talking about?"

"When Wilma asked her where she was living—"

"Oh, hell. Wilma was snooping around, hoping to make her ten percent on one of those cracker box apartments she rents out."

"The point is, she told Wilma she'd found a place west of town."

"So?"

" 'Case you didn't know it," Molly O said, pointing in the direction Vena had taken, "that's east."

"Aw, she probably just got turned around."

"Her kind don't get turned around." Molly O worked at a knot in one of her apron strings. "Woman like that, she always knows exactly where she's going."

"Maybe she needed something from the Texaco. She might've decided to walk down there before she went home."

"The Texaco?" Molly O shook her head at the suggestion. "What for? A tank of gas?"

"Hell, I don't know. Maybe she went to meet her boyfriend. Maybe she went to look for another job. A *real* job."

"But doesn't it seem fishy to you, her saying she lived west, then striking out east? Doesn't that make you just the least bit suspicious?"

"Nope. But then I'm not the suspicious type."

"Well, you'd better be glad one of us is, 'cause if I hadn't had my eyes open, which you obviously did not, then she would've walked out of here with more than a candle."

"That's what this is about? A damned candle?"

"Caney, a thief is a thief. If she'll take one thing, then she'll take another."

"Yeah, you're right. We'd better count the pickles."

"Listen. If she walked in here with a gun and said, 'This is a stickup,' then——"

"Don't make any sudden moves," Caney said as he shaped his hand into a pistol, pointing it at Molly O. "Just hand over your candle."

Molly O waved his hand away, a gesture emphasizing her seriousness. "If she said, 'Empty that cash register,' it wouldn't matter whether she made off with a dollar or a thousand. She'd still be a thief."

Then, with the posture of an attorney winding up her closing argument, Molly O squared her shoulders, offered her hands, palms up, and said, "In this case, we were lucky. All she got away with was a candle."

"Well, since she didn't hold us up at gunpoint, how did she manage to make off with our candle?"

"She snatched it out of the cabinet in the utility room."

"Molly O, we've used those candles for years. You drag them out every time the electricity goes out."

"That don't matter, Caney."

"They're nothing but nubbins now. Hell, some aren't as long as my thumb."

"What's important here is that she took what didn't belong to her."

"And how do you know? Did you see her take it?"

"No, but——"

"Did you have them counted?"

Molly O shook her head. "I saw it in that bag she carries."

"Jesus Christ." Caney shook the last cigarette from the pack he'd opened that morning. "I can't believe you went through her stuff."

"I didn't go *through* it. I just unzipped it and looked inside. It was right there on top."

Caney crushed the empty Camel package, then hurled it against the wall.

"Maybe I'm not as trusting as you are, Caney, but—"

"Look. The woman is working for nothing, wouldn't even eat a meal. She worked seven, eight hours, turned some business and—"

"Oh, honey." Molly O brushed Caney's hair away from his forehead like a mother forgiving a misguided child. "She just took the business from in here. If she hadn't got to them out there, they would've come inside."

"I don't know about that." Caney pulled back, out of Molly O's reach, opened the cash register and began pulling out bills. "I'd say we ran thirty or thirty-five dollars over most Thursdays."

"Well, it's neither here nor there now, is it?"

"How's that?"

"She left here headed for the interstate. Chances are she's already cozied up next to the fool who picked her up." Molly O took the bills from Caney's hand and stuffed them inside a bank bag. "By this time tomorrow night, she'll be God knows where, carrying that pitiful dog around until she finds someone else who'll give her a handout."

"I didn't give her a damned thing."

"And in case you didn't notice, she didn't say 'good night.' She said 'good-bye.' "

"That doesn't mean—"

"Trust me, Caney. We've seen the last of Miss Vena Takes Horse."

"I don't know," Caney said, once again staring out into the night. "I think she'll be back."

Chapter Seven

THE SCHOOL BUS sat at the far edge of a ravine less than a quarter mile behind the Honk. Vena had spotted it earlier in the day while she was out back, getting a box for the dog. She'd wanted to get a closer look, see what condition the bus was in, but when she saw MollyO watching her from the kitchen, she decided to wait until the cafe closed, hoping the night would shield her from view.

She followed the road until it curved away from the Honk before she cut back and crossed an open field. As she crawled through a barbed-wire fence to reach the ravine, she heard a horse snuffle from somewhere nearby.

From what she could tell, the bus hadn't been moved for years. Scrub brush had grown up to the fenders, and trumpet vines snaked over the hood and grille. A couple of windows near the front were cracked, but she didn't see any broken ones, so she supposed the inside might be dry. Still, she didn't expect much.

She hadn't been inside a school bus since she was eleven, when she whipped Braz Iker, a fight that left her facing an angry principal who suspended her bus privileges for a week, a suspension she considered to be a reprieve rather than a punishment. After that, she and Helen never rode the bus again, preferring instead to hitch rides when they could catch them and to walk when they couldn't.

But the fight on the bus wasn't the only time Vena and Braz had tangled.

Their first confrontation took place when Vena was in the third grade, the day he called Helen a blanket ass, laughed at her braids and made her cry, an experience which prompted Vena to stab him with a pencil. The skirmish that ensued left Vena with a swollen lip and sprained ankle.

Then, having discovered his power over the Takes Horse sisters, Braz never passed up a chance to get to them.

When he taunted Helen for wearing shoes bought for a quarter at his cousin's yard sale, Vena wrestled him to the floor of the bus where he punched her in the stomach and made her throw up. When he ripped open Helen's lunch sack and produced what he claimed was a buffalo sandwich, Vena shoved him down the steps of the cafeteria, for which she paid with a black eye. And when he fooled Helen into believing she'd been invited to a Halloween party given by one of the town girls, Vena hit him in the neck with a rock, a lucky throw for which Braz retaliated by repeatedly slamming her head against the jungle gym.

Though she always came away from such confrontations bruised and bloody, she knew Helen suffered more . . . Helen, who chopped off her braid and flung her yard sale shoes into an abandoned well; Helen, who went hungry at lunch rather than bring a bologna sandwich from home; and Helen, who cried herself to sleep because she was the only girl in her class not invited to a Halloween party.

But Vena was tough in a way that Helen would never be, tough enough to take on a boy two years older and thirty pounds heavier than she was, the boy she finally whipped the day after her mother was first taken away to the state asylum.

Vena was sure that the news about her mother would have spread quickly after she was found mutilating herself in the Indian church, strapped into a straitjacket and hauled away by an ambulance with sirens blaring. Still, she thought that the Iker family might not have heard since they lived ten miles out on the river road.

But even before she and Helen slid into seats near the back of the bus, Braz started chanting, "Crazy old Indian, gone to the loony bin."

Helen covered her ears and, screaming, began rocking back and forth while Vena hurtled over two rows of seats to get to Braz, then, powered by fury, pummeled him until his face was a mass of welts and cuts and his front tooth was sliding down his chin in a stream of blood.

But that had been a lifetime ago, a time when Vena still believed she could protect Helen from anything.

Now, as she picked her way across the ravine, she wished for the innocence of her eleven-year-old self, the girl who was just beginning to suspect that a bullying white boy was not the worst life would offer.

Before she could pry the doors apart far enough to squeeze through, she smelled the heavy odor of mice and mildew. When she stepped into the gloom and chill of the stairwell, her flesh roughened with goose bumps.

She moved slowly, her face snagging cobwebs as she felt her way to the aisle. After she jostled her things onto a seat in the front, she lit a match, then held the flame over the box.

"How you doing, girl?" Vena whispered.

The dog lifted her face to the light, her eyes yellow in the reflection of the flame. A moment later, energy spent, her head sank back into the folds of the blanket.

Vena lit the candle she'd taken from Caney's cafe, then moved tentatively down the aisle. There was little to see—a man's well-worn western boot, a thermos missing its lid, a couple of paperback books and an unopened can of motor oil.

But in the back of the bus, Vena found a few surprises.

The last two rows of seats had been removed to make room for a thin mattress, the striped ticking stained and dotted with mouse droppings. And heaped in the corner, a tangle of horse blankets souring with mold.

Not much, she thought, but more than she had hoped for. She did, after all, have a bed, a dry place to sleep and silence—an improvement over the motel in Kansas City where she stayed while the dog was at the vet's.

She'd paid fourteen dollars a night for an airless room with bloodstains on the carpet, a pillow that smelled of soured breath and a crap game in the next room, dice crick-cracking from the time she checked in until she left three days later.

The motel did, however, provide a few luxuries not available in the bus, luxuries like heat, lights and water.

But Vena had greater regrets to deal with than the absence of utilities.

She wrestled the mattress up, pounded it as free of dust as she could, then flipped it over. As it *whump*ed to the floor, a family of field mice scurried away, tiny gray immigrants heading for safer territory.

As soon as Vena shook out the blankets and spread them over the mattress, she moved herself and the dog into their new one-bed efficiency. Then, though she was feeling a little empty, she put aside Caney's sandwiches for later. She could wait, but the dog couldn't.

She opened the frayed denim pouch containing antibiotics, gauze pads, cotton balls and plastic liners, all given without charge by the vet in Kansas City.

Dr. Anna, a painfully thin woman who spoke with a quick German accent, had said little to Vena, but she never stopped speaking to the dog. As she set up for the transfusion and got an IV started, she praised the dog for her bravery; while she administered the anesthesia, she explained the procedure; when she removed the tourniquet Vena had applied, she offered encouragement. Even after the animal was sedated and beyond hearing, Dr. Anna continued to converse with her patient, her voice filled with apology as she sawed away what was left of splintered bone.

Three days later, when Vena came to pick up the dog and settle the bill, she put forty-six dollars on the counter—two folded twenties and six crumpled ones. But Dr. Anna had taken only the twenties, then marked the bill paid in full, with nothing in her expression to suggest she was losing money, nothing in her manner to hint at rebuke.

Then Vena had spent more than four dollars of her last six on baby food for the dog and a bottle of aspirin for herself. And though she was almost out of cigarettes, she had decided to hang on to the last of her money.

She'd smoked her last Winston earlier in the evening, just before she left the Honk. By then she'd made a few tips, enough to buy a new pack, but she didn't. She figured she could survive the night. The dog, however, was another matter.

Vena crushed the antibiotics into powder which she sprinkled into a plastic bowl she'd brought from the cafe, then poured in a few dollops of baby food.

"Ah," she said, "tonight you're lucky. It's turkey, your favorite."

After she eased the dog from the box onto her lap, she held the bowl beneath its mouth. The dog took a few laps, then, exhausted, rested its head on Vena's leg.

"Well, I guess you did the best you could."

When Vena folded the cover back to tend to its wound, the dog began to tremble.

"Easy, girl. I won't hurt you."

After she removed the stained dressing that covered the stump of the amputated leg, Vena cleaned the wound, then covered it with a fresh gauze pad. Next, she cleaned the dog's hindquarters where it had soiled itself. Finally, she removed the dirty plastic liner and slipped a new one into place.

Finished, she rewrapped the dog, laid it on the mattress and covered them both with the blankets. As the dog warmed against her chest, Vena said, "Don't you worry about this place. When you're able, we'll be on our way."

A moment later, the dog licked Vena's hand.

"You're welcome, lady. You're very welcome."

Vena closed her eyes then, inviting sleep, but she was visited, instead, by the voice of a familiar but unwelcomed guest.

Miss Takes Horse? This is Sheriff Jorge Rulfo in Eddy County, New Mexico, and I'm afraid I've got some bad news for you.

Vena started to hum a tuneless melody, hoping the sound would drown out the voice, but she knew better. She'd tried that trick before.

I'm sure sorry I had to be the one to tell you, and especially three weeks late, but we've had a tough time tracking you down.

She thought about getting up to go outside, just sit in the chill night air for a while, but she was afraid if she moved, she'd wake the dog, and it had been through enough for one day.

Well, the way it looks, she was living in an abandoned shack out in the Paduca Breaks. Her nearest neighbor, if you can call him that, lived a good four, five miles away . . . an old hippie, calls himself Wolf. He says your sister might've had some mental problems. 'Course, I'm not sure Wolf's quite right in the head, either.

One night a couple of months ago, she'd turned back to Jack Daniel's, her old remedy for getting through a bad night, but she found out liquor was no match for this.

Anyway, Wolf said he'd seen your sister walking around out there night and day, talking to herself and setting fire to timber, scraps of paper, a mattress. Anything that'd burn. Said he only talked to her once when she came asking for a butcher knife to cut off her hair.

Sometimes she stayed awake all night, thinking she'd be safe to sleep during the day, but the voice was always waiting, no matter when she closed her eyes.

No, ma'am. From what I've been able to put together, it looks like an accident. Somehow, she set her clothes on fire.

Just before Vena drifted off, she realized she had left the candle burning. But the voice was silenced now, and she didn't dare move for fear it would speak again.

Besides, she thought, no one was going to notice a light flickering in the windows of a deserted bus.

And she was nearly right.

Chapter Eight

$\mathcal{B}$UI KHANH'S JOB at the Dallas Auto Detail lasted less than three hours. He wasn't quite sure what he had done wrong, but the boss, Apostolos Kartsonakis, had no doubts about the reason.

Apostolos hadn't been enthusiastic about hiring Bui in the first place because he had trouble understanding him. Bui's opening line, "Please needs to working cars cleaning," caused Apostolos to shake his head in confusion. And if anyone knew the value of learning the language, it was Apostolos, who had come to America with an English phrase book in one pocket and five drachmas in the other.

Still, two of the regular detailers hadn't shown up, and cars were already jammed all the way to the street when Bui walked in asking for a job. Besides, as Apostolos often said, "Beggars can't be chewers." But when he turned Bui over to the manager of the cleaning crews, he told her to make sure Bui didn't talk to the customers.

Sheniqua, an energetic woman with skin as dark as Bui's, operated on only one speed—fast-forward. Her rapid-fire instructions whizzed past Bui like bullets, most far wide of their mark. But he paid careful attention as she demonstrated the equipment and showed him the supplies.

Ten minutes later, Bui joined one of the crews, three men wearing blue shirts stitched with their names. When a new Mercedes was pulled forward in the line, they swarmed it.

One of Bui's jobs was to apply wax to the car after it had been washed and dried. He was expected to work quickly to stay ahead of Milton, the man with the polishing machine, the man who taught him the meaning of "Get your ass in gear" and "Okay, let this shit wagon roll."

By the time Bui's crew moved on to the next car, a black Volvo, he was beginning to enjoy the feel of the sun on his back and the deep, rich smell of car wax. He also liked listening to the other workers, some who spoke languages he had never heard before.

For the first time since he left Houston, Bui started to feel safe again.

He had been trying to convince himself for the past five days that the yellow-haired woman had recovered from her injury, that the money he gave her had paid for her damaged car and that the police had more important work to do than search for him.

On that first night, as he walked away from Houston, the lights of every passing car made him step into the shadows and turn his face away. Even as he crawled out of the train car the next day in Nacogdoches, he was certain the barking dogs he heard were coming for him.

That evening he paid two hundred dollars for a car with one door wired shut and no backseat. The woman who sold it to him lived in a sagging house with peeling paint, bars on the windows and a dozen other cars in the yard, most in worse shape than his. The woman did not ask Bui for an insurance form; he did not ask her for a title.

He drove to Dallas that night, slept in his car and started looking for work the next morning in Little Asia where he blended in with thousands of other Orientals. But the restaurants needed no cooks, the coffeehouses were full of waiters and the meat markets had enough butchers. So he drove into a part of the city where signs in the windows said HELP WANTED.

He had tried a beauty shop, two liquor stores and a motel before he stopped at the Dallas Auto Detail.

Just before Bui and his crew finished their third car of the morning, Milton handed him the buffer and told him to finish while he went to take a leak.

And that's when the trouble started.

At first, Bui was afraid Sheniqua would see him doing Milton's job, but he was also afraid not to keep working because the owner of the car, a woman dressed like a picture in a magazine, was watching him from the window of the customers' lounge.

Bui worked the buffer in slow, easy loops, but when the woman came out of the building to stand a few steps behind him, the loops seemed less easy.

"I have an important meeting at noon," she said.

Bui glanced at her and offered a tentative smile. Her hat, a soft shade of gray, matched her hair and the silk suit she was wearing.

"I have to be on time."

Though he didn't understand all the words she used, Bui could tell she wanted him to hurry. When she raised the sleeve of her jacket to check the time, the diamonds of her watch sparkled blue in the glare of the sun.

"How much longer do you think you will be?" she asked.

Bui nodded, still smiling.

"Do you speak English?"

"Yes, I am learning to speak English," Bui said, careful to enunciate and glad now for the opportunity to use the sentence he had learned from the beginner's language tape.

"Can't you work any faster?"

"Yes, I am learning to speak English," Bui said as fast as he could.

"No! Not *speak* faster," she said. "*Work* faster."

Bui tightened his grip on the buffer as he jerked it fitfully from side to side.

"Perhaps you should call back the other man. . . ."

But Bui had stopped listening to words he did not understand.

He had used the only response he knew to answer her questions, and he did not think she wanted to hear it again.

The woman continued to speak, but Bui had no time now for either smiles or nods. He bent to the work, the buffer skimming across the surface of the car. If Milton was not coming back to rescue him, he would have to rescue himself.

By the time he went after the last smear of wax, the muscles across his shoulders felt full of fire and his arms had numbed from wrists to elbows.

Finally, finished, he switched off the machine, stepped back and turned to the woman. Then, with a courteous bow of his head, he said, "Okay. Let this shit wagon roll."

After Apostolos yelled at Bui in two languages, neither of which Bui understood, he took him to his office where he stuffed a twenty-dollar bill into his pocket, kissed him on both cheeks, then said good-bye to him at the door.

Several of the detailing crews were taking their lunch break when Bui left the office and started across the lot. Most didn't even try to hide their grins as he passed, and when someone whispered, "Shit wagon," a few laughed out loud.

When Bui saw his own crew bunched together, he would not look into their eyes. But as he passed near them, a hand gripped his shoulder and Milton said, "Take it easy, kid."

Smiling, Bui blinked back tears. When he walked away, he was still wearing the warmth on his skin from Milton's strong, dark fingers.

Then, just before he reached the sidewalk, he heard footsteps coming up behind him.

"*Không may mắn, bạn tôi.*"

Stunned at hearing his own language, Bui wheeled and stared into the face of a teenage boy wearing one of the detailers' blue shirts with TRAN NGUYEN written above the pocket.

"*Bạn? Bạn có thể² gọi tôi?*"

The boy made a shushing sound as he gestured toward the other workers, but Bui didn't seem to notice. The words, which had been locked inside him for so long, began to spill out, the staccato sounds of Vietnamese coming with sudden rush, punctuated only by quick stabs of breath.

"Come on," the boy said, pointing to the street, but Bui's hurry now was not in leaving.

"Bạn có thê² quiṕ tôi đuợc không," Bui said, hoping the boy could intervene for him with Apostolos.

"Hey, man. Not here, not in front of these guys." Taking Bui by the elbow, the boy steered him to the street.

Like a child with no sense of direction, Bui let himself be propelled down the sidewalk, then pulled into the doorway of a squat, empty building.

"Hãy nghe tôi." The boy's tone sounded warmer and more sincere in Vietnamese.

Ten minutes later, Tran Nguyen left Bui with an empty money pouch and the assurance that he would make Apostolos change his mind.

Bui understood such dealings. Several hundred dong given to the father of a beautiful girl could secure a lovely wife; several thousand slipped into the hands of a government official could provide passage to a new country. And here in America, four hundred sixty-six dollars would buy back a job.

Bui hoped that Apostolos would not demand all the money, but even if he did, it would be a small price to pay. The Vietnamese boy had told him about the bonus the workers got every month, a bonus that sometimes ran as much as eight hundred dollars.

For the first hour he waited, Bui thought of all a good job would bring—a nice car for Nguyet to ride in, a beautiful house and garden, trips to Disney World and the Grand Canyon.

During the second hour, the sky darkened and rain began to fall. Within minutes the detailers started to leave work, running to their cars with their blue shirts sticking to their backs.

Still, the Vietnamese boy did not return.

Perhaps, Bui thought, the boy did not have enough influence to beg his case. Or maybe had not shown the proper respect. Bui had seen the result of such mishandled attempts many times. A government permit, bought and paid for, could get lost. An apartment secured with a thousand dong might require another thousand before the deal was done. So much could go wrong.

The rain had stopped before Bui finally stepped out of the doorway, but the clouds hung low and a chill wind picked at bits of trash in the gutters.

A chain hung across the entrance to the empty parking lot, its asphalt surface washed clean by the rain.

When Bui found the door unlocked and the office bright with light, he believed he might still have hope for a blue shirt with his name. But when he found Apostolos alone, his face full of confusion and surprise, Bui knew the Vietnamese boy had taken his money and run away.

By the time Apostolos pieced together the story, his face was red with rage.

"That little some-o-bitch!" Apostolos screamed. "Lying little some-o-bitch!"

But this time Bui didn't struggle to understand what he was hearing, didn't try to make sense of the words.

"*Malaka!*" Apostolos pounded his desk. "Thieving chicken-squat *malaka*," he yelled, reaching for the phone. "Well, the police will pin his skinny ass to the wagon."

"No!" Bui heard the echo of his own voice as he pleaded with the yellow-haired woman in the middle of the Houston street. "No police!"

But Apostolos was already dialing, even as Bui backed out the door.

An hour and fifty-two miles later, with the fuel needle pointing to E, Bui remembered the twenty-dollar bill Apostolos had put in his pocket that morning.

He pulled off the highway at the next station, a truck stop, and filled the car with regular.

Inside, he paid for the gas, then waited for his change at the counter where a sheet of glass covered a map of the United States. When the clerk dropped two coins on the glass, Bui picked them up from the places where they fell—a quarter on top of Nevada, a penny on Tennessee.

Then, without knowing why, Bui placed the flat of his hand over the map, pressed his palm into the middle of the country and spread his fingers wide. But his reach was too small to cover it . . . the breadth of his hand too narrow to stretch from east to west, the width too short to touch north or south.

He studied his hand there on top of America and wondered how he could ever find his place in a country so big.

He had left his home with a dream . . . a dream that had walked with him across Vietnam, sailed with him on the South China Sea, lived with him in a refugee camp in Malaysia. And now that dream seemed as lost as he was.

"Where you headed, partner?"

Bui turned to the man standing beside him, a big man with red hair twisting from beneath a cap with GLOBAL TRANSFER printed across the front.

"Saw you ponderin' over this map, thought you might need some help."

Bui nodded, more for the sake of courtesy than from understanding.

"Well, tell me where it is you're tryin' to get to, and I'll show you the way."

Bui narrowed his eyes in concentration and watched the man's lips, waiting for more information.

"Just show me where you're goin'," the man said as he tapped his finger against the glass.

Uncertain, Bui let his gaze wander over the map, taking in the strange shapes and odd-sounding names. Finally, he reached out and touched a spot near the center of America.

"Oklahoma? Why, hell, partner, you're almost there. See, you're gonna cross the Red River . . ."

Bui walked out of the truck stop into swirls of tiny flakes of ice. He had seen snow only in pictures—white banks piled against houses, cars half-buried, the round shapes of snowmen with hats atop their heads.

He smiled at the thought of Nguyet seeing snow for the first time, imagined her eyes wide with surprise, could see her spinning, mouth open to catch the taste of it on her tongue.

Bui's car, holding the snow in its creases and dents, was painted in soft patterns of white. And when he crawled inside, the vinyl seat covering, now stiff with the cold, made cracking sounds as he slid across it.

After he turned the key in the ignition, the motor caught once, then died. He pumped the gas pedal several times before he tried again, but the engine, sputtering, would not fire.

Bui was anxious to get back on the road, to drive into the darkness and snow. He had miles yet to travel, but he would not be traveling alone. His dream had resettled inside him, the dream that would ride with him across a river named Red to a land called Oklahoma.

When Bui turned the key again, the car roared to life.

"Okay," he said, grinning. "Let this shit wagon roll."

Chapter Nine

CANEY HAD BEEN WATCHING for her since sunup, though he had no reason to expect her at that time of morning. Even so, as soon as he had the coffee going, he was back at the front window, waiting.

When he saw her coming, he hurried to fill two cups, then slid one across the counter for her. He tried to wipe the smile off his face before she walked in, but couldn't quite get it done. He was glad she was there, and no way in hell could he hide it.

"You're out early," he said, sounding more pleased than he had a right to.

"What time do you open?"

"Whenever the first customer walks in."

Vena, unsure if Caney was teasing or telling the truth, looked at the Coors clock mounted above the jukebox.

"It's not even six."

"Doesn't matter," he said. "If you're hungry, then you're the first customer. And if you're the first customer, then we're open."

"Okay." Vena smiled. "I'm hungry."

"Great! How do you like your eggs?"

"Scrambled. Let me put the dog in the back and I'll help you."

"She doing any better?"

"Not much."

When Vena came back from the utility room, Caney was already in the kitchen, slapping a thick slice of ham onto the grill.

"Smells good," she said as she soaped her hands at the sink.

"You had her a long time?"

"What?"

"The dog."

"Found her a few days ago in Kansas." Vena took a handful of eggs from the refrigerator and began cracking them into a bowl. "She'd been hit by a car."

"What do you do, travel the country looking for—"

"How many of these will you eat?" Vena jumped in so quickly that Caney's question got lost.

"None for me." Caney flipped the ham over, then brushed butter on two slices of bread. "So, you come from Kansas?"

Vena feigned attention to the eggs, whipping them to a froth. "You already had breakfast?"

"No. I just make it a rule not to eat my own cooking."

"That bad, huh?"

"Well, good enough to keep the doors open. Can't manage to find a cook who'll stay more than three days."

"Maybe you're too hard on the help."

"Yeah," Caney said in mock sincerity. "That's how I whipped Molly O into shape."

"What time does she come in?"

"Whenever she damn well wants to."

Vena glanced toward the front, half expecting to see Molly O at the door. "Doubt she's going to be thrilled to find me here."

"Look, Vena, I don't know what got into her last night, but don't pay any attention to it."

"Is she a relative? Or . . . a friend."

"Little bit of both, I guess. She's been with me since I opened this place. Loyal as a brood hen. And she likes to mother me. Too much. But that's just her way."

Vena poured the beaten eggs on the grill as Caney turned the toast, his arm brushing against her hip.

"Sorry," he said.

They were quiet while Caney finished with Vena's breakfast. She carried her plate to the dining room and slid onto a stool while Caney wheeled to the other side of the counter, handed her a knife and fork, then freshened their coffee.

He watched her as she ate, but she was too hungry to feel self-conscious.

"This is good," she said between bites. "You're a better cook than you give yourself credit for."

"Well, it's hard to mess up ham and eggs."

"So you open this place whenever someone shows up, and you don't close till nine?"

"Seven days a week."

"When do you get a chance to get out?"

"Oh, if we had someone dependable in the kitchen, Molly O could run the Honk without me, but . . ." Caney was quick to turn Vena's attention back to her food. "You want some jelly?"

"That'll do it for me." Vena laid her knife and fork across her plate. "Best breakfast I've had in a while."

"Now you're just trying to butter up the cook." Caney poured more coffee, then offered Vena a Camel.

"I'm quitting," she said, but before Caney pulled the pack away, she held out her hand. "But I'm not quite there yet."

Caney lit her cigarette, then his own.

"You know," he said, "Molly O was probably right about this being a slow weekend. We're not likely to get a crowd in here today and tomorrow won't be any better."

"I don't know." Vena gestured toward the window. "Looks like you're getting off to a good start."

Caney looked up just as Life Halstead opened the door and stepped inside.

"Morning, Caney. Ma'am." As Life took his stool at the counter, he craned his neck trying to see into the kitchen.

"Guess she's sleeping in this morning," Caney said.

"Never knew her to do that."

"Well, sometimes we all break the pattern, don't we?"

"Not me."

"You ready for your breakfast?"

"Yeah, I suppose," Life said with reluctance. "But Molly O always takes care with my eggs, Caney. Makes sure the whites ain't runny and the yolks ain't hard."

"I'll do my best, Life."

Caney rolled into the kitchen, and after Vena crushed out her cigarette, she picked up her plate and followed him.

"Can I help?"

"I guess I can handle this."

"Then I wonder if I could ask you a favor?"

"Shoot."

"If you've got a shower back there in your room, I'd sure like to use it. See, they haven't turned the water on at my new place yet."

"Help yourself. Towels and washrags in the hall closet."

"Thanks. I won't be long."

"Take your time."

Caney's bedroom felt familiar to Vena in the way that one motel room seems like a hundred others. The walls were unadorned except for a framed print of a mountain scene, picked, no doubt, by Molly O for the colors that matched the bedspread.

The room was spare and neat. Vena imagined that Molly O did the cleaning, slipping in sometime every morning to smooth the covers back on the bed, empty Caney's ashtray and straighten the stack of paperback books on the bedside table.

Vena located the linen closet in the hallway leading to the bathroom. When she opened the door and reached in to grab a towel, she saw that the top shelf was crowded with trophies. She didn't count them, but figured there were twenty-five or thirty, heavy trophies each topped by a brass figure, a rider perched on the back of a bucking horse.

She stood on tiptoes to reach the tallest of these, pulled it down and read the plaque on the base.

CANEY PAXTON

FIRST PLACE   BAREBACK EVENT

HIDALGO COUNTY RODEO, 1971

Molly O arrived just in time to listen to Life's whispered complaints about the mess Caney had made of his eggs. As evidence, Life had saved two small clumps of congealed yolk which he'd hidden beneath his toast. He wanted to make sure Molly O felt the sting of guilt over the damage her tardiness had caused.

But Molly O was a little stingy with her remorse, owing, perhaps, to the strain of facing the first early hours of a gray Christmas Eve. Try as she might, she just couldn't manage to force regret and joy at the same time.

She did, however, offer to prepare Life a fresh meal, but once he'd gotten a whiff of her White Shoulders and watched her smooth the bib of her apron across her breasts, he hungered for more than the taste of eggs.

After she'd removed the offending plate, Molly O went around the dining room picking up stray icicles which had fallen to the floor. She had intended to rehang them on the sagging line overhead, but finally decided it would be a waste of energy since the decorations would be coming down in just two more days. As she tossed them into the trash near the door to Caney's bedroom, she froze like a bird dog on point.

"Do you hear water running?"

The question was intended for Caney, who was still in the kitchen, but Life, his bad ear turned to Molly O, thought she was talking to him.

"No more water for me," he said, "but I'll take a little more coffee."

"Caney," Molly O yelled. "Either you forgot to turn off your bathwater, or you didn't jiggle the handle on the stool."

Caney tried his best to avoid answering, but Molly O was not one to be discouraged by silence.

"I said, you forgot to turn off—"

"No, I didn't forget," Caney called from the kitchen.

"Well, I'll go check because I can hear water running somewhere."

"It's the shower." Caney's admission was barely audible.

"The what?" Molly O feared Life's deafness was catching. "Did you say the—"

"It's Vena." Caney sounded like a child confessing that he'd just shaved the family cat. "Vena's taking a shower."

Caney peeked at Molly O to see how she was taking the news, but if he had expected her to blow up, he was in for a surprise. Molly O simply pursed her lips, then nodded her head—gestures of a woman accustomed to disaster.

Minutes later, when Vena came out of Caney's room, Molly O, filling ketchup bottles at the end of the counter, didn't look up, not even when the two exchanged mumbled good-mornings.

Vena went straight to the kitchen where Caney was pouring pancake batter onto the grill. "Thanks for the use of your shower," she said. "I was beginning to smell a lot like the dog."

"Not that I noticed."

She was dressed in faded jeans and a blue flannel shirt, creased but clean, with a smell that reminded Caney of lavender. Her hair, shiny and damp, hung down her back in a single braid, but one thin strand, twisted loose from the rest, lay against her cheek and curled across the hollow of her throat. Caney was thinking of how it would feel to brush it away from her face, to let the silkiness of it slide through his fingers, when Molly O poked her head into the pass-through.

"My short stack ready yet?"

"Almost," Caney said, as he flipped the pancakes, their undersides already too brown.

For the next hour Vena made herself scarce in the dining room by helping Caney out in the kitchen. She chopped onions and sliced tomatoes, then washed dishes at the sink when she found out the dishwasher hadn't worked since September.

Molly O had little business out front—Soldier and Quinton and Hooks, of course, and half a dozen breakfast orders for workers coming off the late shift at the peanut plant.

She came into the kitchen only once, but stayed just long enough to tell Caney they were running low on napkins.

Bilbo and Peg Porter came in for biscuits and gravy, then stayed to visit a while. They showed up more often now that Peg had given up cooking, but Bilbo didn't mind. He said Peg had been a lousy cook even before she got sick, so eating out suited him just fine.

A smoker since she was fifteen, Peg had developed emphysema and was now permanently hooked up to oxygen. Bilbo, a three-pack-a-day man, refused to heed the warning printed on the oxygen canister Peg carried around with her, but he was considerate enough to blow his smoke away from his wife's blue-tinged face when he exhaled.

Then, just before nine, the breakfast run all but over, six cars pulled in, one following the other.

A trucker lingering over coffee at the counter said, "Better roll up your sleeves and put on your work gloves, girl."

Molly O, taking a break with the crossword puzzle, tossed her newspaper aside and hurried to the front window.

"You got a damned convoy coming in," the trucker said.

"We've got a what?" Caney yelled from the kitchen.

As the cars parked, they began spilling out sleepy-eyed children, yawning teenagers, tired-looking men and women, some clutching squirming toddlers, one shouldering a crying baby.

"My word!" Molly O said. "Where am I gonna put all them?"

Caney wheeled his chair to the kitchen door, then whistled through his teeth when he saw the crowd gathering outside.

"Might be Gypsies," the truck driver said. "They travel like that, in convoys."

"They don't look much like Gypsies to me." Molly O spoke with the authority of someone well acquainted with Gypsies even though the only one she had ever seen was a dark, turbaned woman billed as Madam Zola, who told fortunes at the county fair. "Anyway, I hope they're not. The only word I know in Gypsy is séance."

As the first of the group shuffled inside, Molly O asked, "Are you all together?"

"Yes," an older man said, "one big family going home for Christmas."

Relieved to know her conversation would not be limited to "séance," Molly O said, "Well, you come right on in and I'll get you seated." But before she had the words out of her mouth, Vena was already pulling chairs aside so tables could be rearranged.

"I can do this myself," Molly O hissed, but Vena, ignoring her, hoisted one side of the table while Molly O grabbed the other, and for a few seconds it looked like the two were squaring off for a tug-of-war. Then, with a barely perceptible shrug of one shoulder, Molly O signaled a temporary concession, and in one motion, they lifted at the same time and moved the table next to the one beside it.

By the time everyone was inside, tables and chairs stretched across the room. And by squeezing in the two high chairs Molly O kept in the utility room, all thirty-four travelers had seats or laps to sit on.

Vena brought water to the tables while Molly O put out silverware and passed menus around. They both poured coffee as long as it lasted, then Vena put on a fresh pot as Molly O started taking orders.

Caney had already started to gear up in the kitchen before Molly O came to the pass-through and handed him her order: nineteen breakfast specials—eight with bacon and eleven with ham; seven early risers—two with short stacks, five with biscuits; four bowls of oatmeal; two waffles; and an omelet with cheese and green peppers.

"Think you can manage back there until I get the drinks?" Molly O asked.

"I could probably use a little help."

Vena, moving in beside Molly O, said, "I'll get the drinks."

"Oh, it won't take me but a minute. Some milk, a pitcher of orange juice, few cups of hot tea. Then I'll be free to give Caney a hand."

"Well, you'd better hump it up," Caney said, "because we just got busier."

Vena and Molly O turned to see five elderly women coming through the front door.

"I'll get them set up," Vena said.

"No!" Molly O's voice was edged with anger. "That's my job."

"Okay. Then I'll help out in the kitchen."

"Thought you said you couldn't cook."

"I'm not great, but I can probably save Caney some time."

"Look. Caney and me have handled more than this all by ourselves. And we've been doing it for a long time."

"Hell," Caney said, "we haven't had more than two dozen customers in here at one time since the Kiwanis Club showed up a couple of years ago."

"And we took care of them just fine, didn't we?"

"I wouldn't say that. It took us over an hour to get all the orders out."

"But we managed, didn't we?" Molly O flipped a handle on the coffeemaker and began filling cups. "And we can manage now," she added, cutting her eyes at Vena. "Like I said, I'll take care of the tables, then I'll help Caney in the kitchen."

"Then what the hell am I supposed to do?" Vena asked as she slapped a wet rag down on the counter. "Stand here and watch?"

"Well, since you're the carhop," Molly O said, "I guess you'd better go hop a car."

"Now I've had just about enough out of you—"

"Dammit!" Caney grabbed a meat cleaver and hacked through a slab of bacon. "We've got forty mouths to feed and I can't—"

"Please to excusing me."

The voice came from a small, dark foreign man who had passed silently through the dining room and stood now, just inside the kitchen, bowing his head in respect.

"My name Bui Khanh," he said. "And I am cooker."

Chapter Ten

THE RUSH THAT HIT the Honk in the morning didn't let up until midafternoon, and even then the dining room never completely emptied out. But most of the later traffic came from the locals who stopped by to take a look at Bui Khanh. They could hardly believe that Caney Paxton had, within a two-day period, hired not only a carhop by the name of Takes Horse, but also a foreign cook with a name they couldn't even pronounce.

Molly O, believing Bui to be an Eskimo, spent most of the morning reciting bits of information about igloos and whale blubber, facts she had gleaned from an issue of *National Geographic* in her doctor's office. She shared with anyone who would listen the record low temperature at Point Barrow, Alaska, and the largest known glacier in the Arctic Ocean. By the time Caney set her straight, Molly O had half the people in Sequoyah wondering how an Eskimo could ever survive an Oklahoma summer.

But the revelation that the new cook was Vietnamese sent Molly O into a tailspin. She made a three-dollar mistake on one of her tickets, snapped at Life Halstead when he teased her about a run in her panty hose and dropped a handful of silverware that went clattering clear across the floor.

By then, her energy and spirits flagging, her tirade against Vena had all but played itself out, though her misgivings had not, especially after she saw Vena plugging the pay phone with quarters for a long-distance call.

But Molly O decided to keep her suspicions to herself for the time being, as she figured Caney had about all he could handle for now. She kept her eyes on him as much as she was able, sneaking sideways glances whenever she thought he wouldn't notice. And though she didn't pick up on any outward signs of agitation, she felt sure he was just putting up a good front, a trick she couldn't seem to manage.

When she got zapped by a hot flash that left her feeling light-headed, she slipped back to the bathroom to wash her wrists with cold water and dab at her neck with wet paper towels. By the time she returned, several orders had stacked up on the pass-through which sent her running with plates lined three deep on each arm. But in her hurry, she made the mistake of delivering a bean burger to a woman who ordered a chef salad and serving cheese fries to a man who asked for red-top stew.

As she offered a garbled apology, Molly O scooped up the plates and started for the kitchen, but halfway there, turned around and went back to the same table where she reversed the orders, thinking that would take care of the problem. It didn't. And when both customers began to complain, Molly O, unnerved by the mixup, picked up the plates again and, with a bean burger in one hand and cheese fries in the other, started to cry.

Vena, who had been keeping Molly O at a distance since morning, stepped in and straightened out the orders which were intended for other customers, then led her, without a peep of protest, to an empty table.

"Miss." A man at an adjacent table motioned for Molly O. "I need some more coffee."

"I'll get it," Vena said, and without waiting for an objection, she rushed for the coffeepot.

Then, with Molly O watching, Vena refilled not one cup, but three, served two more lunch orders Caney had ready and mopped up a spill of milk.

When she finally rejoined Molly O, she was ready, half expecting renewed hostility, but she was in for a shock.

"Thanks," Molly O said, sounding like she meant it. "I appreciate you helping me out." As another hot flash reddened her face and neck, she grabbed a menu and began to fan with it.

"You want to call it a day?" Vena asked.

"No, I need to stay."

"I can cover for you in here."

"I'll be all right. Guess I'm just tired." Molly O cast an anxious glance toward the kitchen. "And Caney'll be exhausted."

"He seems to be managing okay."

"Always has."

"He told me you've been with him since he opened this place."

"But I've known him since he was born. Watched him take his first steps. Saw him start to school. Put him on his first horse." Molly O looked beyond Vena then, staring into the past at a smiling six-year-old perched on the back of a dun-colored mare. "Lord, that boy was crazy about horses. Couldn't talk about nothing else."

Still feeling a little uncertain despite signs of a truce, Vena pulled up a chair and slipped into it, her movements tentative and slow, just in case she was misreading Molly O's mood.

"I don't think he was happy unless he was on a horse," Molly O said. "His first rodeo, he was fourteen. Skinny, scared, but hell-bent to win. And he did."

"I saw some of his trophies."

"Oh, he was good. Won about every event he entered, I guess. All through school, he was off riding somewhere half the time. His Aunt Effie, the one who raised him, she couldn't keep him home. Why, he didn't even walk across the stage at his own graduation 'cause he was on the road to Wyoming." Molly O drew a ragged breath. "That was his last rodeo."

"Is that how it happened? Is that how . . ."

"You mean his legs?"

Vena nodded, waiting.

"Oh, no. Wasn't rodeo that did that to him. I don't suppose in all the time he was riding he ever got more'n a few bruises. No, he never got hurt on a horse."

"Then how did he end up in that wheelchair?"

"Vietnam," Molly O said, then she put her hand to the hollow of her throat as if to soothe some pain there. "Caney got hurt in Vietnam."

Vena felt a shiver run up the back of her neck as she looked into the kitchen where Bui Khanh's face was framed by the pass-through.

"He fell out of a helicopter over there." Molly O's hands went limp in her lap. "Broke his back."

"My God." Vena closed her eyes, hoping to black out the image of Caney falling through space.

"He never talks about it, and with Caney it's hard to figure what goes on in his head, but I know he still . . ." Molly O looked up when Bui Khanh came from the kitchen with a tray of clean cups and saucers. "Why, of all places in the world, did he come here?" she whispered. "And why did Caney give him a job?"

"Maybe he's so desperate to get out of here that he would've hired whoever walked in."

"What are you talking about?"

"He said he wouldn't be so tied down here if he could find a steady cook."

"We've had steady cooks before. One stayed more'n three years, but Caney didn't go anywhere."

"You're saying Caney didn't take a vacation, not once in three years?"

"Why, he hasn't been out that door since the day we rolled him in here."

"You mean . . ."

"I mean, Caney Paxton hasn't been outside for twelve years."

Caney had known from the first that it would be a mistake to hire Bui Khanh.

For starters, Bui didn't know diddly about English. When Caney had said, "Sorry, but I don't think I can use you," Bui had pulled off his jacket, pushed up his sleeves and tied a cook's apron around his waist, his face beaming with pride. And after Caney said, "Well, I can give you a day's work, but only one," Bui, still smiling, shook Caney's hand and said, "Yes, work very hard, thanks you, very much work."

But even if Bui had known the difference between gravel and gravy, he couldn't cook a lick. The toast he grilled was limp and soggy, the sausage patties hard as hockey pucks. He busted the yolk on every egg he fried but called them all "sunday size up."

Besides, Caney knew even if Bui picked up a little English and learned how to fry an egg, he wasn't going to stick around long. As soon as he could put together some traveling money, he'd drift over into Arkansas and hire on at one of the poultry plants or take off for St. Louis or Kansas City where he might find factory work.

But whatever he did, he wasn't going to stay in Sequoyah where his dark Asian features made him stand out like bamboo in a row of cotton. Caney knew, without a doubt, that no one on Main Street was going to take Bui for one of their own. And with TV images of Vietnam still more painful than surgery without anesthetic, Bui was likely to get an uncomfortable reception.

And if Caney couldn't make sense of watching this Vietnamese man drink coffee from a Batman mug, or dry his hands on a Santa Claus towel, or put on an apron that said I HATE HOUSEWORK, then how could the others?

But the *real* reason not to hire Bui Khanh was that each time Caney looked into his face, he saw the eyes of the lone peasant in a rice paddy watching him fall from the sky—the last pair of eyes that would see Caney's body before it broke itself apart.

Chapter Eleven

CANEY HAD JUST FINISHED basting the turkey and was sliding it back into the oven when he heard the front door slam.

"Merry Christmas," Molly O called, her voice so full of glad tidings that Caney was almost convinced. But when she married her way inside, the holly-jolly smile she was wearing looked about as real as the plastic snowmen dangling from her earlobes.

"The door was open, Caney. You forget to lock up last night?"

"Guess so." The truth was, he had unlocked the door as soon as he got up in case Vena showed up early again. But he wasn't about to admit that to Molly O.

"I should've stayed till you closed. Should've locked up myself."

"You were beat. No reason for you to hang around."

"You do much business after I left?"

"Vena had some heavy traffic at the curb."

"On Christmas Eve?"

"She stayed busy right up till we closed."

"I don't understand it. We go for years without one soul pulling in here for curb service. Then, all of a sudden, looks like we're running a used-car lot." Molly O shook her head. "Doesn't make sense."

"Might not, but it makes money. We turned out more orders yesterday and the day before than we've had for the whole month."

"Good thing you took on a new cook, then, isn't it?" Molly O studied Caney's face, looking for some reaction. "But I was kind of worried when he showed up. I mean, when I found out he was from Vietnam . . . well, I was afraid you might be upset."

"Hell, I was upset." Caney's forehead wrinkled with displeasure. "He couldn't cook."

"Then why'd you hire him?"

"I didn't. I paid him last night when he left and told him not to come back." Caney pushed away from the counter and rolled toward the kitchen door. "But it didn't have nothing to do with Vietnam. Not a damned thing."

"Well, I guess—"

"If I'm going to pay someone to cook, then he ought to be able to cook. Right?"

"Right."

Molly O followed Caney into the dining room where he parked behind the counter. He was just reaching for his cigarettes when he noticed the brightly wrapped package beside the cash register.

"Now I know why you left the door unlocked," she said.

"Why?" Certain Molly O knew the truth, Caney could feel his face redden.

"So Santa could get in."

"Oh, yeah." His sheepish smile sat crooked on his face.

"Well, open it," Molly O said.

"I think I'll wait until you open yours. That way—"

"Then I'll go get it."

"No, not right now. See—"

Before he could stop her, Molly O had rounded the counter and stepped through the door of his room where she came to a sudden stop.

"What in the world . . ."

The room looked like it had been searched by the CIA. Clothes poked from dresser drawers; newspapers and magazines littered the floor; storage boxes and garment bags spilled out of closet doors; and a yellowed baby quilt hung over the side of an antique trunk.

"You forgot where you hid my present, didn't you?"

"No, I didn't." Caney tried to sound injured, but Molly O wasn't fooled.

"You put it in the suitcase on the bottom shelf of your closet."

"Damn," Caney said under his breath.

"Good thing you're not Santa Claus. Kids wouldn't get any toys till 'long about April when you finally remembered where you put them."

"Seems pretty strange to me that you know where to find your own present."

"Well, it's a good thing one of us does," she said. "Next year, why don't you just let me hide it myself."

Caney knew the package was right where Molly O said it was, right where it had been since it was delivered last summer. And though he couldn't recall with much detail what he had bought her, Molly O could describe it with accuracy.

Every August when she got her JCPenney Fall/Winter Catalog, she left it at the Honk along with a string of strong hints about what she wanted for Christmas. This year it was a rayon pantsuit with a double-breasted jacket and rhinestone buttons . . . the right style, the right size, the right color. Molly O made sure Caney wouldn't go wrong.

But he wasn't nearly as certain about the other gift, the one he had tucked into the side pocket of his wheelchair.

Last night when he had found it in his Aunt Effie's trunk, it had looked like a delicate treasure. This morning, though, in the light of day, he realized what a silly gift it was . . . a whatnot, a gimcrack Vena would probably laugh at.

But it was too late to come up with anything else. Nothing in town would be open except for Wal-Mart, but asking Molly O to pick up a gift for Vena would be a bad mistake. Caney knew that for sure. And Aunt Effie's trunk had little else to offer beyond his first pair of cowboy boots or his grade school art awards or his worn copy of *The Black Stallion*.

"Caney, it's beautiful," Molly O said as she came from his room. She held the jacket of the pantsuit against her, posing. "Exactly what I wanted."

"I'm glad you like it."

"Now, open yours."

"Okay, but if this is—"

Caney and Molly O turned toward the front door as it opened.

"Good today," Bui Khanh said as he closed the door behind him. Then, bowing and smiling, he hurried past them. "I am cooker for work to do," he called as he disappeared into the kitchen. "Much cooker. Many work. And happy Christmastime."

Vena hurried back inside, her hands buried in the pockets of her jacket. "It's turning colder," she said.

"Beats me why anyone would want curb service in this kind of weather," Molly O said as she watched Vena prepare a tray for one of the pickups parked outside.

"Maybe they're just trying to pretend."

"Pretend what?"

"That it's not Christmas."

"Well, if it works, then I'm going to go eat in my car," Molly O said as she went to start a fresh pot of coffee.

She'd been trying to stay busy to get past the pain of missing Brenda, but the people in the Honk weren't helping her mood which was turning as dark as the sky.

Life was there, of course, making sure she noticed how lonely and pitiful he looked on his first Christmas without Reba, but she couldn't help feeling sorry for him, remembering how she felt that first year without Dewey.

And just as she had predicted, Henry Brister showed up, still unable to cut up his food because of the bandages on his hands. Henry had lost both his thumbs in an accident at the plastic factory, just after his wife ran off with a John Deere sales rep from Shreveport. Poor Henry, Molly O thought. No wife . . . no thumbs.

Duncan Renfro had managed to stray from home again and wandered around the kitchen measuring for nearly an hour before Soldier and Hooks took him back to Ellen, who was in bed with the flu.

Wanda Sue had stopped by, but only for coffee and gossip. She said she knew for a fact who had torched the Bottoms Up Club over in Marble City, but if she told who'd done it, her life would be in danger. She even had the nerve to whisper that Henry Brister's wounds had healed, but he was keeping the bandages on so he could keep drawing workmen's comp.

Bilbo and Peg Porter had been in, but they didn't stay long. Peg's oxygen canister was running low and Bilbo smoked his last Carlton, a brand Caney didn't carry.

Wilma Driver came by to pick up two takeout orders. Her husband had finally passed his kidney stone, but now he was down with shingles.

Through it all, Molly O tried to keep a smile on her face, convinced that her cheerfulness, even though it was faked, might make the others feel better. But when she served Christmas dinner to a family of three—father, mother and teenage daughter, whose laughter sounded so much like Brenda's—her misery settled on her so hard she couldn't shake it.

She thought of going on home where she could nurse her hurt in private, but the idea of returning to the empty trailer made her feel even worse.

When the phone rang just after two, Molly O rushed to answer, the sound of Brenda's voice already playing in her head.

"Honk and Holler," she said, her breath quickened with excitement. But a moment later, when she heard a man's voice on the line, her shoulders sagged with the weight of disappointment. Then she turned and held out the phone to Vena.

"It's for you."

Vena took the phone, speaking softly with her mouth pressed close to the receiver, but Molly O had no interest in the call.

She wandered to the kitchen doorway, but didn't invite conversation as she watched Caney trim the last of the turkey from the bone. When Bui came in the back door dragging a ladder, he set up such a racket it made her teeth ache.

After his surprise appearance earlier in the day and Caney's refusal to let him near the grill, Bui, undaunted, had declared himself a "fixer" and, in spite of Caney's objections, had spent most of the morning taking the dishwasher apart. And when he put it back together, no one seemed more surprised than he was that it worked.

Fueled by success, he had gone into such a frenzy of repair Caney didn't have the heart to try to run him off again, so Molly O figured he'd be around, at least for a while.

When she drifted back to the front, Vena, just hanging up the phone, expected she'd have to fend off questions about the call, but Molly O didn't ask. Instead, she turned strangely silent until she heard a car engine and glanced outside.

"Looks like you've got another one." Molly O gestured toward the lot as a battered Cadillac pulled in, but she lost interest even before it parked.

The driver was a long-haired man with a thick dark moustache, his passenger a girl wearing a tight sweater and large silver earrings.

"I think they're coming in," Vena said when the girl opened her door and stepped out of the car. But as she started for the Honk, the man backed the car out and pulled away.

"Well, one of them's coming in," Vena said as she watched the girl tug her tight skirt over her hips and run her fingers through her hennaed hair.

Molly O looked up then, narrowing her eyes to bring the girl into focus.

> *Ankle-strap shoes too adult for her feet . . .*
> *head haloed in copper curls,*
> *mouth painted sunburst coral*

"Brenda," Molly O said, her voice as soft and light as the snowflakes just beginning to feather the air. "My Brenda's come home for Christmas."

Chapter Twelve

As soon as Brenda stepped inside the trailer, she tossed her purse on the couch, then zeroed in on the TV.

"You get TNN?"

"What's that?" Molly O asked.

"God, Mom! Nashville Network." Brenda punched buttons but got nothing more than static and snow. "What's wrong with this thing?" she growled, slapping the side of the set.

"The picture's better at night."

"Why don't you have it fixed?"

"You're the only one who watched it much. I hardly ever turn it on."

"Look, a TV's like a car," Brenda explained, her voice edged with irritation. "You got to fire 'em up ever' once in a while or they won't start."

"You sure you don't want something to eat? I could make you a salad or some—"

"I'm stuffed." Giving up on the TV, Brenda took off her jacket and dropped it on the back of a chair. "Didn't you see the turkey Caney piled on my plate?"

"Well, I think I'll put on some potato soup so when your friend comes—"

"No, don't do that. He won't stick around long enough to eat. We've got a lot of miles to cover."

"Now how long does it take to eat a bowl of soup? He can't be in that big a hurry."

"You don't know Travis."

"I guess I can fix him an egg sandwich." Molly O braced for an attack when she added, "If he shows up," but Brenda, peering at a picture of herself and her daddy, seemed unperturbed by the remark.

"He'll show up."

"You sure he knows how to get here?"

"He knows." Brenda fingered a trophy she'd won in a talent contest when she was ten, then flipped through some of her old copies of *American Songwriter* and *Country and Western Stars.*

"Nothing's changed," she said. "Not even the magazines."

"Your room's just like you left it, too. Still full of your stuffed animals," Molly O said, oblivious to the tone of renunciation in Brenda's voice. "I wish you could stay the night, honey. Sleep in your old bed."

"I told you we have to be in Vegas tomorrow night."

"I'm just worried about the roads. They say this snow's moving in from the west, right where you're headed."

"Well, Travis didn't even want to stop 'cause he said coming here was gonna cost us three or four hours, but I just had to come to tell you the news."

Molly O felt a squeezing sensation in her chest. She had been here before, waiting for "the news," the news that Brenda had started on birth control . . . that Brenda was quitting school . . . that Brenda was leaving home.

"What news?"

"Me and Travis are gonna get married."

Molly O grabbed one of Brenda's old magazines and began fanning the flames of another round of hot flashes.

"I knew you'd be surprised."

"Surprised don't even begin to catch it. Why, I don't even know this . . . this Travis."

"Well, you're not the one marrying him, are you?" Brenda squared her chin and locked her lips together, a gesture she had affected when, just shy of her first birthday, she was told not to eat the leaves of an ivy plant.

"How long have you known him, Brenda?"

"Long enough."

"What about your career? All your plans?"

"None of that's changed. Travis is part of my career now. He's the one who hires the musicians, arranges our tunes, books our gigs. And he's the one who takes care of me."

"Sugar, do you think you're ready for marriage?" Molly O reached for Brenda's hand, but she pulled away. "I mean, you're just so young."

"Mom, how old were you when you got married?"

"Sixteen the first time, but—"

"Well, I'm almost eighteen." Brenda struck a practiced pose which amplified the curves of her hips and breasts.

"But I didn't have your talent, I didn't have your dreams."

"And you weren't pregnant, either."

Breath put on hold, fan stilled in midair, Molly O whispered, "Brenda, are you—"

"About two months, I figure."

"You're going to have a baby." Molly O said the words as if to test their truth.

"Yeah, that's usually what comes of getting pregnant, isn't it?"

"How did this happen? I thought you were on the pill?"

"God, Mom, it was an accident, okay? We were on the road, I ran out of pills. What difference does it make now? I'm pregnant!"

"So that's why this Travis just put you out at the Honk." Her voice rising with anger, Molly O slapped the magazine down on the coffee table. "That's why he hightailed it out of there the way he did."

"I told you, he had to find a filling station to get a tire fixed. And why are you calling him 'this Travis'? His name's Travis Howard."

When her hands began to tremble, Molly O walked to the window, staring out at the falling snow. "You mind telling me when this wedding's going to take place?"

"Well, Travis says we need to wait until—"

"Wait?" Molly O wheeled, poised to pounce. "Why wait?"

"Just listen, this is the best part. Travis wants us to finish this gig in Vegas and another one we have booked in Denver, then come back here, find us a place and—"

"A place here? In Sequoyah?"

"That's right."

"You'd give up show business and come back home?"

"We're not gonna give it up entirely, just put it on hold till the baby comes. And I'll keep writing music, maybe play a gig around here once in a while." Brenda shrugged to show the simplicity of her plan. "It'll all work out."

Her anger cooling, Molly O nodded. "It might." Then, with a smile threatening, she said, "It just might."

"There's one thing, though. I guess I ought to see a doctor. An OB-GYN."

"Are you having problems, Brenda?" Molly O tried to hide her alarm. "If you are—"

"Oh, I've been having this pain here"—Brenda touched a spot low on her belly—"but it's not that bad."

"Don't take any chances, honey. You get yourself to a doctor, make sure everything's all right."

"But see, me and Travis don't have any insurance and the band's money is tight right now, so I was wondering . . ."

"I've got almost four hundred dollars," Molly O said as she hurried to the kitchen.

"You still keep your money frozen?"

"Sure do."

Molly O pulled a box of waffles from the freezer, dug out a plastic bag crammed with bills and handed it to Brenda.

"Mom, I'm gonna pay you back, you know that."

"Don't you worry about it. Just get to a doctor and see to it that my grandbaby is okay."

When a horn honked outside, Brenda went to the window. "That's Travis."

"Well, he's coming in, isn't he?"

"I don't think so."

"But I want to meet him."

"He wants to meet you, too. But he said you'd be pissed right now, so he wants to wait until we come back."

"You go out there and tell him I'm not mad. Not one bit. Tell him—"

Travis honked again, several short bursts suggesting his impatience.

"I'd better go." Brenda grabbed her jacket and purse.

"Brenda . . ."

"With the snow and all, we really need to get back on the road."

Blinking back tears, Molly O enfolded Brenda in her arms. "Take good care of yourself, darlin'. And remember, call me. Soon! Call collect."

After Molly O waved from the window until the car was out of sight, she began to wander the room, straightening Brenda's magazines, inching the talent trophy back into place, touching the two-year-old face in the framed photograph.

Pausing before a mirror over the couch, she stared at her own reflection. "Merry Christmas," she said, pushing a limp wisp of hair away from her face. Then, smiling at herself without feeling foolish, she whispered, "Merry Christmas, Grandma."

Bui entered the church by the same window he had crawled through the night before, careful not to rattle the stiff plastic shade as he slid inside. Hardly breathing, he listened for sounds and let his eyes adjust to the darkness before he closed the window. Then, still clutching the paper sack he had carried with him from the car, he felt his way down the hall until he came to the room where he would sleep again.

He covered the small shaded lamp with a shirt from his sack, hoping his shadow could not be seen at the window.

The room looked exactly as he had left it that morning while the sky was still dark. The same scraps of paper remained in the trash can, books stacked crookedly on the desk were undisturbed and the telephone cord was still twisted beneath the typewriter.

Satisfied that his intrusion of the previous night had not been detected, Bui slipped next door to the bathroom where he washed himself. When he finished, he carefully dried the sink with paper towels before he turned out the light in the windowless room.

He didn't know if sleeping in a church was a crime, but he suspected it was. And if he got caught breaking the law here, the police were sure to find out about Houston and the woman with yellow hair. He would have to be very careful in the church, make sure he left no traces of his coming and going.

He was ready now to write the letter he had been saying inside his head for two days. From the drawer of the desk, he took a pen, an envelope and a sheet of paper with "AME Church of the Living God" printed at the top. Then he began to write.

Em yêu Nguyệt,

   Anh rồi Houston vā bây giờ anh sống ở² . . . a town that is small and quiet. My job is very important, I think, for the man who owns the cafe has legs that do not walk, so he travels in a chair with wheels. His name is Mr. Chaney, a man with sad eyes. He is not a good cook, so he is glad for my skill with food.

   I am also in charge of repair in the restaurant as Mr. Chaney is unable to take care of the equipment. Today I fixed a big problem with the machine that washes dishes. Nguyet, in America machines do much work. One called "microwaver" boils food within the time of a breath and another executes with electricity bugs that fly. So much here is surprising.

   One woman who works with me is Miss Ho, and though she has a Vietnamese name, she does not look like us. Another woman has the job of carrying food to people who eat in cars. I think these people are not allowed to come inside our restaurant, but I do not know why.

   I am learning to speak English now. Mr. Chaney talks to me

many times and he often speaks in a very loud voice, so I can understand him.

The place where I am living is like a mansion with too many rooms, but believe me when I say it is not expensive for me here. One room of this house has beautiful windows with glasses of colors and a piano which I hope to learn to play.

Nguyet, my transfer to this city is fortunate for us. I believe we will have a good life here. The people are kind, much kinder than in the city of Houston where it is easy to find problems.

I cannot send more money to you now because the cost of my transfer was very great, but in my next letter, I hope to send you the rest of the money for your passage.

Nguyet, I think of you every minute of every day and at night, as I sleep, I smell the sweetness of your hair and feel the smoothness of your skin on my fingers. My love for you . . . *anh yêu em mãi mãi.*

> *Yêu em,*
> Bui

After he sealed the letter inside the envelope, Bui ran his hands across his eyes. He had slept poorly the night before, listening to strange sounds, waking to dark shapes and shadows not yet familiar to him. Now he had little energy left, but enough for what he had yet to do.

He picked up his sack, then crossed the hall to a pair of heavy wooden doors. After taking off his shoes and placing them side by side against the wall, he slid the doors apart and stepped between them.

Though this was the second time Bui had stood inside the great room, he was just as transfixed by its beauty and tranquillity as the first time. The stained-glass windows, softly lit by streetlights outside the church, shimmered in shades of green and amber, and the pews, stretching to both sides of the room, smelled of dark, rich wood.

Against the far wall, a raised platform held four elegant high-back chairs, a pulpit carved with intricate designs and an upright white piano.

Bui bowed at the door, then started down the aisle, moving slowly and with reverence, for he knew he was in a sacred place. At the front of the room, he stopped before a long, narrow table covered with red velvet cloth. Candles stood at each end in tall silver holders between vases of delicate purple flowers.

He put his sack on the floor, then carefully removed the Buddha he had brought from Houston and placed it in the center of the table. With matches from his pocket, he lit the candles.

When he stepped back and clasped his hands before him, he bowed, first to his Buddha of stone . . . then to a carving on the wall—the statue of a man, hands and feet nailed to a wooden cross.

Then Bui Khanh knelt to pray.

Caney switched off the Honk sign just before seven. He hadn't had a customer for more than two hours, so he was shutting down early tonight.

The tracks of Bui's car, the last to pull out, were barely visible now, filled in with another half inch of the snow still coming down.

Vena came from the back with the dog, then slid the box onto a chair. "I'm going to take off, Caney." She turned up the collar on her jacket and buttoned it at the neck.

"Hate to see you out in this weather," Caney said.

"I'll be all right."

"It's freezing out there now."

"Yeah, but I don't have far to go."

"You know, I was just thinking . . ." Caney felt his mouth go dry. "Maybe . . . well, no reason you can't stay here tonight," he said, lowering his eyes like a shy teenager.

But there was nothing shy about Vena's response.

"Oh, is that how it is? I can work here *if* I sleep with the owner. Part of my job description, right?"

"No, I . . . I didn't mean . . ." Caney licked at lips so dry he could feel their heat. "That's not what I meant."

"Then what did you mean?"

"See, I have a couch, there's a couch in my room . . . and, well, I just wanted you to know . . ." He was rushing now, trying to get it all out, trying to make her understand. "I thought about the couch and you're welcome to it, some extra blankets and a couple of pillows, so you could—"

"No, thank you," she said, but the "thank you" sounded less than sincere.

"Well, I just wanted you to know."

A silence settled between them then, holding them in place until, moments later, headlights swept across the window.

"Now who the hell is that?" Caney said as a vehicle pulled to a stop, too far back on the darkened lot for them to make it out in the blowing snow. "Is someone coming for you?"

"No."

"Probably some damned kids."

"Maybe that guy who brought Molly O's girl."

"Well, whoever it is . . ."

"I'll go out and see."

"No, you don't have to do that. If they want something—"

"I'll be right back," Vena said.

She couldn't tell until she got past the headlights that the vehicle was a truck she had seen before and the driver a man she recognized from her first night at the Honk.

"We're closed," she said.

"You mean it's too late for a drink? Didn't know it ever got too late for a drink."

"Caney's not selling beer tonight anyway."

"Why not?"

"It's Christmas."

"Well, it's not really beer-drinking weather, is it?"

"Doesn't seem to be."

"Yeah, need something a little stronger than beer for a night like this." He reached between his legs for a fifth of Wild Turkey, uncapped it and took a long, slow swallow. "Now this'll make you forget you're cold, Vena."

Vena tried not to look surprised at hearing him say her name, but he caught the sudden tilt of her head.

"Oh, I make it my business to know the names of good-looking women," he said. "And I don't like to drink with strangers." He winked then to make sure she understood. "I'm Sam. Sam Kellam." Smiling, he passed the bottle through the window and held it out to Vena.

"No."

"Aw, go on. You look like you need something to warm you up." Sam leaned farther out the window. "Warm you all the way up inside, Vena."

"I said no!"

"Whoa now. I just came to offer you a drink . . . and a ride."

"I don't need a ride."

"That right?" Sam let his eyes range over the empty parking lot. "Then how you gonna get home, huh? You gonna take a bus?"

Vena cut her eyes away, looked off into the night. "There's no bus in this town."

"Oh yes there is. And it's not very far from here. Not far at all. You know, I wouldn't mind a little ride in a bus myself. Take a little of this to relax," Sam said, waving the bottle in Vena's face, "then get all cozy in the back of a bus. Let someone else do the driving. You know what I mean?"

"I don't give a damn about what you mean."

Vena tried to step away from the truck, but Sam grabbed her arm, pulling her close to the window, so close she could smell the sourness of his breath.

"What's your hurry? You tired? Yeah, I bet you are. On your feet all day. In and out, in and out. Time you pulled off those boots, put your legs up—"

Vena twisted out of his grasp and started for the Honk, but she hadn't taken more than three steps before Sam gunned the truck, tires spinning on the snow as it careened past Vena, then slid to a stop, blocking her path to the door.

"I might be seeing you on that bus. Might get on it myself. And when I do, Vena, I'll do the driving." Then he accelerated and the truck, fishtailing, shot away.

Vena was shivering when she stepped back inside the Honk, a chill caused less by the weather than by her encounter with Sam Kellam. She'd run up against plenty like him before, a few of them even dangerous, but none who made her feel the way he had.

"Whew," she said, blowing on her hands. "It's colder than I thought."

"You're freezing," Caney said.

"Yeah." Vena hid her hands beneath her jacket so Caney couldn't see them trembling.

"Who was that out there?" Caney asked.

"Some kids. Just out having fun."

"Now, this is a hell of a night to be—"

"Caney, when you asked me to spend the night . . ."

"Look, Vena. I was just offering you my couch. Nothing more to it than that."

"Well, if you're still offering, I'll take you up on it."

"Sure," Caney said, clearly delighted. "You bet."

"You mind if I keep the dog in your room? Sometimes at night she—"

"No problem. You go on back, get her settled. I'll lock up, fix us something to drink. Be there in a jiffy."

"Don't go to any trouble for me, Caney."

"You're no trouble, Vena. No trouble at all."

Cocooned in Caney's heavy flannel robe and a nest of thick blankets, Vena took the mug he offered, then blew at the steaming liquid before she took a cautious sip. "Um." She ventured another taste. "This isn't just ordinary hot chocolate, is it?"

"No. It's a secret family recipe."

"What's in it?"

"That's the secret. And if I told you, my Aunt Effie would come out of her grave raising hell."

"You come from a big family, Caney?"

"Not much family at all. My parents weren't married. Hell, they were just kids. He took off when he found out she was pregnant. She stuck around till I was three or four, then my aunt took over. Well, actually, she was my great-aunt." Caney tapped a cigarette from his pack and held it out to Vena.

"Thanks, but I really am quitting."

"What about you?" Caney asked. "Your folks."

"My mom and dad are gone." Vena's voice was even, without emotion.

"Any other family?"

Vena pressed the back of her hand against her lips as if she might hold back the words. "No," she said. "I had a sister." Then she turned to stare at the blinking lights of the Christmas tree, her face bathed in color, then cast in darkness. "She died a few months ago."

"Sorry. I didn't mean to make you feel bad."

"You didn't." Vena drained the last of her drink, then, forcing a lighter tone, she said, "This is nice, Caney. I mean, it feels like Christmas, doesn't it? Snow, hot chocolate . . . the tree. Sort of like one of those Hallmark cards."

Caney slipped his hand into the pocket of his chair and pulled out the gift he had kept there all day.

"Merry Christmas," he said, handing it to Vena.

"Oh, Caney. I didn't . . . I don't . . ."

"It's just something I had when I was a kid."

Vena peeled the tissue paper back to reveal a tiny clear figure, a prancing horse of spun glass. With her fingertips, she traced the delicate lines of the horse's body and the smooth spirals which shaped its tail and mane. Then she held it up so that the lights on the tree sent gleaming flashes of reds and greens through the fragile glass.

Smiling, she looked up and whispered, "Merry Christmas, Caney." Then she placed the horse in the palm of her hand and gently closed her fingers over it. "Merry Christmas."

Chapter Thirteen

CANEY HAD HEARD every sound Vena made from the time he turned out the light until the sun came up.

He'd listened as she pounded her pillow into submission, wrestled blankets to defeat, forced the cushions of the couch to a truce. He'd heard her get up once, feeling her way to the dog where she stroked and soothed until it stopped whimpering; then she'd gone to the window where she'd stood for a long time, looking out into the night.

Soon after she'd settled down on the couch again, he could tell when her breathing slowed that she'd given herself to sleep . . . knew, too, she was dreaming when he heard a soft whine of protest before she murmured, "No. Don't." A warning whispered in the dark.

But as soon as the sky began to turn pink Caney went out like he'd had a whiff of ether.

Sleep carried him so far under that he didn't hear Vena stir, didn't hear her fold away her bedding or tiptoe to the bathroom. But when he did begin to surface, in those few free moments drifting between dream and reality, he floated past watery images of a woman, dark hair spilling across a pillow, face turned toward dim light. And resting in her hand, a small glass horse.

When he awoke to the sound of the shower, he felt time rewinding itself, felt again the wonder of other mornings—rousing on the first day of summer vacation; opening his eyes to the sight of a key on his dresser, the key to his very own car; waking on a fast-moving train to the view of a city skyline—knowing in those first delicious moments he had something to feel good about, something to make him feel alive.

And today, that something was Vena Takes Horse.

When she stepped out of the bathroom, she was dressed in jeans and a plaid shirt, her hair wrapped in a towel, her feet bare.

"Did I wake you up?" she asked.

"No."

She sat on the end of the couch, took a brush from her duffel bag and pulled the towel from around her head.

"Snow's stopped," she said.

"That's too bad. I was hoping we'd get snowed in."

"You wouldn't have much business."

"Yeah." Caney grinned, obviously pleased by the idea.

"But if nobody could get in, then we couldn't get out."

"That'd suit me just fine." Caney scooted himself up on one elbow and watched Vena brushing her hair. "There's nothing out there I want anyway."

As Vena reached into her bag for a barrette, the dog spied her and, struggling, pushed itself up on its two front legs, then hung its head over the side of the box.

"Hey, girl. Looks like you're feeling a little bit better."

"Is that what you named her? Girl?"

"I hadn't really thought about it."

"How about Harvey? That's a good name."

"For a female?"

"Harvette? Harvelina?"

Vena laughed then, the first real laugh Caney had heard from her.

"Harvey was a little terrier my aunt got me when I was seven or eight," Caney said. "Only dog I ever had."

"Lord, we had so many pets we ran out of names."

"You live on a farm?"

"More like a zoo. My sister took in strays. Dogs, cats, rabbits, squirrels—whatever needed a home. And it didn't matter if they were sick or pregnant or hurt, Helen kept them all. Once she had so many dogs she named two of them Lucky."

"Were they?"

"I guess so. They both got distemper and I thought for sure I'd lose them, but they pulled through."

"You took care of them?"

"Had to. Helen went all to pieces when her animals were sick. She couldn't stand to see them suffer, so she made me doctor them."

"How'd she swing that?"

"She was my big sister. And I was crazy about her. Besides, I liked messing with the plants and—"

"Whoa! I'm lost here."

"Our grandpa taught me a little about Cherokee medicine."

"I thought you were Crow."

"My dad was Crow, but my mom was Cherokee. So was my husband."

"Oh." Caney tried not to let his expression change when he asked, "You still married?"

"No. That was a long time ago." Vena pulled on a pair of socks, then reached for her boots. "Anyway, my grandpa showed me how to mix up salves, poultices. Teas. Berry wines."

"Now how do you get a squirrel to drink wine?"

"Well, sometimes I treated people, too."

Caney made a face of surprise.

"Nothing very serious," Vena said. "Toothaches, colds, rashes. Now and then my mom had some kidney trouble."

"Seems pretty serious to me." Caney reached for a cigarette. "How do you treat kidney trouble?"

"Make a tea out of devil's shoestring."

"Sounds like a rock band."

"Oh, some of the plants have great names. Turkey beard. Lady's thumb. Jack-in-the-pulpit. Mountain ditney."

"So what do you use that stuff for?"

"Poison ivy, ringworm, snakebite."

"You treated snakebite?"

"Yeah. Helen had a cat named Peabo. Lord, she loved that cat. One summer Peabo tangled up with a rattlesnake and got bit on the thigh. Leg swelled up three times its size.

"Helen came apart. Couldn't sleep, wouldn't eat. Said if Peabo died, she was going to starve herself. And I was afraid she might. So I mixed up a poultice of mountain ditney and kept it on that cat for a week. Day and night."

"Did Peabo live?"

"Only six more years."

"Damn! You ever think about going to medical school?"

"Me? No! Helen was the smart one. Valedictorian in high school, honor student in nursing school."

"Wait a minute. You treated your mother, you saved the two Luckys, you saved Peabo. Your sister couldn't stand to see anything in pain, yet it was your sister—"

"Who became an RN."

"But you're the one who had the cure for snakebite and poison ivy and kidney trouble."

"Yeah, I had some cures"—Vena's eyes suddenly seemed to lose their light—"but I didn't have what Helen needed."

Molly O was hardly through the door of the Honk before she made her announcement.

"I'm going to be a grandma!"

Caney, momentarily at a loss for a reaction, forced an uncertain smile.

Vena lifted her coffee cup in the gesture of a toast and said, "Congratulations."

Life moved quickly to take advantage of the moment, grabbed Molly O around the waist and danced her across the floor.

Bui, with absolutely no idea of what was happening, was nevertheless caught up in the celebratory mood and fell into a wild excitement of bowing.

Throughout the morning, Molly O repeated her news many times, but most of her customers, at least those as old as she was, responded by pulling out pictures of their own grandchildren, whom they declared to be not only beautiful, but talented and sweet as well.

The exception was Wilma Driver.

"This is my grandson Ronnie," she said as she flipped through pictures in her billfold. "He's nineteen, ugly and stupid. Doesn't work, doesn't go to school, doesn't bathe."

Trying to sound unfazed, Molly O asked, "What does he do, Wilma?"

"Drugs. Now this one is Erin, fourteen. She's trying to sleep with every boy on the football team before her junior year. If she does, she wins five hundred dollars."

"Now who would pay her to do a thing like that?"

"The football team. Here's Robby, the best-looking one of the bunch. Well, he will be if they can do something with his ears. He's an eleven-year-old pyromaniac. Set the garage on fire twice, burned down his sister's playhouse and he's a suspect in the arson of the bookmobile. And guess what he wants to be when he grows up?" Without waiting for an answer, Wilma supplied one. "A fireman."

"Oh, Wilma, I can't imagine—"

"Wait, there's one more. Ashley. She's eight, and according to her, an alien. Claims she's from a planet called Klynot and refuses to eat anything green. Says if she does, she'll turn to slime."

But Molly O was too happy to let one grumbling grandmother spoil her day. As soon as Wilma left, she grabbed the JCPenney catalog and started making a list of the baby furniture she intended to put on layaway that very day.

Shortly after noon, a young man dressed in overalls, heavy boots and a baseball cap crawled out of a mud-splattered pickup and ambled toward the door. Hamp Rothrock at twenty still looked too lean and boyish to be called handsome, but Molly O could tell he'd be a knockout by the time he hit twenty-five.

He'd gone steady with Brenda for almost a year; she'd gone

steady with him for eighteen days. They had broken up just before Hamp's graduation, when Brenda, a sophomore, quit school for the first time. As far as Molly O knew, Hamp had never dated another girl.

"I'll swear, you're getting better looking every day," Molly O said.

Hamp, grinning, turned almost as red as his hair.

"How's your daddy, Hamp?"

"He's doing okay. About finished with his chemo. Two more treatments."

"They think that'll take care of it?"

"Yes, ma'am. That's what they say."

"That's good news. Your daddy's a fine man."

Hamp nodded, twisting the work gloves he held in his hand.

"So what can I get for you today? We have a meatloaf special."

"Nothing, really. I just came in to ask about Brenda. Bobby Swink said he thought he saw her in town yesterday."

"He probably did."

Hamp let his eyes slide over the dining room. "Is she still here?"

"No, she didn't stick around long."

"Oh," he said, trying to hide the disappointment behind a smile. "She still singing her music?"

"She sure is. Matter of fact, she's on her way to Las Vegas. She's booked into a club there."

"Well, that's fine. That's what she wanted. And she deserves it, too. She has a real pretty voice."

"I know she'd appreciate that, Hamp."

"You know when she might be coming back through?"

"She's going to be here before too long, but—"

"She is?" Hamp pulled off his cap and ran his fingers through his hair as if he needed a head start to get ready for Brenda's return. "You know when?"

"I'm not sure, but . . . Hamp, she's getting married."

As the news settled inside him, his boyish smile brittled and threatened to crack. "Anyone I know?"

"He's not from around here. Truth is, I don't even know him yet, but I will. Him and Brenda's gonna have a baby, Hamp."

"Oh." Hamp sucked his bottom lip between his teeth and bit down hard. "I bet she's happy."

"Yeah, she seems to be."

"Brenda'll be a good mother." Hamp cupped his hat back on his head as he took a step toward the door. "Guess I better be getting back. Got some calves to take to the auction in Broken Bow."

"Hamp, you take care of yourself, you hear?"

"Yes, ma'am. I'll do that."

Molly O watched as Hamp hurried back to his truck, and as he pulled away, she saw him wipe the back of his hand across his cheek.

Right after lunch, Molly O started taking down the Christmas decorations. While she was rolling up a strand of red tinsel, Bui sidled up, then stood waiting until she noticed him standing beside her.

"Miss Ho," he said, holding out his letter. "Can you mailing for me?"

"Sure, Bui."

"But I cannot to knowing what is this." He tapped the upper corner of the envelope.

"The return address? Here." Molly O took the letter and wrote the address of the Honk. "Now," she said, "it's ready to go. I'll take it to the post office when I go downtown to make the bank deposit."

Bui pulled some bills from his pocket, neatly folded ones, and handed them to her.

"I've never mailed a letter to France before."

"My wife," Bui said, running his finger across Nguyet's name on the envelope.

"Your wife lives in France?"

"Wife in Vietnam. But no can mailing to Vietnam. Cousin in France can mailing."

Molly O nodded like she understood.

After she finished with the tinsel and packed the Barbies away, she started taking ornaments from the Christmas tree.

"Want me to get that?" Vena said when the phone rang.

"Yeah."

"Honk and Holler," Vena said into the receiver. "Yes, it is." She lowered her voice so that almost all her conversation was muffled. But once, when her voice rose with frustration, Molly O heard her say, "I know it was a long time ago, but . . . Look, are you sure you're spelling it right? Yes. S-a-n-c-h-e-z. Carmelita Sanchez."

Minutes later, when she hung up, Vena brushed past Molly O on her way to the kitchen to ask Caney for a cigarette. As she bent for a light, her hand was trembling.

"You okay?" he asked.

"Just a little ragged, I guess. Nothing a hit of nicotine won't cure."

"You didn't get enough sleep. Tonight, I'll take the couch, you get the bed."

"Oh, no. I'll go to my place. They should have the utilities on today."

"Vena, stay here tonight. Tomorrow night. As long as you want."

"Caney . . ."

"Hell, no point in you paying rent when you can stay here for nothing."

She started to walk away, but at the door stopped, and with her back to him, said, "Caney, you need to know . . . I'll be moving on."

"Well, I didn't think you came to stay. Didn't figure you planned to make a career working here."

"Just so you understand." She turned, then studied his face. "I won't be around long."

Caney grinned at that. "Hell, none of us will, Vena." He shook his head. "None of us will."

When they heard the tinkle of breaking glass followed by a moan from Molly O, they hurried out front where they found her kneeling behind the counter, picking through pieces of her nativity scene.

"I broke it," she said.

"What?" Caney asked.

"The baby. I broke the baby Jesus."

Chapter Fourteen

By the end of the week, Sequoyah had turned almost balmy. The last traces of the Christmas snow disappeared as the temperature climbed into the seventies, prompting the old-timers to warn that such weather was sure to spread some new strain of influenza for which they were quick to blame Asians, causing them to view Bui with even greater suspicion.

But on Sunday, a clear day with a warm southern breeze, most folks were giving little thought to the flu, Asian or otherwise.

The cafe filled early, first with bands of yawning duck hunters, then with an odd assortment of bikers. Though they called themselves the Harley Hellions, they were a docile bunch of circus people who wintered in Hugo every year.

Caney was churning out orders as fast as Molly O and Vena could pick them up while Bui, determined to be helpful, bused tables when he wasn't burning toast.

By the time the churchgoers arrived for breakfast, the Honk was packed. Five members of the Lord's Ladies' Bible Class were waiting impatiently for a table and had just reminded Molly O for the second time that Sunday school started promptly at nine-thirty.

And that's when the power went out.

Caney tried to call the electric co-op in Sallisaw for almost an hour before he finally got through on the emergency line to report the problem. But his wasn't the first call they had received.

A traffic accident on I-40 had sent a propane transport truck barreling into an electric substation where it overturned, knocking out power to most of the county. Four thousand gallons of propane would have to be pumped from the damaged truck into another transport before the co-op crew could begin repairs, which would certainly take most of the day.

While Caney finished up the last of the orders, Vena and Molly O served the last of the coffee. Then, with no lights inside or out, and with the ice machine and coffeemaker shut down, the Honk closed for the first time in nearly twelve years.

The problem of what to do with the food in the freezer was solved by Life Halstead who offered the use of his sister's meat locker over in Stony Point. The only problem, Life explained, was transportation because his truck was in the shop. But, he added, if Molly O would take her car, he'd be glad to go along.

When she agreed, Life tried not to show his joy over the power outage, but secretly he was thrilled that he would have her to himself for a while. And if he got lucky, he might have her all day.

"I was thinking," he said, "that when we leave Stony Point, we might take us a drive."

"Life, going to Stony Point is a drive."

"But we could go on, drive up the Winding Stair, have supper at that fancy place at the top."

"The Wilhelmina Lodge?"

"They tell me while you sit there eating, you can look out the window and see the clouds down below."

"That sounds nice, Life, but I don't think so."

"Why not? You're off work, it's a right nice day and we're heading in that direction anyway."

"This'll be a good time for me to get some things done at home."

"What things?"

"Oh, I need to do my hair, catch up on some ironing."

"Your hair looks great and there ain't a wrinkle on you. Besides, the electricity is out."

"Life, I just—"

"Come on, Molly O. We'll have fun."

"Well, we'll see," she said, but when she smiled, Life knew he had her.

While Life and Bui loaded the freezer packages into her car, Molly O finished up in the dining room, then carried the last of the dishes into the kitchen where Caney was cleaning the grill.

"Where's Vena?" he asked.

"I don't know."

"Is she outside?"

"Caney, I don't think I've seen her since the power went out."

"She might be in the utility room."

"No, I just took some towels in there."

"Maybe she's in the bathroom."

"Probably." Molly O rinsed a stack of plates at the sink, then loaded them into the dishwasher. "Well, that's about the best we can do without electricity," she said as she pulled off her apron. "Tomorrow morning I'll—"

They both looked up as the back door flew open and Vena, breathless and windblown, stuck her head inside.

"I've got a surprise for you, Caney."

"What?"

"Come out and see."

Caney wheeled to the doorway with Molly O right behind him. Outside, tethered to the handle of an old refrigerator, stood a magnificent sorrel gelding.

"He's a beauty, isn't he?" Vena said.

Caney looked stunned. "Where'd you get this horse?"

"That field back of the school bus."

"Well, whose is it?" Molly O demanded.

"That's Brim Neely's gelding," Caney said. "Does Brim know you have one of his horses?"

"I don't think so. At least not yet."

"You mean you just took it?" Molly O's eyes were wide with disbelief. "You stole Brim's horse?"

"Guess I'm just living up to my name."

"Why, Vena?" Molly O said, shocked by the enormity of the crime. "Why'd you take Brim's horse?"

"Thought I'd take a ride. And I'm hoping you'll go with me, Caney."

"Why, Caney's not able to ride!" Molly O put her hand on Caney's shoulder, a protective gesture.

"Why not?"

"Well, for one thing, he can't get on it."

"Sure he can. We'll help him. Bui and Life can lift him and I'll—"

"And for another, he's not well enough." Molly O looked to Caney, as if for confirmation, but he was staring at the horse.

"What do you say, Caney? Think you're up to it?"

"He most certainly is not!"

Caney pulled his eyes away from the gelding to look at Vena, his face grimaced with confusion.

"Vena, I . . . I told you . . ."

"You told me there was nothing out there you wanted."

Caney made an almost imperceptible nod of his head.

"Well, that's fine," she said. "Because we're not going after anything."

Caney looked again at the gelding, tried to see himself settled on its back, but the image was blurred, the picture unfocused.

He closed his eyes then, worked to make his body remember the way it felt to ride, when the power of the animal beneath him had been his power, when the rhythm of its movement had been his rhythm. But that was alien to him now, as alien as walking.

"I don't think I can," he said, his voice strained and thin.

And I'm hoping you'll go with me, Caney.

He thought he should offer her some kind of explanation, but he didn't know what to say. How could he make her understand that in here his life had boundaries and borders. In here he didn't need a compass to know where he was or a map to know where he was going.

. . . I'm hoping you'll go with me . . .

He wanted her to know that in the Honk he didn't need a watch to tell the time or a calendar to know the day. Mornings began with the first customer; nights ended with the last. Yesterday was the meatloaf special, today the liver and onion plate, tomorrow the chicken strip dinner.

. . . go with me, Caney . . .

In here he knew what to expect. The smell of hot grease and stale beer, the flicker of red and blue neon, the taste of ketchup on fries, the clink of spoons against coffee cups. Days as predictable as Life Halstead.

Suddenly, Caney grabbed the wheels of his chair, gave them a powerful jerk and popped the chair over the threshold. Clearing the door frame, feeling the heat of the sun on his face, he squinted against the glare.

"Don't do this," Molly O said as Caney moved out of her reach.

Just beyond the door, he hesitated, wiped the back of his hand across his mouth, then wheeled slowly to the side of the gelding, breathing in the musk of the animal, the smell earthy, ancient.

When he put his hand on the neck of the horse, his palm pressed against flesh warm and solid, muscles quivering beneath his touch, he was filled with an old knowing.

And the gelding's heart seemed to be beating in time to his own.

Vena didn't know Caney had only opened his eyes twice since they'd left the Honk. The first time, they were crossing a shallow stream, their flank exposed to snipers crossing in the thick brush on the far bank. The second time he'd looked, they were passing between two sweet gum trees where he spotted the trip wire strung just inches off the ground.

But even with his eyes closed, Caney knew when the gelding carried them down a sharp incline that the valley below would be dotted with land mines. He knew, too, when the horse clopped across the wooden planks of a narrow bridge that shape charges would be wired to the supports beneath them. And he knew with certainty when they approached the top of a gentle rise that the NVA patrol would be waiting . . . watching and waiting for them to come.

Caney might have ridden sightless for the rest of the morning if it hadn't been for the whirring of a distant sound coming from somewhere behind them, a sound that had followed him halfway around the world and, until now, had only been the black echo of his dark dreams. But here it was again, this time in the Oklahoma sunlight, this time real, vibrating in the hollow of his throat, exploding in the center of his chest.

Snatching the reins from Vena with one hand and slapping the gelding's rump with the other, he sent the startled animal into a sudden gallop across a meadow where a herd of Guernseys had already started to scatter.

By the time Caney looked over his shoulder, the chopper had cleared the ridge no more than a quarter mile behind them, coming in low and fast. He snapped the reins and yelled, a strangled cry lost under the roar from the sky.

When the helicopter swooped just above a stand of pecan trees towering fifty, sixty feet in the air, Vena looked up and pointed to the words CARE FLIGHT stenciled beneath its belly; but by then the dark shadow was passing over them, the *whop-whop-whop* of the rotor blades flattening weeds against the ground, snapping tree branches, pelting the meadow with leaves and loose branches.

Vena could feel the shuddering of Caney's chest against her body, tremors so violent that she reached back and hooked her arms around his waist, locking them together. The gelding, frantic now with the roaring above him, was streaking across the field, head up, ears back, body glistening with sweat.

And then, as quickly as it had come, it was gone, lifting over the eastern peak of the Winding Stair, disappearing beneath a soft bank of clouds.

Chapter Fifteen

CANEY DIDN'T MENTION the horse or the helicopter for two days following his ride with Vena. In fact, he didn't talk at all if he didn't have to.

As they rode back to the Honk that afternoon, Vena had asked a couple of questions about Vietnam, but Caney hadn't answered. She wasn't surprised, though. He'd been through an ordeal, and she figured he'd talk about it when he was ready.

The electricity was still out when they got back, but Bui, who'd stayed to help Caney get off the horse, was waiting for them when they rode up. He'd spent the time while they were gone putting together a makeshift ramp up to the concrete slab outside the back door. But as soon as Caney was settled in his chair, he wheeled onto the ramp and inside the cafe without comment.

Vena led the gelding back to the pasture, then removed the bridle and saddle and put them back in the barn where she'd found them.

Before she turned away, she stroked the gelding's muzzle and said, "Sorry about the rough ride, boy."

When she latched the gate and struck out across the field, the horse followed her to the corner of the fenceline.

Caney was in the bathroom when she got back. She could hear

water running in the tub while she sat on the couch, brushing her hair. She thought about bringing him a beer but decided her best move was to leave him alone for a while.

She drifted into the cafe, to the kitchen, and watched Bui through the back window as he worked to improve the ramp, an attempt, she imagined, to gain Caney's approval. She started to heat water to make herself a cup of instant, then changed her mind. Instead, she filled a pail with warm soapy water, then went to the utility room, scooped up the dog and walked outside to join Bui.

The dog had, in the past few days, started dragging itself out of the box for a few limping steps around the small space between the washer, dryer and hot-water tank by the door. Balance, it discovered, was hard to come by on only three legs, but it was learning.

"Ah," Bui said when Vena came through the door, "sun good for dog."

"Thought I'd give her a bath. Might cheer her up a little."

"I help."

While Vena worked a sponge gently around the wound on the dog's hindquarter, Bui rubbed its head, murmuring, *"Không sao dâu,"* as if he were soothing a frightened baby.

"You know, Bui, there's really no need for you to stick around here. Why don't you take off, go on home."

"I go to home at night. Day, I work for Mr. Chaney, much work to do."

After the dog's bath, Vena sat with it in her arms, the sun warming and drying its coat, while Bui went to work caulking around the back windows and relining the door with new strips of insulation. He worked silently, flashing Vena a smile from time to time, pleased to have her company, even without conversation.

As soon as the sun started to descend and the air began to cool, Vena took the dog back inside. The cafe was bright with light. The refrigerator and the deep freeze hummed and the sign out front glowed in the evening dusk. Electricity was once again zapping the Honk.

After she freshened the dog's bed and settled it inside the box,

Vena went to the bedroom. Caney, in his chair reading, didn't look up when she stepped inside the room.

"You hungry, Caney. Want me to fix you—"

"No," he said, his eyes never lifting from his book.

Vena went to the kitchen, made herself a ham sandwich and a cup of coffee, then sat in the dining room, eating alone.

When she saw a car pulling in, she called out to Caney. "Looks like we've got customers. Want me to let them in?"

She waited, then, unsure he had heard her, went to the bedroom door. "Caney, should I—"

"We're closed," he said, his voice flat and hard.

After she switched off the Honk sign and turned out the lights in the dining room, she watched the car drive away, then sat in the dark, wondering if she shouldn't get back on the road herself.

She had a little money now, enough to head out. And when that was gone, she'd do what she'd always done. She'd land somewhere, anywhere, work a few days, a few weeks, then move on. Her life.

But the dog could use a little more time. Though it looked like she was going to pull through, there was still the danger of infection. Best to leave her where she was for now.

Another reason to stay, at least for a while, was to see if one of the calls she'd made would pay off. She'd left messages everywhere she could think of to try to locate Carmelita, and though she hadn't had any luck so far, she knew if she left now, she'd have to start all over to find her. And Carmelita was the only one who might be able to piece together for her the last two years of Helen's life.

But maybe, Vena thought, she was just fooling herself. Maybe she was just looking for an excuse to stick around the Honk. And if she was, the man in the next room had something to do with it.

Chapter Sixteen

*B*UI ENTERED the darkened sanctuary exactly as he had every night for the past week. But tonight was the first time he'd had an audience.

She was sitting in the center of the third pew, wearing a brown cloth coat and a gray cap lined with rabbit fur. She had been twisting the straps of a cracked plastic purse between her gnarled black fingers until she heard the wooden doors slide open behind her. When she turned toward the shaft of light and saw the dark figure of a man with a chunk of stone in his hands, her fingers tightened on the purse and she pulled it to her chest, her movement quiet and slow so as not to draw his attention.

But Bui didn't see her there in the dim light, didn't hear the quick catch of her breath or the rustle of her coat as she tried to make herself small inside it.

Silently and shoeless, he padded down the aisle past the pew where she was huddled, placed his Buddha on the altar table and lit the tall candles in their silver holders.

He might have completed his prayers, might have left the sanctuary without ever knowing she was there if he hadn't heard the whispered voice coming from the darkness behind him.

". . . the Lord is my helper, and I will not fear what man shall do unto me . . ."

She had thought she was praying inside her head, hadn't even felt her mouth shaping the words until Bui whirled to face her. As his eyes searched the darkness at the edge of the flickering light, a taste like hot copper burned at the back of her throat.

Bui, still in motion when he saw her, went rigid. Neck twisted, limbs bent, body a figure of misangled parts, he looked like a child caught in a game of statues.

They stared at each other then, fixed and silent, two unlikely icons in a darkened church, each sculpted by terror of the other.

Then they watched. And waited.

Finally, the woman, clutching her purse with one hand, raised the other above her head, a gesture of surrender.

While Bui's eyes followed her movement, her fingers lifting toward the ceiling, he tried to decide what he should do. He could run, but he had nowhere to go. He could explain, but he didn't believe he could make her understand. So he did the only thing he could think to do. He raised his hand, too. And for a few moments, they seemed to be practicing a secret rite shared only by the initiated of some strange alliance.

"I have some money," she said, "and a watch I bought at a garage sale for a dollar. It doesn't keep good time, but I guess you get what you pay for."

She inched forward, then, hitching her shoulders up, rolled her head from side to side. "I'm gonna have to put my arm down now 'cause of my bursitis." Moving slowly, she lowered her arm while she shook her hand to restore feeling. Then she opened her purse, pulled out a few limp bills and held them out to Bui.

"I've got eighteen dollars and six quarters," she said, "but I need the quarters for the laundrymat."

Bui stared at the money, his face creased with confusion. Then he pulled his hand down to dig in his pants pocket, took out the twenty dollars Caney had paid him that evening and offered it to the woman.

"Why, I don't want your money," she said. "I thought you wanted mine. Isn't that what you're after?"

"I giving you—"

"Or did you come in here to bust things up? Come to defile this holy place?" Her voice rose and her eyes flashed with anger. "Well, I'll tell you this, mister. You can take my money and my watch, but I won't let you harm God's house. No sirree!"

"No," Bui said, uncertain of her message, but sure of her fury.

"Then what are you doing with that big rock?"

"Rock?"

"Don't act like you don't know what I'm talking about." She pointed an accusing finger at the altar. "I can see it there on the table."

"Ah," Bui said with sudden understanding. "Not rock. Buddha."

"What?"

"Buddha."

"I'll just see about that." She stood, her face grimacing with the effort, then shuffled her way to the end of the pew and started up the aisle.

She was older than Bui had thought, older than the sound of her voice, a strong and steady voice. She was stooped so that her coat sagged lower in the front, almost to her ankles which were thick and misshapen, causing her to walk on the insides of her feet. And her hair, twisting from beneath her cap, was so white it gave off its own light.

She was careful to keep some space between herself and Bui when she reached the table and bent over the stone.

"Well, I swan," she said. "I saw one of these in a Chinese restaurant once. They say if you make a wish and rub its belly, you'll get what you asked for."

Bui smiled and nodded, cheered by what he believed was an improving relationship.

Then the woman took a step toward him and in the candlelight saw clearly, for the first time, the features of his face.

"Why, I declare. You're a foreigner, aren't you?" She moved even closer. "What are you? Mexican? Japanese?"

"I Vietnamese."

"Vietnamese? Why, I've never seen one of you before, except on television when I watched the war over there." Then, without hesitation, she reached out and touched Bui's cheek, letting her fingertips examine the smoothness of his skin.

Bui's breath quickened. He had not felt the touch of fingers on his face since he'd left Nguyet, and the soft, cool sensation made images painted in green and gold swim just behind his eyes.

Then the woman put her hand to her own face, rubbing the skin beneath her eyes.

"Now isn't that something? We feel just the same," she said, smiling at the pleasure of her discovery. "My name is Galilee." She offered him her hand. "Galilee Jackson."

"My name Bui Khanh."

"Boo Can? Now that's a new one on me. I knew a man called Boo Ray once, but he's been dead more'n thirty years. A fancy man, a sweet-talking dancing man. Always smelled of lilac.

"Boo Ray danced with me one night at the Big Ten Ballroom in Tulsa. Danced every song and, oh, we looked fine. I wore a silk dress, blue . . . sapphire blue, and when he whirled me around the floor, the dress would slide around my hips and swish across my thighs and it felt like it was made of honey."

She returned then, leaving the fancy man back in the Big Ten Ballroom still dancing with the girl in the blue silk dress.

"Boo Can, huh? Well, it's an unusual name, but it seems to suit you. Suits you just fine to my way of thinking."

"I thinking, too."

"So," Galilee said, turning her attention once again to Bui's statue, "you're a Buddha."

"Yes, Buddha."

"Well, I expect there's room for all of us in heaven. I knew a Jewish man once, used to come through selling shoes out of his car. And my mother worked for a Catholic family a long time ago. They seemed like fine folks. I've got nothing against the Jehovah's, either, or the Scientists or even the Baptists, though I had a run-in with one when I worked at the school cafeteria. A Baptist woman who decided my name should be shortened to Gal. But I can't hold that against all Baptists now, can I?"

Galilee took a half step, shifting her weight from one leg to the other. "Say, you mind if we sit? I stand too long, my arthritis gives me fits." Then she looked down at her deformed feet. "I should've kept on dancing, I guess."

She hobbled to the first pew, eased herself into it, then patted the spot beside her for Bui.

"You married, Mr. Boo?"

"Yes, I married." Bui took out his billfold and opened it to show Galilee a picture of Nguyet. "My wife," he said.

"Oh, she's a pretty girl. Looks enough like you to be your sister."

"Many sisters and wife, all in Vietnam."

"That's a long ways off, isn't it?"

"She coming," Bui said. "Nguyet coming to living with me."

"Well, that's good, 'cause it hurts to be alone, hurts real bad. I was married, too, but my man Clarence, he's gone now."

"Husband dead?"

"No. He just drove away one day and never came back. I still don't know why, doubt I ever will. We had a good life, 'least I thought we did. He left when our girl was three. She never saw him again, either."

"Bad. Very bad."

"The church is about all I have left now. My girl, Jubilee, she lives in Michigan, but she changed her name when she went north. Says Julie's a better name for business. And I think that's a pretty name, all right, but not as pretty as Jubilee. You know what I mean?"

Bui nodded as if he did.

"Just listen to me go on. Talk, talk, talk. But it's nice to have someone to talk to. You come here a lot?"

"Yes, I here a lot."

"A church is a good place to come to, that's for sure. 'Course, this isn't the church it used to be, no sirree. Why, on Sunday mornings, there isn't enough of us to fill five pews. You see, we're an old congregation. And getting older. So many have passed now, and those still living, well, they're like me. Or even in worse shape. That's why a lot of us don't get out much now, not even for church.

"When we had transportation, we could make it most Sundays, but our bus got hit by a dump truck nine or ten years back. For a while, we had a few drivers to come by for us, but they're either dead or too old to drive now. 'Course, I'm lucky 'cause I live just down the road, so I can walk when the weather's nice if my arthritis isn't kicking up.

"But when we had our bus, I never walked 'cause our driver, Brother Marvin, always stopped for me. He'd slide the door open, smile and say, 'Mornin', Galilee. Come on in and let me carry you down the road.' And I'd settle in the seat right behind him, which I always figured he saved just for me.

"Then I'd watch him drive. Oh, I loved to watch Brother Marvin drive. His big hands curled around that steering wheel. Beautiful hands. Long slim fingers. Why, he could've put his hands around my waist till his fingers touched and he'd have had room left over.

"And when he leaned forward to open the door, the muscles across his back would bulge up under his starched shirt like hard dark plums.

"He had a nice head full of hair, too, not a speck of gray. A young man, fifty at the most. And his neck, thick and strong, skin so smooth, color of cinnamon. I had to sit on my hands to keep from reaching up and stroking Brother Marvin's neck. Oh, he was so . . ."

Galilee clamped her hand over her mouth, a futile attempt at silence.

"Lord, Lord," she said, shaking her head in sorrow. "Here I am, sinning again and me right here in God's house."

Bui shook his head, too, an indication to Galilee that he was as sorrowful about her sin as she was.

"I pray about my sins, Mr. Boo. 'Course, I'm too old to do much more than sin in my head, but sin is sin whether it's an act of the body or an act of the mind. And my mind's a nest of sin. Not *all* sin, mind you. I don't think about stealing or killing, and I try to keep the Sabbath holy . . . but lust and malice? I just can't seem to conquer them two.

"Now I keep thinking I'll grow too old for lust, but looks like I'm gonna carry it to my grave. And malice, to my way of thinking, is just as much sin as any of the rest.

"It's only natural, I guess, that I'd feel malice for my man Clarence after he did what he did to me and Jubilee. But my wickedness doesn't stop with Clarence, no sirree. My malice stretches in a hundred directions. Tax men, dump truck drivers, pawnbrokers. Republicans and bankers, which is one and the same to me. Chiropractors. Fortune-tellers, too. Oh, the list goes on and on.

"Sometimes I get so discouraged by my hateful heart, I think I'll just give up. Then the Lord talks to me, tells me to get myself down here to the church and pray. Pray hard. So I do, but it doesn't seem to do any good. I just can't stop sinning."

Bui sighed deeply, which Galilee took for a sign of compassion.

"You don't talk much, do you, Mister Boo? My husband was a quiet one, too. Never had much to say. But I figured that's because he was all the time reading. You read a lot yourself?"

"No, cannot to reading English."

"You can't? Oh, that's a shame. You need to learn to read. Why, I bet I could teach you. I taught my Jubilee to read before she even started school. She read good, too. Always had her face over a book, just like her daddy.

"Me, I don't read as much as I used to. Right after my man Clarence left, I took up them Harlequin romances for the most part of five years. Read one just about every day. 'Course, they just kept me stirred up with sinful thoughts. Finally, though, I quit those and took up the Bible. Figured it'd take a while for me to balance things out. Good and evil, you know. Love and hate. But it's hard to find that kind of balance. Seems to me most folks never do. They'll tip over one way or the other.

"So now, I just read my Bible, though you might find that hard to believe since I told you about my lust.

"But I don't want you to get the wrong idea about Brother Marvin, 'cause he was a good man. Spent his whole life in service to God. Visited the shut-ins. Taught the men's Bible class. And he did all the work needed doing here at the church. Why, he could fix just about anything. He was our electrician, plumber, bricklayer, painter. I'd come down here and help him sometimes. Sort his nails, clean his brushes, hold the ladder for him.

"But he's gone now. Killed in the bus that day right after he left off Sister May Ruth. By God's grace, she was his last passenger. Now, without anyone to keep things up, this old church is in a pretty mess."

"Yes," Bui said, looking around. "Very pretty."

"Oh, it used to be, but it's falling to ruin now. See up there in the corner, ceiling tile all stained and sagging? Another hard rain and that tile's going to come right down on our heads. And those two windows covered with plywood got busted out in a hailstorm more'n two years ago. Our back door won't lock, either, and the toilet tank leaks. All falling to ruin.

"But repairs cost money and need strong young men like Brother Marvin, so I don't know . . ."

"I can fix."

"You can fix what?"

"I fixer. Can fix window, can fix door, can fix . . ." Bui pointed to the sagging ceiling, a word not yet in his vocabulary. "Top?"

"Ceiling?"

"Yes, I fix ceiling."

"Why, Mr. Boo, that'd be wonderful, just wonderful. But we couldn't pay you for your time. There's not enough money in our—"

"No money, no sirree! I fix for no money."

"Oh, we couldn't ask you to work for nothing. We couldn't do that. But I tell you what I'll do. If you'll help us out here in the church, I'll teach you to read English."

"Me? To reading English?"

"Sure! I'd be more than glad. I'd love to do it if you want me to."

"I want."

"Then we've got a deal. Brother Marvin's tools are still out back in the shed. So's that church bus, a pitiful tangle of metal, but you can get around it. Couple of ladders out there, too.

"And if you need anything else, you let me know. I live up the road 'bout a quarter mile. Yellow house. Closest one to the church. You can't miss it. You come by there and I'll fix you a cup of cocoa and we'll talk. I sure enjoy your conversation."

Galilee Jackson pulled herself up, buttoned her coat and started up the aisle. When she reached the door, she stopped and turned back to Bui.

"You think you'd like to come to worship with us on Sunday, or will you be looking to find your own church?"

"My church?"

"Yeah, the place where Buddhas go."

"My temple far away."

"Yes, I reckon it is. But you remember this, Mr. Boo," she said as she turned and limped through the door. "It don't matter what house you go to . . . just live the life. Just live the life."

And then she was gone.

Chapter Seventeen

CANEY STAYED in bed all morning, pretending to sleep just as he had pretended to read the day before when his eyes had followed every word of every line on every page. But he had no recollection of the story and could not have named the title, even if he'd been asked.

He started to get up twice, but each time sank into his pillow, unwilling to make much of an effort. His back was stiff, his muscles ached and his head throbbed from lack of sleep.

He'd nearly drifted off once, but then the helicopter had come rushing at him, its blades cutting through the air above his head. After that, he made sure his eyes stayed open.

When he'd heard the raccoons in the trash cans just before dawn, he thought of getting his gun and shooting every one of the little bastards, but instead, he'd buried his head in his pillow to shut out the noise.

He'd heard Vena stirring just after first light, heard her pull her clothes on and slip into the cafe in the dark. And he'd heard Molly O arrive a few minutes later, knew when she tiptoed into the room and watched for the rise and fall of his blankets, evidence he was still alive.

He'd heard, too, fragments of conversation coming from just

outside his door, Molly O and Vena, whispered words not intended for him to hear.

"... a stupid stunt, Vena ... not a cowboy anymore ..."

"... going just fine until this helicopter ..."

"... for the love of God ..."

"... asked him about Vietnam ..."

"... did he tell you ..."

"... no, never said a word ..."

And for a moment, Caney thought he might call to her, ask her to come in and sit on his bed while he told it, told her all of it; but he felt his throat tighten and his mouth go dry the way it had each time the balding psychiatrist at the VA hospital had turned to him and smiled.

Caney, I don't believe we've heard from you yet.

They had called him Doc Tremble because of the way his hands would shake when they told their stories. Sometimes it was so bad he couldn't light his pipe or write notes on the pages of his clipboard. But he showed up every Monday and Thursday and gathered them into a circle for what he called their "Common Hour."

Don't you have something you'd like to talk about today, Caney?

No matter how hard Doc Tremble tried, Caney remained silent. Sometimes, after the lights went out in the ward, Caney would lie awake, trying to come up with something to say at the next session. But he just couldn't seem to find the words.

Don't you see, Caney? That's why it's called the Common Hour.

In spite of the fancy title Doc had given to their therapy sessions, Caney knew he didn't belong, knew he couldn't claim to have anything in common with those men ... men missing eyes, hands, testicles ... men fed through tubes in their bellies ... men who held themselves and rocked, staring, seeing nothing. Those men had given up parts of their bodies, pieces of their minds, to kill an enemy they couldn't see, to save friends they couldn't forget, to take a piece of ground they couldn't own.

Since we're out of time today, how about we start with you on Monday, Caney? You have any objection to that?

Those men had a right!

But a kid? An ignorant, clumsy kid falling out of a helicopter like some ten-year-old tumbling out of a treehouse? The only right he had was to keep his damned mouth shut.

When Caney finally wheeled out of the bedroom, Vena and Molly O tried to act like it was business as usual for him to start work in the middle of the day. But they watched him when he wasn't looking, watched and waited to see what was going on.

He spent most of the day in the kitchen, even when he had no orders to fill, but he was sullen and snappish, finding fault and insult in almost everything they did.

He growled at Vena because he couldn't read her tickets, and he jumped on Molly O when she wasn't waiting at the pass-through for each order she turned in.

When Wilma Driver pointed out that he'd left the cheese off her burger, he'd come whizzing out of the kitchen and rammed a slice of Swiss between the meat and the bun.

And as Life Halstead sliced into his rib eye, he made the mistake of saying it was too rare. Caney responded by spearing the steak with a fork, rushing to the kitchen and slapping it back on the grill. When he returned, the object impaled on the tines of the fork looked like a chunk of ebonite, and when he dropped it onto Life's plate, it clanged like a horseshoe striking tin.

But it was Bui who got the worst of it.

Caney fussed at him for leaving the door to the pantry standing open and yelled when Bui dropped too many onion rings into the deep fryer sending grease boiling over the top. When a fluorescent bulb began to flicker, Caney shouted for Bui to take care of it, then griped at him for making too much noise when he dragged the ladder inside to replace it. And when three tables emptied at about the same time, he complained that Bui was too slow in clearing them and warned that he'd better hump up or he might find himself out of a job.

By the time evening came, everyone knew that the best way to deal with Caney Paxton was to steer clear of him. Everyone, that is, except Sam Kellam.

Vena saw the black pickup when it pulled in, but she pretended not to notice as she attached a tray to the window of the familiar GMC. The 4-H boys came in now three or four times a week, each trying to outdo the others in gaining her attention. But this time she lingered, let them flirt with her longer than she usually did, giving Sam plenty of time to saunter inside the cafe.

Caney was behind the register writing checks when Sam came in. He grunted a hello, hardly taking time to look up.

Molly O put a glass and the beer he ordered on the counter, but Sam shoved the glass away and drank straight from the bottle.

"You look bushed, Molly O."

"Well, it's been a long day," she said as she picked up a couple of dirty cups and headed for the kitchen.

"Your carhop's really pulling them in, Caney."

"Uh-huh."

"Looks like a car auction out there."

Caney tore a check out of the book and attached it to a bill on the counter.

"Surprising what a good carhop can do for you, huh?"

"Yeah."

"She must be giving you some special kind of service." Sam grinned, a lopsided smile to show he knew what was *really* going on, but Caney ignored him.

When Vena slipped inside, trying her best to be unnoticed, Sam swiveled on the stool to give her his "undressing you" appraisal.

"Say, Vena, I missed you on that bus. And I don't get much of a kick from riding by myself. But from what I hear, you traded the bus for a horse." Sam took a long pull at his bottle, then wiped the back of his hand across his mouth. "What'd you all do out there? Play cowboys and Indians?"

Caney and Vena exchanged a glance, then she went to one of the back tables and bent over her half-finished meal which was growing cold.

Sam drained the last of his beer, then held the bottle up to Vena. "How about another one of these?"

"I've got it," Caney said, already reaching into the cold case beneath the counter.

"Yeah, Caney, from what I hear, this is about the busiest place in town. Business so good you've had to hire on extra help."

Caney set the fresh beer on the counter, picked up the empty and flipped it into the trash can beneath the window.

"And folks say this place has gone international. A real melting pot."

"Maybe folks talk too much."

"That they do, Caney. That they do. Matter of fact, there's an ugly rumor going around that you hired yourself a gook. But I tell them not to go spreading lies. I tell them there's not an ounce of truth to that because I know you're too smart a man to do something that stupid."

When two middle-aged couples got up from one of the front tables and brought their check to the register, Caney took their money and mumbled, "Good night." As soon as they walked out the door, Bui rushed from the kitchen with a plastic tub.

"Well, looks like I was wrong, Caney," Sam said. "Looks like what I heard wasn't no rumor after all."

Caney pulled a cigarette from his pocket, keeping his eyes on Sam as he lit it.

"Looks like a gook, smells like a gook, then it must be a gook." Sam watched Bui as he cleared the vacated table.

"What's your name, gook?"

Bui, so intent on his work, so desperate to please Caney, was oblivious to the conversation taking place at the counter.

"Hey," Sam yelled. "I said, 'What's your name?' "

Molly O, hearing the anger in Sam's voice, came to stand in the kitchen doorway, one hand pressed against her chest. Vena shoved back from the table where she had been eating, the legs of her chair screeching against the floor.

Bui, smiling despite the certainty that the man's question was not prompted by friendliness, said, "My name Bui Khanh."

"Boy, huh? Well, Boy, looks like you're doing all right for yourself here in the good old U.S. of A."

"U.S.A. very good."

"Yeah, it's a damned good place 'long as you've got a job and people to kiss your ass."

"Sam, where are you going with this?" Caney asked.

Sam spun, leaned across the counter. "What the fuck you think you're doing, Caney? What's that little slant-eyed bastard doing here?"

"Sam, why is it that you—"

"We got boys from this town never came back from Nam. Bill Ott's boy and that Finch kid. Minnie Harwell's husband, Frank. So what are you doing with him here, huh? Rubbing our noses in it?"

"Well, Sam, if you've got shit on your nose, you might've had it stuck in the wrong place."

Sam's eyes narrowed as splotches the color of raw meat spread across his cheeks. "We left a lot of good men over there, Caney, and it just might be the gook you got working here fired the bullets that killed them."

"That goddamned war's been over for twelve years, Sam. What's the use of—"

"That mean we're supposed to love them now? Pat them on the shoulder, give them jobs Americans need?"

"You need a job, Sam? 'Cause if you do, I can probably take you on."

"What the hell is it with you, Caney? You think because you came back in a wheelchair that you've got it all figured out? Well, let me tell you something. We didn't fight that war just so we could—"

"We? Why, I didn't know you were in it, Sam. I heard you waited it out up north. We, my ass!"

Moving slowly, Sam eased his shoulders forward, laid both arms flat on the counter and curled his hands into fists.

"Mr. Chaney," Bui said, his voice tight with tension, "I go to home now. Okay?"

Sam turned, eyes locked on Bui. "You going home now, Boy?

Well, you be mighty careful. You have some kind of accident, you get busted up, you'll be in a hell of a mess. Can't work, can't drive, might be you won't be able to feed yourself or wipe your own ass. Might be—"

"Mr. Chaney?" Bui began to move toward the counter. "I finish work now and—"

Without warning, Sam grabbed his beer bottle by the neck and swung it toward Bui, but Caney caught Sam's hand on the backswing, sent the bottle hurtling through the air and, before it crashed into the Coors sign on the front window, had Sam's arm pinned to the counter, wrist bent like a chicken wing.

"Now you listen to me," Caney said, his voice barely more than a whisper. "You mess with him, you'll have to worry about me the rest of your life. Every time you crawl in some woman's bed, every time you turn the key in the ignition of your truck, every time you see something move in a shadow."

Sam, his lips stretched tight against his teeth, eyes squinted in pain, said, "Yeah, what'll you do, run me down with your wheelchair?"

Caney applied more pressure to Sam's wrist until it made a popping sound. Sam groaned, sweat beading his forehead.

"Sam. You fuck with him, I'm gonna fuck with you."

As Caney released Sam's arm, he shoved him away from the counter. "Now, get your ass out of here."

The only one inside the Honk who moved before Sam's truck roared away was Caney. He grabbed his pen and checkbook and went back to paying bills.

Then, without looking up, he said, "Bui, clean up that broken glass."

Vena didn't know what woke her until she saw the flare of Caney's lighter across the room. He was sitting at the window, a thin shaft of moonlight slanting across his face.

He didn't turn as she raised herself to one elbow but kept his eyes fixed on something outside in the dark.

"We knew it would be a hot insertion," he said. "The four-five-four was pinned down in a valley with the VC right on top of them, so we couldn't get any artillery in there to clean things up before we landed."

Caney took a slow drag of his cigarette, the smoke curling toward the windowpane.

"I was in the third Huey, the last in formation, and I could see the first two go in, VC popping them with everything they had. Antiaircraft, machine guns, grenades.

"The pilot took us in fast. We knew he wasn't going to set us down, didn't want to give the VC a target any longer than he had to, so guys started jumping while we were still fifteen feet off the ground.

"Me and the kid beside me had our feet on the skids, just about to jump, when we got hit. Blew the kid's leg off, right at his knee. Sliced clean away.

"He leaned forward, watched it fall . . . and when it hit the ground, he pointed to it and yelled, 'There it is,' like he thought he might go back and get it."

Caney stopped talking and smoked a while, the room so still Vena could hear the hiss of burning tobacco at the tip of his cigarette.

"The pilot gave it the juice then and that Huey shot straight up, just like a damned rocket. Three, four hundred feet. He was trying to get us out of there, and he might've made it, too, but we took another hit."

Vena eased off the couch, pulled Caney's robe around her shoulders, then slipped across the room and sat on the edge of his bed.

"There was this tremendous jolt, threw me and the kid back across the floor, that chopper shaking like hell. Then it flipped over on its side and everything started sailing out. The kid went first, skidded right by me.

"And I remember feeling so sorry for him. He had all that way to fall. All that time to think about it."

Ash from the cigarette dropped, drifting across Caney's shirt.

"He was a kid," Caney said.

He dropped the cigarette into an ashtray and watched until the red embers burned out.

"He was just a kid."

For several moments they sat unmoving and still. Then Vena reached into the silence and took Caney's hand, slipping her fingers through his where they rested, framed in a wedge of moonlight.

Chapter Eighteen

CANEY HADN'T NOTICED that Molly O had stopped wearing her ring, a narrow turquoise-and-silver band she'd always worn on the third finger of her right hand. He didn't know that when she was home doing dishes or rinsing out her underwear, the ring would slip off her finger and fall to the bottom of her sink. He hadn't missed it, had no idea she'd put it away in the small wooden jewelry box on top of her dresser.

Life didn't miss the ring, either, but since he paid more attention to Molly O's body than anyone else, he should've noticed that her slacks were beginning to hang loose across her hips and her blouses looked a little roomy.

Wilma Driver had noticed a change when Molly O's face started to thin, but she couldn't quite pinpoint the difference. At first she thought Molly O had bought new frames for her glasses or switched to a lighter shade of makeup, but she finally chalked it up to a new hairstyle which prompted her to call the Hair Shed and schedule a cut and perm.

Bui had too many problems of his own to pay attention to these small changes in Molly O's appearance, but he did compliment her one day on a new dress she was wearing. He couldn't have known, of course, that it had been hanging in her closet for three years along with all her other size fourteens.

But Vena had been watching. And she hadn't missed a thing.

When she first realized Molly O was passing up her morning doughnut and scraping her half-eaten cornbread into the trash, she imagined a New Year's resolution was at work. And when she saw her cut her meatloaf into small bites and slip the plate back to the utility room, she thought an animal lover was in the making.

But when she saw Molly O, an ardent nonsmoker, snitch one of Caney's cigarettes, and when she saw her wearing the same stain on the same blouse two days in a row, she knew something more serious than a diet was on her mind.

Vena thought it might be explained by a new stage of menopause, the next step beyond hot flashes, whatever that might be. Depression, maybe. Perhaps the prospect of becoming a grandmother, a subject Molly O hadn't mentioned lately, had brought on the fear of growing old.

Or maybe, she reasoned, Molly O had gone and fallen in love, but she looked too unhappy for that to be the cause. Or she might be stewing about Caney, though his dark mood had been lifting little by little since the day of the horseback ride.

She could, of course, just be worried about money. After all, who wasn't?

Finally, though, Vena realized she had no way to know, not her business to find out. And even if she asked, she was certain Molly O would never confide in her.

But she was about to be surprised.

When the last of the morning diners had cleared out, Caney reminded Molly O about the bank deposit.

"Do you have it ready?" Molly O asked.

"Yeah, it's under the register."

Molly O pulled off her apron, picked up the deposit and grabbed her purse.

"I'm going to stop by Wal-Mart," she said. "You need anything?"

"Not that I can think of."

"You mind if I go with you?" Vena asked. "I need to pick up a couple of things."

"Well, it's okay with me, but if Caney gets busy . . ."

"Caney, you think you and Bui can manage if I go along?"

"Sure. Nothing going on here."

"Okay," Molly O said without enthusiasm, "but we'll have to be back to help with lunch."

"I won't slow you down."

As they crossed the lot to her old Ford, Molly O said, "My car's kind of a mess right now. I've been buying a few things for the baby."

"A few things for the baby" turned out to be a plastic baby seat, a diaper bag, a Rubbermaid bathtub, boxes of baby bottles, a bassinet, a sterilizer, stacks of crib blankets, a potty chair, eight deluxe-size packages of disposable diapers and more toys than Santa could fit in his sleigh.

Vena helped shift enough of it to wedge herself into the passenger seat, but only by holding a large plastic duck on her lap.

As Molly O steered the car onto the highway, she said, "I got that duck for fifty cents. You know, you can pick up this stuff at garage sales for almost nothing, but you go to buy it new, it costs a fortune.

" 'Course, not all of it's used. I clip coupons for disposable diapers and every time the IGA has double coupon days, I save two dollars a package. It'd make more sense for Brenda to use cloth diapers, but she's never been one to take the sensible route. I can't see her washing a dirty diaper in the toilet the way I did. No, I can't see her doing that at all."

As the car picked up speed and began to shimmy, a naked rubber doll on the dash bounced off into Molly O's lap. She was doing forty, driving only a little faster than she was talking, a sudden departure from the past few days when she'd had so little to say.

"I wish now I'd kept Brenda's things. She had a white baby bed with little gold angels painted across the headboard, and a four-drawer chest to match. And I made curtains for her room, pink with ruffles at the bottom. I got her a music box, too, with a china doll on top that turned around when I wound it up. Played . . . oh, what was that song?"

Molly O tried to hum the tune, but gave up after the first few notes.

"I kept all that stuff for years, but I don't know why. I was forty-one when she was born. I knew there wouldn't be any more babies. But it was hard to let it all go. Her little gowns, her highchair, that precious crib."

As Molly O increased her speed to fifty, the shimmy worsened, causing the baby bottles to rattle and the potty chair to clack against the back window.

"Finally, I gave it all away, all except the rocking chair. My mother rocked me in it when I was a baby and I rocked Brenda in it till she was almost big enough to rock me."

Molly O was lost in thought then, silenced for the first time since they'd gotten in the car, prompting Vena to jump into the conversation.

"How's she doing?"

"Why, she's been dead for almost ten years."

"No, I meant Brenda."

"Oh, she's great. Just great! A touch of morning sickness now and then, but that's to be expected, isn't it? She's gained four pounds, but she says she's not showing yet, so she's still performing. Making good money, too. And she says she and that Travis are saving like you wouldn't believe."

When Vena saw they'd entered a forty-mile zone, she expected Molly O to slow down. Instead, with her foot heavy on the gas, she had them moving at sixty and gaining.

"She's been real busy planning their wedding. They're going to get married at the Love Eternal Chapel where the windows are all shaped like hearts, which I think is so sweet. She's already picked out her dress, white with seed pearls stitched on the bodice, but she decided not to get a veil and I'm glad 'cause Brenda's got such beautiful hair. It'd be a shame to cover it up on her wedding day.

She's decided on a bouquet of pink carnations with sprigs of baby's breath which will be just perfect since she's—"

When the car started drifting to the right, Vena saw that the needle on the speedometer was nearing seventy.

"Maybe you ought to slow down a little," she said, but the car continued to accelerate, still tending to the right.

"Molly O?"

"She picked out her ring last week . . ."

They were moving dangerously close now to the edge of the asphalt. Beyond that, a narrow graveled shoulder gave way to a steep drop to a bar ditch.

". . . a cluster of diamonds set in a—"

"Watch it!" Vena yelled as the right front tire dropped onto the shoulder.

Molly O made a rasping sound which Vena took for fright, but when she glanced at Molly O's face, she saw she was crying.

Vena grabbed the wheel. "Molly O, I want you to take your foot off the gas," she said, trying to conceal her panic.

". . . wants me to come for the wedding," Molly O whimpered.

"Take your foot off the gas!"

Molly O lifted her foot and slumped in the seat, sobbing.

"Now, listen. Do what I say, exactly what I say. Gently . . . very gently, put your foot on the brake. Good. Now, press. Easy, easy."

Vena was doing her best to hold the wheel steady, prepared in case Molly O stomped on the brake which was certain to send the car into a skid.

". . . something borrowed and something blue . . ."

"Just keep pressing down on the brake. That's it, good."

". . . loan her my locket . . ."

"A little more pressure, Molly O, but take it easy."

As the car began to slow, Vena brushed a pile of baby blankets off the seat and scooted over, crowding Molly O against the door.

"I've got it now," she said, placing both hands on the wheel. "You can let go."

Molly O's hands fell limply to her lap as she eased the brake pedal to the floor and the car rolled to a stop.

For several moments, neither of them spoke.

Finally, Vena put the car in park. "I'll drive," she said.

When she stepped out, her legs buckled, and as she made her way around to the driver's door, she staggered and nearly fell.

She gently nudged Molly O to the far side of the seat, then slipped beneath the wheel.

"She never called," Molly O said, her voice breaking.

Vena's heart was pounding like a sprinter's at the end of a race. "What? Who are you talking about?"

"I haven't heard from Brenda since she was here. Christmas Day." Molly O snuffled. "Not a word."

Vena's fingers were still trembling as she readjusted the rearview mirror.

"I waited nearly a month, thinking she'd get in touch with me, but when she didn't, I called information in Las Vegas, you know, thinking she and that Travis might have a phone, but the operator said she didn't have a listing.

"Well, I didn't think much about that 'cause Brenda said they'd only be there a little while, so I thought maybe it wouldn't make any sense, them getting a phone."

Vena waited until a truck passed, then eased the car back onto the road.

"So then I called that club where they were booked, the Lucky Lady, but they said they didn't know what I was talking about. Said they'd never heard of Brenda O'Keefe or Travis Howard."

Molly O wiped her nose with the back of her hand, then dug in her pocket for a tissue.

"That's when I really started to worry. Edna, down at the library, let me take a Las Vegas phone book home and I started calling all the casinos there. Started with the A's, the Aladdin, and worked my way down the list."

Vena kept the car steady at thirty, five miles below the speed limit as they entered the outskirts of Sequoyah. When she finally relaxed her grip on the wheel, she realized her nails had been digging into the palms of her hands.

"So last night I got to the H's, the Hacienda. The guy I talked to said Brenda's band wasn't booked there, but he knew Travis. Told me he was playing some dump, that's what he called it, 'some dump,' called the Seven-Come-Eleven.

"And sure enough, that Travis was there. I had to call back three times before I caught him on a break, but I got him."

Molly O's fingers had found the naked doll in her lap, and she began absently smoothing back its nonexistent hair.

"He was mad 'cause I called. Real mean. And when I told him I wanted to talk to Brenda, wanted to know where she was, he said, 'How the hell should I know? She split three weeks ago and I don't give a good goddamn where she is.' That's what he said."

"Well, it sounds like they've had a fight," Vena said. "But chances are they'll be back together before you know it and—"

"That's what I figured. She's mad, staying in some motel, making him wonder where she is. That sounds just like something Brenda would do.

"But I just have to talk to her. See, when she was here, she was having a pain in her side. Promised me she'd get to a doctor, but—"

"Then she probably has. And if anything had been wrong, she'd have called you. Sounds to me like the best thing for you to do right now is wait for her to call. And try not to worry."

"I can't do that. No way I'm not going to worry about Brenda. And as far as waiting, I'm not too good at that, either. I've already started calling all the motels in the book. I'm already up to the Boulder."

"That's going to get expensive."

"Yes, but it doesn't matter. I don't care what it costs. I guess it sounds crazy, but I feel like she's lost. The way I'd feel sometimes when she was little and I couldn't see her playing in the backyard, or when we'd be at the store and I'd turn around and she was gone.

"I'm just crazy, I guess. But sometimes people do crazy things when someone they love is lost."

Molly O, her eyes red and face puffy from crying, had insisted on waiting in the car.

"I'm not going in there looking like this," she said. " 'Cause you can't go in Wal-Mart without running into someone you know."

Vena would discover, too late, that she was right.

She picked up the skein of blue yarn Molly O had asked for, then, from a table of Christmas leftovers—a mishmash of ornaments and decorations—she found something to give her as a surprise.

After she got herself a box of tampons, she headed for the checkout stand, but before she got there, a hand reached out and caught her by the arm.

"Hey, pretty woman," Sam Kellam said as he spun her around to face him. "Did I get lucky and catch you on your day off?" He tapped the box and grinned. "Picking up some supplies for Caney?"

"Look, I've got to go."

"Why? You think the Honk'll shut down if you're not there?"

"Molly O's waiting in the car."

"She knows how to drive. Let her go on."

Vena tried to turn away, but Sam tightened his grip on her arm and held her in place.

"I'll take you back," he said.

"No, you won't."

"Why not? You afraid of me?"

"Judging from what happened the last time you were in the Honk, I don't think I have much to be afraid of."

Sam's face flushed, but he managed a thin, tight-lipped smile. "You mean because I didn't beat the shit out of your boyfriend? Now what kind of man would take advantage of a cripple?"

"You're a slimy son of a bitch."

"What's wrong, Vena? You don't like me calling your hump a cripple?"

Vena noticed that a woman pushing her shopping cart up the aisle gave her and Sam a wary look as she dashed past them.

"Or could I be wrong? You fucking the gook?"

When Vena wrenched herself free and spun away, the box of

tampons slipped from her fingers and sailed across the floor. But she didn't care about that now.

Sam made no move to follow, but yelled after her, "Or are you taking on both of them at the same time? What one can't do for you, the other one can. That it?"

Everyone at the front of the store was staring as Vena rushed to the checkout and shoved her purchases onto the counter.

"Guess it's hard for a woman like you to find one man who can do it all," Sam shouted.

"Hurry, please," Vena said to the checker, a middle-aged woman who looked like she wanted to run.

When her bill was totaled, she tossed down five dollars, grabbed her plastic sack and hurried away.

"Ma'am? You forgot your change," but by then Vena was already out the door.

When she slid into the car, she was working hard not to let her anger show. She figured Molly O had enough on her mind just then without worrying about Sam Kellam.

"Here's your yarn."

Molly O opened the bag and looked inside as Vena fumbled the key into the ignition.

"Good, it's exactly the color I wanted." Then she reached to the bottom of the sack where she found a small ceramic figure—a tiny baby Jesus from Taiwan.

"Oh, Vena."

"Well, since you have the rest of the manger . . ."

"Yes," Molly O said softly. "Not much point to a manger without you have the baby."

Chapter Nineteen

By THE TIME the AME congregation learned that Bui was sleeping in the basement of their church, they didn't care. By then they would have let him sleep on the altar if he'd wanted to.

At first, they hardly noticed evidence of his handiwork but focused instead on their service to the Lord.

When five women gathered in the church kitchen early Monday morning, their minds were on Sister Zibeon, friend and faithful member for over sixty years. They had come together to prepare a meal they would serve following her burial at the Rest Haven Cemetery that afternoon.

Not until one of them started rinsing vegetables at the sink did she notice the drain was once again running freely. And when another started outside to empty trash, she was surprised to find that the back door no longer caught on the door frame but could be closed and locked securely again.

On Monday afternoon, when three members of the Hope Missionary Society met in the Reverend's study to plan their annual banquet, they concentrated on preparing their program—not on the ceiling fan. They didn't notice it had been cleaned and oiled, blades tightened, brass trim polished, burned-out bulbs replaced and the globe, emptied of dead insects, scrubbed with soap and water. Even Sister Nadine, whose hearing was still good, failed to realize the fan no longer hummed and whined, a sound that had always set her nerves on edge.

Tuesday morning when the Ladies' Auxiliary met in one of the small Sunday school classrooms, Sister Eunice, the first to arrive, was surprised to find the sliding wooden door, jammed for months, had been rehung, fitted snugly back into the metal track it rolled on. Sister Cordelia, the last to show up, commented on what a bright clear day it was, never realizing that the windows facing Sticker Creek had been scraped clean of pigeon droppings and scoured with a stiff-bristled brush.

At Wednesday evening service, no one in the sanctuary, fourteen including Reverend Thomas, noticed that the frayed carpet at the door had been concealed by a new strip of aluminum tacked neatly in place. Nor were they aware that the half-inch crack snaking up the west wall had been plastered and sanded smooth. And because they were huddled together on the front row, they couldn't see that the hymnal racks which had come loose from the backs of the pews had all been screwed back into place.

Thursday's choir practice was sparsely attended because one of the altos was suffering from gout and their only soprano was at the bedside of her brother, who'd just had a stroke. But not one of the seven who did assemble noticed that the vestry had been mopped and waxed or that a three-foot strip of loose baseboard had been retacked to the wall.

The Friday Singles Club had not met in the recreation room for nearly three months, not since the only male, Brother Samuel, had remarried on the day he turned seventy-one. But if they had come together, they would surely have been pleased to see that the piano stool missing a leg was now standing firmly on all four and the door to the cabinet where they kept their checkers and dominoes was adorned with handles once again.

On Sunday, though, they finally started paying attention when twenty-two of them straggled into the sanctuary and found the pews waxed and gleaming, and the chandelier suspended from the arched ceiling, shimmering with light, each glass prism washed and polished by a careful hand.

By whose hand, they could not guess.

The following week they had bad weather—rain, then sleet and snow. The temperature stayed below freezing until Friday, prompting cancellation of choir practice, the Ladies' Auxiliary meeting, and the Hope Missionary Annual Banquet. Even the Wednesday night service was called off, the first time since a flu epidemic the previous winter had put nearly half the congregation in their sickbeds and scared the others into staying home.

But by Sunday the weather had warmed and the slush on the streets had mostly disappeared, conditions which prompted thirty-two members and one guest to come to church.

As they made their way to the front steps, keeping their eyes on the sidewalk to avoid loose stones and deep cracks in the concrete, they didn't notice the patch of new shingles on the roof, damaged last spring by the broken limb of a sycamore tree. And as they entered the small vestibule, they paid no attention to the framed painting of the Last Supper which had been straightened and wiped free of cobwebs.

But when they entered the sanctuary, they did not move far beyond the door before they stopped and stared in silent wonder.

The plywood covering the broken windows was gone, and where there had been cracked and shattered glass, windows were whole again, their new panes glistening in shafts of sunlight. The sagging ceiling tiles had been removed and in their place, new ones fitted neatly into the metal supports. And the walls, only last week stained and discolored, had been freshly painted a pristine white.

At first they were hushed as, turning, their eyes swept the room. Then, as they moved down the aisles, they spoke in whispered conversations, their hands fluttering, pointing out to their neighbors the marvels they might have missed. By the time they were settled in their pews, their voices were quavering with excitement.

Even as Reverend Thomas took the pulpit, they were still buzzing with questions, leaning forward, then back, as one, then another, offered some explanation as to how such a miracle had been performed.

"Brothers and sisters," the Reverend intoned, "we cannot question this morning that the Lord has blessed us."

"Amen."

"And we know today, as we have always known, that God does hear our prayers."

"Hallelujah."

"Amen."

"A benevolent God who has sent one of you among us to restore His house."

"Praise the Lord."

"And now, whoever you are, we would like to recognize you for your most unselfish contribution . . . for putting your hand to the repair of this holy place of worship."

Thirty-two heads turned to see who would stand.

"We would surely like to offer you our thanks."

Long moments of silence passed.

"Then we must suppose that whoever you are, you have beautified God's house for His glory and not your own. As Proverbs twenty-nine, verse two tells us, 'Let another man praise thee and not thine own mouth.' So we honor your silence and lift our thankful voices to God.

"Let us pray. Our Heavenly Father . . ."

As Reverend Thomas led them in prayer, and as they stood with bowed heads and closed eyes, they could not see the smile that graced Galilee Jackson's face. But even if they had, they would most certainly have attributed it to the joy in her heart for God's blessing.

"Oh, Mr. Boo, you should've seen their faces," Galilee said as she placed Bui's cocoa on the coffee table. "I just wish you'd been there.

"Now, at first, they guessed Reverend Thomas was the one did all that work. Sister Maybelle says to me, 'It had to be the Reverend. No one else here's able to lift a hammer, let alone climb a ladder.'

"So I reminded her that the Reverend works six days a week over at the plastics plant. See, Mr. Boo, he has to work another job, given the little dab the church can afford to pay him.

"And at night, well, ever' night 'cept Wednesday and Sunday, he baby-sits his grandbaby 'cause his daughter works the late shift at the nursing home and no way she can pay a sitter on her salary.

"Your cocoa too hot, Mr. Boo?"

Bui took a sip to show her it wasn't, then swished the scalding liquid in his mouth until it cooled enough to swallow.

"So then Sister Maybelle considers what I said and she says I'm right, so she starts to squelch the notion that the preacher did it, and that runs through the crowd and pretty soon they're all nodding their heads, saying, 'No, 'course the Reverend didn't do it,' like they'd realized that all along.

"Well, that sets them off again, all of them guessing who it might've been. Then somebody said it could've been Jennings Washington on account of him being so handy with tools and the like. But we all know Jennings ain't been in a church but one time in his whole life and that was the day he married Grace Abbott. 'Course, they kept their voices down to a whisper so Sister Grace wouldn't hear, 'cause she was sitting right there in the third pew.

"Well, they guessed and guessed, but they couldn't come up with a name. By then they were squirming in their seats, anxious for Reverend Thomas to take the pulpit, figuring he'd solve the mystery for them.

"But when the Reverend got up and told them he didn't know, they were stunned. Just stunned. And when he asked for whoever done it to stand up, you should've seen them. Twisting their necks like a bunch of chickens. And I did the same, 'cause I figured if I didn't, they might guess I knew a thing or two about it.

"Oh, I came this close to telling them, Mr. Boo. Just this close."

Galilee held her thumb and index finger close together to illustrate for Bui, who studied the gesture with curiosity.

"But you know why I didn't?"

Bui shook his head, still puzzling over the strange sign Galilee had made with her hand.

" 'Cause they got enough misery in their lives to think about. Brother Junior, his wife in the nursing home, doesn't even know who he is, but he goes to see her ever' day, bless his heart. Brother Arnold? Got sugar diabetes so bad, he'll end up getting his feet cut off, just like his daddy did.

"Sister Martha, whose granddaughter is . . . well, there's just no nice way to say it."

Galilee leaned forward and lowered her voice. "She's a lady of the night, if you get what I'm saying."

When Bui realized some response was required of him, he leaned forward, too, and nodded.

"And Sister Hannah, God love her, her home burned down last spring, and oh, she had such lovely things. Now, she's living with her son and daughter-in-law and their six kids in a two-bedroom trailer."

"So many bearing so much sadness."

Galilee shook her head, then reached for her cocoa. "So I said to myself, 'Galilee, no reason you have to pop up and tell them about Mr. Boo right now. Give it some time, let them wonder. Let them get their minds off their troubles and think about something good, something fine, even if it's just for a little while.'

"Now you know why I didn't speak up, don't you, Mr. Boo?"

Bui nodded as if he had taken in every word.

"Well, we've spent enough time jawing. Wish we could just sit here all morning talking, but we can't. No sirree. We've got work to do."

Bui followed Galilee to the dining room and sat down at the table while she got out the tablet in which he practiced his ABCs and the books she was using to teach him to read—the same books she'd learned to read from when she was a child.

"Okay, let's take up where we left off Saturday morning," she said as she handed a small, thin book to Bui.

"Look, Molly O, you want to take some time off, go out there and look for her yourself?"

"Where would I look, Caney? I already called every place I could think of."

"Maybe you ought to call her boyfriend again," Vena said.

"I did."

"And?"

"He's gone, too. Got fired at that club a few days ago."

"Well, maybe he and Brenda got back together and went on to Denver. Didn't you say that they had a gig there when they finished in Las Vegas?"

"That's what she said."

"How about I make some calls to Denver. See what I can find out."

"I don't know, Caney. I just don't know."

Molly O had her purse in one hand, the other on the doorknob, but she looked like she'd forgotten where she was going . . . or just didn't care.

"Go on and get your hair done," Caney said. "Might make you feel better."

"Well, whether it does or not, I'll be back by ten."

As she walked out, Bui drove across the lot, his trunk door open, slapping air. He waved at Molly O, then pulled around the building to park in back.

Vena refilled coffee for Bilbo and Peg at the front table, then took an order for a waffle and a breakfast special to the pass-through and handed the ticket to Caney, who had wheeled into the kitchen.

When they heard a banging noise coming from out back, Caney said, "What the hell was that?"

"I don't know, but Bui's out there, I think."

Vena hurried to the door and yanked it open as Bui struggled to remove something from his trunk. When he finally managed to lift it, they saw him grappling with a large object covered with a stained tarpaulin.

Staggering with the weight, he carried it, chest high, to a grassy spot beneath the pecan tree in the back. When he finally lowered it to the ground, he leaned against it, waiting for his breathing to slow.

"What've you got there, Bui?" Caney asked.

Bui turned and smiled, then, like an artist unveiling a creation, he jerked the tarp off with a flourish.

"A doghouse!" Vena squeezed past Caney and went outside. "Bui, did you make it?"

"Yes," he said proudly.

Made from scrap lumber in the basement of the church, the doghouse resembled a barn—almost. Bui had painted it red and covered the pitched roof with sheets of tin, but he'd turned the corners up in the style of a Buddhist temple.

"I make for dog a home."

Vena squeezed Bui's hand. "She needed a home."

"Everyone need home." He looked away then, staring off across the Oklahoma countryside, but seeing a place halfway around the world.

"It's perfect." Vena knelt and peered inside. "Just the right size."

"You like dog home?"

"Oh yes, Bui, I do."

As Bui hunkered down beside her, he said, "Miss Vena, dog got name?"

"What?"

"Name for dog?"

"Just dog, I guess."

"No, dog not name."

"Well, I suppose we could call her—"

"I got name. I got name for dog."

"Okay, Bui. You built her a house, you get to name her. What do you have in mind?"

"Spot."

"Spot?"

"Dog name Spot."

"Hell, Bui," Caney said from the doorway. "She doesn't have a spot on her."

"Dog name Spot," he said with authority.

"Okay, then. Spot it is."

Vena stood and dusted off the knees of her jeans. "Well, I'll go get Spot and we'll see how she likes her new home."

"No, first I make for Spot the panse."

"Pants?" Vena asked.

"Pants!" Caney laughed.

"Yes, I make for Spot the panse."

"Well, if you think Spot needs pants, then get after it, pardner," Caney said. "But she's gonna look pretty damned foolish."

"Good," Bui said, convinced that "pretty damned foolish" was something he could achieve.

Vena hadn't been gone more than ten minutes before Caney found an excuse to stay near the front window, watching for her to come back.

She took off now and then during the lull between lunch and dinner. She was hardly ever gone more than fifteen or twenty minutes, so Caney figured she just went to the Texaco station up the road, but he didn't know why.

He hadn't guessed she went there to use the phone.

She still hadn't managed to get a lead on Carmelita, but she had reached a nurse at Sun Valley Hospital in San Antonio where Helen worked for eight years. And though the woman couldn't tell her much since she'd only been there five months before Helen left, she'd given Vena the names of a few people who might be more help.

Vena had been able to get in touch with only two of them so far, as they'd left Sun Valley a few years earlier, but both had given her pretty much the same information: they had liked Helen, but spent little time with her outside the hospital, and they were shocked to learn she had died.

But each of them had told her about a Mickey Murasaki, an anesthesiologist who had been Helen's friend.

Vena had tried to reach him several times without any luck, but today he answered on the first ring.

"Sure," he said, "I knew Helen pretty well . . . and I was so sorry when I heard she was dead."

"Were you close to her?"

"Yeah, I was. And because I was, I've heard a lot about you. We went to dinner every few weeks, a movie or concert now and then. A couple of years ago we went to a conference together in San Francisco."

"Mr. Murasaki, can I—"

"Call me Mickey."

"Okay. You don't have to answer this if you don't want to, Mickey, but . . . well, were you and Helen . . ."

"Involved? No, I'm of a different persuasion. But we liked each other. Really liked each other. And I still have trouble when I think about her."

"Mickey, do you know why she left? What I'm trying to find out is what happened to her there in San Antonio."

"Vena, I don't know, and that's one of the things that bothered me, still bothers me.

"I came in one day last spring and found out she'd called in sick. That wasn't like Helen at all. She never missed a day of work that I know of. Helen was a dedicated nurse, the best I ever worked with. She really cared about her patients. Too much, maybe. She took their troubles home with her.

"So I called to see what the problem was, see if she needed anything.

"She said she was okay, told me not to worry. But she sounded different. I don't know . . . sad. Anyway, she said she'd be back the next day.

"But she wasn't. And she didn't show up the day after that. So I went to her apartment. But when she didn't come to the door, I asked the manager to let me in to check on her. He said she'd moved out."

"Did he tell you where she went?"

"He didn't know. Said she just handed him her key and left. Didn't take her furniture, TV, anything.

"And that was it. She was gone. Didn't call me, didn't call the hospital, didn't turn in a resignation. She just left. I never heard from her or about her until someone here told me her sister called and said Helen was dead."

"Had she said anything to make you think she might be leaving?"

"Not a word. But she was real funny about her private life. Never talked much about anything more than her work."

"The last few times you saw her, did she act like she was troubled about anything?"

"To the contrary. She was up! Happier, more talkative than she'd ever been. Said leaving the burn unit was the best decision she'd ever made."

"I didn't know about that."

"Well, it was time. The burn unit's rough, and Helen had been there for almost three years. Then she lost a sixteen-year-old who'd been critical for weeks. And that did it for her. That's when she asked for the transfer."

"To what?"

"Pediatrics. She'd only been there three months before she took off. And that's what's so weird. She just loved working with the babies."

Caney was making a stab at figuring his income tax, a project that always brought out the worst in him. But today he was saying little, even when his totals didn't jibe. He didn't want to add to Molly O's dark mood, which had not been lifted by her trip to the beauty shop.

She'd been finding small jobs to do while they weren't busy, jobs that required no thought and no conversation.

When Life walked in, she was filling salt shakers, unmindful of her long-held superstition which required her to toss a few grains over her shoulder each time salt was spilled.

Life had been in the Honk for breakfast and lunch, but they were two hours away from supper, and he never showed up unless it was mealtime.

But his timing was only a little less strange than his appearance.

He'd changed out of his overalls and work boots into clean starched khakis, a white dress shirt and a dark blue sport coat just a tad too tight across his belly. His hair was perfectly parted, slicked with Brylcreem, and he smelled of soap and aftershave, something lemony and sweet.

"Hey, Life," Caney said. "You preaching or politicking?"

"Neither one."

"You look nice, Life," Molly O said, knowing how much a compliment could mean to someone who needed it.

"You're a little early for supper," Caney said.

"Yeah. I guess."

"Get you something?"

"No," Life said, doing his best not to look at Molly O.

Caney had never seen Life so serious and distant, but he pretended not to notice and went back to his paperwork.

Finally, to break the silence, Life said, "Guess I will have some coffee."

Molly O filled a cup and slid it onto the counter without speaking, but just before she pulled away, Life stretched his hand toward her and brushed his fingers across her wrist.

"You want some pie with that?" she asked, figuring his touch was a signal for food.

"No."

He added sugar to the cup but never stirred it, never raised it to his lips. Then, after several seconds of intense concentration, he said, "Caney, do you mind if I have some time alone with Molly O?"

Caney tried to cover his surprise while he fumbled to recap his pen. "Why, sure, Life. No problem."

Molly O looked as puzzled as Caney, who snatched up slips of paper, shoved them beneath the counter and hurried to the kitchen.

He was hardly out of sight before Molly O said, "What's the matter, Life?" a look of concern on her face.

"Well, I was wondering . . ." He stopped and listened as pounding came from behind the Honk. "What's that?"

"Bui's making a pair of pants for the dog."

"With a hammer?"

"I think they're some special kind of pants, probably some Vietnamese thing. I don't know, maybe it's got something to do with his religion. Now, you said you was wondering."

"Yeah."

Life pulled himself up, squared his shoulders and began the speech he'd been rehearsing for a week.

"You're going through a very bad time right now, Molly O, so this maybe isn't the best time to ask, but I have to.

"You know times haven't been the best for me. I mean, I don't have much farm left . . . and after burying Reba, well, that pretty much wiped out what little I did have put aside. Now understand I'm not complaining. It had to be done."

"Yes," Molly O agreed. Burying Reba certainly seemed appropriate . . . considering she was dead.

"Now I'm telling you all this 'cause I want to be honest about the situation I'm in before I ask if you could see your way clear to . . ."

Molly O shook her head.

"Life, I'd help you if I could, I really would. But I'm running pretty short right now myself. My phone bill last month was almost two hundred dollars, but I could let you have—"

"Oh, no! Nothing like that. . . . I didn't mean . . . No, that's not what I came to ask. . . ."

The front door opened as Vena stepped inside and forced a smile. "Hi, Life." Though the phone call had left her shaken, she was trying not to let it show. "You're early, aren't you?"

Life's shoulders slumped and his chin dipped toward his chest. "I guess I am," he said with the realization that his attempted proposal had been thwarted once again.

As Vena started for the kitchen, she almost collided with Bui as he ran through, dashed into the utility room and returned with the dog tucked under his arm.

"I make for Spot some panse," he said, nearly breathless with excitement.

"Well, let's go see," she said, feigning enthusiasm she couldn't feel just then.

Vena followed Bui through the kitchen, but before she reached the door, he stopped her.

"Not look," he said.

"What?"

Bui demonstrated by shutting his eyes. Vena followed suit, then let him take her hand and lead her outside.

"Look now!"

Chicken wire stretched around a ten-foot square of winter grass . . . and in the center sat the doghouse.

"A fence!"

"Yes, I make for dog some panse," he said, then he lifted Spot over the fence and put her inside the yard.

Casting forlorn eyes at Vena, the dog took a few hobbling steps.

"See Spot run," Bui said clearly.

After she sniffed at a clump of chickweed, Spot squatted and peed.

"See Spot jump," he said, enunciating every word.

And when the dog limped inside her new home and curled herself at the door, Bui wound up his recitation, his voice confident and strong.

"See Spot run and jump," he said with the dignity of a learned man.

Then, smiling, he bowed.

Vena, touched by Bui's kindness, found some relief from the sadness that ached inside her when she hugged him against her and whispered, "Thank you," as her eyes filled with tears.

Chapter Twenty

MOLLY O HADN'T MISSED a day of work at the Honk since she'd found her fourteen-year-old daughter naked in the backseat of a car with a drummer in a band called Hard Drivin'.

After running the drummer off with the threat of castration, Molly O had delivered a burning lecture to Brenda who had yawned and padded off to bed where she'd fallen into a deep and untroubled sleep. In the next room, Molly O had wept, pacing the floor and praying for guidance.

She'd only wanted to settle her nerves when, still sleepless at three the next morning, she uncapped her last husband's last bottle of Jim Beam, just a hot toddy to help her calm down. But she ended up drinking it all, then woke up suffering the agonies of a hangover, the only time in her life she'd ever been drunk.

She'd never even taken off for a vacation, though she'd planned one, a graduation gift for Brenda. They were going to Nashville for a whole week, take in the Country Music Hall of Fame and the Grand Ole Opry, stay in a motel with a pool and swim every day.

But that all fell through when Brenda dropped out of school again, this time for good, and ran away with a guitar player in a band out of Nashville.

When Molly O found the note Brenda left, she gave some

thought to drinking again, but decided against it. Instead, she pulled herself together and went to work, knowing the best place for her to be that day was with Caney.

Even when she was under the weather, Caney couldn't get her to stay home. She'd worked with bronchitis, a sprained wrist, pleurisy, migraine headaches, and once with ten stitches in her arm, the result of falling off a merry-go-round at the fair.

So on Monday when she wasn't in by seven, Caney knew something was wrong.

"You okay?" he asked when she answered the phone.

"Oh, I was gonna call you, Caney, but I fell asleep."

"What's going on?"

"I've caught a darned cold. Cough kept me awake most of the night and I think I'm running a little fever."

"Well, why don't I get in touch with Doc Warner, get him to call you in a prescription."

"No, honey, don't do that. It's just a cold, nothing to do but wait it out."

After Caney hung up, he tried to convince himself she was right. But a cold had never kept her home before.

He stayed busy for the next couple of hours as Vena turned in a steady stream of orders. They could have used Bui's help, but he came in later now because of his lessons. When Galilee started teaching him to read, he'd proudly announced that he was a student. But when Caney had asked him questions about his school and his teacher, he'd become as secretive and vague as he was about the place where he lived.

So this morning, with almost more business than the two of them could handle, Vena and Caney didn't slow down until nearly ten.

As soon as he grabbed a cup of coffee, Caney started to call Molly O back, but hung up halfway through dialing for fear he might wake her again.

"Look, Caney," Vena said, "if you're worried, why don't I go over there and check on her. I can borrow Bui's car, take her some soup, a carton of juice."

"Yeah." Caney nodded. "She says it's a cold, but I don't know. The way she's been dragging around."

"Oh, she'll probably feel better when she hears from her daughter."

"That damned Brenda!" Caney shook a cigarette from his pack. "Her and her goddamned country musicians. Dewey wouldn't have stood for it."

"Is Dewey her daddy?"

"Was. Got killed in a car wreck when Brenda wasn't much more than a baby. Hell of a good guy, the only one of Molly O's husbands that was worth a damn."

"How many husbands has she had?"

"Four. Three of them while she was a teenager."

"Jesus!"

"Married the first time when she was sixteen, some asshole who beat hell out of her for a couple of years.

"She caught the next one fooling around with her older sister . . . and the third time, turned out the creep was already married to a gal out in New Mexico.

"After that, she had the good sense to stay single till she was almost thirty, when she met Dewey O'Keefe. He came in here with a drilling crew, bunch of hard-drinking boys, stirring up trouble in one town, then another.

"But Dewey wasn't like that . . . and he wasn't a kid. I guess he was ten, twelve years older than Molly O. She said they met at a dance hall one night, got married a week later. When the drilling crew moved on, he stayed.

"They settled down, bought a house next door to my aunt. Wanted a family in the worst way, but Molly O couldn't seem to carry a baby more'n three or four months. She'd had two miscarriages by the time I went to live with my Aunt Effie.

"I was almost five then, so Molly O and Dewey took up with me, figured they weren't going to have any kids, so they played mom and dad with me.

"They put up a swing in their backyard, got me a big plastic swimming pool. Took me to movies and carnivals, the zoo in Tulsa."

"Did they spoil you, Caney?"

"Hell, yes. Even got me a pony. Dewey rode some rodeo when he was young, started teaching me calf roping when I was seven or eight.

"Then my aunt died when I was in the ninth grade, so I moved in with Molly O and Dewey. By that time, their house felt just as much home as my aunt's did.

"The next year, Molly O got pregnant with Brenda."

"And all of a sudden, you weren't their kid anymore," Vena said.

"That's what I figured, but it wasn't like that. They treated me just the same as they always had. Made me feel like her big brother. When I went off to Vietnam, Molly O wrote me all the time, sent me pictures of Brenda, called her my baby sister.

"When I came back, Molly O and Dewey were waiting for me at the VA hospital in Kansas City. They stayed in a motel for almost a week, came to be with me every day.

"A month later, Dewey got killed."

Caney turned his face away while he pretended to look for matches.

"Molly O had to sell the house and moved into a trailer 'cause the only job she could find was part-time at the IGA.

"So when I wrote her about opening the Honk, she jumped right in it. Took over everything needed to be done to get it open . . . well, all except that damned sign. I have to take the blame for that."

Caney shook his head and grinned.

"I managed to screw that up all by myself."

Vena waited for almost a minute after she knocked, shifting the box she carried from one arm to the other. Finally, she tried the door, found it unlocked and eased inside.

Molly O had fallen asleep on the couch, knitting needles resting loosely in her hands. Her head was tilted at an awkward angle and her glasses had slipped down the bridge of her nose.

"Hello," Vena said softly.

When Molly O stirred, one of the knitting needles fell into her lap.

"I hope I didn't scare you."

"Oh, Vena," Molly O said, straightening her glasses. "No, you didn't. I heard your voice in my dream, but I couldn't see you because the boat was so crowded."

"How are you feeling?"

"Pretty good."

"Yeah, I can tell."

"Well, you know how it is with a cold. Head's all stopped up, throat's scratchy. And that cough syrup makes me feel dopey."

"Caney was worried about you, so I thought—"

"I told him it wasn't anything serious."

"He sent you some lunch." Vena set the box on a bar dividing the kitchen and living room.

"Looks like he sent enough for the whole trailer park."

"How does vegetable soup sound to you?" Vena held up a plastic container.

"Oh, I couldn't eat a thing."

"Maybe there's something else here that might taste good."

As she rummaged in the box, pulling out packages, jars and bottles, Vena held them up for Molly O's approval.

"We have a Hershey with almonds, dill pickles, peanuts . . ."

Molly O groaned.

"Banana Bikes, crackers, juice, doughnuts, bubblegum . . . and pigskins."

Molly O's laughter led to a fit of coughing; Vena waited until it passed.

"And he sent you a bouquet," Vena said as she pulled out a dusty vase stuffed with faded plastic roses which had been in the front window of the Honk since it opened.

Obviously pleased, Molly O said, "Ain't he something?"

Vena put the vase on top of the TV, then leaned close to study two black-and-white snapshots propped against the cable box. In one, Caney, at seven, was astride an Appaloosa colt, a slender man with a receding hairline holding the reins. In the other, the same man, nearly bald, held a frowning baby.

"This must be Dewey O'Keefe," Vena said.

"Oh, Caney told you about Dewey."

"It's funny. He looks like I thought he would from hearing Caney talk about him."

"Dewey was crazy about that boy. So thrilled to have a son. Didn't matter that another man fathered him, that didn't matter to Dewey at all.

"And when Brenda came, well, he just couldn't get over the wonder of me and him creating a child." Molly O dabbed her eyes with a tissue. "I see him in Caney, in Brenda . . . and now, with her baby coming, I'll have another part of him with me."

"Have you heard anything yet? About Brenda?"

"No, but every time the phone rings . . . Well, I try to keep my mind occupied. Read my magazines, do a little knitting."

"What are you making?"

When Molly O held up the half-finished bootie she was working on, Vena recognized the blue yarn she'd bought at the Wal-Mart a few days earlier.

"Hard to imagine, isn't it," Molly O said, "that a foot can be that tiny."

Grabbing for more tissues, Molly O tried to cover a sneeze. "Vena, I'm scared to death I'm gonna give you this cold. No sense you staying here breathing my germs. What would Caney do with both of us out sick?"

"You sure I can't fix you something before I go? Maybe a nice bowl of pigskins?"

Molly O made a face. "I'll pass, but I'd drink a glass of juice. And I probably ought to take a couple of aspirin."

"Where are they?"

"In the bathroom."

Vena went down the hallway and opened the first door she came to.

The room, light and airy, smelled faintly of baby oil. White dotted swiss curtains covered the windows, beneath them a small chest painted pale yellow, stenciled with hearts. A changing table was neatly arranged with stacks of receiving blankets, diapers and gowns. A folded quilt covered the seat of a high-backed pine rocker standing in the corner.

On a table beside a white wicker crib against the far wall rested a framed photograph of Dewey O'Keefe, placed there by a woman who trusted the miracle that the heart of his heart was beating in the child of his child.

Chapter Twenty-One

THE MAIL NEVER CAME before two or two-thirty, but Bui started watching long before then.

He'd been expecting a letter from Nguyet for over a week, each day growing more anxious when the mail carrier had nothing for him. But today he was certain his waiting would end because last night he had seen Nguyet in his dream.

She was writing to him by candlelight and as her hand moved across the page, he heard her voice whispering the words as she wrote them.

> *I do not think I can make you hear with words on paper what is in my heart because you are so far away. I have started many letters, but this one I will finish for I have something I must tell you . . .*

Then a wind turned suddenly against her, lifting her hair from her shoulders, ruffling the paper on which she wrote.

> *. . . for I have something I must tell you . . .*

She did not look up, did not take her eyes from her writing as a current of air began puffing at the candle.

. . . something I must tell you . . .

With each flicker of light, she was disappearing, her voice growing fainter and more distant until at last it was silenced.

Too late, Bui reached for her in the darkness, but she was gone.

"She's just got a bad cold, Life," Vena said as she set a blue plate special before him. "Probably be back tomorrow or the next day."

"Well, you never can tell. Friend of mine over in Poteau, he had a cold one day, the next week he was dead of pneumonia."

"We could use some more tea over here," Bilbo Porter said.

Vena grabbed four menus to deliver to a table of secretaries from the courthouse, refilled tea for Bilbo and Peg, then wrote up Wilma's order for a club sandwich and took it to the pass-through.

"Where the hell is Bui?" Caney said as he flipped two beef patties on the grill.

"Standing out there by the mailbox."

"Why?"

"Said he's going to get a letter today."

"Mail won't be here for—"

"I told him that."

"He's gonna do me a lot of damned good out there."

Vena left Caney growling in the kitchen, then went to the register where a young couple waited to pay their check.

As soon as they walked out, the phone rang.

"Can you get that?" Caney yelled.

"Honk and Holler," Vena said into the receiver, then pulled out her pad and began to write. "You want those with mustard or mayonnaise?"

"Hey, Vena," Bilbo shouted. "How you gonna hook a tray on that one?"

Vena turned to see a horse and rider coming across the lot. The rider was a burly man in his sixties, the horse the gelding she'd taken from the pasture the week before.

"You suppose Brim's gonna order something for hisself or something for the horse?" Bilbo laughed.

"What?" Vena said to the caller as she continued to stare out the window. "Sorry, you said hold the onions on two?"

She turned her face to the wall as Brim Neely walked in. Then, just as she hung up the phone, Caney came out of the kitchen wiping his hands on a dish towel.

"Finish up those burgers for me, will you?"

"Caney . . ."

"Looks like I've gotta see a man about a horse."

Vena went into the kitchen, but stood near the door to hear what Brim Neely had to say.

"Sorry to come at your busy time, Caney, but . . ."

Take me back to Tulsa, I'm too young to marry . . .

Someone had plugged the jukebox, so Vena heard more of steel guitars and fiddles than she did of the conversation out front.

". . . knew he'd been ridden, but couldn't figure who the hell would . . ."

". . . got in a little trouble, but . . ."

Yonder comes a gal with a red dress on / Some folks call her Dinah . . .

". . . reckoned I had me a horse thief . . . said he saw you and a woman . . ."

". . . hard not to get caught . . ."

". . . goes crazy at the sound of gunfire . . ."

Take me back to Tulsa, I'm too young to marry . . .

Vena stepped out of the kitchen and walked purposefully toward Brim Neely. "I'm the one who took your gelding," she said. "Caney didn't have anything to do with it."

"Yes, ma'am."

"So if you've got a problem . . ."

"No, ma'am, I ain't got a problem. Seems to me everything's settled." Brim moved toward the door.

"Thanks, Brim," Caney said.

"You know, when you called, I figured some of my stock got loose. Reckoned if one of those damned steers got close to the Honk, it'd be hamburger by now."

"Got to turn a profit somehow, Brim."

"Well, I best be getting on. You take care."

Vena watched as he unhitched the gelding from a bumper guard out front and led him around the side of the building.

"Caney, I feel like a fool. I didn't mean to cause you any trouble."

"There's not gonna be any trouble."

"Then why was he here?"

" 'Cause I bought the gelding."

"You what?"

"He's a fine animal, Vena. Well bred, healthy. Apparently he's spooked by gunfire, but other than that . . ."

"Where are you gonna keep it?"

"Back there in my pasture."

"Your pasture?"

"Yeah, Brim leases it from me."

"But I don't understand why you wanted to buy a horse. You don't even—"

"Well, I figured it was the only way to keep you out of jail." Then, grinning, Caney rolled back into the kitchen. "You finish those burgers up for me?"

As soon as Bui had closed the drapes in the Reverend's study, he sat at the desk and switched on the lamp. Then he reached inside his shirt for Nguyet's letter which lay warm against his skin.

When the mail carrier had handed it to him earlier in the day, Bui had known he would not read it until he was alone in the church. Feeling Nguyet's words pressed against his body had been enough to bring him to this moment.

After he removed the outer envelope addressed to him by his cousin in France, he studied the smaller one inside, his name printed neatly by Nguyet's small hand. He smiled as he imagined how she had gripped the pen tightly in her slender fingers to write the strange name of the town where he lived.

Then, as he withdrew the pages from inside, he dizzied at the scent . . . the incense Nguyet burned each night at the altar, the mint plants she tended in her garden, the smell of the jasmine soap with which she bathed her skin.

He unfolded the pages and smoothed out their creases, his fingers tingling as they swept across the words.

> *Anh yêu Bui,*
> *Em có vài tin buồn* . . . hurts my heart to say we can never be together now. For my need to come to you in America has cost me too much.

Bui blinked his eyes to clear his vision, certain he had misread the words.

> Because I was too impatient to wait, I borrowed from my sister's husband all the money he could give. I paid it to a man taking many people on his boat to Malaysia, but my money was not enough. He demanded more. Much more than money.

"Ông ta muốn gì?" Bui whispered. *"Cái gì?"*

> On the night I was to meet him and the others to begin the voyage, I discovered he had left me behind. The boat had sailed, not at the time he told me, but two days before.

Bui felt the pain twisting inside him, the force of it rising in his chest.

> So now I have nothing but shame, a shame that lives inside me, for I am carrying a child. But not the child of the man I love. . . .

As Bui lifted the letter to his lips, the empty church echoed with the sound of his keening.

Molly O had a hell of a time getting to sleep. She couldn't breathe through her nose, coughing left her gasping for air and her throat felt like she'd swallowed nails.

She'd finished off the cough syrup, enough to make her woozy, inhaled nose drops until she thought she'd drown. Then she'd slathered her chest with Vicks and rubbed some onto the soles of her feet, therapy learned from her mother, who swore the procedure opened clogged passages and induced sleep.

There might have been something to it because sometime near two, Molly O fell into a heavy, dreamless sleep, so exhausted she heard nothing . . . not the wind chimes clanking on her neighbor's porch, not the episode of *Andy Griffith* running on her TV in the living room . . . and not the pounding at the door.

But she came wide awake at the sound of one word spoken outside her window.

"Mom."

As she hurtled down the hall, her greased feet slipped on the cold linoleum and, flying through the kitchen, she jammed her hand on the refrigerator. But she didn't care about a trail of footprints in Vicks or the pain in her wrist.

Nothing else mattered now that her baby was home.

She flipped the lock, flung the door open and rushed into the chill night air.

"Brenda, Brenda, Brenda," she chanted as she enfolded her daughter in her arms, rocked her back and forth, and cried.

"Hi, Mom," Brenda said, her mouth crushed against Molly O's wet cheek as she was whisked inside.

"Oh, honey, I've been so worried about you. Where have you been? Why didn't you call me?"

"No, don't turn on the light," Brenda said too late.

"Here, let me look at you."

Brenda turned her face away from the light, but not before Molly O glimpsed the bruise on her chin, the scratches down the side of her neck.

"My God! How did you—"

"An accident, that's all."

"Honey." When Molly O turned Brenda toward her, she discovered the injuries were less alarming than the pallor of the girl's skin, and her eyes, which looked old and empty.

"Brenda, what's happened to you?"

Molly O tried to hold her, but Brenda twisted away and dropped onto the couch.

"What's happened? Why, I'm a star, haven't you heard? The greatest country music star Las Vegas has seen since Dolly Parton. I packed them in at the Golden Nugget, a real hit."

"Why, that's wonderful, darlin'," Molly O said, trying to sound like she believed her own voice.

"Don't suppose you got any cigarettes, have you? I'm about to die for a smoke."

"You think it's wise for you to be smoking?"

"Wise!"

"Well, they say it's not good for you when you're carrying—"

"God, here we go again. I just walked in the door and you're already on my case. What is it with you? I thought you'd be glad to see me. Welcome the prodigal daughter home. Oops, 'daughter' doesn't work, does it?" She giggled. "Has to be a son, right? 'Cause that's the way it is in the Bible."

She laughed then, sharp brittle sounds that carried heat.

"Oh, watch this." She pointed to the TV. "This is where Andy tells Opie about the birds and bees."

"Let me fix you something to eat," Molly O said. "I've got some soup in the box, or I could make you a sandwich."

"No."

"When did you last eat? You look so—"

"Let me see." Brenda screwed up her face to let her mother know she was thinking. "I had breakfast at seven, dinner at noon—straight up, and supper at six. Three balanced meals, too. Milk, lots of milk because it builds strong bones and healthy bodies. Bread, which is the staff of life. Spinach, too. You know I always eat my greens 'cause they clean you out. You taught me that. And—"

"Brenda, are you—"

"Wait, I'm not finished. Fruit. Fresh fruit. None of that canned stuff for me. And meat, of course. Piles and piles of flesh." She nodded. "Yep, something from each of the basic food groups. I learned that from my home ec teacher, Miss Twitchface. Oh yeah, vitamins. I dropped a whole fistful of vitamins today, just to be on the safe side. B_1, B_2, B_3 . . ."

"Honey, I wish you'd—"

"And acid. The body needs acid. Nitric acid, folic acid, benzidine acid. I make sure to get my minimum daily requirement of acid."

"Brenda, are you okay?"

"I'm great! Just great! Don't you think I look great?" she asked as she jumped off the couch. Pushing her tangled hair back from her face, and hiking up her dirty jeans, she struck a model's pose. "So what do you think? Huh? Don't I look great?" With her hands on her hips, she paraded around the bar to the kitchen. "Don't I look like one of them Las Vegas showgirls? Might need to get a tit job, but—"

"I think what you need is some sleep. I'm gonna fix you a bed here on the couch."

"What happened to my old room? You rent it out?"

"No. I took your bed out and—"

"Oh, heave the bed out and the little bitch won't come back 'cause she'll have no place to sleep. That it?"

Molly O eased herself to the couch as if sudden movement might make her break.

"Brenda, why are you talking like this? Are you mad at me or something?"

"Me? Mad? Just because my mother threw out my bed?"

"I took the bed out because I turned your room into a nursery." Then, trying for a brighter tone, Molly O said, "You want to see it? I fixed it up real cute. Put in some—"

"I don't want to see it."

"Found a sweet crib, made some curtains. And look." She dug in her knitting basket on the floor beside her and pulled out the bootie she had started. "I'm making—"

"There's not any baby."

"No! No, that's not right." Molly O held up the bootie, proof that a mistake had been made. "Honey, you're just run-down, that's all. Have you seen a doctor? Brenda, you promised me you'd see a doctor."

"I did. And now . . . there's no baby."

"Brenda, what are you saying? You didn't . . . Oh, God, Brenda. Are you telling me that you . . . that you . . ."

The room was silent except for the hum of the refrigerator.

Finally, leaning against the kitchen sink, staring out the window into the darkness, Brenda said, "No. No, the doctor said it was because I'd had too many greens. You know, that's the thing about greens. They just clean you out. Clean as a whistle. Don't leave anything behind, do they?"

But Molly O didn't answer. And though she didn't know it, her fingers were moving mechanically, pulling the stitches from a bootie that never quite took on the shape of a tiny foot.

Chapter Twenty-Two

MOLLY O CAME BACK to work three days after Brenda got home, even though Caney had threatened to shoot her if she did. They'd argued about it in a half dozen phone conversations, but finally reached a compromise when she agreed to take off early, promising to leave as soon as the lunch trade wound down.

She convinced him that getting out of the trailer for a few hours would be good for her and he couldn't argue with that. Being with Brenda twenty-four hours a day would be an endurance test he feared Molly O couldn't pass right now.

He tried to talk to Brenda once, but Molly O couldn't get her to come to the phone, so he didn't try again.

By the time Molly O returned to the Honk, the regulars already knew Brenda was home because someone had spotted Molly O shepherding her into Doc Warner's office. But they didn't know what was going on, and Caney wouldn't tell them. He figured Molly O would find her own way of breaking the news, and he was right.

When they asked her about Brenda, she said she'd lost the baby, but she offered no details. And because they remembered that Molly O herself had suffered several miscarriages, they accepted her explanation and quietly offered their condolences.

The only strange reaction came from Bui. When he heard what happened, he went out to his car where he sat slumped behind the wheel and wept for nearly an hour.

During the lull between breakfast and lunch, Caney fixed her a plate of meatloaf and mashed potatoes, but she didn't do much more than push the food around with her fork.

When Vena sat down beside her, Molly O included her in a conversation which, until that moment, she'd been having inside her head.

"She needs some time alone, you know, time to think, to pull herself together."

Vena nodded, a good listener.

"She's not herself right now. Sleeps most of the time, but even when she's awake, it's like she's not there. She doesn't talk. Never turns on the TV or picks up a magazine or newspaper. I went to the library and checked out some books I thought she'd like, but she hasn't even touched them.

"Doc Warner's got her on an antibiotic for the infection. And he gave her some pills for depression, but he says it'll take a few days for them to kick in.

"I can't get her to eat much of anything. I've tried all her favorites. But she just doesn't have any interest in food. None at all."

Molly O pushed her mashed potatoes into the shape of a hill, then made an indentation in the top, transforming it into a volcano.

"I try not to think about what she did, destroying her baby. How can anyone do that?" Lifting her eyes from her plate, she looked surprised, as if she'd only just noticed Vena. "How could she do that?"

"I don't know, Molly O. Maybe she couldn't see any other way out. It's hard when you're scared and alone. It's real hard."

"No," Molly O said, speaking to her food again. "I just can't understand it.

"That reminds me of a song my mother used to sing. 'We'll understand it, all by and by.' But I don't know. There's so much I don't understand about what's happened. Guess I still haven't reached the 'by and by.'

"Brenda got her voice from my mother, you know. She sure didn't get it from me, 'cause I can't sing a lick. But you ought to hear Brenda. The sweetest voice you ever heard.

"She started singing before she could talk, humming tunes she made up. By the time she started school, she knew every country song on the radio. Won a talent contest when she was only ten. Got to sing on a TV show in Tulsa.

"She's loved music her whole life. 'Course, at her age, it's pretty hard to think about a whole life, 'cause seventeen's just a little tiny piece of life, isn't it?

"But you know what worries me most?"

Vena shook her head.

"She's just so . . . so *angry*. Now I don't blame her for being mad at that Travis. I'd like to kill him myself. But Brenda's mad at the whole world, including me. Lord knows I haven't been a perfect mother, but I've loved her to death since the day she was born.

"But maybe something more happened to her out there in Las Vegas, something I don't even know about. Maybe even meaner than I can imagine. Oh, I wish I could stop thinking like that, but my mind just won't leave me alone. Seems like—"

"Miss Ho?"

Molly O turned to Bui who was offering her a cup of tea, but his hands were trembling so badly that most of it had sloshed into the saucer.

"Miss Ho," he said, his voice as shaky as his hands. "Very sorry for baby. Very sorry . . . and I . . . ." With his eyes tearing up, he placed the cup and saucer on the counter, then hurried away.

"Poor Bui. He's a sensitive soul, isn't he?"

"He's been pretty strange the last couple of days," Vena said. "Don't know what's going on."

"I suppose it's hard for him here without his wife, his family. No one who speaks his language. And he doesn't understand us most of the time." Molly O shook her head. "I guess he hasn't got to the 'by and by' yet, either."

*   *   *

The dining room had emptied quickly after lunch and Molly O, true to her word, had left as soon as her last customer walked out. Caney was fixing himself a sandwich while Bui loaded the dishwasher, so Vena figured it was a good time for her to disappear for a while.

She was sorting through her tips to make sure she had enough quarters for the phone at the Texaco when a shiny new van pulled in and parked. She waited for the driver to open his door. When he didn't, she headed outside to take his order. As she approached, he rolled down his window.

"How you doing today?" she asked.

"Well, my prostate's enlarged and I'm legally blind," he said as he removed a pair of sunglasses. "But my urologist is out of town and my seeing-eye dog died."

Vena grinned. "Can I get you something?"

"I'm coming inside if your door is wide enough for my creepy-crawler."

He winked when he saw Vena's confusion, but it didn't take her long to catch on as he swiveled the driver's seat around, then hoisted himself out of it and into a wheelchair beside him. Almost immediately, the van door swung open and a hydraulic lift began lowering him to the ground.

"Elevator going down," he said. "First floor—shoes, blues and bad news. Mezzanine—bloomers and rumors. Ground floor—everybody out."

A few seconds later, he was rolling toward the front door of the Honk with Vena walking beside him.

Like Caney, his upper body was powerfully built, but both legs ended at his thighs where his khaki pants were doubled beneath his stumps.

"Don't suppose you have a cup of coffee so strong it'll make me howl?" he asked.

"That's the only kind we serve."

She held the door open as he came inside. Caney, just coming out of the kitchen, slowed when he saw them.

"Hey, looks like you and me drive the same kind of jalopy," the man said. "They get poor gas mileage, but they handle well. Name's Austin Tyler. You must be Caney Paxton."

"Yeah," Caney said as he shook the hand that was offered.

"I'm from Farmington, Missouri. On my way to San Diego. Got a date out there with a little chick named Lily Rene Tyler, four days old. My new granddaughter."

Vena set a cup of coffee on the counter.

"Thanks."

"You've got a long drive in front of you," she said.

"Well, I've got plenty of time. Just so I get there before she graduates from college." He blew on his coffee, took a cautious sip. "Anyway, I'm not traveling fast. Thought since I was going to make the trip, I'd get off the interstates, see a little of the country, meet some new people."

Austin Tyler offered a Marlboro to Vena, who shook her head, and to Caney, who pulled out his Camels.

"I stopped at the edge of town to fill up with gas and an old boy at the station, we got to talking about Nam and he said I ought to come by here and meet you, Caney."

He took a more aggressive sip of coffee as he waited for some response from Caney, but he didn't get one.

"Said he thought you were at Cam Ranh Bay."

"I don't know where he heard that."

"I was there from '69 to '71. 21st Infantry."

"That right?"

"You ever at Long Binh, Caney?"

"No."

"What outfit were you with?"

"I wasn't."

Austin Tyler was thrown off for a moment, then he grinned. "Special Forces, right? You guys." He shook his head. "Still doing that covert thing, aren't you?"

"I wasn't in Vietnam," Caney said, his features immobile, showing nothing. "Never been in the military."

He shot a quick glance at Vena, but stunned by the lie, she turned away and busied herself at the coffeemaker.

"But that fella at the Fina station told me you were. Said that's how you . . ."

"This?" Caney patted the arms of his chair. "No, I did this water-skiing."

"Then why'd he say you were in Nam? Why the hell would he do that?"

"Maybe he was pulling your leg."

Tyler thought about that, then he laughed.

"Sorry you came out of your way," Caney said. "But since you did, coffee's on the house. I'll throw in a piece of pie, too, if you like cherry or apple. And I won't even lie and tell you it's homemade."

"I thank you, Caney," Tyler said, crushing out his cigarette. "But I guess I'll get back on the road."

"I'll talk to that guy at the Fina. Tell him to get his facts straight."

"Aw, I needed a break anyway. And besides, it was good to meet you. Good to meet both of you. Here." He pulled out his billfold. "Let me give you my card. If you're ever in my part of the country and you need your TV fixed, you give me a call."

"Sure."

"And thanks for the coffee."

Vena and Caney watched as he returned to his van, rolled onto the lift and disappeared inside. Neither of them spoke until he was at the wheel and pulling away.

"Caney, why did you tell him you weren't in Vietnam?"

"He was there. He didn't need me to tell him what it was like."

"But you—"

"Vena, that guy served two tours over there. You know how long I lasted?"

"No."

"Forty-two days."

"Are you ashamed of that? That you got hurt after forty-two days? Caney, a lot of boys didn't make it that long."

"You're right. And you know why? Because they stepped on mines, walked into ambushes, got their heads blown apart. But I never heard about a damned one of them fell out of a helicopter."

Vena went back to take her shower while Caney was shutting down the kitchen and locking up for the night. But when she came out of the bathroom twenty minutes later, he was still in the cafe.

She pulled his bathrobe on over the T-shirt she slept in and went out to find him feeding quarters into the jukebox. The only light in the dining room came from the neon beer sign in the window and the colors reflecting from the old Wurlitzer.

"What's going on?" she asked.

"I'm just winding down."

"Want a beer?"

"Sure." He began punching numbers on the jukebox. "What do you want to hear?"

"Play B seven."

She opened two beers, took one to Caney, then sat down at a table beside him to drink hers.

"Hand me the salt, will you?"

"Oh, I forgot," she said, passing the shaker to him, then watching as he sprinkled salt into the neck of the bottle.

"You're the only person I've ever seen do that."

"I never drank beer before I went to Vietnam. Hated the taste. But over there . . . Well, I learned that if I salted it, it didn't taste so bad."

"Caney, can I ask you something about what happened to you in Vietnam?"

"Okay," he said, smiling to cover his reluctance.

"When we went riding, you told me about the other guy who fell out of your helicopter. You said he was only a kid."

"That's right."

"Well, I was wondering. How old were you?"

"Seventeen."

"Then he was no more a kid than you were."

"But there was a difference," Caney said. "I knew he was going to die. No way he could survive a fall like that."

"But you believed you could?"

"I *knew* I would! Knew I was never going to hit the ground because someone . . . or something was going to save me."

"You mean . . ."

"Like maybe there'd be a net to catch me. I'd been to a circus, saw a woman fall off a high wire into a net. It saved her . . . why couldn't it save me?

"And if there wasn't a net, there'd be something else. A plane would fly over and drop me a parachute . . . or I'd land on a cloud.

"The first time I was ever in a plane, I was six, going with my aunt to her brother's funeral. As the plane started to climb, I got scared. Scared it would crash. But my aunt told me not to worry. She said planes didn't crash, they landed on clouds. And I believed her."

Caney paused as if he were listening for the voice of his aunt to confirm the story, to justify the lie.

"Or maybe, I thought, I'd be rescued by one of those superheroes I believed in. Comic book stuff.

"Once I was wading Sticker Creek, fishing for perch. Got my foot tangled in an old trotline that had floated downstream. Now I wasn't about to drown. Hell, the water wasn't more'n a foot deep and I was probably nine, ten years old. But in my imagination, I was tangled in the cables of a ship buried on the bottom of the ocean. I wasn't scared though, because I knew that just when I couldn't hold my breath another second, Aquaman would save me. Aquaman or Daredevil . . . Captain America."

Caney's breath quickened as he leaned forward to stare at something only he could see.

"As soon as I felt myself slide out the door of that helicopter, nothing between me and the ground but air, all those things went through my mind. And everything seemed to slow down, like I was falling in slow motion. Plenty of time for a rescue.

"I could feel myself starting to spin, to tumble." With one hand, Caney made a circular motion above his head. "Dizzy. Afraid I was going to pass out. I spread my arms, cupped my hands as if I could hold the air. Trying to ride the currents.

"I could see the ground getting closer, but I didn't see any net that would catch me. There was no damned parachute to grab hold of. No Superman coming to save me."

Caney wiped away a rivulet of sweat threatening his eye.

"So I started looking for the best spot to land . . . something to aim for. A grove of trees, great leafy trees, soft enough to cushion my fall.

"A river. I'd go in feet first, go all the way to the bottom, then push off. Come up, swim to the bank. Stretch out in the mud, lay in the sun."

When the bottle slipped from his fingers and crashed to the floor, Caney didn't hear it, didn't feel the spray of beer across his arm.

"But I don't have time. I'm too far from the river, too far from the trees.

"Then I see the rice paddy, sun reflecting off it like arrows pointing 'Here! Here!'

"Water not deep, but maybe . . ."

Words tumbling out now, Caney's face twisting with the telling.

"Then I see a woman down there in the water. A tiny woman wearing one of those pointed bamboo hats. She's in water up to her knees.

"And she's looking at me. Her head's tilted back, her hand shading her eyes as she watches me coming.

"I call out to her, tell her to wait for me . . ."

Vena watched Caney watching himself fall, his eyes wild as the ground rises to meet him. Suddenly, she jumped up, reaching him in two strides.

"Caney?"

"I can't be sure she hears me, but . . ."

Vena put her hands on the arms of his chair and leaned into his face as her song, B7, began to play on the jukebox.

"I'm so close I can see a scar just below her eye, a scar that curves toward her temple——"

"Caney!"

"But I'm scared she'll leave before I get there."

Vena straddled him, wedged her knees between his thighs and the sides of the chair, leaned into him until his heart was pounding against hers.

"Dance with me, Caney!"

She put her arms around him, pressed her cheek to his and began to move her body to the music as she hummed the tune.

"Dance with me," she whispered.

He was saved then, just before he hit the water. Caught by the faint warmth of breath on his ear.

"Come on, Caney. Dance."

Moving stiffly, mechanically, he put his hands on the wheels of the chair but could not turn them.

"Vena," he said, his voice choked.

"Don't talk. Just dance."

"Can't . . ."

"Sure you can."

He tried again, turned the wheels tentatively.

"You're doing fine," Vena said. "Just fine."

As he slowly rolled the chair forward, then back, she could feel his breath easing, the tension beginning to drain from his shoulders as he let her sway him to the rhythm of the music.

He gave himself to her then, filled with the wheat smell of her hair as she slipped her cheek into the curve of his neck.

When he began to whisper along with the music, she lifted her head and looked into his face. Wiping tears from his cheeks, she kissed his eyes, then put her lips to his.

When he took his hands from the wheels to encircle her waist, pressing her closer to him, she felt his heat and hardness against her.

And while they kissed again, he waltzed her off the dance floor, the music fading behind them.

Chapter Twenty-Three

VENA WASN'T THE FIRST woman Caney had been with since Vietnam, but she was the first in more than three years.

The last had been Naomi Watts, an English teacher at the middle school. Caney didn't know it then, but their brief and clinical couplings were part of her research for a romance novel she was writing about a beautiful young socialite involved in a passionate love affair with a dispirited paraplegic.

Caney heard several months later she'd sold her book and moved to California to try to peddle it to the movies.

Before Naomi, he'd been visited from time to time by a prostitute from Ft. Smith, her phone number passed along to him by a trucker whose pockets were filled with such numbers.

A plain-looking woman named Lou, she had always complained about the long drive required to make a "house call" to the Honk, for which she demanded Caney pay, in addition to her minimum fee of twenty-five dollars, thirty cents a mile for driving expenses. And she insisted on per diem—a grilled cheese sandwich and onion rings.

But their relationship ended when Caney discovered that Lou was leaving her four-year-old son sleeping in the car while she was inside the Honk conducting business.

There had been one other woman Caney had seen a few times, a former classmate named Linda whose marriage of nine years dissolved when her husband left her for a teenage girl. Linda, in her bitterness, had turned to drink, the result being that her nights with Caney had become long drunken hours during which she devised fantastic schemes for luring her wayward husband back.

Beyond those dismal involvements, Caney had had only one other encounter, that with a nurse in the VA hospital in Kansas City on the night he arrived there.

She had been making her rounds of the ward he shared with nineteen other men when she'd found him crying. At first, she offered him medication for pain, but she discovered she didn't have a pill for what he was feeling.

She stood beside him as, sobbing, he talked of all that had died in him in Vietnam—his youth, his legs, his manhood. Then, moving quietly, she had pulled the thin white curtain around his bed, and taken from her pocket a bottle of lotion that smelled of peppermint.

She began to work the lotion in small, tight circles across his chest, his shoulders, down onto his belly, his skin warming to her touch. Then, when she slid her hand beneath the drawstring of his pajamas, he had tried to look away, but she wouldn't let him.

Smiling, she had leaned close, so close he could feel her moist breath on his face, as, without hurry, her sweet urgings proved to him he was still alive.

But now, Vena Takes Horse had slipped into his life, filling his days and nights with something new, something untouched by Vietnam.

The regulars had come to expect Caney's occasional bouts of moodiness, days and nights when he grew surly or silent, when he had little interest in their stories, when he snapped at them for complaining about their food or stubbing out their cigarettes in the remains of their eggs, when he grumbled about them tying up the phone or spilling coffee on his newspaper.

They had never taken offense, though. Instead they had excused his sudden fits of peevishness because he was one of their own, returned to them with the scar of battle pinned to the breast of a uniform . . . a uniform tailored to fit a body reshaped by war.

But this new Caney had them baffled.

What was happening, they wondered, when he began to laugh at their jokes, when he encouraged their exaggerations about the car deals they'd made and their lies about the feats of coon hounds they'd raised?

Why, they questioned, was he always smiling and when had he started whistling the song that was B7 on the jukebox? And why wasn't he upset when they tracked in mud and why didn't he get mad when they complained that the beans were too salty, the liver too dry?

At first, they figured it was the weather. Spring had descended on them almost overnight. Sidewalks were lined with jonquils, yards brightened by flowering tulip trees, the countryside alive with blooming dogwoods.

Some credited Caney's improved humor to the upturn in his business. The Honk was seldom empty and sometimes so crowded at noon, customers had to wait for tables.

But they never guessed that the changes they were seeing in Caney had anything to do with a woman because they tended to agree with Bilbo, who said, "It's a shame, but I don't believe the boy's equipment is in working order."

When Hamp Rothrock came through the door, Molly O waved him to a table in the corner where their conversation was less likely to be overheard.

"Thanks for coming, Hamp," she said. "I know you're busy with the farm since your daddy's sick."

"Oh, I'm not that busy. Besides, I had to come into town anyway to go by the feed store."

Molly O fidgeted with an earring while she tried to decide how to start, but Hamp jumped in and made it easy.

"My mom said she saw Brenda in Doc Warner's office last week."

"Yeah, she's been home for a while now."

"Is she okay?"

"No, Hamp. To tell you the truth, she's not doing too good."

"What is it?" Hamp said, his voice edged with alarm. "What's wrong with her?"

"Well, she lost the baby."

"Oh, I'm sure sorry to hear that."

"She'll get over it, I suppose. Just going to take her some time."

"She gonna be here long?"

"I think she might be, but . . ."

"Is her husband with her?" Hamp asked, trying not to sound too interested.

"No, she didn't get married. That fell through."

Hamp glanced away, hoping Molly O couldn't read his expression.

"But I'm worried about her, Hamp. Real worried. She's okay physically, but she seems so sad. So depressed."

"Anything I can do?"

"Well, that's why I called. I was thinking that maybe if you could go by and see her . . ."

"She wants to see me?" he asked, unable to conceal his excitement.

"She might."

"But she didn't say she wanted to."

"She's not saying much of anything these days, at least not to me. But I think she might talk to you. You're about the only friend she has left here."

"You know I'd love to see her."

"Now, I can't say just how she'll react 'cause she's in such bad shape. Hamp, she has no interest in anything. Not even music."

"Brenda? I can't image Brenda without her music."

"I know. That's what worries me. But you two used to play together and—"

"Oh, mostly just school stuff. And a few weddings. But we never got any real work except for a couple of dances at the Elks Lodge."

"You still play the guitar?"

"I play at church now and then."

"Well, I was thinking that if you took your guitar with you, she might pick a few tunes. Maybe she'd start thinking about writing again."

"She used to write such great songs. I always knew she was gonna make it. She had so much talent."

"Hamp, I think you'd be good for Brenda right now. You might be able to bring her out of it."

"You think it would be okay if I went by this evening?"

"This evening would be great."

"About seven? Seven-thirty?"

"Good. I'm gonna work late tonight, leave you two alone so you can visit."

"Okay then," Hamp said as he scooted his chair back and stood to leave.

"Just one more thing."

"Yes, ma'am?"

"Let's not tell her this was my idea."

"Sure, if you say so."

"I think it's best," Molly O said. "She's not too crazy about my ideas these days."

Bui had written only a few lines before the pen began to slide in his hand. While he used his shirttail to dry his sweaty palm and fingers, he tried to decide what to say next. Though he had practiced the letter in his head for many days, putting the words on paper carried a risk, the risk that she would not hear his heart speaking.

Biting at his lip, he picked up his pen again.

   I know the months ahead will be hard for you there, but do not listen to those who will speak to you of shame. And when they look at you with hard eyes to make you smaller, do not think of guilt. Guilt does not belong to you, Nguyet, or to the baby you carry, a baby who will laugh with the sound of your laughter . . . see the beauty of the world with your eyes.

I want you and our child here with me, a child made of your body and my love. How could you think I would not want you both?

Bui paused when he heard the front door of the church rattle against the wind.

Do you not know that any part of you is precious to me? Do you not believe that without you, my life is nothing?

Come to America, Nguyet, and we will make for our child a good life . . . and for ourselves, a new beginning.

After he folded the letter around the money he was sending, Bui went to the window and pulled the curtain aside to stare at the moon, knowing that in a few hours it would shine on another part of the world. And he wondered if Nguyet would look at it and think of him.

Chapter Twenty-Four

WHEN LIFE SAW CANEY unlock the front door, he grabbed the notebook off the seat beside him, then scooted out of his pickup where he'd been waiting for nearly an hour. He knew Molly O and the morning coffee drinkers wouldn't be far behind him, so if he was going to have any time alone with Caney, he'd have to hurry.

He'd been carrying the book around with him for the past three days while he tried to decide what to do. At first, Molly O had teased him about going back to school, but when she pressed him about what was in the book, he'd felt the color burn in his face as he lied.

"Morning, Life," Caney said. "See you're still working on your taxes."

"No, this ain't tax stuff." Life slid onto his regular stool and put the notebook on the counter in front of him. "Nothing like that."

"Oh, I thought I heard you tell Molly O—"

"Well, I did, but I wasn't truthful with her about that."

"How come?"

"That's what I want to talk to you about, Caney. See, this here's real private." Life patted the black notebook tenderly. "I never showed it to nobody before. But I'd like you to take a look at it."

"Me?"

"Yeah." Life pushed the book across the counter to Caney. "I need another man's opinion, a man I can trust."

"I don't know, Life. If it's something that secret . . ."

"I've give this a lot of thought, Caney. I feel like I'm doing the right thing here."

"But—"

"You'd be doing me a real favor if you'd read it," Life said.

"Well, okay."

Caney opened the notebook which was filled with at least an inch of loose-leaf paper. On the first page there were two long paragraphs. One written in pencil, one in pen, they were separated from each other by several blank lines. Each paragraph was dated—the first March 4, 1941, the second, March 5.

Grinning, Caney said, "I never figured you to be one to keep a diary, Life," but when he began to read, his grin quickly faded. And as his eyes moved down the page, they widened in surprise.

"Is this some kind of joke?"

"No joke."

"This is hot stuff, Life." Caney turned the page where the next entry was dated March 6. After he read that, he riffled through all the pages, watching decades fly by until he came to the final entry written on November 10, 1983.

"What are you going to do with this?" Caney asked.

"I was hoping you could tell me."

"Well, I don't know a damned thing about writing, but I think you're pretty good. You've got a wild imagination, I'll say that for you, but if you're thinking about trying to get this published, I'd change this guy's name to Bob or Bill. Something like that. You use your own name, everybody'll know—"

"I didn't write it."

Caney looked puzzled. "Who did?"

"Reba."

"Oh, come on." Caney smiled, seeing the humor, but he could tell from the look on Life's face that he was serious as death. He was telling the truth.

"Reba?!" Caney shook his head, as much from astonishment as to shake loose the image of Mrs. Life Halstead.

Reba . . . a short, heavy woman who went to the Holy Ghost Tabernacle and spoke in tongues. Reba . . . a hardworking farm wife who made the best peach cobbler in the county and milked their Holsteins every morning before breakfast. Reba . . . a quiet, shy grandmother who wore loose brown dresses and sensible shoes.

Caney slammed the notebook closed and shoved it across the counter. He felt like a kid who's just been caught peeking in his neighbor's bathroom window.

"I found it in her dresser drawer the day after she was buried."

"You didn't know about this till then? That she was keeping a record of every time you two had sex?"

"We didn't have sex, Caney. We made love."

"You sure as hell did!"

"Reba was the only woman I was ever with," Life said, fighting tears.

"From what I just read, she was enough."

"Yes, she was. She truly was." Life pulled out a handkerchief and wiped the corners of his eyes. "But she's gone now and . . . Caney, I think you know how I feel about Molly O."

"I guess I do."

"Well, here's what I'm wondering. Do you think I should show this to her?"

"To Molly O?"

"Yeah. I been thinking that she might be a little more interested in me if she saw what Reba had to say."

"You mean kind of like providing references?"

"Something like that."

"You want my honest opinion, Life?"

"I do, Caney."

"Okay. I think if you show her this . . ."

Caney looked out the window as Molly O parked her Ford out front.

"Uh-oh. Here she is," Caney warned.

"Go on. You think if I show her this . . ."

"We'd better talk about this later, Life. She's gonna walk in here in just a second."

"We have time, Caney! Now, what did you start to say?"

"Here she comes."

"Dammit!" Life slapped the counter. "If I ever get to finish one conversation in this place, I'll—"

"Morning, Life. Caney."

"How you doing?" Caney asked.

"Great. Just great. Spring is here and love is in the air."

Life and Caney exchanged guilty glances.

"Hamp Rothrock went by to see Brenda last night. Still there when I got home, sitting beside her on the couch. Now I could be wrong, I suppose, but she seemed happy to be with him. 'Course, she wouldn't want me to think she was happy, but I could tell. He stayed till almost eleven. And after I went to bed, I heard her in the living room playing her guitar."

As Molly O went behind the counter to put her purse away, she said, "Why, Life, you don't even have a cup of coffee."

"No, I don't," he said, his face pulled into a pout.

"Caney, where's Vena?"

"She took the gelding out. Said she might ride to the lake."

"Well, you made a smart decision not to go with her."

"Yeah." Caney rolled to the window. The sky was cloudless, the sun bright, the countryside greening. "Real smart."

When Molly O handed Life his coffee, she said, "I see you're still carrying that notebook around with you."

"Uh . . ."

"But you're not fooling me."

"I'm not?" Life laid a protective hand across the book.

"Those aren't farm accounts. That thing's full of love letters, I'd bet."

"Well, you could be right," he said. "You sure could be right."

The newspaper usually came about the time Soldier and Quinton showed up for their morning coffee, but today Big Fib Fry, the carrier, was running late.

"Suppose he's been picked up by another UFO?" Quinton asked.

"Guess he's gettin' on right friendly terms with those aliens. They've had him . . . what? Four or five times now?"

"Yeah, but you notice ever' time they get him, they let him go real fast."

"Hell, wouldn't you?"

"From what I hear, Big Fib's got more on his mind right now than aliens," Wanda Sue said from her perch at the counter.

"What's that?"

"I hear he's carrying on with the wife of one of our city councilmen. But don't ask me who, 'cause I ain't gonna repeat it."

"Now I admire that," Soldier said. "A woman who don't pass on gossip."

While Wanda Sue pulled off her glasses and used a napkin to clean them, Soldier winked at Quinton as he took out his pocket watch.

"But I will tell you this, the woman in question's at least ten years older than Big Fib."

"Paper here yet?" Caney asked as he came out of the kitchen.

"Nope."

"Guess Fib got beamed up again," Caney said.

"Huh-uh." Wanda Sue shook her head. "He's stopped off at his girlfriend's."

"Who's his girlfriend?"

"She's not telling."

"No, but I will tell you this. She's going to Houston next month to get a face lift."

"Well, here comes the fishing king."

As Hooks Red Eagle climbed out of his battered pickup, Molly O filled a cup with coffee and took it to Soldier and Quinton's table.

"You get 'em today, Hooks?" Soldier asked when the door opened.

"Caught a couple of decent catfish. They go twenty, twenty-two pounds. Saw an old boy in a johnboat pull in crappie as long as my arm."

"Lake's warming up."

"Man, that water's smooth as glass today. No wind. Beautiful. Just beautiful."

"I'll bet it is," Caney said.

"Say," Hooks said, "I heard old man Spence died last night."

"That right?"

"She lives right next door to the Spence place," Wanda Sue said with authority.

"Who does?"

"The woman in question."

"Hell, Wanda Sue. Ain't but one house next door, and that's Frances and Luter's place."

"Now, you did not hear it from me." Wanda Sue pointed her finger at Quinton to place blame where it belonged.

"Hear what?" Hooks asked.

"That Big Fib's having an affair with Frances Dunn." Then, to make sure everyone present realized the significance of the revelation, for which she would later blame Quinton, Wanda Sue added, "*Mrs.* Luter Dunn."

Soldier checked his pocket watch and held up two fingers. "Yes sir, if there's anything I admire, it's a woman who can keep her mouth shut."

Just then Big Fib Fry's pickup came flying in, and as it circled the lot, the newspaper sailed out and landed on the concrete strip that fronted the Honk.

"About damned time," Soldier said as he pushed his chair back, but before he got to his feet, Caney opened the door, and to the astonishment of all those watching, he wheeled himself outside.

"What's he doing?"

"Why, he—"

"Went right out the door!"

"Never seen him—"

"Outside!"

"What the hell is going on?!"

*   *   *

"See where those branches fork?" Caney pointed to the bois d'arc tree out back.

Bui leaned across Caney's shoulder and peered through the kitchen window.

"I believe you can hang a chain from each of those branches, then wire the bar to them." Caney kept his voice low. "You think you can manage that?"

"I can fix, Mr. Chaney," Bui whispered, clearly pleased to be a part of Caney's secret.

"I'll call the lumberyard and have them put the order together. You think you could go in and pick it up this afternoon?"

"Yes sirree!"

Caney glanced into the dining room to make sure Vena and Molly O were still busy, then he refolded the sheet of paper with the sketch he had drawn and handed it to Bui.

"Two chicken strip baskets," Molly O called as she slid a ticket onto the pass-through.

Caney winked at Bui, then headed for the grill.

Bui had just walked out of the lumberyard carting Caney's order when he noticed Sam Kellam and two other men hunkering against the front of the building.

As Bui loaded the materials into the trunk of his car, the men started laughing, but he didn't look up.

When he slid beneath the wheel and reached for the key in the ignition, he heard a sound like the rustle of dry leaves just seconds before he noticed the burlap bag in the seat beside him. And though he had never heard the sound before, he knew what was convulsing inside the bag even before the snake began to slither toward him.

His first impulse was to yell and pull back in fear, the same cold fear that had gripped him each time he came upon a python or cobra in the jungles of Vietnam where he had felled trees for wood.

But he remained perfectly still, breath suspended, eyes unblinking as he fought to find control.

Then, moving imperceptibly, he inched his left hand toward the door and eased it open, never taking his eyes from the snake as it disentangled itself from the bag and slid over his thigh, moving toward heat.

Bracing himself for what he was about to do, Bui drew a silent, even breath, felt the fingers of his right hand tingle as he drew it slowly and steadily into position, then, with startling speed, lunged, grabbed the snake just behind the head, hurled himself out the door and in one smooth motion flung the rattler into the air—five feet of twisting, contorting snake soaring in an arc toward the building.

The two men, one on each side of Sam, saw what was coming in time to scramble away, while Sam, still locked in a crouch, holding a match to a cigarette, looked up, too late, as the rattler slammed into his chest and fell squirming into his lap.

"Goddamn!" he yelled as he struggled to rise, but, unbalanced, fell back against the building, hands clawing at the agitated snake writhing against his belly. Then, frantic, Sam managed to roll away and bound to his feet, dropping the rattler to the ground where it began to coil between his boots.

By then, his two companions, well out of the way, were hooting with laughter while Sam danced a wild fandango—whirling one way, then the other, frenzied and furious as he stomped and hopped until the snake slithered across the sidewalk and into a grate in the gutter.

Bui, unhurried, crawled back into his car and started it up. But for one brief moment, he and Sam locked eyes before the car pulled away.

When Vena got the call she'd been waiting for, her skin turned clammy and roughened with goose bumps. But she didn't know if what she was feeling was relief or dread.

"Oh, Carmelita. I've left messages for you from San Antonio to Portland," she said.

"Well, one of them just caught up with me. A doctor I worked for in Phoenix. He said when he saw a slip of paper with

'Carmelita' written on it, he knew it had to be me even though the last name was different."

"What do you mean?"

"I got married. But when the husband walked out, the name walked with him, so I'm back to Sanchez again. Didn't Helen tell you?"

"No."

"Vena, where is that girl? I haven't heard from her for months. Can you believe that?"

Vena felt suddenly so light-headed she leaned against the wall for support. All this time she'd waited for Carmelita to fill her in on the last two years of Helen's life. But now, it seemed, she had waited for nothing.

"You know, we talked almost every week, sometimes for two hours. My husband, well, my ex-husband, complained about the phone bill all the time."

"Carmelita—"

"But the last time I called her, her phone had been disconnected, so I figured she'd moved. Then I called for her at the hospital, and they said she'd quit, which just didn't make any sense.

"So I waited for her to call me, but she didn't. And I tried to find you, but you left a cold trail. In the meantime, I made a couple of moves myself and—"

"Carmelita, I have some bad news." Vena could hear a sharp intake of breath on the line. "Helen's dead."

"Madre de Dios."

"I . . . I thought you might have heard."

"No." Her voice breaking, Carmelita said, "Vena, I just can't—"

Vena could picture her there at the other end of the line. Small, dark-haired Carmelita, her beautiful face distorted with grief.

"I don't know what to say." Carmelita fought for breath. "She was the best friend I ever had. I loved Helen like a . . ."

"Sister."

"Vena, I'm so sorry. I'm so sorry for you."

"I'm okay." Vena felt far from "okay," but sometimes the biggest lies slipped out easier than the truth.

"When's the funeral? I'll be there, you know that."

"She was buried eight months ago."

Vena fought against the image of Helen's grave, a still-life—one spray of yellow roses atop a fresh mound of earth—but the picture was too vivid, like a framed painting she looked at every day.

"Vena, what happened?"

"I got a call from a sheriff in south Texas. He said she died in a fire. He seemed to think she might have set it herself."

Vena could hear Carmelita crying again.

"Apparently, she was living in some abandoned place in the middle of nowhere."

"Why? What was she doing out there?"

"I don't know, but something happened to her in San Antonio, something that made her snap. And she ran."

"I don't understand any of this, Vena. The last time we talked, I guess it was last spring, she sounded so happy. She'd met a guy she was crazy about and . . ."

"Did she tell you who it was?"

"I asked her, but she said it wasn't anyone I'd know. He didn't work at the hospital."

"But you think they were serious?"

"*Helen* was serious. No question about that. She was already talking marriage and they'd only been seeing each other for a few weeks.

"I told her to slow down, but you know how she was with men. She tried too hard to be what they wanted. And every time one of the bastards walked out on her, she'd get so depressed she scared me."

"You think that's what happened, Carmelita? You think this guy dropped her and—"

"Pushed her over the edge? It's possible, I guess. She was so desperate to find someone to love, someone who'd love her. You know, all she ever really wanted was a family."

Vena lost her breath for a moment, then closed her eyes.

"Vena, did you ever talk to Helen after . . ."

"After the mess I made of things in San Antonio? No, I wanted to, but . . ."

"Don't do this to yourself, honey. She wouldn't want you to."

"I let her down so many times, Carmelita. And I thought now, even though it's too late, I might be able to make it up to her somehow. I know that doesn't make any sense, but—"

"Look, why don't you come to Chicago. I'm at Cook County Hospital, settled in and planning to stay. Come up here and stay with me."

"I don't think so, Carmelita. But thanks."

"Will you at least call me? You're the closest thing I have to Helen and I don't want to lose you again."

"Yeah, I'll call."

"Vena, Helen always loved you . . . more than anyone in the world. I hope you know that. She worried about you, but she said you'd find your place someday."

"Well, I haven't found it yet."

Chapter Twenty-Five

$\mathcal{M}$OLLY O HAD been in bed for nearly an hour before she heard Brenda and Hamp go outside. As they talked quietly on the front porch, she lay very still, trying to make out what they were saying, but she couldn't pick up a word.

Ten minutes later, when she heard Brenda come back in, she got up, pulled on her robe and padded down the hall to the kitchen.

"Have a good time?" she asked, hoping she didn't sound too interested.

"I guess."

"Thought I'd have a glass of milk. Want some?"

"No."

While Brenda put her guitar in the case and gathered up sheets of music, Molly O poured her milk and carried it into the living room.

"You two sound so good together. Better than most of the singers I see on the TV."

Brenda rolled her eyes.

"I mean it. What was that last song I heard you all sing?"

"Something new."

"Is that the title?"

"No, I mean it's a new song. I just finished it today."

"And Hamp's already learned it?"

"Well, there's not much for him to learn. He just harmonizes with me on the chorus."

"He's good, though, isn't he?"

"He's okay."

"I'm so glad he's going to sing with you at the concert because he—"

"Don't call it a concert!"

"Why?"

"Because it sounds so stupid. It's not a real performance, like for a real audience."

"Oh, you're going to have an audience, all right. Everyone I know is going to be there. And I'm going to ask Danny Starr to come and take some pictures."

"Who's that?"

"Soldier's grandson. He works for the newspaper."

"I don't want any pictures in the paper."

"Why not?"

"Look. You asked me if I'd come down to the Honk some night and sing. Four or five songs, you said. Now, all of a sudden, I'm going to give a concert and you're doing publicity, for Christ's sake."

"Well, honey—"

"I can just see it. A front-page story in the *Sequoyah Weekly Ledger.* 'Brenda O'Keefe appearing in concert at the Honk and Holler Opening Soon.' God."

"What's wrong with that?"

"Mom. Wake up! It's *not* the Grand Ole Opry. It's the Honk." Brenda plopped down on the couch. "I wish I'd never said I'd do it because this whole idea is stupid."

"I don't think so."

"That's because you're my mother. But what do you think those freaks I went to school with would say? Oh, Phyllis Ford would love it. She was always hoping I'd be a flop."

"Honey, you're not a flop. You just—"

"I just came crawling back to Sequoyah the same way I left. A nobody."

"Brenda, you're seventeen and—"

"Oh, God. Please don't give me your 'you've-got-your-whole-life-ahead-of-you speech.' I've heard it so many times, I know it by heart."

"But things are looking up for you now, Brenda. You came home sick and confused, but now you're better. You got rid of that Travis . . . and now you've got Hamp."

"Hamp's just a friend. Don't try to make something more out of that."

"But he's a good friend, Brenda. And because of him, you're writing music again. Great music. And in a few nights, you're going to give a con—" Molly O slapped her hand over her mouth.

"I'll tell you what, Mom. You rent a place with a stage and lights, bring in some backup musicians and some sound equipment, and we'll call it a concert. Okay?"

"Well, Miss Smarty Pants, I remember when all you needed for a concert was a spoon."

"Not the spoon story again," Brenda wailed, but she wasn't very convincing. She loved to hear the story as much as Molly O loved to tell it.

"Your daddy used to dress you up every Saturday in jeans and a fancy western shirt, put you in your cowboy boots and cowboy hat and take you all over town to sing. And you were just barely out of diapers.

"He'd take you to the barbershop, filling station, the VFW. The pool hall. Wherever he could find you an audience.

"And he'd put you up on a counter or a table and hand you a spoon and you'd pretend it was a microphone."

Brenda giggled and covered her face in mock embarrassment.

"You'd tap your feet, shake your little butt and belt out 'On Top of Old Smokey' or 'Honky-Tonk Angel.' Oh, you knew two or three dozen songs.

"You weren't shy about singing, either. You didn't have to be begged. You knew how to work a crowd, too, 'cause you knew if you put on a good show, the audience would pay up. And they did. Why, some Saturdays you made three or four dollars."

"Not bad. You think I might pick up a little change at the Honk if I sing into a spoon and wiggle my butt?"

"Why, I'd pay fifty cents to see that myself." Molly O put her arms around Brenda and pulled her close. "Might even go a dollar."

Shifting in sleep, Vena rolled to her side, one hand coming to rest in the crook of Caney's arm. As she pressed her cheek into the pillow, she cried out, a strangled sound that woke her.

"You okay?" he asked.

"Yeah." She propped herself up on one elbow and rubbed her hand across her eyes. "What time is it?"

"Twelve-thirty."

"Is that all? Feels like it should be morning."

"That's because you're having a bad night."

"Am I keeping you awake?"

"No." Caney ran his finger around the curve of her jaw. "What's wrong, Vena? You got demons chasing you?"

"More than you can imagine."

"Tell me about your demons."

"Why?"

"Because I want to know everything about you."

"Oh, I don't think you do, Caney. I don't think you'd like it."

"Everything. Your favorite color, how old you were when you learned to tie your shoes, who your first boyfriend was. I want to know where you got the scar on your calf and why you had a skull tattooed on your arm. I want to know it all."

"Green. I like green. And Helen tied my shoes until I was seven. My first boyfriend was Richard Bearpaw, a boy in second grade, but I dumped him when I found out he was scared of spiders. The scar came from a barbed-wire fence, and I got the tattoo the last time I ran away from home."

"The last time?"

"Yeah. I took it up as a hobby after Inez came to live with us."

"Who's Inez?"

"The woman Dad married two months after Mom died. He said me and Helen needed a woman to look after us, but that was just an excuse. Mom had been in and out of psycho wards for two or three years and we'd managed all right on our own. We needed Inez like we needed gangrene."

"The wicked stepmother, huh?"

"Three days after she moved in, she burned every picture of Mom we had. Said it was best for us. Told Dad she was only trying to help us get through our grief.

"I think he felt bad about it, but he didn't say anything. That wasn't his way.

"The damage was done, though. Once Inez discovered she had the upper hand, she made our lives miserable."

"And you ran?"

"Found out I was good at it, too. But Helen wasn't. We wouldn't be gone more than a few hours before she'd start worrying about her animals. Back we'd go. I went without her a couple of times, but I never stayed away long. I couldn't leave her there by herself.

"So we stuck it out until the day Helen graduated. By then, she'd found homes for the few animals Inez hadn't killed or run off, and we left for good."

"Where'd you go?"

"Austin. Helen got a job in a bank and I started my sophomore year in high school. We lived in a crummy little apartment, didn't have a car, shared a bed and what clothes we had, but we were happy.

"I got a part-time job waiting tables and we saved every dime we could because we had this dream that we'd both go to nursing school after I graduated. Something we'd talked about since we were kids.

"Then Helen started dating a guy I couldn't stand, a know-it-all who wanted to tell everyone what to do. Nagged me about my grades, told Helen how to fix her hair, how to dress. Said we'd be stupid to go into nursing because it didn't pay anything.

"But she was in love, wanted to please him, I guess. Before long she enrolled in night courses at a business college—his idea, of course. She began to ride me about studying, threw a fit when I made a D in math. She started to sound just like him.

"By the time they got engaged, I'd already figured out that she didn't need me around anymore, so I dropped out of school, got on a Greyhound and went to Santa Fe."

"Why Santa Fe?"

"I saw some pictures in a magazine. It looked glamorous."

"Was it?"

"Oh, yeah. I worked in a bakery icing cakes. Met a guy, a roofer. I got pregnant and he got lost, so I had an abortion and moved on."

Caney shook his head.

"Heard enough?" Vena asked as she started to roll away, but Caney caught her hand and pulled her back.

"No. Where did you go then?"

"Knocked around Arizona, a couple of years in Texas. Got in some trouble in Abilene. Owner of a liquor store where I worked had me arrested. Said I stole a hundred dollars from the register. I didn't, but I spent a night in jail before Helen showed up and bailed me out.

"After the jerk back in Austin had dumped her, she'd gone on to nursing school, got a job in a hospital in Las Vegas, so I went back there with her. That's where we were when we found out Dad had died."

"Did you go home?"

"Not much point. He'd been dead five months before we heard about it. Seems Inez had him cremated before he was cold, sold our place the next week and she was gone. Never heard a word from her."

"God, what a sweetheart."

"Anyway, I stayed in Las Vegas for a while. Worked as a cocktail waitress, a blackjack dealer, bartender. Started drinking. Got arrested one night for DWI. Helen to the rescue again.

"I headed north then. Wyoming, Montana. Worked at a dude ranch for a while, a couple of training stables, ran some rodeo stock. But that came to a halt when I got thrown from a stallion, broke my arm and collarbone. Helen sent the money for the hospital and doctor bills.

"She'd moved to San Antonio, wanted me to come live with her, but I went to California instead. Met Tom Sixkiller, got married. Another big mistake.

"Tom was a decent guy . . . too decent, I suppose. But I wasn't much of a wife." Vena rolled onto her back and stared at the ceiling. "After I left him, I drifted down to San Antonio. Stayed with Helen and her roommate, Carmelita Sanchez.

"I wasn't there long before Helen started talking about helping me go to nursing school. Hell, I was thirty years old and she still believed I could be somebody.

"I don't know why I said yes. To please her, I guess. She gave me a thousand dollars for my tuition. She acted real happy, tried to pump me up, but I suspect she knew I'd screw up again. And I did.

"I took the money, had a few drinks, bought a car and wrecked it that night."

"What did she say?"

"I didn't stick around to find out, couldn't face her. Couldn't stand to see the disappointment in her eyes. I'd seen it too many times before."

"So . . ."

"I left town. Didn't even say good-bye. And I never saw her again."

Vena was quiet for several moments, then she wiped her eyes on the heels of her hands before she shifted, rolling onto her side again, facing Caney.

"Well, there you have it. I told you it wasn't a pretty story."

"I wasn't expecting a fairy tale." Caney used his thumb to wipe a tear from Vena's temple. "You made a few mistakes. Who hasn't?"

"Caney, I didn't make a few mistakes. I hurt the one person in my life who cared about me."

"Well, now there's someone else who does."

"Weren't you listening to me?" Vena sat up and hugged her knees to her chest. "After what you just heard, do you—"

"Hell, Vena. I don't care what you've done. I didn't know the person you were . . . I only know who you are now."

"Caney, people don't change. We get older, maybe a little smarter or maybe not, but underneath, we're still the same."

"That's not the way I see it."

"Look. I've messed up my own life and lots of others. I don't want to mess up yours."

"Hell, go ahead. Mess it up. Listen, the day I watched you climb out of that truck and walk in here, I knew my life was gonna change. Hoped it'd get better, didn't figure it could get much worse, but if that's how things turn out . . ."

"Caney, I told you from the beginning—"

"That you wouldn't stay. Well, I won't ask you to. I'm not gonna push my luck; I'll settle for what I've got."

He reached for her shoulders, eased her down onto his pillow and cradled her head into the curve of his neck.

"But for now," he said, "for tonight . . . that's enough for me."

Chapter Twenty-Six

CANEY HAD WATCHED the whole thing from out back of the Honk, watched as Bui approached the gelding, taking mincing, tentative steps, holding the nylon halter out as if he were offering it as a gift.

"Don't hold it in front of you, Bui," Caney said to himself. "He sees it coming, he'll never let you get close."

But once again Bui neared the gelding with the halter held before him at arm's length, and once again the gelding jerked his head and backed away.

Bui had said he was not afraid of the horse, but Caney could tell from the way he jumped each time the gelding reared his head and snorted, that he was terrified. The animal knew it, too.

While Bui waited again for the horse to settle, Caney could see his lips moving, and though he was too far away to hear the conversation, he knew Bui was pleading for a little cooperation.

Caney smiled, wondering if the gelding could understand Vietnamese.

Then, holding the halter at his side, Bui began to inch close again.

"That's the idea," Caney whispered. "Go slow."

Bui got near enough this time to stroke the gelding's muzzle with one hand; with the other, he slid the halter over its neck until he could reach under and pull both ends together.

Because the halter was twisted, he had to work at getting it buckled, but he stayed with it, even as the gelding backed up, dragging him along. When he finally got it fastened, he turned toward the Honk and waved to let Caney know everything was all right, and Caney shot back a thumbs-up salute.

As Bui led the gelding toward the gate, he moved like a crab, looking back to make sure the horse wasn't gaining on him.

While Caney waited, he wheeled his chair to the side of the tall ramp he'd had Bui build and pushed against it to test its strength. It felt sturdy enough, but the pitch was steeper than he'd figured on. Still, he thought he could manage it.

Vena and Molly O had watched Bui working on it for the past couple of days, but when they asked what it was for, Caney said he guessed it was another of Bui's secrets. Then, when he'd chained the bar to the limbs of the bois d'arc tree, Molly O said it looked like a trapeze, and she got the notion that Bui was thinking of joining a circus.

When Caney looked up, the bar high over his head was swinging gently in the morning breeze.

Bui had arrived early, just as he'd promised, right after sunrise. Caney, already up and dressed, had slipped out while Vena was still asleep. He didn't want her watching in case this crazy plan didn't work, didn't want her to see him hanging up there like some kind of helpless Tarzan, or worse, to see him fall on his ass.

Bui was smiling as he crossed the yard, leading the gelding to Caney.

"You're a good man, Bui," Caney said. "You did fine, just fine."

"Yes, Mr. Chaney. I not fear of horse." Bui patted the gelding's flank to prove it.

"Oh, I could see that all right."

"Horse my friend now. Like me very much, I think so."

"No question about it."

As Caney took the halter from Bui, he said, "You saw where

Brim Neely put the bridle and saddle in the shed yesterday, didn't you?"

"I saw."

"Well, if you'll bring those out here . . ."

"I get, Mr. Chaney. Lickety spit." Bui beamed. "New American words. Lickety spit. Mean very fast." He laughed as he dashed for the shed.

"You been well trained, fella," Caney said as he smoothed the coat on the gelding's withers. "Now, let's see how you're gonna deal with me."

When Bui came back, he put the saddle on the ground beside Caney and handed him the bridle.

"Here, Bui. You take the halter again."

Caney reached in his shirt pocket and pulled out a chunk of apple. When the gelding lowered its head to take it, Caney pressed just behind the ears to make sure the head stayed down after the apple was gone. Then Caney took the bridle in his right hand while he slipped the thumb of his left in the gelding's mouth so he could guide the bit into place.

"Horse have big teeth," Bui said. "Much bite, I think so. Take off finger."

"Naw, he wouldn't bite off your finger. Besides, if he did, he probably wouldn't swallow it."

Bui giggled.

"Can you unbuckle the halter now and slip it off?"

"I can do it, Mr. Chaney."

Once the halter was removed, Caney looped the reins over the horse's neck, then tethered them to the arm of his wheelchair.

"Now, let's see if we can get that saddle on him."

Bui picked up the saddle and moved in beside Caney who grabbed the pommel; then lifting together, they swung it onto the gelding's back.

"Bui, go around to the other side, reach up under the saddle and pull out the girth and stirrup leathers. They're caught under it."

After Bui fumbled the tangled girth from beneath the saddle, he grabbed hold of the stirrups and pulled the leathers free. Then

Caney reached under the gelding's belly, pulled the girth toward him, threaded the latigo through and tied it off.

"You did fine, boy," Caney said as the horse lifted his head and snuffled.

"All right. We're ready for the hard part." Caney pulled the reins loose from his chair and handed them to Bui. "Try to maneuver him right under the bar, while I see if I can get up this thing."

As Caney rolled around to the down side of the ramp, he passed Spot's fence where the little dog was watching with interest the goings-on around him.

"What do you think, Spot? Think this is gonna work?"

The dog wagged her tail.

Bui said, "Spot thinks horse is very big dog. A new friend, she thinks so."

Caney figured Bui might be right since Spot hadn't barked, not once. But then Spot wasn't much of a barker.

When Caney rolled into position at the bottom of the ramp, he wiped his palms over his pant legs, then took a deep breath before he grabbed the wheels of his chair and started grinding his way to the top.

In the beginning, he decided it was easier than he had thought. But by the time he was halfway up, his arms were quivering with the strain.

As he worked to gain the final couple of feet, he was panting and making growling sounds each time he got a new handhold and forced the wheels forward.

"You can do, Mr. Chaney," Bui said. "I know you can do."

With one last powerful lunge, Caney rolled the wheelchair over the lip of the incline and onto the platform Bui had built at the top.

"You champion now." Bui flashed a smile of admiration. "Like Muhammad Ali."

"You bet," Caney said between gulps of air.

Caney flexed his hands to restore feeling back to his fingers, then shook his arms and rolled his head from one shoulder to the other.

The gelding, growing impatient, snorted, then pawed at the ground.

"You're right, buddy." Caney reached down and scratched the gelding between the ears. "It's time to get on the road. You ready, Bui?"

"I ready."

Caney reached above him for the bar, stretching his upper body as far as he could to reach it, and found that Bui's measurements were just about perfect.

When he curled his hands around the thick cylinder of steel, he tested it with a yank which sent the chains holding it clanking. Then he grasped the bar tightly and, straining, began to lift himself from the chair. And though he hadn't chinned himself since he'd left rehab at the VA, he still had the strength to get the job done.

He pulled himself up far enough to free his legs from the chair, and with them dangling almost over the gelding, he said, "Okay, Bui. Help me get there."

Bui, still holding the gelding in place with a tight grip on the reins, grabbed Caney's legs and guided him to a position over the saddle.

"You there, Mr. Chaney."

As Caney lowered himself, Bui was able to maneuver him onto the saddle.

"Well, I'll be damned," Caney said. "It worked. What do you know about that? It worked!" And then he laughed and Bui laughed with him.

Finally he took the reins from Bui, then reached down and shook his hand. "Thanks."

"You welcome, Mr. Chaney."

Then Caney flicked the reins and the gelding began to trot toward the open field.

Bui stood watching until the horse and rider disappeared into a thick stand of evergreens, then turned and started for the Honk where he saw Vena smiling at him from the bedroom window.

Caney was hardly out of sight of the Honk before he felt the first stirring of fear rise, but he fought against it, fought to keep his mind and body centered on the old familiarity of movement and rhythm, the smell of horse and leather, the feel of an early morning breeze on his skin.

He struggled to keep his eyes fixed on the ground directly in the gelding's path, would not let himself think about what might be creeping up behind him or what could be waiting up ahead, rode in silence, neck bowed, head lowered, the curled brim of his stained Stetson blocking the view of all but a few feet of earth.

He didn't know how long he'd ridden that way until the gelding waded into the stream they'd crossed weeks earlier and stopped to drink. Then, though Caney tried to resist, he was unable to keep from cutting his eyes to the far bank. But where before snipers had been in hiding, he saw now a doe and her fawn grazing near the water's edge which was lined with flowering dogwoods and red maples.

Then, tentatively, he began to steal quick, short glances around him as the gelding headed across a wide valley where plum and pear trees and crabapples bloomed.

When he passed between the sweetgum trees where he'd seen the trip wire before, he discovered the wire's mysterious transformation into vines of honeysuckle and ivy, and as the gelding carried him into the mouth of the valley, instead of land mines, he saw a field exploding with black-eyed Susans and Indian paintbrush.

Then the horse climbed a rise thick with yellow daisies, and at the top, where an NVA patrol had been waiting for Caney weeks ago, he was met this morning by a wild turkey foraging beneath a stand of cottonwood trees.

At the edge of a ridge, he looked down on a field covered with bluebonnets and sunflowers, and while he let the gelding graze in the meadow where the helicopter had roared in, filling the sky with its dark terror, Caney watched a red-tail hawk gliding on a current of air.

In the remnant of the orchard near Ted Kyle's now collapsed old home place, he picked a green apple smaller than a golf ball and almost as hard, but bit into it anyway, the sourness sweet with the memory of others he'd tasted in another time.

He rode to the lake and watched a bass break water in a cove where he and Dewey O'Keefe had fished on Sundays, sharing a breakfast of Vienna sausage and hard biscuits, taking turns bailing water from a leaking johnboat.

He saw a black snake sunning on a slab of granite, felt the rough bark of a bois d'arc and smelled earth fresh turned by a tractor in a field where he'd shot at his first deer and missed, perhaps intentionally.

He watched scissor-tailed flycatchers rise from a black gum tree, and from a far hill, he heard the bellowing of coon hounds, reminding him of how grown-up he'd felt at nine, crouched around a predawn campfire with Soldier and Quinton, sharing strong black coffee and lies as they listened to their blueticks bay.

He watched a crawdad back into its mud tunnel beside a narrow creek, then smiled at the memory of himself and Carl Phelps cutting school to catch crawdads with bacon tied to the end of a string.

By the time the sun had centered itself in the sky, Caney's eyes were bloodshot from its brightness, his arms burned from its heat. A dull pain spread between his shoulder blades while a muscle spasm gripped his lower back. A bee sting reddened and swelled on his elbow, and his fingers, unused to the grip of a saddle horn, had stiffened, yet he was filled with the boyness of his life . . . whole and free, alive again.

Chapter Twenty-Seven

As Reverend Thomas took the pulpit, the congregation of the AME Church steeled themselves for bad news.

They knew it was coming. Not because of the solemn expression that creased the Reverend's face with deep furrows. They were used to that look, figured it came with the burden of trying to deliver them to the Kingdom of Heaven. No, today it was not the preacher's face that gave him away. It was his feet.

On those mornings his toes weren't tapping out the rhythm of the spirituals the choir sang to open up the service, they knew something unfortunate, perhaps even tragic, was about to be revealed to them. And today, his spit-polished black Florsheims had remained rooted to the floor, even when the choir sang "Praying My Way to the Promised Land," his favorite, the song that always caused his feet to dance.

Now, fearing to hear the worst—that one of their number had passed over, they looked anxiously around them to see who was missing.

"Brothers and sisters . . ."

At the sound of his rich, deep voice, they grew silent with the dread of the news he was about to give them.

"The sermon I had prepared for you today was inspired by the beautification of our house of worship. For each time we come together, we marvel at yet more evidence of the wondrous skill of our benefactor, who continues to remain anonymous.

"Why, in just this past week alone, my study has received a fresh coat of paint, the trash stacked behind the shed has been removed and the supplies and materials in the basement have been reorganized and neatly stacked against the walls.

"My Scripture for today's sermon was to have come from Second Corinthians. 'Every man according as he purposeth in his heart, so let him give; not grudgingly, or of necessity: for God loveth a cheerful giver.' "

Ordinarily, the reading of Scripture would be met with a chorus of amens, but now the congregation was stilled by foreboding.

"But you will not hear that sermon prepared for you this morning. I'll save that for another time. A time when my heart is less troubled than it is today."

"Here it comes," Sister Hannah whispered to Galilee, who was already rigid with premonition.

"While I was in the basement this morning, I made a shocking discovery."

Reverend Thomas waited until the agitated whispering ceased before he went on.

"My friends, our holy house has been invaded by an intruder."

A collective groan, shy of only one voice, rumbled through the sanctuary.

"As Christians," the Reverend continued, "we strive to follow God's commandments, including that which comes to us from Exodus, chapter twenty, verse four.

" 'Thou shalt not make unto thee any graven image that is in heaven above, or that is in the earth beneath, or that is in the water under the earth.' "

"Amen" rose in a subdued quartet of voices as Reverend Thomas reached beneath the podium and took out an object covered by a brown towel.

"But as we know, there are those who do not heed the commandments of the Lord."

Then, with a dramatic flourish, the preacher pulled the towel away to expose a stone Buddha, the sight of which charged the congregation with alarm.

Sister Cordelia, still traumatized by the recent vandalism of her house, recoiled in fear at the memory of a rock hurled through her kitchen window by a nine-year-old neighbor boy. Brother Junior, his emotions raw after visiting his wife in the nursing home earlier that morning, began to weep. Brother Samuel, who had suffered two heart attacks, slipped a nitroglycerin pill beneath his tongue. And Sister Hannah, always at the edge of hysteria, shouted, "Lord, help us," which so startled her husband that he jumped and cracked his shin on the pew in front of him.

"I ask you now, as servants of our Father in Heaven, if any one of you can shed some light on what this unholy idol is doing in God's house?"

The congregation fell silent again as, leaning forward and back, they examined the faces of their friends and neighbors. Then they turned, as if in orchestrated movement, and watched, incredulously, as Galilee Jackson struggled to her feet.

"Oh, Mr. Boo, my legs were shaking so bad I didn't think they'd hold me up. Just the way I felt when I was a girl in school and had to stand to recite my lessons. My insides gone to jelly, mouth drying up, hands all quivery.

"I was getting up real slow, partly because these worthless old bones was thinking about going on strike, and partly to figure out what I was gonna say if I could get my mouth to work. Then out of my blue memory comes a skinny, ashy-legged ten-year-old girl jabbering in my bad ear, reminding me of the day I was called on to recite a poem by Mr. Countee Cullen.

"Now it was a long poem, but I had it memorized. Why, I'd said it for my mama at home near a hundred times and never missed a word. But that day at school, standing there in front of my classmates and my teacher, it was a different thing.

"I guess I was over halfway through that poem, word after word just tumbling out when all of a sudden, my mouth stopped working. Stopped just like that."

Galilee snapped her fingers to show Bui the suddenness with which muteness could strike.

"I could hear the words in my head, but I couldn't say them for the life of me.

"Then, when some of the boys started to snicker and point at me, the awfulest thing happened. I started to cry, which only made them laugh harder, the whole class by then, even the girls. And then, I wet myself. Wet myself standing right there by my desk where every student in that room and my teacher, too, could see the puddle forming around my feet."

Galilee shifted in her chair, discomforted by the image of her ten-year-old self, which now, over a half century later, still caused her pain.

"Well," she said, getting back to her story, "my mind played back over that embarrassment as I got to my feet in church, wondering if my mouth would fail me again.

"So you know what I did, Mr. Boo?"

Bui shook his head.

"I prayed. I prayed a silent prayer, asked God to give me the words to tell them about you, tell them about your Buddha and how you come to be living and working in the church.

"And glory to the Lord, my prayer was answered. I told it all without ever stopping, not even once. Just told the whole thing straight out.

"But when I thought I'd said all I had to say and was about to sit down, Mr. Countee Cullen's poem flashed into my head, and this time the words didn't get stuck there. No, sirree!

"Without even knowing I was going to say 'em out loud, the words just came sliding out, my voice as soft as churned butter, and my mouth working fine. Real fine."

Galilee leaned forward in her chair, then closed her eyes as she began her recitation.

> Lord, I fashion dark gods, too
> Daring even to give You

Dark despairing features where
Crowned with dark rebellious hair,
Patience wavers just so much as
Mortal grief compels, while touches
Quick and hot, of anger, rise
To smitten cheek and weary eyes.
Lord, forgive me if my need
Sometimes shapes a human creed.

When Galilee opened her eyes, they were brimmed with tears.

"Well, Mr. Boo, when I finished, they were so quiet, froze in their seats like statues, and the preacher, he looked like a statue, too.

"Then, after what seemed an awful long time of silence, Reverend Thomas bowed his head and we bowed ours as he asked God what he should do, but before the words was hardly out his mouth, a breeze kicked up and set that chandelier to swinging. And all those little glass crystals you'd polished sent tiny beams of light dancing all over us, and as they went spinning, they made sweet tinkling sounds like music, which was surely a joyful noise unto the Lord.

"Well, the preacher didn't hesitate after that. He just wrapped that towel around your Buddha *real* careful and said he was gonna put your stone right back where he found it, and then he led us in prayer again.

"And you know what he asked for, Mr. Boo?"

"No."

"He asked God to keep you folded safely in his arms."

Chapter Twenty-Eight

$\mathcal{B}$Y THE DAY of Brenda's concert, Molly O was already worn out. But she couldn't let up. Not now. Not after she'd worked so hard to make it happen.

She'd started her promotion nearly a week ago when she hand-lettered two dozen index cards which she slipped into the sleeves of all the menus.

SEQUOYAH'S OWN BRENDA O'KEEFE

NASHVILLE RECORDING STAR WILL APPEAR LIVE
AT THE HONK AND HOLLER OPENING SOON THIS
FRIDAY, APRIL 4TH, AT EIGHT O'CLOCK P.M.

ADMISSION IS FREE! AND SO IS THE COFFEE!

Molly O figured she might be stretching the truth just a bit in using the term "recording star," but she had, after all, given Brenda two hundred dollars for studio time to put one of her songs on a cassette. And though only one radio station in Nashville had aired the tape a couple of times, that seemed enough to justify star status, at least to the folks at the Honk.

She'd had to be creative to come up with something for the newspaper since Brenda had thrown such a fit about it. Finally, she'd written a small notice for the classified section, just thirty words which had ended up sandwiched between an ad for the sale of three pygmy goats and another for six dozen Vidalia onion sets. Molly O felt pretty sure Brenda wouldn't see it as she appeared to have no interest in raising goats or onions.

For the posters, Molly O dug out of her scrapbook a photo of Brenda singing at the Kiwanis pancake supper just before she'd dropped out of school and gone off to Nashville. Terry Stillman at the photography studio downtown had blown the photo up and printed eight-by-ten glossies which Molly O taped to large pieces of poster board. She'd put one in Bilbo Porter's Grease-and-Go, one at Hook's bait shop, one at the Goodwill and another in Wilma Driver's Century 21 office.

Then Molly O spent most of one day on the phone, calling to extend personal invitations to Mrs. Miles, Brenda's kindergarten teacher, who'd cast her as the Singing Heart in a Valentine's Day play; Julia Campy, Brenda's first piano teacher; Mr. Dunn, director of the junior high band in which Brenda had played cymbals and bass drum; Dutch Swain who owned Gold-N-Guns where Brenda had pawned her great-grandmother's antique clock so she could buy a Gibson guitar, which, according to Dutch, had belonged to Tanya Tucker; Leroy Jeleski, owner of a liquor store and tattoo parlor, who'd called Molly O when Brenda, at thirteen, had demanded he tattoo the devil's face on her butt; and Carl Phelps, the sheriff, who'd kept Brenda out of jail after he'd found her smoking pot behind the high school with a boy from Poteau.

When Molly O completed her last call, Wanda Sue, who'd been at the counter drinking coffee most of the day, said it sounded to her like the Rolling Stones were coming to the Honk. But Molly O didn't care what Wanda Sue said. She was only trying to make sure Brenda had an audience.

The next day she drove to Ft. Smith and spent three hours shopping. Her feet were killing her by the time she started back to Sequoyah, but the seat beside her was heaped with packages for

Brenda: a white silk blouse with soft ruffles at the sleeves, a light blue denim skirt and vest trimmed with fringe, navy blue boots with silver tips on the toes and earrings shaped like tiny guitars.

When she got home, Brenda took one look at the new outfit and said she wouldn't wear it even *if* she did show up. Molly O tried to pretend she didn't take the threat seriously, but secretly she was afraid that Brenda might really back out.

But when Hamp came by that evening and he and Brenda resumed their rehearsal, Molly O told herself that everything was going to be all right. Most likely.

With time running out, she turned her attention to the Honk and, with the help of Bui, Caney and Vena, gave it, as nearly as they could manage, the look of a nightclub.

While Bui put together an elevated platform which would serve as a stage, Caney worked out a way to rig up a spotlight.

Molly O and Vena covered all the tables with red tablecloths borrowed from the community center and rearranged the furniture to make room for some folding chairs Life brought from the pool hall.

Vena placed three dozen candles around the room, then filled small vases with wild roses she'd found growing in the field behind the Honk.

When everything was ready, Bui set the tables with cups and saucers, Caney turned down the lights, Vena lit the candles and Molly O took a nerve pill.

By seven-thirty, only a handful of regulars had arrived which sent her into a tailspin, but only fifteen minutes later, the tables were full, all the stools at the counter were taken and people were still drifting in.

By eight, the Honk was packed. But Brenda still wasn't there.

"Well, where is the Nashville recording star?" Wanda Sue asked, her voice oozing accusation.

"Oh, she'll be here," Molly O said with all the assurance she could muster, then she retreated to the kitchen to fan the flames of a hot flash that was wilting her hair.

She didn't want to imagine what was going on at the trailer, but couldn't stop the picture playing in her head. She could see Brenda, arms folded, face set in a scowl, as she shook her head, refusing to budge, while Hamp . . .

The dining room erupted with applause as Brenda and Hamp stepped through the door.

"Thank you, Jesus," Molly O whispered as she dabbed at her damp forehead and tried to puff up her hair.

She found a place to stand at the end of the counter beside Life, watching as Brenda gave Caney a kiss, then, making her way through the crowd, was stopped again and again by a touch, a hug from people who'd known her all her life.

When she and Hamp reached the stage and removed their guitars from their cases, Bui turned on the spotlight, causing Brenda to look up in surprise and shade her eyes for a moment.

She was wearing the new outfit Molly O had bought her. The skirt, a size six, was a bit loose around her tiny waist, but Molly O had to guess at the size since Brenda had lost so much weight.

Her face was still pale, but now, with a touch of color on her lips and cheeks, her clear, smooth skin looked iridescent beneath the light above her. And her eyes, dull and clouded for these past few weeks, sparkled with excitement.

Her hair, freshly washed and shining, fell across her shoulders in soft, loose curls the color of cinnamon, and when she tilted her head, Molly O could see she was wearing the earrings she'd bought her.

"She's a beautiful girl," Life said. "A real beautiful girl."

"Well, thank you, Life." Molly O patted his arm. "I think she is, too."

While Brenda tuned her guitar, Hamp whispered something that made her laugh. Then, a moment later, when she looked out into the audience, the room grew quiet.

"Good evening," she said. "It sure is nice to see you all here tonight. I'm Brenda O'Keefe and this is Hamp Rothrock, but I think most of you know us."

Hamp strummed a chord.

"This first tune we're going to do is one I wrote a few days ago. It's called 'Lost Love and Heartbreak.' I hope you all like it."

> When I was young, I didn't care for love songs
> I thought all that despair was just for show
> But I'd never felt a broken heart in those days
> And you have to feel it for yourself to know

When Brenda began to sing, no one in the audience made a sound. No clink of cups against saucers, no whispered conversations, no shuffling of feet or scraping of chairs.

> This is a song of lost love and heartbreak
> For all those who've been put back on the shelf
> And if you don't feel like feeling sorry for me
> Hope you don't mind if I feel sorry for myself

They were entranced by this girl, by her clear, true voice, touched in a place they kept closed and guarded. But now, for these few moments, they let themselves remember, feel again the sweet pain of first love.

> With all the problems in this world to sing of
> I have some nerve to sing about my own
> But my problems seem worse than the rest right now
> Do broken hearts hurt more than broken bones

Brenda kept her eyes on her fingers as they found their place on the frets, but she couldn't hide the pain that played across her face.

> I tried to write a happy song
> But I'll be damned if I could
> 'Cause this song is a song of love
> And love ain't always good

As the last sound of the song softened to silence, Brenda lowered her head and the room settled into a stillness like suspended breath. Then one, then another, then more began to applaud, gently at first, as if too much sound might break the spell, then louder and louder until the air was charged with their rhythm.

Caney caught Molly O's eye and winked at her as Brenda started her next song, a folk song about a fisherman who, after thirty years of trying, finally catches "Old Willy," but can't bring himself to keep it, which made Hooks Red Eagle cry.

Between numbers Vena and Bui refilled coffee and served soft drinks and beer. By the time Brenda finished another love song, Bilbo Porter, usually not much of a drinker, had downed three bottles of Miller and was starting on his fourth.

After two more ballads, Brenda changed the mood when she sang an upbeat song she'd written called "Stop the Presses."

> Listen up, I'm warning you
> 'bout a new subversive plot
> To discredit the fine reporting
> in the newspaper you bought
> If you don't read the papers
> how the hell you gonna know
> If the ghost of Old Abe Lincoln's
> in bed with Molly O

The crowd, hooting and laughing, turned to look at Molly O, whose eyes widened in surprise at hearing her name in Brenda's song.

> Man, if you don't think that's news
> I've got some news for you
> You ain't gonna read 'bout talking bears
> in the *Saturday Review*
> Stop the presses,
> we don't need no more pills

If we'd all try Oprah's diet
it'd be the cure for all our ills

Soldier Starr shook his finger at Wanda Sue, a loud and long-winded fan of Oprah's diet, which had, over an eight-month period, enabled her to lose two pounds.

Don't get me wrong, I don't believe
in everything I read
But I don't want to overlook
some info I might need
If The Boss is getting married
I think I got a right to know
Just who it is I'm losing to
and where they're gonna go

Bilbo, inspired by both music and beer, jumped up and broke into a jig he called the Beto Shuffle which caused his arms to jump and twist like the jointed legs of a wooden puppet. And the crowd went wild.

I'm always keeping up
with foreign policy and stuff
But well-rounded readers know
That *Newsweek* ain't enough
What intellectual college boy
could ever ask for more
Than to read the gospel truth
in line at the grocery store

Still shuffling, Bilbo let out a whoop that later he would claim was required when performing the Beto.

So stop the presses
How can I sleep in peace
If Loni Anderson's selling arms
in the Middle East

> Stop the presses
> let me get my thrills
> A man from outer space
> is paying all Joan Collins' bills

When the song ended, the Honk exploded with cheers as Bilbo collapsed into his chair beside Peg and took a quick hit of her oxygen before he had a coughing fit and ordered another beer.

Brenda and Hamp played for nearly an hour. She stopped to sip water a couple of times, but her voice never sounded tired or thin.

When she announced her last song, the audience moaned with disappointment.

"Thanks for your encouragement," she said, "but a good rule in show business is to quit while you're ahead. And me and Hamp seem to be ahead right now, so we're gonna close with a song I call 'I Knew I Could Count on You.' "

> I've never known more certainly
> Just what I wanted in my life
> But you gave me no room to wonder
> I knew that lovin' you was right

Brenda smiled at Hamp as he joined her in the chorus.

> I knew I could count on you
> To push and pull me through
> I knew I could count on you
> To count on me, too

Vena, who had moved in beside Caney, felt him reach for her hand, and she gave it.

> God saw me in my despair
> Saw that I needed someone to care
> I needed you to make everything right
> And bring some love into my life

Everyone waited until Hamp struck the final note; then, leaping to their feet, they clapped, cheered and whistled.

Brenda stood and blew them a kiss. Hamp, nodding shyly when someone called out his name, tried to back away to let Brenda have her moment, but before he was beyond her reach, she slipped her arm around his waist and pulled him in beside her, then, together, they bowed.

Molly O, her eyes fixed on her daughter, was crying quietly as she whispered, "Oh, Dewey. I wish you were here tonight."

Chapter Twenty-Nine

VENA HAD BEEN FIGHTING off the fear that she was pregnant for over a month. In the beginning, she tried to tell herself she was worrying over nothing. After all, her periods had been erratic since the abortion when she was seventeen, so being late wasn't unusual for her. Sometimes she went seven or eight weeks without starting, but this time there was something else, something she couldn't quite grab hold of.

But she thought it might be connected to the dreams.

They started that first night she'd been with Caney, but they didn't have anything to do with him or with a baby. They were always about Helen.

In the dreams, she and Helen were at the home place, a tacky ranch eighteen miles from Thorndale, Texas, where their father worked as a well digger when he could find work, sold and traded horses when he couldn't.

He'd always liked calling their place the Takes Horse spread, but it didn't spread very far . . . six acres of scrub oak with a gray four-room house, barn and chicken coop, a shallow creek and a dozen junkers—mostly pickups wrecked on the central Texas farm roads. Bashed-up, burned-out hulls lined up like rotten teeth against a fence that sagged like a frown.

But in Vena's dream, it always looked better.

She would see herself, a child, walking across a neat lawn toward the house, a white house now with green shutters, windowboxes brilliant with flowers of yellows and reds, and on the porch, Helen, an adult, wearing a heavy coat and a man's hat pulled low on her forehead.

"I've been waiting for you, Vena," she would say as she came out to meet her. "I've got something for you."

Then Helen would take her hand to lead her to the pet cemetery out back where they had buried Helen's animals, the ones too sick or injured for Vena to save, and others found dead on the road or in the fields.

"I think it's here." Helen would point to the graves, mounds of dirt with tiny wooden crosses on which she had carved the names she'd given to the animals buried there.

Then she'd begin to dig with her hands, scooping out dirt quickly until she uncovered a squirrel or bird, cat or possum, dog, raccoon.

"Not here," she'd say, moving on to another grave, her digging becoming more frenzied with each one.

Then the dream would shift somehow and Helen would be in the barn, searching through the horse stalls, the tack room, the hayloft. By then she was panicked, bolting from place to place.

When she ran from the barn to the chicken coop, Vena followed, but more slowly now, her legs beginning to feel heavy, her feet weighted. With chickens flying, Helen tore into their nests, crying now and calling to Vena, "I think it's here," but her hands always came up empty.

Then she was galloping across a field planted in corn, but the crop was dead, the stalks so dry they rattled, dust swirling around her in dark clouds as she raced on. Vena, falling farther and farther behind, could hear Helen shouting from the distance, "Hurry, Vena!"

She could see Helen far ahead, but the dust, thicker and black, smelled of smoke that choked off her breath. If only, she thought, she could make it to the creek.

Then suddenly, the field burst into flame, the cornstalks blazing as, still, Helen called, "Hurry! Hurry!"

Vena tried to shout a warning as the fire spread before her, but it was too late. She could see flames begin to lick at the tail of Helen's coat, then, catching, crawl upward across her back, her shoulders, her hair.

And the last thing Vena would see was the hat Helen wore as fire flashed through the crown.

"Mr. Chaney," Bui said, starting out the back door with a load of trash, "is bus for you?"

"What?" Caney was dipping chili into a plastic bowl.

"Bus."

Caney looked up to see Bui pointing through the door.

"Yeah. I used to drive it to rodeos."

"Bus can go?"

"Nah. It was shot when I parked it there. And that was fourteen years ago."

"What wrong with bus?"

"Oh, the carburetor's bad, it needs a new brake drum. Grease pan's got a hole in it."

"I fix."

"Hell, Bui. It'd cost more money than it's worth. It'd have to have some tires, a new muffler . . ."

"Cost is free."

Caney clapped a lid on the bowl of chili, then turned to Bui.

"How's that?"

"My friend have other bus, some pieces still good."

"Parts, you mean?"

"Yes. Some parts can use for fix your bus. Can trade old for new. Bad for bester. I fix bus for no money, I think so."

"Well, if that's what you want to do, it's okay by me."

"Thank you, Mr. Chaney. Good to have bus go."

"What the devil you gonna do with it? Start your own bus line?"

"Yes, but only Sunday. My bus be a Sunday bus." Bui smiled, then went through the door, the screen slamming behind him.

Caney wheeled out front where Wilma, talking to Molly O, was waiting for the chili.

"Well, I thought she was great, just great," Wilma said. "I mean she is *so* talented, Molly O. I had no idea."

Molly O beamed. "Yeah, it was a good night, wasn't it?"

"Good? Why, it was wonderful. You know, when she goes back to Nashville—"

"Oh, she's not going back."

"She's not?"

"No. I believe she's got other things on her mind now."

"Like what?"

"Well, she and Hamp are getting pretty close."

"Oh, I could tell from the way he looked at her that something besides music was going on."

"I think things might be getting pretty serious between them."

"Here's your chili, Wilma."

"It's for Rex. He's home complaining of his gallbladder. So what does he want? Chili." Wilma made a face of disapproval, then pulled two bills from her purse and handed them to Caney. "Guess I'd better get down to the office. Got a couple of houses to show to Frances Dunn. You hear that she and Luter are splitting up?"

"Is that right?"

"I hear she's involved with someone, but I don't know who."

"Ask Wanda Sue."

"Oh, I won't have to ask. She'll volunteer it." Wilma slid off the stool, grabbed her purse and chili. "See you all later."

As soon as Wilma was out the door, Caney said, "You know, Molly O, you might be setting yourself up for another disappointment."

"How's that?"

"This thing you're building up about Hamp and Brenda."

"Now don't get the wrong idea, Caney. I'm not butting into that. That's their business."

"I have a hard time believing Brenda's through with show business."

"But things have changed now, Caney. After what she's been through, losing the baby and all."

"Molly O, she didn't 'lose' that baby."

"Well, same thing. You know, she's still so young that something like that—"

"Yeah, that's what I'm talking about. She's seventeen, pretty damned unpredictable. I'm just not sure you ought to be encouraging this business with Hamp right now."

"Oh no, Caney. I'm not. That's between her and Hamp. Last thing she needs is to have me trying to push her into something before she's ready."

"You feeling okay, Vena?" Molly O asked.

"Sure."

"Well, you're looking a little peaked, I've noticed. Kind of pale."

"Guess I didn't get enough sleep."

Molly O knew that Vena was sharing Caney's bed now, had known it for weeks, but she'd been too worried about Brenda to get into that. Besides, Caney seemed happy, really happy, for the first time since he'd come back from Vietnam.

"Why don't you sit down and let me get you a bowl of soup. Get off your feet for a while."

"Thanks, but I'm not hungry yet." Vena could feel a sourness in her mouth at the thought of food. "Maybe a little later."

Bui came from the kitchen with a tray of clean plates. Just as he set them down, he glanced outside and saw the mail truck pulling up, which sent him dashing out the door.

"That Bui is sure anxious about the mail these days."

They watched as he took the mail from the carrier, then ripped open a letter and stood beside the road reading it.

"Must've got what he was waiting for."

Moments later, he wheeled, sprinted across the lot, then burst through the door, his face wet with tears.

"My baby borned!"

"Your wife had a baby?" Molly O said in amazement.

"Yes! Baby girl! Wife and baby leave Vietnam soon. Come to America to living with me."

"Congratulations, Bui," Vena said. "Why didn't you tell us you were going to be a father?"

"Big surprise."

"Bui," Molly O said, hoping she didn't sound too much like Wanda Sue, "when did you say you left Vietnam?"

"More than two year."

Molly O, in what was a rare instance for her, was speechless.

"Take long time to make good baby," Bui explained. "Long time." Then, laughing, he hurried to the kitchen to tell Caney the news.

"Hamp, I hope I'm not becoming a pest," Molly O said.

"I'm glad you called. I wanted to talk to you, too."

"I just had to tell you how much I appreciate you getting Brenda involved in her music again."

"Well, it was your idea, really. But it was a good one."

"She's feeling so much better now. Feeling better about herself, and part of that is because of you."

"Mrs. O'Keefe, I think you know how I feel about Brenda."

"I do, Hamp. And I think she feels the same way about you."

"You do?" Hamp let out a breath and smiled. "That's what I'm hoping for."

"Me too. You're good for her."

"You know, I've . . . well, I've loved her since the first time I saw her, in seventh grade. But when we started to go together, when she said she'd go steady with me . . ."

"Oh, that's been ages ago, Hamp. She's changed, grown up, matured."

"That guy who was gonna marry her, the one who got her pregnant . . ."

"He's out of the picture, I can promise you that, Hamp. She never even mentions him anymore."

"I'm glad to know that."

"No, the only person she ever talks about is you."

"Really?"

"It's the truth."

"You know, I been thinking . . . Well, it might be too soon to talk about it, but . . ."

"What, Hamp? You can talk to me about anything."

"Well, I've been thinking that maybe I might ask Brenda to marry me. I mean, if that's all right with you."

"Oh, Hamp. Nothing could make me any happier than to see you two married, settled down. Starting a family."

"We could live out at my place. My folks have a trailer out there. Used to have a farm hand living in it, but it's empty now."

"It'd be perfect, Hamp. Just perfect!"

"Well, I wanted to talk to you about it first, see what you thought. See if it seemed too soon after her getting all tangled up, losing her baby."

"I don't think it's too soon at all! Besides, the best way to get over a miscarriage is to get pregnant again. The sooner the better."

"Okay, then. I'm gonna give this some more thought, but—"

"Good idea. Don't rush into anything, but don't wait too long, Hamp. You never can tell what tomorrow will bring. Just never can tell."

Molly O had gone home before seven following a brisk dinner trade. Since then, Vena had handled the dining room and the curb, enough business to keep her on the move until eight-thirty when everyone had cleared out except for a couple of beer drinkers at a table inside. But she could tell they were looking for more action than the Honk offered, so she figured they wouldn't stay much longer.

"Caney, I think I'm going to go on back and take a hot bath. I'm beat."

"You go on. Soon as those two leave, I'm gonna close up."

"Need any help?"

"Nah, Bui's still around."

"Where is he?"

"Out back."

"Gone to give Spot and the gelding their midnight 'snake'?"

"Yeah." Caney grinned.

"He's making a habit of that now, isn't he?"

"You know, after I saw how jumpy he was around the gelding, I never thought he'd go near a horse again. Now, he's treating the damned thing like a pet. If you've noticed that the stew's a little shy of carrots, it's because Bui's sneaking them out of the vegetable bin so there'll be enough for the gelding."

"You think he'll ever get up the nerve to ride him?"

"Might be. I haven't seen him back off from anything yet."

"Okay," Vena said as she started for the bedroom. "I'm going to go soak for a while."

"Don't you want something to eat first? I didn't see you have any supper."

"Yeah, I had a bite," she lied, then she turned and walked away.

The beer drinkers left a few minutes later and Caney turned off the sign, then went to the back door where he watched Bui coming back, his flashlight bobbing across the dark field.

But what he couldn't see was Sam Kellam's pickup pulled off on a dirt road a hundred yards east of the pasture. And Bui didn't see it either.

Chapter Thirty

$\mathcal{A}$s MOLLY O WANDERED the aisles of the Super Saver, she hummed the tune to one of Brenda's songs, and once, when she was going for a bag of potato chips, she even did a little dance step.

In the days following the concert, with her worry about Brenda fading, she was often surprised to find herself singing and dancing. But she wasn't embarrassed, even when someone in the Honk would notice and make some crack about it. She felt too happy to care.

She and Brenda were getting along so well now that she'd started leaving work right after supper, anxious to be at home. Since the concert, Brenda had been a different person, and they'd been able to talk, really talk, for the first time ever. One night they'd even talked about the abortion, and though Brenda didn't actually say she was sorry about it, Molly O could tell she was.

She was so eager now to get home that she hated taking the time to shop for groceries, but tonight she needed to pick up some snacks Brenda had asked for: Baby Ruths and Cap'n Crunch, Pop-Tarts and Cracker Jacks. And butter pecan ice cream.

When she turned down the frozen foods section, she was surprised to run into Life, but he wasn't at all surprised to see her.

He'd followed her to the Super Saver, had been following her ever since she'd entered the store. He'd started to catch up with her several times already, but he enjoyed watching the way she walked as she pushed the shopping cart ahead of her, so he'd been content just to stay behind. But now, as she turned down the last aisle, he figured he'd better make his move.

"Why, hello, Life. You're doing your shopping kind of late, aren't you?"

"No, this is the time I usually come here. It's not so crowded."

"Well, you must not need much."

Suddenly aware that he had no basket and nothing in his hands, Life reached quickly into one of the freezers and picked up the first thing he touched, a package of frozen lima beans.

"Well, I ran out of these."

"Lima beans? Why, you hate lima beans."

"No I don't," he said defensively.

"You sure do. Every time Caney has them on the lunch special, you have me substitute a salad."

"Yeah, but I eat them every evening."

"Life, you eat at the Honk every evening."

"I mean later. Like for a midnight snack."

"A midnight snack of lima beans?"

Seeing that this conversation was not going the way he planned, Life fought the urge to throw the lima beans back in the freezer, but instead, he decided to get to the opening line he'd been rehearsing.

"You know, it's funny me running into you here, 'cause I been meaning to talk to you about something."

"Life, you see me three times a day."

"Yeah, but sometimes it's kinda hard to finish a conversation with you at the Honk. Always someone buttin' in."

"What did you want to talk about?" Molly O pushed the cart forward a few steps, then reached into the freezer and pulled out a gallon of butter pecan ice cream. "Brenda just loves this," she said. "And I'm doing everything I can to fatten her up, but—"

"I was wondering if you'd like to go over to Poteau some night and take in a movie?"

"Oh, I don't think so. I haven't been to a movie in years."

"Well, it's not like you'd be taking up a bad habit if you went to one."

"Is that what you wanted to ask me, Life? Seems like you could've said that while I was pouring your coffee."

"No, but I thought if we was to go to Poteau, we might go out to dinner, some quiet place where we could talk. See, I've got something serious on my mind and—"

"Mrs. O'Keefe!"

A woman Life had seen at the concert rushed up and grabbed Molly O's hand.

"Hello, Mrs. Miles."

"I just wanted to tell you how much I enjoyed hearing our little girl sing the other night."

"I'm glad you came."

"I tried to get a short word with you after the concert, but there was such a crowd. Too many big people." Mrs. Miles shuddered. "You know, I get so nervous when I'm in a crowd of big people. I break out in a rash, teensy bumps all over my neck."

Life nudged Molly O's shopping cart with his boot.

"Oh, Mrs. Miles, this is my friend, Life Halstead. Life, Mrs. Miles was Brenda's kindergarten teacher."

"Yes. Brenda was my little singing valentine. A tiny talent on the big stage. And that voice! That marvelous voice coming from that wee girl. Oh, it just . . ."

Mrs. Miles was still talking as Life backed away.

". . . I knew then she was going to be a star. A shining little star. Why, when she put on her valentine costume with all those itty-bitty hearts . . ."

As Life rounded the end of the aisle and headed for the check-out, he sighed and shook his head. He didn't know what had gone wrong, but he figured it was the lima beans.

*   *   *

"I'm home, honey," Molly O called as she lugged two sacks of groceries to the kitchen cabinet.

"Brenda?"

After she switched on a couple of lights, she walked down the hall to check the bathroom and Brenda's bedroom, but both were dark.

She figured Brenda had gone to dinner with Hamp, and though she was glad they were together, she couldn't help but feel a little lonely. She'd gotten used to coming in and finding someone waiting for her.

She flipped through the mail, mostly junk and a few bills, including the one from Hazel's where she'd charged Brenda's outfit, but she decided not to think about that until payday.

She'd just slipped out of her shoes and turned on the TV when the phone rang.

"Hi, Mrs. O'Keefe. Can I talk to Brenda?"

"Why, she's not here, Hamp."

"Do you know where she is?"

"No, I just got home. As a matter of fact, I thought she was probably with you."

"I haven't talked to her all day."

"I called her around eleven, I think, just before I got busy with lunch. She was getting ready to wash her hair."

"Did she say anything about going out?"

"No. I can't imagine where she could be."

"Oh, she probably just went out for a while with one of her friends."

"I kind of doubt that. As far as I know, you're the only friend she's seen since she's been back."

"Maybe she walked over to the Quik-Trip."

"Hamp, I completely forgot. I talked her into going out to Wal-Mart today to put in her application."

"Well, it's almost seven. Seems like she'd be back by now."

"There's a good chance they already put her to work."

"Really?"

"Yeah. I talked to Little Fib Fry—you know, he's the store manager now—and he said he had a part-time slot open and if she wanted it, he'd hire her, so she might already be on the job."

"Boy, that sure seems strange. I just can't imagine Brenda working at Wal-Mart."

"Well, I can't say she was thrilled about the idea, but like I told her, she can work there till something better comes along. Might take a while, things being the way they are here right now, especially her without a high school diploma."

"Look, Mrs. O'Keefe, I think I'll run out to Wal-Mart, see if she's still there, but if I miss her, will you ask her to give me a call when she gets in?"

"Sure. Hamp, have you said anything to her yet? You know, what we talked about?"

"Not yet, but that's why I was hoping to see her tonight."

"Then I'll be sure she gets hold of you, Hamp. You can trust me on that."

As soon as Molly O recradled the phone, she noticed the grocery sacks still on the cabinet.

"Oh, my gosh."

The ice cream was already half-melted when she took it from the sack and opened her freezer. She had to shuffle packages around to make room, shoving meat and vegetables and waffles . . .

Waffles!

The box had been ripped open and the plastic bag, the bag where she kept her money, had been pulled out and emptied.

"No," she whispered. "No, baby. No."

She didn't run to Brenda's room, didn't even hurry, but by the time she stepped inside, she was so tired that she crawled onto her daughter's bed.

She sat in the dark for several minutes before she summoned enough energy to turn on the light, but there wasn't much to see because Brenda hadn't left much behind—three dirty socks, a can of hairspray, two guitar picks and enough hurt to fill a fifty-foot Skyline in the Cozy Oaks Trailer Park.

Chapter Thirty-One

MOLLY O CAME ON to work the next morning, weepy and exhausted. She hadn't slept for twenty-eight hours, but it wasn't the first time she'd spent a night walking the floor in despair.

When Caney found out what Brenda had done, he was so furious that he raged around the rest of the morning, his anger splattering like bacon in hot grease. He banged around in the kitchen, slamming skillets onto burners, hacking the meat cleaver into the cutting board, knocking cans of corn and peas from the pantry shelves and cussing onions and eggs as if he'd found them sneaking around telling lies.

But once, when Molly O came back to the sink to wash her hands, he'd grabbed her around the waist and buried his head in her chest, held her without a word, then rolled away and smacked five pounds of ground beef, punishment, perhaps, for whatever grief that cow had brought to its mother.

Vena, though a good listener, could think of little to say that would ease Molly O's pain. She saw too much of her seventeen-year-old self in Brenda, and the memories of what she'd put Helen through were still too raw.

Bui wasn't quite sure what was going on, but while he was bus-ing a table, scraping uneaten food into a pan for Spot, Molly O said what a shame it was to see so much good food going to waste.

"And with the little children starving in China," she said, which caused her to cry, leaving Bui with the impression that her sorrow was caused by her tender feelings for hungry children, especially those in China.

Oddly enough, Molly O found her greatest comfort in Life, who stayed through the morning, listening, patting her hand and opening up to her about his own daughter, something he'd never done before.

"She was a mess, I'll tell you that. Reba did her best with the girl, tried to keep her in church, steer her away from trouble, but that church stuff don't always work out when a girl takes to sin like a kid to mud.

"I guess Reba had some notion of what laid ahead when her girl was born, so she named her Chastity, like she thought the name would make some kind of difference. She just as well have called her Screwin' Around. It seemed to fit her better."

"Oh, Life. You oughtn't to say such a thing."

"Wait now, hear me out."

Molly O nodded, then wiped her nose with a balled-up paper napkin.

"When Chastity was fifteen, she ran away from home for the first time. Came back three months later with one of them venal diseases. Like to've broke Reba's heart, but she didn't give up, no way. Reba was like that. Determined.

"Well, the girl wasn't back no time before she started drinking, running with a hard crowd and got herself knocked-up. But she got drunk one night, fell out of the back of a pickup and she didn't have to worry no more about having a baby. At least not that one."

Molly O said, "Life, I had no idea you and Reba had been through something like that. And here I am telling you my troubles."

"No way you could know, Molly O. We was living in Indiana then, a long time before we come to Oklahoma.

"Anyway, a few months later, Chastity took off with a guy just out of prison. Had a kid by him, little boy named Jake. Then she lived with a fella for a while down in Alabama. He gave her a two-inch scar across her forehead and another baby before he kicked her out.

"By then, she was a drunk. Got arrested, I don't know how many times. Public intoxication, prostitution, resisting arrest.

"Me and Reba finally went and got the kids to come live with us, and let me tell you, when we left the rat-hole Chastity was living in, I figured it was the last time I'd see her alive, given the direction she was headed.

"But then, the damnedest thing. Chastity was dancing in one of them naked clubs down in Georgia when she met a guy in some hamburger joint. A machinist named Don Buck, a real decent fella. And believe it or not, Chastity got herself together, got married, came got her kids and settled down.

"They been married now, over twenty years. Got grandkids, go to church regular. A real comfort to Reba before she died, I'll tell you that."

"I love stories with nice endings, Life." Molly O started crying again. "Just like a fairy tale. But with Brenda . . ."

"Look, the point I'm trying to make here is that things ain't settled with Brenda yet. There's more to come. Some good, some bad, but all you can do is wait. She's going in another direction now, one you didn't pick out for her, but it's her direction."

"But she didn't even leave me a note."

"What the hell was she gonna say? 'I stole your money, lied to you, broke your heart.' She didn't need to tell you what you already knew."

"I just wish I could—"

"Molly O, people change. Look at us. We're not who we was at seventeen or thirty or fifty. Hell, I ain't who I was yesterday.

"But here's what you have to hang on to. All the things you taught Brenda, they're inside her now, like little seeds. You planted them there and someday they'll start to grow. And when they do, she'll remember what her mama told her about right and wrong."

"You really think so, Life?"

"I sure do."

Molly O managed a feeble smile.

"But while you're waiting for that to happen, you got your own life to live."

"I'm not sure I know how."

"Well, I'll tell you how you're gonna start. We're gonna get out of here, go out to the lake and have a picnic."

"Oh, I couldn't do that. Leave Caney here at lunchtime."

"Caney," Life called back to the kitchen, "think you can fix me and Molly O up with a picnic lunch?"

"A what?"

"A picnic. You know, a few sandwiches, maybe some potato salad. Something cold to drink."

"Sure, Life," Caney said, unable to hide his surprise. "I'll have it together in no time."

"Good. 'Cause we're in kind of a hurry." Life smiled at Molly O. "We've already wasted too much time as it is."

Vena poured herself a cup of coffee, then joined Bui at the table where he was eating a late supper.

"You like American food?" she asked as she watched him pour soy sauce over his meatloaf and mashed potatoes.

"American food very good." He took a bite, then made a face of approval. "But Vietnam food bester." He paused as he mentally ran through one of Galilee's lessons, then corrected his mistake. "Vietnam food better."

"I've never tasted it."

"My wife come, you eat Vietnam food. You like it, I think so."

"When will she get here?"

"Maybe soon, maybe late. Hard to knowing. She leave Vietnam in boat, then boat go where boat go."

"What does that mean?"

"Sometime boat go to Thailand, sometime Malaysia, sometime

Indonesia. Boat go where boat go." He shrugged then to show he understood the nature of fate. "My boat go . . . my boat went Malaysia. Many days of sea, then two years in refugee camp."

"Two years?"

"Very hard to getting papers for America. Must wait long time." Bui added more soy sauce to his potatoes. "I rat catcher in my camp. Camp fourteen. Catch many rats," he said with pride. "More over one thousand. Win prize for best rat catcher."

"Is a refugee camp like a prison?"

"No! Not like prison. In Vietnam, I stay in prison long time. Prison bad, very bad."

"Bui, you mind if I ask you why you were in prison?"

"In prison for stealing rice from boss of black market." Bui could see Vena's confusion. "Do what have to do. Mother sick, sister sick. Not enough rice, so I steal. Go to prison. But . . ." He turned his hands up, palms open, "Mother well, sister well."

Vena shook her head.

"World keep go turning round," he said, then he smiled.

"Yeah, I guess you're right. World just keep go turning round."

Bui poured the pan of scraps into Spot's bowl while the little dog waited patiently.

"Eat all, Spot." Bui gently cupped the dog's chin in his hand and raised its head. Then, his look solemn, his voice serious, he said, "Remember, Spot. Little childs in China starving."

He waited until he was satisfied that the dog was eating with good appetite, then stepped over the low fence and switched on the flashlight as he started across the field.

The night, warm and still, was dark, the light of the quarter moon only slicing now and then through a tear in the thick blanket of clouds.

He smiled to imagine Nguyet with him here on a night like this, holding tightly to his arm, jumpy at the sounds of crickets and cicadas, rushing her steps as stiff weeds brushed against her ankles.

Bui liked being in the open at night. No roof, no walls, just space—space that stretched all the way to Vietnam. But tonight, though he would not know it until too late, he was not the only one crossing this field of darkness.

"*Phong Ma*," he called, his voice echoing in the heavy, still air.

He hadn't told Caney and Vena that he'd given the gelding a name. *Phong Ma*. Wind Dancer. For now, the name was a secret that only he and the horse shared.

When Bui unfastened the gate, the clank of the chain caused the man who was following, hidden now by the bus, to stop and rub at his wrists . . . the wrists of the bloody, naked boy long ago chained to the door of a church.

As Bui walked into the pasture, he could see the horse coming to him while, snuffling, he smelled Bui's familiar scent and the scent of the carrot.

"Hello, my friend," Bui said when they met. "You are happy to see me, I think so."

The gelding dipped his nose, sniffing at Bui's pocket.

"Oh, you think something hide there," he said as he pulled the carrot out and held it before him. But before the horse could take it, Bui, laughing, ran in a wide, slow circle with the gelding trotting along behind him.

When Bui stopped, he waited until the horse neared, then took several running steps backward.

"*Phong Ma*. You must come quick."

Finally, Bui stood still, holding the carrot behind his back while the gelding nudged him in the chest with its nose.

"Okay, my friend. You work hard for carrot, now is yours."

Unmindful now of the animal's teeth, Bui held the carrot until the horse took the last bite, neither of them noticing the dark figure slipping soundlessly through the open gate.

Then, suddenly, the gelding lifted his head and snorted.

"What the matter? Want more carrot?" Bui teased. "Well, I have surprise. I bring two." But when he offered the second carrot, the horse backed away. With his head high, his ears down, he whinnied.

From her fence behind the Honk, Spot began to bark—sharp, shrill yelps answering the horse's warning.

"So long, Hooks," Caney said.

"See you folks tomorrow."

Vena was refilling Bilbo's coffee when Hooks fired up his truck. A second later, the dog started barking.

"Sounds like you've turned that mutt of yours into a watchdog, Vena," Bilbo Porter said.

"That's strange. I've never heard her bark before."

"She probably got scared when she heard Hooks crank up that old Dodge," Caney said.

"Yeah, that damned thing clankin' and clatterin'." Bilbo laughed. "Hell, it makes me want to bark."

When Bui heard a twig snap somewhere behind him, he turned toward the gate and saw a dark figure moving across the pasture, coming toward him.

"Miss Vena?" he called, but there was no answer.

When he directed the beam of the flashlight across the field, he saw the face of the man called Sam Kellam.

"What you want?" Bui asked, his voice pitched high with alarm. Then he saw a glint of steel as Sam raised a gun and fired.

Bui felt a jolt of pain in his hand when the flashlight was ripped from his fingers and, still shining, cartwheeled through the air.

"What was that?"

"Huh?"

"That noise."

"I didn't hear anything."

"Sounded like a shot."

"Probably Hooks' truck backfiring."

The gelding, frenzied now, whinnied and stamped the ground, then reared, legs windmilling the air.

Holding his injured hand before him as if offering it in greeting, Bui took a step forward as Sam fired twice more.

The first bullet spun Bui like a wind-up toy, the second slammed him to the ground.

"Hell, those are gunshots."
"Came from out back."
"Oh, my God! Bui's out there."

The gelding, half-crazed with fear, shuffled from side to side, kicking up clods of dirt that stung Bui's face and arms.

In the weakening beam of the flashlight a few feet away, Bui could see boots crossing the ground in long, quick strides, coming close, and someone said, *"Em yêu Nguyệt,"* but the sound seemed to come from some great distance.

Then, his vision beginning to cloud, he saw in a haze of shadow and light the boots just inches away. Saw the gelding rear again, towering, heard the rough bark of human fear. Another shot fired. A powerful huff of the gelding's breath. A crack of bone.

The shudder of earth as some great weight dropped to ground.

Vena was already out the back door, running, when the last shot was fired.

Halfway across the field, she stumbled and fell to both knees; then, gasping, she pulled herself up and ran on.

Just before she reached the gate, she heard Caney call her name, but didn't have enough breath to answer.

As moonlight broke through the clouds, she saw them—the gelding on its side, legs thrashing, and Bui, still as death.

Then she saw another figure, a man, his legs pinned beneath the gelding's hindquarters. And she recognized Sam Kellam, even with part of his face caved in.

Chapter Thirty-Two

CARL PHELPS and his deputy were the first to arrive, but not by much. A highway patrol trooper pulled in a minute later, followed soon by a city police car, then another and another, until the pasture looked as if one of Big Fib's spaceships had landed, whirling flashes of red and blue lighting the night sky.

The lights and sirens had, of course, attracted so much attention that by the time the ambulance arrived, the parking lot of the Honk was a maze of vehicles, and a steady stream of the curious was snaking across the field, spilling through the fence and into the pasture.

The ambulance driver, slowed by traffic on the road, negotiated his way across the lot and around the cafe, but before he reached the gate, he had to stop twice, once for a stooped old woman walking with a cane and again for a little girl in pajamas and cowboy boots who ran across his path.

Caney had made his way into the pasture just seconds before the sheriff arrived, but he might not have made it at all without help. As he was trying to maneuver the chair across the ravine, it toppled and would have tipped over if Bilbo had not caught up in time to right it and push Caney to level ground.

He couldn't make out much in the dark as he rolled across the pasture, but when Carl pulled in and drove past him, the head-lights of his cruiser illuminated all too clearly what lay ahead.

Sam Kellam was pinned beneath the horse, but Caney could tell it didn't matter. Sam wasn't going anywhere.

The gelding, wild with pain and fear, tried to get up when Carl's cruiser roared in, but his legs, jerking spasmodically, could not purchase ground. When Carl cut off the siren, the animal gave up the struggle, but not before a flailing hoof crushed Sam's watch, leaving it as ruined as the man who wore it.

Bui lay ten feet away, sprawled on his back, his head twisted to the side and his right arm extended as if stretching to pick up a carrot just beyond his reach.

Vena, kneeling beside him, used one hand to brush dirt from his cheek, the other to press against his side where blood seeped be-tween her fingers.

"What the hell happened here, Caney?" Carl asked as he stepped out of the cruiser and slammed the door.

"The ambulance . . ."

"On the way."

Caney rolled in beside Vena, leaned forward and touched her arm. "Is he . . . Can you tell if—"

"He's got a pulse," she said, "but it's not very strong."

Danny Starr, the reporter for the *Weekly Ledger,* pulled up and parked behind Carl's cruiser as two more police cars sped through the gate. When the gelding began to thrash again at the sound of the sirens, Danny hauled his camera out and started shooting pic-tures.

By then, a ring of onlookers was forming, pressing forward as more pushed in behind. Their conversations were hushed except for two teenage boys who laughed in false bravado, too loud and too long. But when a toddler cried, "Mommy, man's got a boo-boo on his head," the crowd was stilled as they parted to let the mother carry her child away.

When the ambulance arrived, the medics hit the ground run-ning, but as they hurried toward Sam, Carl said, "You boys can't do him any good."

As they moved in on Bui, Vena scooted to the side to give them room, then watched without comment while they started to work. But when they tore his shirt open, she got up and stepped to the edge of a twisted knot of bystanders straining for a closer look.

One bullet had ripped into his shoulder where splinters of bone protruded through the skin. The other had pierced his side, just below his ribs, where blood, more black than red, ran in a rivulet across his belly and pooled in the depression of his navel.

Danny had worked his way to the center of activity, aiming his camera first one way, then another, but when he leaned between the medics to get a close shot of Bui, Carl yelled at him to "stay the hell out of the way."

Danny, accustomed to such warnings from the sheriff, got the shot he wanted, then turned to train his camera on Sam and the gelding, while Carl made his way around the medics, then hunkered beside Caney's chair.

"What can you tell me about this, Caney?"

"Not much. I was in the cafe when Bui came out here. . . ."

"What for?"

"Oh, he'd started coming out every night about this time. He liked to check on the gelding."

"Was Sam in the cafe tonight?"

"Huh-uh."

"I heard you two mixed it up in there a few weeks back."

"Yeah, we did."

"What was that about?"

"Sam took in after Bui, and I—"

"So there was bad blood between them then?"

"Hell, Bui didn't even understand what was going on. It was just Sam. You know how he was."

"Did Bui own a gun?"

"Not that I know of. . . ."

"So you figure—"

"I figure Sam was out here waiting for him."

"Look's like it could've happened that way." As Carl stood,

bones popped. "Damned knees." He took a couple of half steps to work the stiffness out. "You got a smoke?"

Caney shook a cigarette from his pack, but before Carl took it, he saw the district attorney coming toward him, trailed by a lawyer from the courthouse.

"Oh, crap," he said as he headed to meet them.

Caney turned his attention back to Bui as one of the medics ran to the ambulance for the stretcher.

Vena moved in beside Caney and put her hand on his shoulder just before someone called his name. They turned to see Hooks and Quinton elbowing their way through the gawkers.

"You okay, Caney?" Hooks sounded like he'd been running.

"Yeah."

Quinton looked him over, then spit into the dirt and shook his head. "We run into Wanda Sue down at the Texaco. She said you'd been shot."

"Hell, by tomorrow, she'll have me buried," Caney said, but with no trace of humor.

"He gonna be all right?" Hooks asked, gesturing toward Bui.

"I don't know." A shiver made Vena rub at goose bumps on her arms. "But he's still breathing."

They watched as the stretcher was positioned and the medics lifted Bui onto it. He had a tube down his throat, an IV in his arm, monitors attached to his chest, but there was no sign of consciousness.

"I'm going with you boys," Caney said, rolling in behind the medics as they moved toward the ambulance.

"Sorry, but we'd have to have clearance to take you."

"I've already got clearance," Caney said.

"No, sir. What I mean is, we'd have to radio in and—"

"I'm going in that ambulance."

When the medics lifted the stretcher inside the ambulance, one climbed inside to tend to Bui while the driver turned to Caney and said, "Sir, it'll take time, and I don't think you want to slow this down."

"No, sir. I don't. So let's just—"

"But I have to have clearance."

"He's got clearance," Carl yelled as he broke away from the DA and came striding toward them. "Mine!"

Then, without hesitation, Quinton and Hooks lifted Caney, chair and all, into the back of the ambulance. The medic shrugged, slammed the doors and crawled into the cab, firing up the siren as he pulled away.

By the time the second ambulance arrived, Vena, with the help of Bilbo and Carl's deputy, had the gelding up and moving—stiff, slow, limping—but moving. And as soon as the medics removed Sam's body, the last of the spectators wandered away, having less interest in a wounded horse than a man half-dead, and another who'd made it all the way.

The vet, Doc Corley, pulled in as Vena was leading the limping gelding into the barn.

Doc had been in Sequoyah for over forty years, but recent back surgeries following a tussel with a Black Angus bull had limited his mobility. He'd been trying for three years to take in a partner to do the heavy work of treating livestock, leaving him to work with small pets, the animals he favored anyway, but so far he hadn't had any luck.

"Well, is this the killer horse?" Doc asked as he shuffled into the barn.

"He look like a killer to you?"

The exhausted gelding stood unmoving, his head hanging, his ears drooping, as Vena rubbed his muzzle.

"So what've we got here?"

"Bullet wound, right foreleg."

Careful to keep his back straight, Doc took his time getting down on one knee. When he reached for the damaged leg, the horse threw his head and whinnied, but Vena had a halter on him and held it steady.

Doc tilted his head so he could see through his bifocals as he examined the gelding's leg.

"Cannon bone's splintered. Bullet's still in there."

"Can you take it out?"

"Don't want to try," he said. "Start digging around in there, sure to damage some tendons."

"So what do you think?"

"Well," he said as he grunted with the effort of standing. "Doubt he'll ever recover from this. I'd say the humane thing to do is put him down."

"You mean without even trying—"

"Lady, I guess I've treated four, five thousand horses. Snakebite, gangrene, broken legs, twisted intestines, crushed hooves . . . and bullet wounds. And in my opinion, this animal oughta be put down. Save him a lot of misery, a lot of pain, and it'll all come to the same thing in the end. Might as well do it now and—"

"No, I can't do that."

"I was under the impression that this horse belongs to Caney. Brim Neely told me that he—"

"It's Caney's, but he'd say the same thing if he was here."

"You sure of that?"

"Yes. I am."

"Okay." Doc reached for his bag. "I'll give him a tetanus shot, start him on antibiotics. And something for pain. But I'll check back tomorrow," he said, cutting his eyes at Vena, "when Caney's here."

When Vena got back to the Honk, she found Duncan Renfro, the only one inside, going silently about the business of measuring the shelves along the back wall. She picked up the phone to call Duncan's wife, but midway through dialing, she saw Life's pickup barrel in and slam to a stop when it hit the guardrail out front.

Molly O jumped out before the truck had even stopped bouncing and hit the door yelling.

"Oh, God! Is it true? Vena, tell me it's not true."

She went limp then and might've fallen if Life had not rushed through the door in time to steady her and lead her to a chair. Crying, she lowered her head to the table.

"He's still alive." Vena slid an arm around Molly O's shoulder. "When he left here, he was still alive."

"How bad off is he?" Life asked.

"I don't know. I stayed here to wait for the vet. Even if Caney knew anything, I doubt he'd try to call, knowing I would be out back, and—"

Molly O raised her head, dazed by what she'd just heard. "Caney? You mean he's—"

"That damned Wanda Sue!" Life pulled off his cap and slapped it against the counter. "She said Caney was dead. Said Sam killed him."

"Well, she got that wrong. Sam's dead. And Bui's in pretty bad shape. . . ."

"I don't understand," Molly O said. "I don't—"

"Look, let's get Duncan out of here first, then we'll go to the hospital."

"I'll take Duncan home," Life said. "You go on and I'll lock up here."

"Then Molly O can go with me in Bui's car."

"But—"

"Come on. I'll tell you about it on the way."

They were all gathered in the surgical waiting room except for Bilbo, who'd gone outside again to smoke. Vena, Molly O and Hooks sat side by side in a line of chairs against the wall while Quinton dozed in the corner and Life paced the length of the room. Caney, with his back to them, stared through a window overlooking the emergency entrance.

At the sound of approaching footsteps, Vena tensed and leaned forward, Molly O's unopened magazine slipped from her lap, Life came to a stop and Caney turned from the window. But when a man in scrubs passed without comment, they slumped with disappointment, then rubbed at tired eyes and stiff necks.

"How about I get us some coffee," Life said.

"Here. I've got some quarters."

"None for me."

"I'll take mine black," Carl Phelps said as he stepped through the door.

"You're puttin' in a late night," Hooks said.

"Looks like I'm not the only one." Carl pulled a chair up beside Caney, sat down and stretched out his legs. "How's he doing?"

"Still in surgery," Caney said. "You get your business settled out at the place?"

"For tonight. Still some loose ends to wrap up, but that kind of thing takes some time. Damned DA's got a notion the Vietnamese fella hit Sam in the head with a rock. He wants an autopsy on Sam, though I think it's a waste of time."

Bilbo, just back from his smoke, said, "Right. Sam shot the kid twice and while he was falling, he picked up a rock and bashed Sam's head in. Shee-ut!"

Bilbo looked for a place to spit, his way of showing disgust, then thought better of it and shook his head instead.

"I went by the Hi-Ho," Carl said. "Found out Sam had been in there for a couple of hours drinking straight shots of Wild Turkey. Did some tough talking, said he was going gook hunting. Tried to stir up some interest, wanted the Mosier brothers to go with him, but they weren't drunk enough to take him up on it, so he left alone. About fifteen minutes before he ambushed the Vietnamese guy, the way I figure."

"Sam could never handle his liquor," Quinton said.

"He was a mean son of a bitch, even when he was sober." Carl pulled off his hat and ran his fingers through his hair. "Guy told me he saw Sam string a German shepherd up by the neck, then beat it to death with a two-by-four 'cause it muddied the door of his truck."

"Shee-ut." Unable to control his anger, Bilbo spit into a potted plant. "Shame that horse didn't bash his brains out sooner."

"Oh, Brim Neely came by your place, Caney. Caught me just before I left. Said he wasn't much surprised when he heard about what happened. Told me that gelding had always gone crazy around guns. Said he threw him once when they came up on some target shooters, and you know yourself that Brim's not been on many could unsaddle him.

"Anyway, I'm going to need a statement from you, Caney. But we can take care of that later, when this is—"

Carl was stopped in midsentence when he looked up and saw Galilee Jackson, Reverend Thomas and several parishioners of the AME Church standing in the doorway.

No one spoke for several moments, then Galilee stepped forward.

"We're here to see about Mr. Boo," she said. "He's a friend of ours."

Chapter Thirty-Three

$\mathcal{T}$HE HONK, closed for three days, didn't reopen until after the funeral on Friday morning. But when it did, those who came didn't come because they were hungry. Most stopped by just to talk, trying to understand all that had happened.

A few came directly from the cemetery. They'd gone simply to pay their respects to Sam's mother and his brother, Don, who came in from Idaho where they'd moved not long after Kyle Kellam died. But though Don had gone into the ministry, he didn't conduct the graveside service for Sam as most had expected. He'd left that up to the Baptist preacher who hadn't known Sam at all, figuring a stranger might find better things to say about Sam than he could.

Many of the conversations that Friday morning took place at Caney's counter where those assembled were as hard-pressed to find praise for Sam as his brother was. But since they felt bound not to speak ill of the dead, and with Sam barely into his first hour underground, they recalled with admiration that his boots were always polished and he'd kept his pickup clean.

But much of the talk following Sam's funeral took place out back where a half dozen men, black and white, were working to restore Caney's bus.

Reverend Thomas, Brother Junior and Sister Grace's husband, Jennings Washington, had brought parts pirated from their wrecked Sunday bus, while the others—Bilbo, Soldier and Hooks, contributed some tools, a couple of good tires and a steering wheel Quinton had found at the junkyard north of town.

But they all brought their enthusiasm for helping Bui repair the bus, a project they'd learned about while they waited together at the hospital on Monday night.

No one, however, was more zealous than Galilee who was in the kitchen preparing chicken and dumplings, purple-hull peas and cornbread.

She had insisted on helping out with the cooking since Caney was spending nights at the hospital and Vena stayed through the days. Molly O was happy for the help and the company, though most of their conversations took place in whispers for fear of waking Caney who hadn't returned from the hospital until almost eight that morning.

They needn't have worried, though. Caney had gone to sleep as soon as he crawled into bed, a sleep so deep he hadn't even heard Vena when she was sick in the bathroom just minutes after he closed his eyes.

When Vena stepped into the cubicle in ICU, she made sure to have a smile on her face, just in case. But nothing had changed. Bui was still in a coma.

The surgeon had repaired the damaged spleen, put in a stint for the contused kidney and treated the busted clavicle. But with the concussion, all they could do was wait. And they'd been waiting for three days.

Vena pulled a chair up beside the bed to do what the nurses had told her to do. Talk, they'd said. Pretend he can hear you. Just talk.

"So, how're you doing today, huh? Yeah, I can tell. You look a lot better."

She reached through the rails of Bui's bed and curled her fingers around his.

"Me? I'm fine. Great. I've got this one little problem, though. Looks like I'm pregnant. You're the first to know.

"Happy about it? No, I wouldn't say that. Well, I'll try, but I don't know if I can make you understand.

"See, Bui, I just don't have the right stuff to be a mother. There's something missing in me, I think. I mean, I don't feel anything for what's growing inside me. And that's pretty sad, isn't it?

"Other women, they get pregnant, they think it's the most wonderful thing ever happened to them. That's all they can talk about. Is it a boy? Is it a girl? They start thinking up names and making quilts. They buy baby beds and teddy bears, start taking vitamins, stop smoking.

"Well, yeah, I have, but that's because they make me so sick. And not just cigarettes, either. Coffee, onions, eggs. Let's not talk about it or I'll be sick again.

"But what I'm trying to say is, I don't see myself holding a baby in my arms and singing lullabies. God, I don't even know a lullaby.

"Now my sister Helen, she would've been a great mother. She loved kids. Talked about having babies when she was just a little girl. Made me play house—she'd be the mother and I'd have to be the baby. Sure, I went along with it. Had to. She was my big sister.

"But me? What I wanted was to go somewhere. Get on a horse and ride as far as I could. Climb into the back of my dad's pickup, no matter where he was going. I just wanted to move.

"I've always been like that. Get on the road, see where it would take me. I figured there was always something new, something waiting for me just down the highway or in the next town or across the next mountain.

"So, that's the story. Probably hard for you to understand, you being so happy about your baby, but—"

A nurse stopped at the door, peered in at Bui, smiled at Vena, then disappeared.

"I guess my time's about up, Bui. . . . I know, but we just get ten minutes with you, and they'll only let us come back here every two hours.

"No, Caney doesn't know, has no idea. He's got enough prob-lems of his own. I mean, what would he do with a baby? And what about when she's older? What if she turned out like Brenda? Hell, what if she turned out like me? Can't stay in one place, can't really call any place home. And you know why? Because home doesn't last. That's for the movies.

"Look what happened to me and Helen. Look at yourself, Bui. You live in a church. Caney lives in a cafe. You ask me, no one has a home anymore.

"So I'm going to get rid of the baby. But it's not the first time for me. No, it doesn't hurt. Not the physical part, anyway.

"The other part? I was only seventeen, so it's hard for me to re-member exactly what I felt.

"Oh, sometimes I'd see a baby and I'd think about mine. But one funny thing . . . see, if I'd gone ahead and had that baby, it would've been born in April. So I picked a date. April eighteenth. Now, every April, on the eighteenth, I sort of go through the birthday thing in my mind. And I think, Today she would've been five. This week, she would be eleven. Next Tuesday, she'd be fif-teen. That's crazy, isn't it? But . . ."

Vena pulled the strap of her purse over her shoulder as she stood.

"You know what, Bui? I've never told anyone this stuff. And I don't know for sure why I'm telling you except I'm leaving and I figure you'll keep it to yourself after I'm gone.

"I can't wait much longer, but I'd like to stick around until you're back on your feet again. Caney never really needed me there, but he needs you. You and Molly O.

"No, I won't be coming back. See, Bui, Caney's a good man. A fine man. He deserves a hell of a lot better than me."

"Excuse me, ma'am." The nurse was the same one who had stopped by earlier. "I'm sorry, but—"

"Sure. I'm going."

Then Vena leaned over and brushed her fingers across Bui's cheek. "You rest now. I'll see you in a couple of hours. And we'll talk again."

*   *   *

Vena didn't usually get back from the hospital until well after dark, when Caney took over. So when she walked in at four-thirty, he knew something had changed.

"What's wrong?" he asked, steeling himself for bad news.

"He woke up, Caney! He woke up an hour ago!"

Molly O whooped as she ran from the kitchen and grabbed Vena in her arms. Caney, a smile spreading across his face, let out a breath he felt he'd been holding for a long time.

"Did you talk to him?" Molly O asked. "Does he seem . . . well, did he make sense?"

"He didn't talk much, didn't act like he remembered what happened, but he asked if he'd had a letter from his wife and he told me to be sure the gelding gets his carrots."

"Oh, thank you, Jesus," Molly O whispered.

"His damned carrots." Caney laughed then, his first in many days.

"The doctor came in just before I left. Said they've got the infection under control, and he thinks the urologist might take the stint out tomorrow, see how his kidney's going to work. But he told me everything looks good."

"I'm going to call Life." Molly O reached for the phone.

"I was reading to him, Caney," Vena said as she slid onto a stool. "Some fishing magazine I found in the waiting room. And when I finished, I looked up and he was looking at me. He said, 'Miss Vena, you go to fishing today?' "

Vena let the tears come then as Caney reached across the counter and took her face in his hands.

"He's going to make it, Vena."

"Yeah. He is."

Molly O hung up the phone and said, "Life's coming right over. He thinks we should have a glass of champagne, but he doesn't like it, so he's bringing a jug of cider."

"I'll settle for a glass of tea."

"You look so tired, Vena. Let me get you something to eat. How about some of Galilee's chicken and dumplings?"

"That sounds good."

Molly O scooted off to the kitchen as the phone rang. "I'll get it back here," she said. "I'll bet a dollar it's Wanda Sue trying to get a scoop on the news."

"She's right," Caney said. "You look worn out."

"How about you? You don't look much more rested than I feel."

"I slept till almost noon."

"How'd things go here today?"

"Fine. Looks like it'll be a while before they have the bus running, but Molly O and Galilee kept things going out here."

"Has she left?"

"Yeah, not long ago. Doc Corley was by again."

"And?"

"He says the gelding's not any better. Thinks an infection is setting in. He's changing the medication, but . . ."

"But what?"

"He still thinks we should put the gelding down."

"What did you say?"

"I said we'd give it a few more days."

Caney had fallen asleep around eleven, while Vena, feigning restlessness, sat in the dining room with a book. She waited until nearly midnight when she heard him snoring softly before she slipped into the kitchen, grabbed a long sharp knife, then stepped outside, closing the door soundlessly behind her.

She had prepared what she would need earlier that evening when she went to the barn to check on the gelding—dead branches and dry twigs for the fire and the bundle she'd hidden nearby.

"Sorry to make you walk on that leg," she said as she haltered the gelding. "But you've suffered enough."

After she led the horse from the barn, she tethered him to a sycamore not far from the kindling she'd stacked. Once she had the fire going, she retrieved the secreted bundle and laid out what was inside. Then she picked up the knife and went back to the gelding.

"This won't take long, boy."

The animal turned his head toward her, his eyes reflecting light from the fire as she cut switches of his mane and tail, whispering words to calm him as she worked.

When she finished, she squatted beside the fire to pour water from a plastic bottle into the dirt, then used her hands to work it into loose, thin mud.

With the fire blazing, she picked up a large strip of clean cotton cloth and waved it back and forth through the smoke coming from the flames, and as she did, she started to chant, words and sounds passed from her great-grandfather to her grandfather to her, from a memory as old as her tribe.

Still chanting, she stripped sage from the stems she'd gathered, making a small pile of the weed in front of her. Then she took a handful of sage and one of horsehair and rolled them together between the palms of her hands.

Finally, she spread mud on the cloth, then worked the sage-and-horsehair mixture into it.

Finished, she went to the gelding, knelt and pressed the poultice to his leg, while the moon cast them in lacy patterns through the branches of the sycamore tree.

Chapter Thirty-Four

MOLLY O AND GALILEE sparred for five days over where Bui would stay when he left the hospital, but Galilee finally won out, her strongest argument being that she'd midwifed fifty-three babies. Caney couldn't quite see the connection, but he was smart enough to keep his mouth shut.

Fresh from her victory, Galilee spent the next twenty-four hours working to make her house patient ready. She aired pillows, bleached sheets, boiled dishes and sanitized the bathroom, growing faint once with the fumes of ammonia.

She hung a small silver bell on the poster of her spare bed, lowered the shades to soften the light and prepared a tray with bandages, alcohol, liniments and salves.

Then she turned down the ringer on her telephone, lettered a "Do Not Disturb" sign for the door, warned the neighborhood children about noise and threatened two barking dogs.

Long acquainted with the cleansing powers of wild greens, she made pot liquor from poke, dock and lamb's-quarters gathered from a nearby field, then squeezed a pitcherful of orange juice to cool in the fridge.

Late that afternoon, with Brother Junior driving her, she went to town. She bought Bui a pair of house shoes at the Mercantile, stopped by Sister Nadine's to borrow a cane and went to the library where she checked out *The Practical Book of Health,* then stayed up half the night to read it.

The next morning she dug new potatoes from her garden and made a pan of potato soup, cut roses from her trellis and arranged them in a tall yellow vase, then swept off the welcome mat in front of her door.

Finally, she said a prayer asking God for guidance, put on a fresh white apron, then sat on her front porch swing to wait for Vena to deliver her patient.

When he came, she bundled him off to bed, and for the next week, she medicated, fed, washed and bandaged, worrying over every grimace and groan.

She applied cold compresses to drive down his fevers, held his head when twice he threw up, massaged sore muscles and aching joints to ease his pain, read to him when he was restless and hurried to his bedside to calm him when he cried out in his sleep.

Eight days later, when he finally emerged, he was fattened, shaved, bathed, free of infection—and regular.

But when Vena arrived to drive him back to the Honk, Galilee went into a fit of anxiety, checking and rechecking his splint and warning against drafts, spicy food, missteps and exertion.

She was still cataloging dangers as she helped settle him in the car. Just before she shut his door, she reminded Vena once again that he was to be returned to her in two hours, hinting that if he wasn't, she might give the sheriff a call.

Then she stood in the street, waving until the car was out of sight.

On Bui's first visit to the Honk, Molly O brought him a pillow to put at his back, Caney made him a special lunch of beef tips and noodles and Vena played "You're the Reason God Made Oklahoma," his favorite song, on the jukebox.

The regulars, alerted to his return, dropped by with gifts and cards, handshakes and hugs.

Life brought him a used book wrapped in brown paper, *Sex: The*

Facts, The Acts, & Your Feelings, but cautioned him not to open it until he was alone. Hooks gave him three pounds of filleted crappie, Wilma Driver presented him with a Century 21 key chain, and Soldier brought a jar of his wife's strawberry jam. Quinton made him a present of a chess set he'd carved from pear wood, and Bilbo and Peg gave him a gift certificate for an oil change at the Grease-and-Go.

They stayed to kid him about the pretty nurses at the hospital and tell old jokes about nearsighted proctologists and bumbling gynecologists.

They laughed at Soldier's story about eating a Vicks sandwich when he was eight, a futile attempt to cure strep throat in time to go to summer camp, and they roared at Bilbo's account of a punishing bus trip to California only three days after he was circumcised at the age of fifty-three.

They brought Bui up-to-date on Big Fib's latest encounter with aliens, told him about the fire in the kitchen of the Dairy Queen and the newest graffiti scrawled on the city water tower: "A boy's best friend is a chicken."

But they didn't mention the shooting, not one word, and when Wanda Sue stopped by, Caney pulled her aside to tell her he would poison her coffee if she even thought about bringing it up.

Bui managed to slip away from them once on the pretext of going to the bathroom, but Vena found him in the kitchen getting meat scraps for Spot and carrots for the gelding.

When he walked out the back door, the dog yipped and ran to meet him at the fence, more excited by his attention than the food he offered. Then, as he made his way across the pasture, the gelding caught his scent and came trotting toward him, the only signs of his wound a slight limp and a pink scab on the shin of an otherwise sound and sturdy leg.

When Galilee called, alarmed that Bui was five minutes late, the regulars, beginning to see signs of his tiring, said their goodbyes and scattered, while Vena and Molly O gathered up his gifts and carried them out to the car.

But Bui held back, waiting until he had Caney alone.

"Mr. Chaney, I ask you a question?"

"Sure."

"Why the man called Sam shoot to kill me with his gun?"

Caney, thrown off-guard, reached for a cigarette and matches, buying time before he answered.

"Well, Bui. Sam was, uh . . ."

"He shoot me because I Vietnamese?"

The question hung in the air like the smoke from Caney's cigarettes until finally he said, "Yes," but when he did, he had to look away.

"Man called Sam fight in Vietnam War?"

"No. He didn't."

"Mr. Chaney, you fight in Vietnam War, I think so."

"I was there."

"Then why you don't shoot me?"

Caney was quiet for several moments, then he said, "I never could come up with a good reason."

The two men locked eyes then as something unspoken passed between them . . . something that had started in another place, in another time . . . something that had forever linked them.

Bui stayed a little longer at the Honk each day until, by the end of the week, he was around for most of the afternoon. But with his strength returning, he began to feel bored and useless just sitting, so he started finding small jobs to do despite Molly O's protests.

About the most he could manage with one good arm was to set up tables with silverware, refill tea and coffee and bus some tables, a few dishes at a time.

The dining room was usually full by noon because the fire at the Dairy Queen had shut it down temporarily; most of that business was coming to the Honk. And with school out, Vena had so much business outside, she was kept running from midmorning until closing time.

She was keeping up, but just barely. Occasional bouts of nausea were dragging her down, so that by early evening she had little energy left.

Caney was unaware that she sometimes disappeared for several minutes at a time, but he'd noticed that she looked tired and was often withdrawn and quiet.

She covered up by saying she might be a bit anemic, a problem she'd had from time to time. And when he saw her sipping a dark-colored liquid from a fruit jar she kept in the cooler, she explained that she'd gathered rattle-bush for tea, good for the blood, that would put her right in no time, though, in truth, the tea was to help her control morning sickness.

Even so, Caney decided she needed some help outside, especially with the hottest part of summer coming on, and though she said she could manage, he hired Quinton's sixteen-year-old grand-daughter, Kim, who was saving money to go to college to study art.

Kim started to work the next day, part-time, the same day Caney acquired a chef.

Bui had been trying for months to help out in the kitchen, but Caney had never let him do much beyond mangle some eggs and burn several loaves of bread.

But now Bui had the advantage of sympathy on his side. Who, after all, could refuse the simple request of a man with a broken body and damaged spirit?

When Caney finally caved in, Bui traded the pathetic expression he'd affected for a triumphant smile as he marched into the kitchen.

Molly O, refusing to allow him to lift anything heavier than a spoon, slid cast-iron skillets onto the burners, hauled pots filled with water to the stove, and rounded up bags and boxes from the pantry, meat and vegetables from the fridge.

When he was finally able to shoo her away, he went to work. He had to substitute certain spices for those he didn't have, and couldn't cook all the dishes he wanted for lack of ingredients not available in the kitchen of the Honk.

Nevertheless, two hours later he presented what he had pre-pared, a Vietnamese feast of ginger beef, caysin pork, chicken sesame and shrimp fried rice.

Caney, knowing his was a steak and potato trade, figured most of the food would go to waste, but for Bui's sake, he hauled out an old chalkboard and wrote at the top, "Saturday Night Special. Asian Delight."

When the dinner crowd began to arrive, they were reluctant to try it, preferring instead their chicken-fried steak and gravy, pork chops and fries, but out of deference to Bui, they said they'd give it a try.

When the food was set before them, bowls served family style, they pretended it was exactly what they'd expected, though they'd never seen the likes of it before.

Soldier was the first to put a forkful into his mouth while the others watched and waited for his reaction. They were silent while he chewed, then swallowed. But when he smiled with pleasure, they eyed each other and hesitantly reached for the nearest bowl.

Most took only small portions on their plates, then, at Bui's urging, spooned on the sauces he'd prepared.

They didn't say much as they fought to keep the thin, slippery noodles on their forks, stabbed at small chunks of spicy chicken, speared slivers of carrots and cucumbers, thrust at fluffy grains of rice and paper-thin slices of green onions, pierced juicy pink shrimps and beef seasoned with ginger.

Minutes later, their plates empty, they dug into second helpings as they licked at lips tingling with sharp, sweet tastes they'd never experienced before.

A half hour later, Caney erased the "Special" from the board. The chef had run out of food.

Vena sat at an empty table in the corner of the room where she watched . . . watched the way Soldier hooked his thumb over the rim of his coffee cup when he raised it to his mouth and how Hooks squinted when he chewed on a toothpick . . . watched the way Bilbo tilted his head to blow his smoke away from Peg's bluish face and how Wanda Sue pulled at her ear when she passed on her latest gossip . . . watched the way Bui bowed shyly to compliments and how Life looked at Molly O like a puppy waiting to be petted.

Watched the way Caney's eyes, the color of spring willows, picked up the light as he studied her from across the room.

She watched, wanting to remember each face, each gesture, each smile, as she saw them for the last time.

And though she made no effort to rise, to push back from the table and pack her things, she knew she had already slipped away.

Chapter Thirty-Five

CANEY KNEW she was gone. Even in half-sleep he could feel the emptiness beside him, could feel that the bed had already lost her heat, that her pillow held only the hollow shaped by her head.

But until he opened his eyes, it would not be real.

She was still sleeping beside him, her bottom lip quivering with the exhale of her breath, her eyelids fluttering as she dreamed. He moved his hand very slowly to run his fingers across the silky strands of her hair on the pillow without her knowing.

Then she stretched in sleep, her toes curling, pointing like a diver going into water, and the sheet across her chest slid below her breasts.

At rest again, her breathing slowed, and from deep inside her came a sound like the purring of a cat.

Minutes later, she rolled toward him, her hand lightly grazing his skin before she twisted her shoulders back and touched one finger to the hollow of her throat.

Finally, she yawned, flicked her tongue across her lips, brushed a lock of hair from her cheek as, slipping from sleep, she opened her eyes, saw him watching her and smiled.

Then, without words, they reached for each other, their bodies coming together as the first copper ray of sun began to slide across the bed.

This morning, though, there was no shaft of sunlight, no purring breath, no shape to reach for.

She'd caught her first ride of the day at the Texaco station just after dawn with a gospel quartet from Little Rock. They took her as far as Waco, their destination, and let her off at a truck stop.

She hadn't thought much about where she was headed, but almost any city would do. Abortion clinics didn't fare well in smaller places, and she wasn't about to face a line of angry protesters carrying pictures of mutilated fetuses or slink in the back door of some dingy doctor's office like she'd done when she was a scared scrawny kid.

By the time the waitress brought her first cup of coffee, she'd decided on San Antonio, only a couple of hours down the road. She knew her way around there, might even be a couple of her old drinking buddies still hanging around, but she had no interest in finding out.

She didn't have to wait long before a driver hauling cattle said he was going her way, but just the thought of smelling cow manure for two hundred miles brought on a sudden wave of nausea, so she passed up the offer.

After a trip to the bathroom, she switched from coffee to tea, ate a few crackers and, feeling better, started asking around again for a ride.

She was anxious to get back on the road because when she'd been moving, she had outdistanced thoughts of Caney. But sitting still, he caught up with her.

Listen, the day I watched you climb out of that truck, I knew my life was gonna change.

She got up quickly, grabbed a newspaper from the counter, then went back to her booth to read.

Hell, Vena. I don't care what you've done. I didn't know the person you were . . . I only know who you are now.

After tossing some change on the table, she picked up her duffel bag and started outside. But before she reached the door, she hooked up with a trucker on his way to San Antonio by way of La

Grange to pick up four hundred cases of beer at a brewery, so she found herself taking an unexpected detour, going south on 77 instead of the interstate.

They hadn't gone far before she began to see familiar territory. Not that she was interested. She hadn't been back since the day she and Helen left twenty years ago, and she couldn't think of a good reason to go back now.

Ten minutes later, when she asked the driver to stop, she was more surprised than he was as she climbed down out of the cab at Hawkins Corner and started walking down a rutted dirt road.

Odel Hawkins' store, where she and Helen had sold pop bottles to buy candy, was boarded up now, the sign out front advertising Dr Pepper riddled with buckshot.

A quarter mile beyond the store, she came to the one-lane wooden bridge over Push Creek where Helen had threatened to jump one day when she was in the fifth grade.

I'd rather be dead, Vena, than be in that dumb play. Miss Lyons could've picked any girl in class to be Pocahontas, but she picked me 'cause I'm the only Indian. And she said I had to put my arm around that stupid Buddy Pitt 'cause he's going to be John Smith. Well, I guess she'll be sorry when she hears I'm drowned.

Almost halfway to the section line, she passed the old Lanford place, but the three-room house where they'd lived was gone now, and in its place sat a double-wide house trailer, bashed in and rusted on one end.

When the road curved downhill at the Heisenberg farm where she used to steal watermelons, Vena stopped to shake a rock out of her boot.

You know what? I don't think stealing watermelons is a sin, Vena. I mean, it's not like taking someone's money or maybe some rich woman's fur coat. 'Cause watermelon, well, it comes out of the earth. And the earth belongs to everybody.

Ezra Settlemyers' house was still standing and still leaning to one side, but now it had a six-foot chain-link fence around it. When Vena stepped into a ditch where she saw a thicket of blackberries, two pit bulls raced from out of nowhere and, running full speed, hurled themselves against the fence as someone inside the house pulled aside a curtain to watch her back away and move on.

After she turned east at the section line, she passed the farm pond where she and Helen used to fish for perch until the day Helen hooked one in the eye when she was nine.

I'm never ever going to eat another creature that has a face, 'cause if they have faces, then they have eyes and they can look at you when you kill them.

The road grew crooked just past the cattle guard, then straightened for a hundred yards before it snaked into the S-curve where Mary Cobb, at twelve, had wrecked her brother's pickup.

But the twisting road was still as familiar to Vena as the jagged scar on her leg, the result of a dare by Jimmy Mendoza to play matador in his daddy's corral. She'd escaped the charging bull called Zore by diving through a barbed-wire fence which sliced open her calf and required twenty-two stitches to close.

She passed the old cemetery where she'd gone with Davey Baysinger, the first boy she ever kissed; hurried by the abandoned cabin rumored to be haunted by the ghost of Cassie Washington who poisoned herself; rested under the lightning-struck oak where Helen had pried from a knothole the blackened Prince Albert can they hid in their secret place.

She walked for almost an hour, a road where every house and hill and hollow held for her some voice, some face, some history . . . collecting moments of her past like a child stuffing fireflies into a jar.

But when she rounded the last bend and saw the place she'd once called home, she came to a dead stop.

The junked cars and pickups were gone, the lawn recently mowed, and the house, remarkably like the one she'd seen in her dreams, was white now with green shutters and windowboxes filled with flowers.

Her heart began to pound, and she felt light-headed as she started toward it.

"Can I help you?" A white-haired man leaning on a cane stood behind a closed screen door, watching her. "You got car trouble?"

"No, I—"

"Don't get many visitors here since the wife died, not unless it's some fool run out of gas or one of those kids driving hell-bent for leather hits that gully this side of the bridge."

"I used to live here," Vena said. "I grew up in this house."

The man opened the door, studying her as he stepped onto the porch.

"Now ain't that something. There was a woman here 'bout a year ago said the same thing. And by the looks of you, I'd say you might be her sister."

"What?" Vena almost went to her knees. "Helen was here?"

"Well, she didn't say her name."

"But you talked to her?"

"Tried, but she wasn't doing much talking, 'least not that made sense. To tell you the truth, I thought there was something wrong with her."

"What do you mean?"

"Like maybe she wasn't quite right in the head. No offense, but she acted real strange, eyes all wild, and she had on a hat and a heavy coat buttoned up to her neck and it musta been ninety degrees that day."

Vena dizzied with the memory of her dream-vision.

"Me and my daughter'd just finished supper and she was fixing to go out and mess with her flowers when she looked through the window and seen this woman standing in the backyard.

"Well, I went out and asked her what she wanted, and she said she was looking for the graveyard. I told her the graveyard was a mile north, but she said no, it was right under her feet. Said that's where someone named Peabody was buried."

"Peabo. Her cat."

"She was real upset, said it'd all changed, asked where was the barn and the chicken house. I told her they got blowed away in a cyclone a few years back, but she walked around out there looking for them like she didn't believe me.

"Then she told me she had to leave something for her sister who'd be showing up here sometime. And I suppose that's you."

"What did she leave?" Vena asked, her voice hardly more than a whisper.

"Well, she didn't leave nothing. I told her I'd be glad to keep it here, whatever it was, in case her sister showed up, but she wasn't having any of that.

"She looked bad. Terrible, to tell you the truth, so I said I'd go get her something cold to drink and I went on in the house, but when I come back out, she was already halfway down to the creek."

At the place where Vena went into the creek, the water was only ankle deep, but by the time she reached midstream, her boots were filled. She pulled them off, emptied them, then, cradling one in each arm, fought for balance on the sharp stones beneath her stockinged feet.

Much of the far bank had washed away, but she could see that the outcrop of rock which shielded the secret place was still intact.

From the day they'd discovered the narrow crevice beneath the rock ledge, just wide enough for the Prince Albert can, she and Helen had hidden small surprises for each other there—arrowheads, fossils, eagle feathers, stones shaped like stars and apples and whales. Sometimes they'd leave buckeyes or a favorite poem, and once, Helen had been delighted to find that Vena had left her a tiny porcelain rabbit with ruby chips for eyes.

They'd even gone there together on the morning they left for good to hide their mother's cheap gold locket which the woman their daddy married had claimed for her own.

When they left, they knew they'd never return to that secret place again, but now, as Vena waded from the water, she felt certain it had been visited one more time.

She tossed her soggy boots on the bank and climbed to the overhang, then reached into the crevice, but her hands were larger now. She forced her fingers between the rough stone, scraping skin from her knuckles and breaking off fingernails until she was finally able to pull the can free.

She scooted down, dropped onto the muddy bank, pried open

the rusted lid and pulled out a folded piece of brown paper torn from a grocery sack.

Her hands were trembling as she unfolded it, but when she saw the writing, she could hardly believe it was Helen's.

The words were jumbled, crooked letters written on top of others, like the scribblings of a child.

My Dearest Vena, I leave this letter because I know you will come for it. I have a baby named Tioga, so tiny he fits into the palm of my hand, a sweet baby who never cries but he is cold. I wrapped him in a piece of sheep wool and put him in the blue jewelry box you gave me but he is still cold. I burn fires to keep him warm but the wind blows out the flames and the sun is too far away. He talks to me sometimes and tells me to let him go but I know when you find us you will make him well. You could always make them well. I was so happy when I had him inside me but then I saw two crows in the same tree and you know what mama always says about that. You were always the strong one but I was too scared by the questions. I found a book with the answers but the pages were burned. Did you know I always wanted to be like you because you are good and have strength. I have always loved you.

Helen

Vena read the letter only once before she pressed the paper tightly between the palms of her hands as if she could force the words into her flesh and warm them.

Then she heard the voices of children playing upstream where she saw two thin brown-skinned girls, herself at six, standing chest deep in the water, keeping Helen afloat, one hand beneath her neck, the other at the small of her back.

Just relax, Helen.

I can't. I'm scared.

Move your hands like I showed you.

But I'll go under.

No, you won't. I'll be right beside you.

Promise?

Cross my heart and hope to die.

Vena watched as the girls began moving downstream, saw herself sidestepping in the water, still supporting Helen as they moved with the current.

Stay with me, Vena, till I'm ready.

I will.

As they slid past her, Vena heard Helen calling, her voice filled with wonder.

I'm doing it, Vena! I'm doing it! You can let me go now. . . .

I'm not scared anymore.

Then Vena slipped soundlessly into the creek, and as the water washed over her, she released the torn brown paper and watched it float away.

Chapter Thirty-Six

BEFORE THE OFFICIAL beginning of summer, Sequoyah was already baking in the heat. Most days the temperature climbed into the mid-nineties with thunderheads rolling in by late afternoon.

A tornado raked the southern edge of town on the sixteenth of June, knocking out electricity for a few hours, uprooting some trees, blowing down what was left of the old drive-in screen and destroying Henry Brister's trailer.

But the trailer had been unoccupied since Henry, by then fitted with prostheses, had settled out of court with the plastic factory for two million dollars, an event which attracted the attention of a number of women anxious to help him recover from the loss of his thumbs and his wife. And on the day of his marriage to a pretty, divorced mother of three, Henry had moved his new family into the finest house on the lake, an area untouched by the storm.

Wanda Sue was still rattling with tales about the woman Henry had married when Big Fib Fry disappeared, news that nearly felled her with gossip overload.

Certain that Big Fib had run away with his paramour, Frances Dunn, who dropped out of sight the same day, Wanda Sue pointed out that she, and she alone, had known from the beginning what was going on.

But a week later, when Frances and Luter returned from Acapulco where they'd celebrated their reunion with a second honeymoon, Wanda Sue turned uncharacteristically silent, at least for a couple of hours.

The disappearance of Big Fib, however, remained a mystery, heightened a few days later when Little Fib found his daddy's straw hat in a soybean field where he swore he saw strange circles of scorched earth, leading some to believe that Big Fib had been abducted by aliens again.

The summer brought other changes, most far less dramatic, but still worthy of comment by Wanda Sue on a slow day.

As a result of a radio trivia contest on a Fort Smith station, Soldier won a three-day trip to Las Vegas. His wife, a Southern Baptist who held that gambling was a sin, declared she was staying home. But Quinton, believing that only by faith would a man draw to an inside straight, accepted Soldier's invitation to go along.

After they checked into the Golden Nugget, they pooled their money and sat down to a game of draw poker. When they checked out the next morning, two days earlier than planned and with less than five dollars between them, Quinton, repentant, confessed that he might have tested his faith a few too many times.

Wilma Driver's three youngest grandchildren came for their annual summer visit of two weeks which caused Rex to come down with a severe case of scaly eczema and left Wilma nearly addicted to Valium.

Erin, just turned fifteen, made off with Wilma's new Lincoln one night, then returned it at three the next morning with a half bottle of orange-flavored vodka in the front seat and a pair of briefs in the back. Robby, the budding pyromaniac, set fire to the doghouse, but fortunately, Wilma's poodle, Nipper, was in her lap at the time. And Ashley, the youngest, sat in the yard every night, holding aloft a strangely shaped crystal to receive messages from her home planet, Klynot, where she claimed Big Fib had been taken.

Hooks Red Eagle had a stroke in early July. Though minor, he was left with enough impairment in his right arm and leg to make it impossible for him to get in and out of his johnboat. But declaring he'd rather be dead than give up fishing, he sold his bait shop and used the money to buy a pontoon boat he could manage, then rigged up a contraption which allowed him to haul in the big ones with the use of only one good hand.

A sudden outbreak of violence and vandalism, blamed on the oppressive heat of midsummer, began when one of Wanda Sue's nephews sent a jack handle flying through the window of the Mercantile because they didn't have the shoes he wanted in his size.

Then a late night fight at the Hi-Ho where the Mosier brothers fought each other over a game of shuffleboard left one with a punctured lung and the other missing the tip of his tongue.

A week later, the little locomotive in the city park was defaced with the word "Niger" painted on its side either by a racist who couldn't spell or someone with an obscure connection to the age-old river which twisted its way through West Africa.

Not even the Honk was spared the mayhem that spread from one side of town to the other.

Kim, a carhop for less than two months, didn't come to work for three days after a neat and studious-looking young man exposed himself to her when she delivered the foot-long hotdog he'd ordered to his car.

But to some, more extraordinary news than even the crime wave concerned Bilbo Porter, who gave up smoking on the evening he rushed Peg to the hospital choking for breath. As he stood over her in the emergency room, watching her fight for air, he vowed he would never again put a cigarette to his lips.

When he stopped by the Honk that night and told them of the pledge he'd made, the bets came down hard and fast, and before he left, he had two hundred dollars on the line that he wouldn't make it a week.

He started walking the next morning, eight or ten blocks each time he wanted a smoke, and he developed a craving for sweets, so he stocked up on ice cream, candy, cookies and pies. By the time Peg was released eight days later, he had walked fifty-six miles, gained nine pounds and had ten twenty-dollar bills stuffed in the pocket of his pants which he had not been able to button because of his bulging belly.

A few nights later, when someone broke into the IGA and stole sixty cartons of cigarettes, those who'd lost their money to Bilbo accused him of being the culprit.

When the Dairy Queen reopened three weeks after the kitchen fire, Caney's business slacked off a little except for Friday nights, when Bui's Asian Delight Special drew customers from three counties and filled the Honk from five o'clock until closing.

Hamp came by the Honk several times during the summer, always to ask about Brenda. He said his friend Bob Swink thought he'd heard one of her songs on the radio, but he couldn't remember the title or the station that played it.

Molly O didn't know where Brenda was, but early in August she'd gotten a phone call—long distance, she judged from the sound—and though no one spoke when she answered, she had a mother's intuition that her daughter was on the other end of the line. For the next three nights she slept on the couch to be near the phone, but Brenda didn't call again.

Life almost managed to complete his proposal of marriage to Molly O while they were playing bingo at the VFW on a Saturday night. But just before the last few words were out of his mouth, she called out, "Bingo!" as she marked B-1 on her card, making her a winner of fifty dollars for filling all four corners.

Then, desperate and with nothing to lose, he gave her Reba's journal to read when he took her home that night.

Three days later, shyly avoiding his eyes as she poured his first cup of coffee, she slid the journal across the counter to him, then turned without comment and hurried to the kitchen to hand Bui the order for Life's bacon and eggs.

The heat of summer held on in Sequoyah until the last Thursday in September when a steady soaking rain fell from early morning until midafternoon, ending a thirty-seven-day drought and twelve straight days of temperatures exceeding a hundred and three, to which caladiums, scarlet sage, nasturtiums and Duncan Renfro succumbed.

Ellen missed him shortly after eleven when she began to listen for the phone call that would signal his sighting. When no such message came, she got in the car and drove to the Honk, but no one there had seen him all day.

She didn't know until that evening that he had managed to climb into the attic of their own house where he'd spent the hottest part of the afternoon measuring the rafters until he dropped dead of heat stroke.

He was buried two days later, wearing his striped carpenter's overalls with a tape measure shoved into each pocket.

Throughout the fall the weather was unusually cold, but not cold enough to keep Caney inside. While Bui cooked for the breakfast trade, Caney took off to ride the gelding. And some afternoons, when it was warm enough, he left after lunch to go fishing with Hooks.

To fill his nights, he took up with Louis L'Amour again, staying up till two or three, reading and drinking coffee in bed.

Mostly, though, he tried not to think about Vena.

But on those days when an eighteen-wheeler would pull up out front, he'd lean forward and look out the window as if he expected to see her crawl down from the cab and walk back into his life.

Chapter Thirty-Seven

THE ONLY CHRISTMAS decoration in the Honk was a bedraggled plastic wreath in the front window. No trees or lights, no frizzy-haired Barbies or candy canes. Even the nativity scene remained packed away.

When Molly O had started hauling in boxes of ornaments and tinsel, Caney had asked her not to put them up this year, an annual request which she annually ignored. But this time she heard a deep sadness in his voice she hadn't heard before.

And she didn't have to guess at the cause.

She had pleaded the case for the wreath, then gave in without further argument, relieved in a way that she wouldn't be faced with reminders of Brenda—the Santa she'd made in second grade that always went at the top of the tree; an old high-heeled shoe decorated with macaroni, sprayed gold and stuffed with plastic holly; the special ornaments she loved—mice made of straw, elves of ceramic and red birds with real feathers.

But now, with Christmas only two days away and the Honk looking like it had been hit by the Grinch, she wondered if she hadn't made a mistake.

"You're running a little late this morning," Quinton said as Soldier came through the door.

Soldier shrugged out of his coat and pulled up to the table where Quinton was just mopping up the last of his biscuits and gravy while Hooks worked on his second cup of coffee.

"Looks like I'm not the only one who slept in," Soldier said. "I see the damned paper's not here yet."

"Nope." Molly O filled a cup for Soldier, then picked up Quinton's empty plate. "Can't say this new carrier's any better than Big Fib."

"Yeah, but as far as we know this one's still living on Earth."

"Little Fib still sticking to that story 'bout his daddy being held captive on Mars?"

"Hell, yes. He's getting as bad as his old man. He keeps on, he'll have to change his name from 'Little' to 'Bigger.' "

"You gonna have breakfast, Soldier?" Caney asked as he came out of the kitchen and settled behind the counter to have a cigarette.

"Not unless Bui's doing the cooking."

"He's not here yet," Molly O said. "Galilee's got him closing in her back porch, making extra room for when his wife and baby get here."

"They still in Vietnam?"

"No, they got out of there," Hooks said. "Bui told me they was in a refugee camp in Malaria."

"Hell, Hooks. Malaria's a disease."

"Didn't Wilma's husband have that once?"

"Rex hasn't had *anything* just once."

"Speaking of disease," Soldier said, "look who's here."

"Morning, Wanda Sue," Caney said as she trooped in and took her usual place at the counter.

"Paper's not here yet?" she asked.

"No, we was just saying that things ain't improved a bit since Big Fib went to Mars."

"Mars?" Wanda Sue pulled at her ear, signaling she had something to tell. "Why, you're not even close. Not even on the right planet."

"I take it you know more than we do."

"Don't I always?"

"Well, I bet whatever it is, we couldn't pry it out of you short of torture."

"He's gone to Jupiter." Wanda Sue gave her stool a dramatic spin to face her audience. "Jupiter, Florida."

"Now what the hell would he be doing in Florida?"

"I imagine you'd hightail it out of here, too, if the Mosier brothers was after you."

"Yeah, I probably would," Soldier said. "But I wouldn't stop at Florida. I'd go on to Cuba, even if I had to swim."

"Seems Big Fib was running around with Jake Mosier's wife and got caught."

Quinton whistled between his teeth.

"So the two Fibs cooked up the idea of making it look like a spaceship took him."

"I reckon if Jake Mosier ever catches up with him, Big Fib'll wish he'd hooked up with them aliens."

When Hooks saw the bus pull in, he said, "Why's Bui driving the bus today? This Sunday?"

"No, Hooks. Sunday comes right after Saturday. Every week. But you keep working on it, you'll get it."

"Bui's car's up on concrete blocks behind Galilee's house," Caney said. "Threw a rod."

"Say," Hooks said as Bui walked in, "I hear you're getting ready for your family to come."

"Yes, Sister Galilee make home for me and wife and baby."

"Well, that's good. Home's important, all right."

"For me, yes. But some people ascared of home."

"Now who told you that?" Molly O asked.

"Miss Vena."

After Bui went to the kitchen, no one spoke or stirred until Caney turned and wheeled into his room.

"I guess I'd better get going," Molly O said as she came from Caney's bedroom, snapping on a pair of dangling rhinestone earrings.

"Wow!" Caney said.

She had showered and changed from her workclothes into a cherry red silk dress with a low-cut neckline, low enough to show the cleavage between the halo of her breasts.

"You look great in that dress."

"Oh, this old thing?"

"Come here and let me cut the price tag off the sleeve of that old thing."

Molly O blushed as Caney pulled out his pocketknife and clipped loose the tag.

"I've never seen you so gussied up before."

"Now, Caney, don't tease."

"Guess this is a real special occasion."

"Life called it the eve of Christmas Eve dinner."

"I never figured Life for a cook."

"He's not, but he says he's been practicing."

"Well, it must be one hell of a meal he's fixing. He hasn't turned up here all day."

When Bui came from the kitchen, wiping his hands on a towel, he said, "Miss Ho, you look too beautiful."

"Thank you, Bui."

"She's going to her boyfriend's house for dinner."

"Caney, he's not my boyfriend."

"Yeah? Try telling him that."

"Look, I hate to take off so early, but—"

"Sure." Caney made a sweeping motion across the empty cafe. "Right here at our busiest time."

"And as soon as I walk out that door, a dozen customers will show up."

"Get on out of here."

"Okay. I'll see you in the morning."

"Oh, you never know. You might still be at Life's in the morning."

"Caney! You're gonna have Bui thinking I'm some kind of loose woman."

"What is loose woman?" Bui asked.

"I'll explain it to you later," Caney said. "After she's gone."

Molly O pulled on her coat, checked her makeup in the mirror, then waved as she slipped out the door.

"Bui, what do you say we call it a night?"

"Yes sir, Mr. Chaney. Kitchen all finished and—"

Caney swiveled to pick up the phone on the first ring.

"Honk and Holler," he answered, "but we're closed."

When he heard the soft intake of her breath, he closed his eyes while he waited through the silence, waited to hear her say his name.

Bui had never driven the bus beyond the outskirts of Sequoyah, never passed another vehicle or even honked the horn. He'd never traveled faster than a safe thirty-five, never failed to yield to another driver and never taken the right-of-way, even when it was his.

But when he reached the highway and pushed the bus to sixty-five, felt the power and speed and authority only he controlled, a strange transformation began to take place.

He found himself overtaking monster trucks, bearing down on sleek sports cars, honking at unyielding drivers puttering along in the passing lane.

The qualities of patience, timidity and compliance instilled by the culture that had shaped him, waned with every mile. And by the time the bus roared across the Red River, speeding into the moonless Texas night, he was charged with boldness, tigerish at the wheel.

Caney, his chair locked in place beside the driver's seat, said almost nothing through the blur of Dallas after midnight, Waco at three, Austin before dawn.

Even when they reached San Antonio in the middle of the morning rush hour, Caney didn't seem to notice as Bui cut his way through the tangle of traffic, squeezing the bus into impossible openings, darting from lane to lane, yelling Vietnamese warnings to those who dared to get in his way.

*   *   *

"There it is." Caney pointed to a peeling, splintered sign that said "Majestic Apartments." But the mustard-colored building suggested even less grandeur than the sign.

The treeless patch of ground surrounding the complex was littered with aluminum cans, two bent bicycle wheels, fast-food boxes and the bottom half of a rusted metal chair.

A swing set missing the swings leaned on three legs near a child's plastic swimming pool where a squashed rubber duck floated in two inches of muddy water.

At the curb a ten-year-old Mustang with four flat tires faced a pickup, the bed piled high with bulging garbage bags.

Bui parked behind the pickup, then hooked the plywood ramp he'd made to the top step of the bus and waited while Caney rolled to solid ground.

He faced a half dozen unnegotiable steps, but Bui pushed the chair up the dirt incline beside them and onto a cracked sidewalk.

"Number fourteen," Caney said. "Hope it's not upstairs."

"If up the stairs, I carry you, Mr. Chaney." Then Bui pointed to the last door on the ground floor. "I see the fourteen."

When they reached the apartment, Caney pulled out a comb and ran it through his hair, then looked to Bui for approval.

"Look okay," Bui said.

Caney took a deep breath, then knocked—three quick raps followed by sounds of movement from inside. Moments later, she opened the door.

She was barefoot, wearing jeans and a plaid shirt, and her hair, longer than when he'd last seen it, was twisted into a braid that hung across one shoulder.

She stared, first at Caney, then Bui, unable to hide her surprise.

"Did we wake you up?"

"No, but I didn't look for you to be here so soon. Didn't think you'd start out last night."

"Bus run good at night, Miss Vena. And fast."

She looked past them to the street where the bus was parked; then, as if she'd suddenly remembered her manners, she swung the door open wider and said, "Come in."

After Bui helped Caney maneuver his chair over the threshold, he started backing away. "Now I go sleep in my bus."

"You can rest in here, Bui."

But he was nearly to the street when he called back, "No, thank you, Miss Vena. I sleep in my bus."

As Caney wheeled into the room, she closed the door, then stood awkwardly before him, one hand stuffed into the pocket of her jeans.

Then in a rush, she said, "How about some coffee?"

"Sounds good."

He wanted to watch her as she moved around the cramped kitchen, but feared she'd look up and meet his eyes, so he pretended interest in her apartment, though there was little to see.

The place was neat, but small and shabby. Not much furniture—a frayed sofa and a mismatched chair with a rip in the cushion, two end tables and a cheap red lamp covered by a faded plastic shade. Leaning in the corner, a skinny Christmas tree, bare except for a half dozen candy canes, stood guard over three gift-wrapped packages on the floor.

"I made this a couple of hours ago, so it's liable to be pretty strong," she said as she handed him a cup, then settled with hers in the chair.

"So . . ." Caney didn't know where to go from there.

"How's everything back at the Honk?"

"About the same, I guess. Bui's trying to teach Spot some tricks, but he's not making much progress."

"And the gelding?"

"I ride him most every day. Just make sure to keep him away from gunfire."

They were quiet then, staring into their coffee. Suddenly, from a nearby apartment, the sound of rap music blared, followed seconds later by hard thumps coming from somewhere overhead.

"How about you, Vena?"

"Me? I'm fine. I work at an animal shelter, just part-time right now."

"Well, saving animals is something you're good at."

"Mostly I'm a janitor and caretaker. It's a no-kill shelter, so—"

"What made you come to San Antonio?"

"Oh, you know. Boat go where boat go."

They laughed then, a relief from the tension.

"How long you been here?"

"Since I left the . . . Almost seven months."

"Wouldn't figure you to stay in one place that long. You planning to be here for a while?"

"I don't know."

"Well, you put up a Christmas tree, so I guess you plan to be around at least until tomorrow."

The sound of a siren close by gave them an excuse not to talk, at least for a few seconds, but when it died away, Vena put her coffee on the table beside her, then picked at a frayed tear in her jeans.

"I'm glad to see you, Vena."

"Are you?"

"Why wouldn't I be? Because you left?" He shook his head. "You were honest with me about that, told me from the beginning you wouldn't stay."

"I started to leave you a note."

"Couldn't find a pencil?" Then, forcing a stiff grin, he leaned forward and set his cup on the table beside her.

"I didn't know what to say."

"How about 'good-bye'?"

"Yes." Vena pulled at her lip. "I owed you that much."

"You didn't *owe* me a damn thing." Abruptly he backed away and rolled across the room to the window where he watched a mangy dog drinking from the plastic swimming pool.

"Caney, I tried to write to you a couple of times."

"Is that right?" he asked, his tone verging on sarcasm.

"I wanted to tell you why I left."

"Oh, I think I know why."

Unnerved, Vena lost her grip on the handle of her cup, sloshing coffee on her jeans.

"Living in the back room of a run-down cafe. Flipping burgers, waiting tables. Same thing one day after another. I couldn't expect you to want that." Absently, he stroked the leaf of a small ivy plant on the windowsill. "I'm surprised you stayed as long as you did."

"You're wrong about that. I liked being there, being with you."

"You have a funny way of showing it. You disappear without a word, put five hundred miles between us . . ."

"You were good to me, Caney. Too good, I guess. And that scared me."

"Kindness kills, is that it?"

"Look, Caney. I can't blame you for being mad, but—"

"Damned right I'm mad!"

"Then why the hell did you come here?" she said, her voice rising with anger.

"Why the hell did you ask me to?" he yelled.

They glared at each other from across the room, and in the uncomfortable silence that separated them, they could hear a woman outside yelling in Spanish and, from nearby, the whimper of a baby.

Caney pulled his cigarettes from his pocket, tipped one from the pack, then, as an afterthought, offered it to Vena.

She shook her head. "I don't have any ashtrays, but I'll get you something."

She came back from the kitchen with a jar lid. When she handed it to him, their fingers touched.

"Thanks," he said.

She opened the window and, standing beside him, stared outside.

"Caney, I've spent my life running away. I ran from home, from my sister, from a husband. Then I ran away from you.

"But all that time, I didn't know the person I was trying to leave behind was me."

She turned, put her hands behind her and leaned against the wall.

"See, I never believed anyone could really love me, didn't think I was good enough. So I ran from people who cared about me."

She shifted, rolled her head to the side and looked Caney in the eyes.

"I figured I was doing you a favor."

She started to walk away, but Caney took her hand and held her in place.

"Vena, I didn't know the girl who had a skull tattooed on her arm or the girl who had an abortion in Santa Fe or the one who went to jail in Abilene.

"I fell in love with a woman who walked into my life carrying a three-legged dog, who put me on a horse and showed me a world I thought I'd lost . . . a woman who wrapped her arms around me and taught me to dance again."

Vena drew a deep breath, then let it out slowly. "And I fell in love with the man she danced with."

Afraid to trust what he'd heard, Caney searched her face for the truth . . . and found it in her eyes.

"Why didn't you tell me, Vena? Why didn't you say it when we were together?"

"Because I didn't know then that I could let you love me."

"And you thought you could stop me by leaving?"

"Yes. But something happened, Caney, and I got another chance."

Chapter Thirty-Eight

THOUGH THE SUDDEN and inexplicable disappearance of Caney and Bui seemed unlikely to be related to that of Big Fib, there were those few who, on hearing the news, ran to their windows to scan the sky for spaceships.

But others, more grounded in reality, surmised that aliens would not have taken the bus, which was also missing, nor would they have granted Caney the opportunity to write the note he left on the counter for Molly O.

Me and Bui are taking a little trip. Might be back soon—might not. Close the damned place down.

The note didn't shed much light on the mystery, but it helped to calm Molly O's initial fear that a kidnapping had taken place.

She didn't have time even to consider not opening up for business, though, since Life had gotten to the Honk ahead of her and, finding the door unlocked, gone inside, turned on the lights and started the coffee. By the time she arrived, Soldier and Quinton were already there, huddled with Life at the counter, puzzling over Caney's message.

Minutes later Galilee phoned, still confused over a cryptic call she'd received from Bui the night before. Then she caught a ride over with Brother Samuel, explaining that she preferred to wait in the company of others as troubled as she was.

Wanda Sue, with her uncanny sense of a story in the making, showed up before nine, and within an hour she had the word out, which brought a steady stream of the concerned pouring in for more news.

Everyone who walked through the door that morning had some theory on Bui and Caney's unexplained departure, theories that ran from the absurd to the less absurd to the divine.

Life reckoned they'd gone to Arkansas to dig for diamonds because of a recent story about a woman who'd uncovered a two-million-dollar stone. Hooks figured they went deep-sea fishing in the Gulf, something he himself had always dreamed of doing, while Soldier thought they'd gone to the Vietnam Memorial in Washington where he'd been once with his brother.

But Galilee believed they were on a quest, their path laid out by the hand of God. And several times throughout the day she quoted Scripture in support of her conviction: "Behold, I shew you a mystery; We shall not all sleep, but we shall all be changed."

Having heard the news downtown, Carl Phelps dropped by just to check things out. But he saw nothing to suggest anything of a criminal nature in Caney's note which was, by then, crumpled and creased and smudged with fingerprints.

But since he was there and it was nearing noon, he ordered lunch. And Galilee, finding comfort in cooking, was just serving him a plate of fried catfish and hushpuppies when the call came.

They all knew it was Caney when Molly O answered, then waved them to silence.

"Where . . ."

Her voice was anxious, her face creased with worry.

"But why . . ."

Life dropped a spoon, which clattered to the floor.

"When . . ."

Bilbo's chair creaked as he leaned forward.

"Are you . . ."

Wanda Sue lit a cigarette.

"I've been worried sick . . ."

Peg coughed.

"Okay," she said, then recradled the phone, the call having lasted only forty-eight seconds.

"He sounds tired," Molly O reported to those assembled. Then, with the disappointment of a journalist who's just missed her story, she added, "He didn't say where they were or what they were doing. But they'll be back tomorrow sometime around noon."

Her account left them quiet, and as they started to drift away, they looked as puzzled as they had when they'd come.

Later that evening, with the cafe empty except for Life and Galilee, Molly O decided to decorate. She didn't know what to expect when Caney and Bui returned, but whatever it was, she would be waiting to offer them a bit of Christmas cheer. And she hoped that wherever her Brenda was, someone would be waiting to do the same for her.

By the time she closed up that night, the Honk had a tree with twinkling lights, walls adorned with cardboard bells and ceiling fans draped with aluminum stars. Frizzy-haired Barbies were posed atop napkin holders, silver icicles were strung across the room, the nativity scene was arranged on the counter and the Oriental-looking baby Jesus was tucked snugly into his bamboo bed.

Christmas morning found Sequoyah shrouded in dark, low-lying clouds threatening rain, but with the temperature in the mid-sixties, there'd be no snow to brighten the day.

By seven-thirty Galilee was in the kitchen with Molly O where two turkeys were already roasting in the oven, a pot of noodles stewing on the stove, and mincemeat and pumpkin pies cooling on the counter.

Kim came in at nine, as promised, and she, along with Life, was preparing to handle business in the dining room.

By eleven folks were beginning to arrive, as hungry to learn the whys and wherefores of Caney and Bui's secret expedition as they were for the food coming out of the kitchen.

Soldier brought his wife, and they were joined by their son, Danny, hoping the mystery would lead to a story for the next issue of the paper.

Quinton and Hooks came in together—Quinton wearing a tie and jacket for the occasion, Hooks still in his fishing clothes.

Wilma surprised everyone when she showed up not only with Rex, looking robust and hardy despite the half dozen prescription bottles he placed on the table, but also with her grandchildren, who, notwithstanding her tales of their wild and weird ways, were quiet and well behaved.

Henry Brister brought his new family, three small children and the pretty, young wife. But now, skillful with his metal thumbs, Henry needed no help cutting up his turkey or buttering his bread or scooping bites of mashed potatoes onto his fork.

Wanda Sue came dressed in a red sweatshirt with a picture of Santa, a finger to his lips, cautioning, "Don't spread this around—but I'm watching you."

Bilbo and Peg took a table near the door—she still hooked up to her oxygen and he, though he hadn't smoked for months, slapping his empty pocket now and then, looking mildly surprised when he discovered his pack of Carltons was missing.

Brim Neely stopped by to pick up two dinners to go as his wife was feeling poorly again, and Carl Phelps and his deputy took stools at the counter where they ate quickly in case a call came in.

Just before noon, with the Honk nearly full, the clouds opened up and loosed a downpour, a deluge which made it impossible to see more than a few feet beyond the front window, so no one saw the bus pull in.

When the front door flew open a few minutes later, the wind-driven rain blew in and so did Caney, the back and shoulders of his shirt soaked through, his hair plastered to his head, rivulets of water running down his face.

And just behind him, Bui, more wet than Caney, held the door open while he tried to shield someone from the rain with a tented piece of black plastic with which she was draped and almost hidden except for her jeans and red boots.

"Merry Christmas," Caney said as he wiped his shirtsleeve across his face.

But there was hardly a murmur from those assembled when Bui lifted the dripping plastic away and closed the door.

Vena seemed not to notice the eyes trained on her as she tucked the corners of a blue blanket around something she cradled against her chest.

Wilma and Molly O exchanged a quick glance, both of them remembering the day just over a year ago when they'd first seen Vena coming toward the Honk, clutching an injured animal in much the same way.

She smiled at Caney as she bent and gently slipped the soft bundle into his arms.

"I'd like you all to meet someone," he said as he peeled the blanket back to reveal a tiny sleeping baby with a shock of black hair, one curled fist pressed against its face.

"This is my son, Caney Paxton the Second. But we call him Pax."

Then, as if he knew he was the focus of attention, Caney Paxton the Second squinted one eye open and yawned, his mouth stretched into a dime-sized O, and kicked one leg free of his blanket, his foot slipping out of a sock no bigger than a thumb.

Molly O was the first to lift the baby from Caney's arms, tears spilling down her face as she thought of Dewey whose love had been passed on from his heart to another's, and now to this one she felt beating against her own.

Then Life slipped in beside her, enfolded her and the baby in his big arms and rocked them gently, his cheek resting against hers, his lips grazing the top of the baby's head.

One by one the others rose from their places, hugging Vena and shaking Caney's hand as they waited to meet little Pax.

And as he was passed from one to the other, he offered no complaint, his serene expression unchanging as if he accepted that this was what his life was to be—a succession of hands cupping his bottom and rubbing his back, fingers tracing the curve of his toes, lips pressing against the soft flesh of his cheeks . . . each testing and touching and tasting some part of him.

Hooks, holding him gingerly in his good arm, declared that he had the hands of a fisherman. Quinton, awkward with babies, commented that he had a good poker face, a look that would give away nothing when drawing to an inside straight.

Wilma proclaimed that the baby had his daddy's eyes, but Wanda Sue argued they were clearly his mother's.

Galilee held the baby's pink face against her black one and whispered, "He shall be like a tree planted by the rivers of water, that bringeth forth his fruit in his season; his leaf also shall not wither; and whatsoever he doeth shall prosper."

Bilbo, recovered from his surprise that Caney's equipment worked just fine, put a quarter in the jukebox when he got hold of Pax. Then, in the center of the floor, he danced the Beto Shuffle, holding the baby securely to his chest.

And through it all, Caney smiled, waiting for his baby to be returned to his arms.

Bui, the last to leave, had intended to go after he brought in the bassinet, the rocking chair and the boxes they'd moved from San Antonio. But when he finished, Caney motioned him to the kitchen where Vena was getting ready to give the baby a bath.

They watched her with the fascination of boys at their first magic show as she slipped the baby into a small plastic tub on the kitchen counter, held spellbound by her wizardry in handling the tiny, slick body. They were sure it was only by enchantment that she could soap and rinse the squirming creature, then, as if by levitation, lift him—dripping legs bicycling the air—before she caused him to disappear into a large, fluffy towel.

They followed her to the bedroom where she opened act two by obscuring their view with a cloud of baby powder, deceptive cover for close sleight of hand—the trick of diapering. She flipped the baby's legs up in a sudden and smooth motion while, undetected, she slipped a diaper under its bottom and, before the powder had settled, magically secured the diaper.

How she managed to propel the baby's limbs into the sleeves and legs of terrycloth sleepers the size of a work glove was beyond their comprehension, but knowing a true magician never reveals her secrets, they didn't ask.

Then, for the finale, she settled Pax against her in the rocking chair, opened her shirt and performed the ultimate feat as the child found her breast.

Caney was in the cafe when Vena tiptoed out of the bedroom and closed the door softly behind her. Her hair, still wet from the shower, was wrapped in a towel, and she was wearing a soft flannel gown.

"Is Bui gone?" she asked.

"Yeah, just a few minutes ago. He hugged me twice, looked like he was about to cry."

"Why?"

"He said it was the miracle of babies. Ours. His. All babies."

"He's a sweet man."

"That he is."

Vena let her head fall forward as she rubbed the back of her neck.

"You want some coffee?" Caney asked.

"No. I'm too tired to lift a cup."

"Tired?" He studied her face. "Or is it something else?"

She looked puzzled. "Like what?"

"Vena, you haven't changed your mind about anything, have you?"

"Changed my mind?"

"About being back here. Being with me."

"Caney, I have a family here. You and Pax. Bui, Molly O . . ."

"I just don't want you to feel like you're stuck. Don't ever want you to think this is the end of the road."

"I've seen the end of the road, Caney, and believe me, this isn't it."

"I'm just scared, I guess."

"Scared of what?"

"That it can't last. That you'll need to go again."

"I'm not going anywhere, Caney. Seems like this is the place I've been heading all my life. I took a thousand wrong turns before I got here, but . . . boat go where boat go."

"Vena, I love you," he said as he reached across the table and took her hand. "It's just hard for me to trust happiness." He swallowed hard, trying to ease the tightness that thickened his voice. "But if you love me, I can do anything."

"Yeah," she said, hinting at a dare, "like what?"

"Oh, play the saxophone. Write poetry. Eat anchovies. Build you a house on that rise back in the meadow."

"Where that stand of oaks shades the creek?"

"They'll be right in your front yard."

"Well, I don't know." She shook her head. "If that's all you can offer, then . . ."

"Wait! I'm not finished."

"I'm listening."

"I'll wear a tie at our wedding, paint your portrait."

"You better be careful."

"Vena, I can do anything as long as you love me."

"Even dance?"

"Like Fred Astaire."

"Now you've gone too far."

"You think so?"

He rolled to the jukebox, dropped in a quarter and punched B7, turned and held out his hand.

Vena pulled off the towel and let it slide to the floor, shaking her wet hair free while she moved toward him.

Gathering her in his arms, pressing her warmth against him, he felt the stir of her breath on his throat when she whispered his name.

Then they danced, circling a floor of cracked linoleum, unaware of the smell of stale grease and onions, unmindful of the blowing rain striking the windows.

They danced, sweeping across a ballroom floor, polished, gleaming, smooth. They danced, filled with the sweet aroma of pine needles and pumpkin and baby powder. They danced, entranced by a crisp, clear sky lit by twinkling stars and a bright, full moon.

They danced, this man and this woman, whirling and spinning together on one magical Christmas night in the Honk and Holler Opening Soon.

Reading Group Guide

A Q&A with Billie Letts

Q. *The Honk and Holler Opening Soon* is such an intriguing title. How did you come up with it?

A. When I was sixteen, I worked as a carhop in Tulsa, at a drive-in where most customers would park on the lot and honk for service. But if they were kids, they'd usually yell or, as we say in Oklahoma, holler. So "The Honk and Holler" seemed an appropriate title. I tacked on "Opening Soon" when I came up with the idea of Caney being drunk when he ordered the neon sign.

Q. The characters in your books are sometimes described as quirky. Do you agree?

A. I don't take offense when people call my characters "quirky," but I suspect the use of the word is simply a short-cut for reviewers. Most people act and react in highly individual ways. We're all a little "quirky."

Q. As you were writing *The Honk and Holler Opening Soon*, did you have a particular favorite among your characters?

A. My favorite? That's a tough one because I get so involved with my characters that they become real to me—so real that naming a favorite seems like a slight to the others. But I will admit that Bui Khanh was great fun to write. I've always liked the "fish-out-of-water" characters, the ones who are set down in an environment that is alien to them. And for Bui, most everything in Sequoyah was a mystery. For instance, in his first few days at the Honk, he thought certain customers ate in their cars because they were not allowed to come inside for service. And I loved teaching him English. I taught Vietnamese students for several years and it was one of the most fulfilling jobs I ever had. With Bui, I had the opportunity to teach again.

Q. Why did you decide to make Caney Paxton, your central character, a paraplegic? What problems did you create for yourself in making that decision?

A. I don't remember *deciding* to make Caney a paraplegic. He "came" to me in a wheelchair. That's the way I saw him from the beginning. As I writer, I encountered the problem of dealing with his movement. Able-bodied characters can walk, stroll, saunter . . . amble, run, trot, dash, scurry. So I had to work to find ways of describing Caney's movements without being too repetitive.

Q. What kind of research went into writing this novel?

A. I tend to think of "real" research as a formal study of textual material. My research was of a different kind. I had to get into the mind and body of a man living in a wheelchair. To do that, I turned to a friend, a quadriplegic, who gave me insights into his life. For the character of Bui Khanh, I relied on Vietnamese students and friends. And to establish the setting and the minor characters, I hung out in a few small town cafes and drive-ins. Not very formal research, but what I learned came from real people who live lives similar to those of my characters.

Q. Several of your characters deal with pregnancy in this story. Brenda chooses to end hers with an abortion; Helen gives birth to a stillborn baby; Nguyet is expecting a child, though it's not Bui's; and Vena, having had one abortion when she was seventeen, leaves the Honk intending to have another. And in *Where the Heart Is*, one of the first things we learn about Novalee Nation is that she is seven months pregnant. Why is pregnancy/abortion/birth such an important issue in your books?

A. I believe the greatest decision a woman has to make in her life is whether to have children. And like it or not, that decision has become one of the great issues of the twentieth century. Everyone has an opinion, so the issue takes on political, social and religious significance. I prefer to keep my opinion out of my work, but I do put my characters in situations where they must make their own choices about bringing another life into the world.

Q. Both of your books revolve around dispossessed, poorly educated people who live from payday to payday. Why do you write about characters who lead such marginal lives?

A. I haven't spent much of my life around wealthy, powerful people, so I don't attempt to tell stories about them. Most of what I know of such people is what I see in movies or read in books. My characters don't make important decisions in corporate boardrooms; they don't call their stock brokers on their cell phones; and they don't shop at Neiman Marcus or drive Rolls Royces. Instead, they have to try to manage to stretch minimum wages to pay rent, buy shoes for their kids, keep their old Chevys and Fords running, and get medical treatment when they have no insurance and no more than a few bills in their pockets. But despite their financial conditions, the working-class characters in my stories try to live worthwhile lives, lives with dignity.

Q. In your first novel, the central character, a seventeen-year-old pregnant girl, lived secretly in a Wal-Mart. In this new book, one character lives in a church, one finds shelter in an abandoned bus, and another lives in a drive-in. Why do you have your characters take up residence in such strange places?

A. I went to school with a woman who, when she was a child, lived with her mother and sister in a chicken coop, their only shelter for several months. I know about a Vietnam vet who lives in a cave in eastern Oklahoma and I read about a man who lived in a crawl space over a shopping mall in California. A man here in Durant was found living in a mini-storage unit one summer when the temperature was 104. My family—father, uncles, aunts—moved from oil field to oil field during the depression, living in tents and on the flatbed truck in which they traveled. Read the papers. Watch TV. Survivors survive—not just in Albania, or Nicaragua, or Indonesia, but also in the towns and cities we all know.

Q. You frequently write about people who lack a family in the traditional sense, yet form unconventional ties that provide them with a sense of belonging. What draws you to this theme?

A. So many families are nontraditional. Many more are made up of "your kids, my kids, our kids" than ever before. More and more children are being raised by grandparents, foster families, single parents, or in institutions. We all need to belong—to love and be loved. So those without a "real" family reach out, and if they're fortunate enough to find the good people—and there are many out there—bonds are formed, families are forged.

Q. Your novels are filled with characters who have suffered great tragedies and experienced deep loneliness. Yet, in the end, the stories you tell are joyous and life-affirming. How do you explain this?

A. Almost everyone I know has suffered some tragedy. Most people have obviously experienced the prolonged sorrow of loneliness. But people have a way of going on, building new lives after divorce, the loss of children, spouses, siblings, parents. They live with loss and sadness, yet find comfort in opening themselves to others. Ah, humanity!

Q. How was writing this book different from writing *Where the Heart Is*? Did you feel that you had to live up to any expectations? Which one was harder to write?

A. I was amazed and thrilled at the response I got from readers of *Where the Heart Is*, so when I started my second book, the fear of disappointing readers almost overwhelmed me. A nasty little voice started whispering in my ear each time I tried to work, a voice insisting that I wasn't going to be able to live up to my readers' expectations. I really struggled to overcome self-doubt.

Q. You've just written the screenplay for *The Honk and Holler Opening Soon*. How does the writing of a screenplay differ from that of a novel? Which do you prefer?

A. I had written several screenplays before I wrote my first book, so I was familiar with the structure— the arc of the story. But those scripts came from my own imagination. Writing the screenplay for *The Honk and Holler Opening Soon* was my first attempt to adapt a book for the screen . . . and in this case, I was adapting my own work. I found it quite difficult, mainly because I had to let go of some of the characters and events in the book. That was painful, but then I remembered a maxim: "A book is not a movie and a movie is not a book." The cliché we so often hear, "The book was better than the movie," is like saying "The airplane is better than the sparrow."

Q. What writers have influenced your writing the most?

A. I suppose that in some mysterious way everything I've read has helped me find the voice that speaks in my work, but there are some that are vivid in my memory.

   The Sound and the Fury by William Faulkner and Toni Morrison's *The Bluest Eye* taught me to listen to the rhythm of language. In Maya Angelou's *I Know Why the Caged Bird*

Sings, I learned about the gift of hope that can come from writing honestly about pain. Flannery O'Connor's short stories made me believe I could write in the language of my Oklahoma culture and tell stories about the people I come from. In *To Kill a Mockingbird*, Harper Lee showed me that storytelling can change people's lives. And in her collection *Woman Hollering Creek*, Sandra Cisneros gave me "Salvador Late or Early," so powerful in its simplicity that I am humbled each time I read it.

Q. What are you doing now? What's next for you?

A. I have a couple of stories banging around in my head right now. Just when I decide to start one of them, the other shouts "Write me! Write me first," so I'm still unsure what my next book is. Maybe I won't know until I sit down at the typewriter a few days from now. But that's the part of writing I love—the surprises.

Discussion Questions

1. *The Honk and Holler Opening Soon* is set in Sequoyah, a very small town in Oklahoma. Is it realistic to believe that a Vietnam vet, a Native American woman, an African American woman and a Vietnamese man might come together under the strange circumstances in the book? Do you find it believable that outsiders such as Bui or Vena could be fully accepted into this insular community?

2. Which of the characters do you feel you have most in common with? Why?

3. Bui Khan, a recently arrived immigrant, understands little of the language and culture of the United States, yet he is in search of the American Dream. What are his chances of achieving that dream?

4. Caney Paxton stayed inside the Honk from 1973 until 1985. What major changes in this culture took place during his period of isolation? How will those changes affect his life outside the Honk?

5. Is the relationship that develops between Caney and Vena believable? Why or why not?

6. What do you believe is the theme of this book? Do you think the author fully developed that theme?

7. It seems that several story lines are not concluded by the end of the novel. Bui Khan's wife has not arrived; Brenda is "lost" out there in the bigger world; Molly O and Life are going out together, but there's no indication how their relationship will end; and though Vena and Caney are together, they still have problems to work through. Why do you suppose the author left so many issues unresolved? Do you find this frustrating?

8. Vena Takes Horse isn't "good at staying still" at the beginning of the book, but at the end, she returns to the Honk. Do you think she's changed enough that she'll stay? Do you think Brenda will return to her mother?

9. Are the problems between Molly O and Brenda common between mothers and daughters?

10. How do the regulars at the Honk contribute to the story?

11. Although all of the major characters in *The Honk and Holler Opening Soon* are adults, the role that children play in this novel is enormous. In fact, many of the novel's pivotal moments revolve around children. Yet Caney, Molly O, Brenda, Vena, Helen and Bui react so differently to the idea of parenthood. Why is that? Is it easier for Caney and Bui to accept the fact that they are going to be fathers than it is for Molly O, Brenda, Vena and Helen to accept the fact they are going to be mothers? Is the connection between mother and child always stronger than the bond between father and child?

Billie Letts on Writing

I was about eight chapters into this book when I ran away from home. With thirty chapters yet to complete, I left husband, home and dogs behind and headed north.

I was going to hide out to finish my book because, as I had explained to my puzzled mate, there were just too many distractions at home. I had forty years worth of photos to organize and mount in albums; dozens (maybe hundreds) of knives to sharpen; a basket of ironing accumulated since 1994—the year I sold my iron in a yard sale; and new washers to install on every faucet in the house, all of which had been threatening to drip for months (maybe years).

Just too many distractions!

I landed in Tulsa, rented a small apartment furnished with a bed, chair, table and lamp. No television, no radio. No old photos or knives, no iron and only two faucets, both outfitted with new washers, so said the building manager.

Nothing to distract me here.

I set to work, writing three sessions a day, seven days a
week. And I was churning out pages—ten or twelve a day.
Why, I thought, I'd be back home within weeks.

Twelve days later the agonies moved in. Not next door or
across the hall or in the apartment above me. They moved into
my nest, slept in my bed, sprawled in my chair. And they
offered not one word of encouragement. Instead, they snick-
ered at the work I was doing, laughed contemptuously each
time I made a false start, and roared when I'd snatch paper
from my typewriter, wad it up and throw it across the room.

By the end of the week, I was paralyzed with fear and
loathing. I feared that the agonies were right—my work was
dreadful—and I loathed myself for listening to them.

I needed help!

I raced to bookstores and carted home tomes on writer's
block. I pressed crystals to my forehead; took herbs advertized
to enhance brain function; gave up coffee, salt and carbonated
beverages; and, following advice from a writer friend, tried
writing naked, assured that free of constraints, I would loosen
up, the creative urge would awaken and the writing would
flow.

Wrong!

Then, several weeks later, I was awakened in the middle of
the night when one of the agonies made a terrible mistake by
whispering an obscenity in my ear. I got up, went to the living room, settled into my chair and read all the pages I had
completed.

And there it was. On page 153 of my draft, I had suddenly
lost my voice. Not the voice I speak in, nothing wrong with
my throat or vocal chords. I had lost my writer's voice, the
voice that tells the story.

After publishing only one book, and less than halfway

through the second, I had started trying to sound like a writer, using a voice so stilted and preachy that I cringed at seeing my own words.

Even my characters' voices had changed. They spoke as if they'd studied linguistics. The morning coffee drinkers had started using standard English and Life Halstead sounded like a Harvard man. Molly O spoke more like a New Yorker than an Okie and Bui Khanh, who had been struggling with the basics of a new language, was able to make subjects and verbs agree, and avoid dangling modifiers.

The agonies, knowing I was onto something, huddled in the corner trying to come up with a new game plan. But it was too late. I had discovered my own undoing.

I went to the typewriter and started to work, joyous to hear an old familiar voice telling me the story of *The Honk and Holler Opening Soon*.

I pretended not to notice when the agonies slipped out the door, determined not to make some snide comment, but I couldn't help but smile as I heard the door close behind them.